THE
HOUSE
ACROSS
THE LAKE

ALSO BY RILEY SAGER

Final Girls

The Last Time I Lied

Lock Every Door

Home Before Dark

Survive the Night

THE
HOUSE
ACROSS
THE LAKE

A NOVEL

RILEY SAGER

DUTTON

DUTTON

An imprint of Penguin Random House LLC
penguinrandomhouse.com

Interior image: Forest reflection © andreiuc88 / shutterstock.com

LIBRARY OF CONGRESS CATALOGING-IN-PUBLICATION DATA

Names: Sager, Riley, author.
Title: The house across the lake : a novel / Riley Sager.
Description: [New York] : Dutton, an imprint of
Penguin Random House LLC, [2022]
Identifiers: LCCN 2021044954 (print) | LCCN 2021044955 (ebook) |
ISBN 9780593183199 (hardcover) | ISBN 9780593183205 (ebook)
Subjects: GSAFD: Suspense fiction.
Classification: LCC PS3618.I79 H68 2022 (print) |
LCC PS3618.I79 (ebook) | DDC 813/.6—dc23
LC record available at https://lccn.loc.gov/2021044954
LC ebook record available at https://lccn.loc.gov/2021044955

ISBN: 9780593472736

Printed in the United States of America
1st Printing

BOOK DESIGN BY LAURA K. CORLESS

I think he did it, but I just can't prove it.

—Taylor Swift, "No Body, No Crime"

THE
HOUSE
ACROSS
THE LAKE

*T*he lake is darker than a coffin with the lid shut.

  That's what Marnie used to say, back when we were children and she was constantly trying to scare me. It's an exaggeration, to be sure. But not by much. Lake Greene's water is dark, even with light trickling through it.

  A coffin with the lid cracked.

  Out of the water, you can see clearly for about a foot beneath the surface before it starts to get cloudy. Then inky. Then dark as a grave. It's worse when you're fully submerged, the shimmer of light coming from above a stark contrast to the black depths below.

  When we were kids bobbing in the middle of the lake, Marnie often dared me to swim past the point of visibility until I touched bottom. I tried many times but never succeeded. Lost in the darkness, I always got disoriented, turned around, swam up when I thought I was headed down. I'd emerge breathless, confused, and slightly unnerved by the difference between water and sky.

  On the surface, it was bright day.

  Just below, the night waited.

  On shore, five houses sit beside the dark water of Lake Greene, ranging in style from comfortably quaint to conspicuously modern. In the summer, when the Green Mountain State is at full splendor and each house is packed with friends, family members, and weekenders, they glow like beacons signaling safe port. Through the windows, one can see well-lit rooms filled with people eating and drinking, laughing and arguing, playing games and sharing secrets.

It changes in the off-season, when the houses go quiet, first during the week, then on weekends as well. Not that they're empty. Far from it. Autumn lures people to Vermont just as much as summer. But the mood is different. Muted. Solemn. By mid-October, it feels like the darkness of the lake has flooded the shore and seeped into the houses themselves, dimming their light.

This is especially true of the house directly across the lake.

Made of glass, steel, and stone, it reflects the chilly water and the gray autumn sky, using them to mask whatever might be happening inside. When the lights are on, you can see past the surface, but only so far. It's like the lake in that regard. No matter how much you look, something just beneath the surface will always remain hidden.

I should know.

I've been watching.

I stare at the detective on the other side of the table, an untouched mug of coffee in front of me. The steam rising from it gives her a gauzy air of mystery. Not that she needs help in that regard. Wilma Anson possesses a calm blankness that rarely changes. Even at this late hour and soaked by the storm, she remains unperturbed.

"Have you watched the Royce house at all this evening?" she says.

"Yes." There's no point in lying.

"See anything unusual?"

"More unusual than everything I've already seen?" I say.

A nod from Wilma. "That's what I'm asking."

"No." This time a lie is required. I've seen a lot this evening. More than I ever wanted to. "Why?"

A gust of wind lashes rain against the French doors that lead to the back porch. Both of us pause a moment to watch the droplets smacking the glass. Already, the storm is worse than the TV weatherman said it would be—and what he had predicted was already severe. The tail end of a Category 4 hurricane turned tropical storm as it swerved like a boomerang from deep inland back to the North Atlantic.

Rare for mid-October.

Rarer still for eastern Vermont.

"Because Tom Royce might be missing," Wilma says.

I tear my gaze from the French doors' rain-specked panes to give Wilma a look of surprise. She stares back, unflappable as ever.

"Are you sure?" I say.

"I was just there. The house is unlocked. That fancy car of his is still in the driveway. Nothing inside seems to be missing. Except for him."

I turn again to the French doors, as if I'll be able to see the Royce house rising from the lake's opposite shore. Instead, all I can make out is howling darkness and lightning-lit flashes of water whipped into a frenzy by the wind.

"Do you think he ran?"

"His wallet and keys are on the kitchen counter," Wilma says. "It's hard to run without cash or a car. Especially in this weather. So I doubt it."

I note her word choice. *Doubt.*

"Maybe he had help," I suggest.

"Or maybe someone made him disappear. You know anything about that?"

My mouth drops open in surprise. "You think I'm involved in this?"

"You did break into their house."

"I *snuck* in," I say, hoping the distinction will lessen the crime in Wilma's eyes. "And that doesn't mean I know anything about where Tom is now."

Wilma remains quiet, hoping I'll say more and possibly incriminate myself. Seconds pass. Lots of them. All announced by the ticking of the grandfather clock in the living room, which acts as a steady beat backing the song of the storm. Wilma listens to it, seemingly in no rush. She's a marvel of composure. I suspect her name has a lot to do with that. If a lifetime of Flintstones jokes teaches you anything, it's deep patience.

"Listen," Wilma says after what feels like three whole minutes. "I know you're worried about Katherine Royce. I know you want to find her. So do I. But I already told you that taking matters into your own hands won't help. Let me do my job, Casey. It's our best chance of getting Katherine back alive. So if you know anything about where her husband is, please tell me."

"I have absolutely no clue where Tom Royce could be." I lean forward, my palms flat against the table, trying to summon the same opaque energy Wilma's putting off. "If you don't believe me, you're welcome to search the house."

Wilma considers it. For the first time since we sat down, I can sense her mind ticking as steadily as the grandfather clock.

"I believe you," she finally says. "For now. But I could change my mind at any moment."

When she leaves, I make sure to watch her go, standing in the doorway while being buffeted by rain slanting onto the front porch. In the driveway, Wilma trots back to her unmarked sedan and slides behind the wheel. I wave as she backs the car out of the driveway, splashes through a puddle that wasn't there an hour ago, and speeds off.

I close the front door, shake off the rain, and go to the kitchen, where I pour myself a supersized bourbon. This new turn of events requires a kick coffee can't provide.

Outside, another gust of wind jostles the house. The eaves creak and the lights flicker.

Signs the storm is getting worse.

Tail end, my ass.

Bourbon glass in hand, I head upstairs, into the first bedroom on the right.

He's exactly how I left him.

Splayed out across the twin bed.

Ankles and wrists tied to the bedposts.

Towel stuffed into his mouth to form a makeshift gag.

I remove the towel, sit on the identical bed on the other side of the room, and take a long, slow sip of bourbon.

"We're running out of time," I say. "Now tell me what you did to Katherine."

BEFORE

I see it out of the corner of my eye.

A breach of the water's surface.

Ripples.

Sunlight.

Something rising from the water, then sinking back under.

I've been watching the lake at a mental remove, which happens when you've seen something a thousand times. Looking but not really. Seeing everything, registering nothing.

Bourbon might have something to do with that.

I'm on my third.

Maybe fourth.

Counting drinks—another thing I do at a remove.

But the motion in the water now has my full attention. Rising from the rocking chair onto legs unsteady after three (or four) day drinks, I watch the lake's glassy surface again break into sun-dappled circles.

I squint, trying to emerge from the bourbon haze long enough to see what it is. It's useless. The movement is located in the dead center of the lake—too far away to see clearly.

I leave the back porch of the lake house, step inside, and shuffle to the cramped foyer just beyond the front door. A coatrack is there, buried under anoraks and rain slickers. Among them is a pair of binoculars in a leather case hanging from a frayed strap, untouched for more than a year.

Binoculars in hand, I return to the back porch and stand at the railing, scanning the lake. The ripples reappear, and in the epicenter, a hand emerges from the water.

The binoculars drop to the porch floor.

I think: *Someone's drowning.*

I think: *I need to save them.*

I think: *Len.*

That last thought—of my husband, of how he died in this same deep water—propels me into action. I push off the railing, the movement jiggling the ice in the bourbon glass next to the rocking chair. It clinks lightly as I leave the porch, scurry down the steps, and spring across the few yards of mossy ground between the house and the water's edge. The wooden dock shudders when I leap onto it and continues to shake as I run to the motorboat moored at its end. I untie the boat, wobble into it, grab a paddle, and push off the dock.

The boat twirls a moment, doing a less-than-elegant pirouette atop the water before I straighten it out with the paddle. Once the boat's pointed toward the center of the lake, I start the outboard motor with an arm-aching tug. Five seconds later, the boat is gliding over the water, toward where I last saw the circular ripples but now see nothing.

I start to hope that what I saw was merely a fish leaping out of the water. Or a loon diving into it. Or that the sun, the reflection of the sky on the lake, and several bourbons caused me to see something that wasn't really there.

Wishful thinking, all of it.

Because as the boat nears the middle of the lake, I spot something in the water.

A body.

Bobbing on the surface.

Motionless.

I cut the motor and scramble to the front of the boat to get a better view. I can't tell if the person is faceup or facedown, alive or dead. All I can see are the shadows of outstretched limbs in the water and a tangle of hair floating like kelp. I get a mental picture of Len in this very position and yell toward the shore.

"Help! Someone's drowning!"

The words echo off the flame-hued trees on both sides of the lake, likely heard by no one. It's the middle of October, and Lake Greene, never crowded to begin with, is all but abandoned. The only full-time resident is Eli, and he's gone until evening. If someone else is around, they aren't making their presence known.

I'm on my own.

I grab the paddle again and start to row toward the person in the water. A woman, I see now. Her hair is long. A one-piece bathing suit exposes a tanned back, long legs, toned arms. She floats like driftwood, bobbing gently in the boat's wake.

Yet another image of Len pushes into my brain as I scramble for the anchor tied to one of the cleats on the boat's rim. The anchor isn't heavy—only twenty pounds—but weighty enough to keep the boat from drifting. I drop it into the water, the rope attached to it hissing against the side of the boat as it sinks to the lake's bottom.

Next, I snag a life vest stowed under one of the seats, stumble to the side of the boat, and join the anchor in the water. I enter the lake awkwardly. No graceful dive for me. It's more of a sideways plop. But the coldness of the water sobers me like a slap. Senses sharpened and body stinging, I tuck the life vest under my left arm and use my right to paddle toward the woman.

I'm a strong swimmer, even half drunk. I grew up on Lake Greene and spent many summer days more in the water than out of it. And even though fourteen months have passed since I've submerged myself in the lake, the water is as familiar to me as my own bed. Bracing, even on the hottest days, and crystal clear for only a moment before darkness takes over.

Splashing toward the floating woman, I search for signs of life.

There's nothing.

No twitch of her arms or kick of her feet or slow turn of her head.

One thought echoes through my skull as I reach her. Part plea, part prayer.

Please don't be dead. Please, please be alive.

But when I hook the life vest around her neck and flip her over, she doesn't look alive. Hugged by the life vest and with her head tilted toward the sky, she resembles a corpse. Closed eyes. Blue lips. Frigid skin. I connect the straps at the bottom of the life vest, tightening it around her, and slap a hand to her chest.

No trace of a heartbeat.

Fuck.

I want to shout for help again, but I'm too winded to get the words out. Even strong swimmers have their limits, and I've reached mine. Exhaustion pulls at me like a tide, and I know a few more minutes of paddling in place while clinging to a maybe/probably dead woman might leave me just like her.

I put one arm around her waist and use the other to start paddling back to the boat. I have no idea what to do when I reach it. Cling to the side, I guess. Hold on tight while also holding on to the likely/definitely dead woman and hope I regain enough lung power to scream again.

And that this time someone will hear me.

Right now, though, my main concern is getting back to the boat at all. I didn't think to grab a life vest for myself, and now my strokes are slowing and my heart is pounding and I can no longer feel my legs kicking, even though I think they still are. The water's so cold and I'm so tired. So scarily, unbearably exhausted that for a moment I consider taking the woman's life vest for myself and letting her drift into the depths.

Self-preservation kicking in.

I can't save her without saving myself first, and she might already be beyond rescue. But then I think again about Len, dead for more than a year now, his body found crumpled on the shore of this very lake. I can't let the same thing happen to this woman.

So I continue my one-armed paddling and numb kicking and tugging of what I'm now certain is a corpse. I keep at it until the boat is ten feet away.

Then nine.

Then eight.

Beside me, the woman's body suddenly spasms. A shocking jolt. This time, I *do* let go, my arm recoiling in surprise.

The woman's eyes snap open.

She coughs—a series of long, loud, gurgling hacks. A spout of water flies from her mouth and trickles down her chin while a line of snot runs from her left nostril to her cheek. She wipes it all away and stares at me, confused, breathless, and terrified.

"What just happened?"

"Don't freak out," I say, recalling her blue lips, her ice-cold skin, her utter, unnerving stillness. "But I think you almost drowned."

Neither one of us speaks again until we're both safely in the boat. There wasn't time for words as I clawed, kicked, and climbed my way up the side until I was able to flop onto the boat floor like a recently caught fish. Getting the woman on board was even harder, seeing how her near-death experience had sapped all her energy. It took so much tugging and lifting on my part that, once she was in the boat, I was too exhausted to move, let alone speak.

But now, after a few minutes of panting, we've pulled ourselves into seats. The woman and I face each other, shell-shocked by the whole situation and all too happy to rest a few minutes while we regroup.

"You said I *almost* drowned," the woman says.

She's wrapped in a plaid blanket I found stowed under one of the boat's seats, which gives her the look of a kitten rescued from a storm drain. Battered and vulnerable and grateful.

"Yes," I say as I wring water from my flannel shirt. Because there's only one blanket on board, I remain soaked and chilly. I don't mind. I'm not the one who needed rescue.

"Define *almost*."

"Honestly? I thought you were dead."

Beneath the blanket, the woman shudders. "Jesus."

"But I was wrong," I add, trying to soothe her obvious shock. "Clearly. You came back on your own. I did nothing."

The woman shifts in her seat, revealing a flash of bright bathing suit deep within the blanket. Teal. So tropical. And so inappropriate for autumn in Vermont it makes me wonder how she even ended up here. If she told me aliens had zapped her to Lake Greene from a white-sand beach in the Seychelles, I'd almost believe it.

"Still, I'm sure I would have died if you hadn't seen me," she says. "So thank you for coming to my rescue. I should have said that sooner. Like, immediately."

I respond with a modest shrug. "I won't hold a grudge."

The woman laughs, and in the process comes alive in a way that banishes all traces of the person I'd found floating in the water. Color has returned to her face—a peachy blush that highlights her high cheekbones, full lips, pencil-line brows. Her gray-green eyes are wide and expressive, and her nose is slightly crooked, a flaw that comes off as charming amid all that perfection. She's gorgeous, even huddled under a blanket and dripping lake water.

She catches me staring and says, "I'm Katherine, by the way."

It's only then that I realize I know this woman. Not personally. We've never met, as far as I can remember. But I recognize her just the same.

Katherine Royce.

Former supermodel.

Current philanthropist.

And, with her husband, owner of the house directly across the lake. It had been vacant the last time I was here, on the market for north of five million dollars. It made headlines when it sold over the winter, not just because of who bought the house but because of where it was located.

Lake Greene.

The Vermont hideaway of beloved musical theater icon Lolly Fletcher.

And the place where troubled actress Casey Fletcher's husband tragically drowned.

Not the first time those adjectives have been used to describe my mother and me. They've been employed so often they might as well be our first names. Beloved Lolly Fletcher and Troubled Casey Fletcher. A mother-daughter duo for the ages.

"I'm Casey," I say.

"Oh, I know," Katherine says. "Tom—that's my husband—and I meant to stop by and say hello when we arrived last night. We're both big fans."

"How did you know I was here?"

"Your lights were on," Katherine says, pointing to the lake house that's been in my family for generations.

The house isn't the biggest on Lake Greene—that honor goes to Katherine's new home—but it's the oldest. Built by my great-great-grandfather in 1878 and renovated and expanded every fifty years or so. From the water, the lake house looks lovely. Perched close to shore, tall and solid behind a retaining wall of mountain stone, it's almost a parody of New England quaintness. Two pristinely white stories of gables, latticework, and gingerbread trim. Half the house runs parallel to the water's edge, so close that the wraparound porch practically overhangs the lake itself.

That's where I was sitting this afternoon when I first spotted Katherine flailing in the water.

And where I was sitting last night when I was too drunk to notice the arrival of the famous couple that now owns the house directly across the lake.

The other half of my family's lake house is set back about ten yards, forming a small courtyard. High above it, on the house's top floor, a row of tall windows provides a killer view from the master bedroom. Right now, in mid-afternoon, the windows are hidden in the shadow of towering pines. But at night, I suspect the glow from the master bedroom is as bright as a lighthouse.

"The place was dark all summer," Katherine says. "When Tom and I noticed the lights last night, we assumed it was you."

She tactfully avoids mentioning *why* she and her husband assumed it was me and not, say, my mother.

I know they know my story.

Everyone does.

The only allusion Katherine makes to my recent troubles is a kind, concerned "How are you, by the way? It's rough, what you're going through. Having to handle all that."

She leans forward and touches my knee—a surprisingly intimate gesture for someone I've just met, even taking into account the fact that I likely did save her life.

"I'm doing fantastic," I say, because to admit the truth would open myself to having to talk about *all that*, to use Katherine's phrasing.

I'm not ready for that yet, even though it's been more than a year. Part of me thinks I'll never be ready.

"That's great," Katherine says, her smile as bright as a sunbeam. "I feel bad about almost ruining that by, you know, drowning."

"If it's any consolation, it made for one hell of a first impression."

She laughs. Thank God. My sense of humor has been described as dry by some, cruel by others. I prefer to think of it as an acquired taste, similar to the olive at the bottom of a martini. You either like it or you don't.

Katherine seems to like it. Still smiling, she says, "The thing is, I don't even know how it happened. I'm an excellent swimmer. I know it doesn't look that way right now, but it's true, I swear. I guess the water was colder than I thought, and I cramped up."

"It's the middle of October. The lake is freezing this time of year."

"Oh, I love swimming in the cold. Every New Year's Day, I do the Polar Plunge."

I nod. Of course she does.

"It's for charity," Katherine adds.

I nod again. Of course it is.

I must make a face, because Katherine says, "I'm sorry. That all sounded like a brag, didn't it?"

"A little," I admit.

"Ugh. I don't mean to do it. It just happens. It's like the opposite of a humblebrag. There should be a word for when you accidentally make yourself sound better than you truly are."

"A bumblebrag?" I suggest.

"Ooh, I like that," Katherine coos. "That's what I am, Casey. An irredeemable bumblebragger."

My gut instinct is to dislike Katherine Royce. She's the kind of woman who seems to exist solely to make the rest of us feel inferior. Yet I'm charmed by her. Maybe it's the strange situation we're in—the rescued and the rescuer, sitting in a boat on a beautiful autumn afternoon. It's got a surreal *Little Mermaid* vibe to it. Like I'm a prince transfixed by a siren I've just plucked from the sea.

There doesn't seem to be anything fake about Katherine. She's beautiful, yes, but in a down-to-earth way. More girl-next-door than intimidating bombshell. Betty *and* Veronica sporting a self-deprecating smile. It served her well during her modeling days. In a world where resting bitch face is the norm, Katherine stood out.

I first became aware of her seven years ago, when I was doing a Broadway play in a theater on 46th Street. Just down the block, in the heart of Times Square, was a giant billboard of Katherine in a wedding dress. Despite the gown, the flowers, the sun-kissed skin, she was no blushing bride. Instead, she was on the run—kicking off her heels and sprinting through emerald green grass as her jilted fiancé and stunned wedding party watched helplessly in the background.

I didn't know if the ad was for perfume or wedding dresses or vodka. I really didn't care. What I focused on every time I spotted the billboard was the look on the woman's face. With her eyes crinkling and her smile wide, she seemed elated, relieved, surprised. A woman overjoyed to be dismantling her entire existence in one fell swoop.

I related to that look.

I still do.

Only after the play closed and I continued seeing the woman's picture everywhere did I match a name with the face.

Katherine Daniels.

The magazines called her Katie. The designers who made her their muse called her Kat. She walked runways for Yves Saint Laurent and frolicked on the beach for Calvin Klein and rolled around on silk sheets for Victoria's Secret.

Then she got married to Thomas Royce, the founder and CEO of a social media company, and the modeling stopped. I remember seeing their wedding photo in *People* magazine and being surprised by it. I expected Katherine to look the way she did on that billboard. Freedom personified. Instead, sewn into a Vera Wang gown and clutching her husband's arm, she sported a smile so clenched I almost didn't recognize her.

Now she's here, in my boat, grinning freely, and I feel a weird sense of relief that the woman from that billboard hadn't vanished entirely.

"Can I ask you a very personal, very nosy question?" I say.

"You just saved my life," Katherine says. "I'd be a real bitch if I said no right now, don't you think?"

"It's about your modeling days."

Katherine stops me with a raised hand. "You want to know why I quit."

"Kind of," I say, adding a guilty shrug. I feel bad about being obvious, not to mention basic. I could have asked her a thousand other things but instead posed the question she clearly gets the most.

"The long version is that it's a lot less glamorous than it looks. The hours were endless and the diet was torture. Imagine not being allowed to eat a single piece of bread for an entire year."

"I honestly can't," I say.

"That alone was reason enough to quit," Katherine says. "And sometimes I just tell people that. I look them in the eye and say, 'I quit because I wanted to eat pizza.' But the worst part, honestly, was having all the focus be on my looks. All that nonstop primping and objectification. No one cared about what I said. Or thought. Or felt. It got real old, real quick. Don't get me wrong, the money was great. Like, *insanely* great. And the clothes were amazing. So beautiful. Works of art, all of them. But it felt wrong. People are suffering. Children are starving. Women are being victimized. And there I was walking the runway in dresses that cost more than what most families make in a year. It was ghoulish."

"Sounds a lot like acting." I pause. "Or being a show pony."

Katherine laugh-snorts, and I decide right then and there that I do indeed like her. We're the same in a lot of ways. Famous for reasons we're not entirely comfortable with. Ridiculously privileged, but self-aware enough to realize it. Yearning to be seen as more than what people project onto us.

"Anyway, that's the long story," she says. "Told only to people who save me from drowning."

"What's the short version?"

Katherine looks away, to the other side of the lake, where her house dominates the shoreline. "Tom wanted me to stop."

A dark look crosses her face. It's brief—like the shadow of a cloud on the water. I expect her to say something more about her husband and why he'd make such a demand. Instead, Katherine's mouth drops open and she begins to cough.

Hard.

Much harder than earlier.

These are deep, rough hacks loud enough to echo off the water. The blanket falls away, and Katherine hugs herself until she rides out the coughing fit. She looks frightened when it's over. Another cloud shadow passes over her face, and for a second she looks like she has no idea what just happened. But then the cloud vanishes and she flashes a reassuring smile.

"Well, that was unladylike," she says.

"Are you okay?"

"I think so." Katherine's hands tremble as she pulls the blanket back over her goose-pimpled shoulders. "But it's probably time to go home now."

"Of course," I say. "You must be freezing."

I certainly am. Now that the adrenaline of my earlier attempted heroics has worn off, a fierce chill takes hold. My body shivers as I haul the anchor up from the bottom of the lake. The entire rope—all fifty feet of it—is wet from being stretched underwater. By the time I'm finished with the anchor, my arms are so spent it takes me several tugs to start the motor.

I start to steer the boat toward Katherine's place. Her house is an anomaly on the lake in that it's the only one built after the seventies. What had previously been there was a perfectly acceptable bungalow from the thirties surrounded by tall pines.

Twenty years ago, the bungalow was removed. So were the pines.

Now in their place is an angular monstrosity that juts from the earth like a chunk of rock. The side facing the lake is almost entirely covered in glass, from the wide, rambling ground floor to the tip of the peaked roof. During the day, it's impressive, if a little boring. The real estate equivalent of a store window with nothing on display.

But at night, when all the rooms are lit up, it takes on the appearance of a dollhouse. Each room is visible. Gleaming kitchen. Sparkling dining room. Wide living room that runs the length of the stone patio behind the house that leads to the edge of the lake.

I've been inside only once, when Len and I were invited to dinner by the previous owners. It felt weird to be sitting behind all that glass. Like a specimen in a petri dish.

Not that there are many people around watching. Lake Greene is small, as lakes go. A mile long and only a quarter mile wide in spots, it sits alone in a thick patch of forest in eastern Vermont. It was formed at the tail end of the Ice Age, when a glacier plowing its way across the land decided to leave a chunk of itself behind. That ice melted, digging a trough in the earth into which its water eventually settled. Which basically makes it a puddle. Very big and very deep and quite lovely to look at, but a puddle all the same.

It's also private, which is the main draw. The water is only accessible by one of the residential docks, of which there are few. Only five houses sit on the lake, thanks to large lot sizes and a shortage of additional land suitable for construction. The northern end of the lake is lined with protected forest. The southern end is a steep, rocky bluff. In the middle are the houses, two on one side, three on the other.

It's the latter side where Katherine lives. Her house sits tall and imposing between two older, more modest structures. To the left, about a hundred yards down the shore, is the Fitzgerald place. He's in banking. She dabbles in antiques. They arrive at their charming cottage on Memorial Day weekend and depart on Labor Day, leaving the place empty the rest of the year.

Sitting to the right of the Royces' is the ramshackle abode of Eli Williams, a novelist who was big in the eighties and not so big now. His house resembles a Swiss chalet—three stories of rough-hewn wood with tiny balconies on the upper floors and red shutters at the windows. Like my family, Eli and his wife summered at Lake Greene. When she died, Eli sold their house in New Jersey and moved here full-time. As the lake's only permanent resident, he now keeps an eye on the other houses when everyone else is away.

There are no lights on in Katherine's house, making its glass wall reflect the lake like a mirror. I catch a distorted glimpse of the two of us in the boat, our reflections wobbling, as if we're made of water ourselves.

When I bring the boat to the property's dock, Katherine leans forward and takes my cold hands in hers. "Thank you again. You truly did save my life."

"It was nothing," I say. "Besides, I'd be a terrible person if I ignored a supermodel in need."

"*Former* supermodel."

She coughs again. A single, harsh bark.

"Are you going to be okay?" I say. "Do you need to go to a doctor or something?"

"I'll be fine. Tom will be back soon. Until then, I think I'll take a hot shower and a long nap."

She steps onto the dock and realizes my blanket is still over her shoulders. "God, I forgot all about this."

"Keep it for now," I say. "You need it more than I do."

Katherine nods her thanks and starts to make her way toward the house. Although I don't think it's intentional, she walks the dock as if navigating a runway. Her stride is lengthy, smooth, elegant. Katherine might have grown tired of the modeling world, with good reason, but the way she moves is a gift. She has the effortless grace of a ghost.

Once she reaches the house, she turns back to me and waves with her left hand.

Only then do I notice something strange.

Katherine mentioned her husband several times, but—for now at least—she's not wearing a wedding ring.

My phone is ringing when I return to the lake house, its angry-bird chirp audible as I climb the porch steps. Because I'm wet, tired, and chilled to the bone, my first instinct is to ignore it. But then I see who's calling.

Marnie.

Wonderful, caustic, patient-beyond-her-years Marnie.

The only person not yet completely fed up with my bullshit, which is probably because she's my cousin. And my best friend. And my manager, although today she's firmly in friend mode.

"This isn't a business call," she announces when I answer.

"I assumed that," I say, knowing there's no business to call about. Not now. Maybe not ever again.

"I just wanted to know how the old swamp is doing."

"Are you referring to me or the lake?"

"Both."

Marnie pretends to have a love-hate relationship with Lake Greene, even though I know it's really only love. When we were kids, we spent every summer here together, swimming and canoeing and staying up half the night while Marnie told ghost stories.

"You know the lake is haunted, right?" she always began, scrunched at the foot of the bed in the room we shared, her tanned legs stretched, her bare feet flat against the slanted ceiling.

"It feels weird to be back," I say as I drop into a rocking chair. "Sad."

"Naturally."

"And lonely."

This place is too big for just one person. It started off small—a mere cottage on a lonely lake. As the years passed and additions were added, it turned into something intended for a brood. It feels so empty now that it's just me. Last night, when I found myself wide awake at two a.m., I roamed from room to room, unnerved by all that unoccupied space.

Third floor. The sleeping quarters. Five bedrooms in all, ranging in size from the large master suite, with its own bathroom, to the small two-bedder with the slanted ceiling where Marnie and I slept as children.

Second floor. The main living area, a maze of cozy rooms leading into each other. The living room, with its great stone fireplace and pillow-filled reading nook under the stairs. The den, cursed with a moose head on the wall that unnerved me as a child and still does in adulthood. It's home to the lake house's sole television, which is why I don't watch much TV when I'm here. It always feels like the moose is studying my every move.

Next to the den is the library, a lovely spot usually neglected because its windows face only trees and not the lake itself. After that is a long line of necessities sitting in a row—laundry room, powder room, kitchen, dining room.

Wrapped around it all, like ribbon on a present, is the porch. Wicker chairs in the front, wooden rockers in the back.

First floor. The walkout basement. The only place I refuse to go. More than any other part of the house, it makes me think of Len.

"It's natural to feel lonely," Marnie says. "You'll get used to it. Is anyone else at the lake besides Eli?"

"As a matter of fact, there is. Katherine Royce."

"The model?"

"Former model," I say, remembering what Katherine told me as she was getting out of the boat. "She and her husband bought the house across the lake."

"Vacation with the stars at Lake Greene, Vermont!" Marnie says in her best TV-pitchwoman voice. "Was she bitchy? Models always strike me as being bitchy."

"She was super sweet, actually. Although that might have been because I saved her from drowning."

"*Seriously?*"

"Seriously."

"If the paparazzi had been around for that," Marnie says, "your career prospects would look very different right now."

"I thought this wasn't a business call."

"It's not," she insists. "It's a please-take-care-of-yourself call. We'll deal with the business stuff when you're allowed to leave."

I sigh. "And that's up to my mother. Which means I'm never leaving. I've been sentenced to life in prison."

"I'll talk to Aunt Lolly about getting you parole. In the meantime, you have your new model friend to keep you company. You meet her husband?"

"Haven't had the pleasure yet."

"I heard he's weird," Marnie says.

"Weird how?"

She pauses, choosing her words carefully. "Intense."

"Are we talking Tom Cruise jumping-on-a-couch intense? Or Tom Cruise dangling-from-an-airplane intense?"

"Couch," Marnie says. "No, airplane. Is there a difference?"

"Not really."

"Tom Royce is more like the guy who holds meetings during CrossFit sessions and never stops working. You don't use his app, do you?"

"No."

I avoid all forms of social media, which are basically hazardous waste sites with varying levels of toxicity. I have enough issues to deal with. I don't need the added stress of seeing complete strangers on Twitter tell me how much they hate me. Also, I can't trust myself to behave. I can't begin to imagine the nonsense I'd post with six drinks in me. It's best to stay away.

Tom Royce's endeavor is basically a combination of LinkedIn and Facebook. Mixer, it's called. Allowing business professionals to connect by sharing their favorite bars, restaurants, golf courses, and vacation spots. Its slogan is "Work and play definitely mix."

Not in my line of work. God knows I've tried.

"Good," Marnie says. "That wouldn't be a good look for you."

"Really? I think it's very on brand."

Marnie's voice drops an octave. Her concerned voice, which I've heard often in the past year. "Please don't joke, Casey. Not about this. I'm worried about you. And not as your manager. As your friend and as family. I can't begin to understand what you're going through, but you don't need to do it alone."

"I'm trying," I say as I eye the glass of bourbon I abandoned in order to rescue Katherine. I'm gripped by the urge to take a sip, but I know Marnie will hear it if I do. "I just need time."

"So take it," Marnie says. "You're fine financially. And this madness will all die down eventually. Just spend the next few weeks focusing on you."

"I will."

"Good. And call me if you need anything. Anything at all."

"I will," I say again.

Like the first time, I don't mean it. There's nothing Marnie can do to change the situation. The only person who can get me out of the mess I've created is me.

Something I'm not inclined to do at the moment.

I get another call two minutes after hanging up with Marnie.

My mother making her daily four p.m. check-in.

Instead of my cell, she always calls the ancient rotary phone in the lake house's den, knowing its annoying ring makes it more likely I'll answer. She's right. In the three days since my return, I've tried to ignore that insistent trilling but have always given in before five rings.

Today, I make it to seven before going inside and picking up. If I don't answer now, I know she'll keep calling until I do.

"I just want to know how you're settling in," my mother says, which is exactly what she told me yesterday.

And the day before that.

"Everything's fine," I say, which is exactly what I told *her* yesterday.

And the day before that.

"And the house?"

"Also fine. That's why I used the word *everything*."

She ignores my snark. If there's one person on this earth unfazed by my sarcasm, it's Lolly Fletcher. She's had thirty-six years of practice.

"And have you been drinking?" she asks—the real purpose of her daily phone call.

"Of course not."

I glance at the moose head, which gives me a glassy-eyed stare from its perch on the wall. Even though it's been dead for almost a century, I can't shake the feeling the moose is judging me for lying.

"I sincerely hope that's true," my mother says. "If it is, please keep it that way. If it's not, well, I'll have no other choice but to send you somewhere more effective."

Rehab.

That's what she means. Shipping me off to some Malibu facility with the word *Promise* or *Serenity* or *Hope* in its name. I've been to places like that before and hated them. Which is why my mother always hints at the idea when she wants me to behave. It's the veiled threat she's never willing to fully reveal.

"You know I don't want that," she adds. "It would just cause another round of bad publicity. And I can't bear the thought of you being abused by those nasty gossip people more than you already are."

That's one of the few things my mother and I agree on. The gossip people are indeed nasty. And while calling what they do abuse is taking it a bit too far, they certainly are annoying. The reason I'm sequestered at Lake Greene and not my Upper West Side apartment is to escape the prying gaze of the paparazzi. They've been relentless. Waiting outside my building. Following me into Central Park. Covering my every move and trying to catch me with a drink in my hand.

I finally got so sick of the surveillance that I marched to the nearest bar, sat outside with a double old-fashioned, and gulped it down while a dozen cameras clicked away. The next morning, a picture of that moment appeared on the cover of the *New York Post*.

"Casey's Booze Binge" was the headline.

That afternoon, my mother showed up at my door with her driver, Ricardo, in tow.

"I think you should go to the lake for a month, don't you?"

Despite her phrasing it as a question, I had no say in the matter. Her tone made it clear I was going whether I wanted to or not, that Ricardo would drive me, and that I shouldn't even think about stopping at a liquor store along the way.

So here I am, in solitary confinement. My mother swears it's for my own good, but I know the score. I'm being punished. Because although half of what happened wasn't my fault, the other half was entirely my doing.

A few weeks ago, an acquaintance who edits celebrity memoirs approached me about writing my own. "Most stars find it very cathartic," she said.

I told her yes, but only if it I could call it *How to Become Tabloid Fodder in Seven Easy Steps*. She thought I was joking, and maybe I was, but I still stand by the title. I think people would understand me better if I laid out my life like Ikea instructions.

Step One, of course, is to be the only child of Beloved Lolly Fletcher, Broadway icon, and Gareth Greene, a rather milquetoast producer.

My mother made her Broadway debut at nineteen. She's been working nonstop ever since. Mostly onstage, but also in movies and television. YouTube is chock-full of her appearances on *The Lawrence Welk Show*, *The Mike Douglas Show*, *Match Game*, several dozen awards shows. She's petite, barely five feet in heels. Instead of smiling, she twinkles. A full-body sparkle that begins at her Cupid's bow lips, spreads upward to her hazel eyes, and then radiates outward, into the audience, enveloping them in a hypnotic glow of talent.

And my mother *is* talented. Make no mistake about that. She was—and still is—an old-school Star. In her prime, Lolly Fletcher could dance, act, and land a joke better than the best of them. And she had a powerhouse singing voice that was somewhat spooky coming from a woman so small.

But here's a little secret about my mother: Behind the twinkle, inside that tiny frame of hers, is a spine of steel. Growing up poor in a Pennsylvania coal town, Lolly Fletcher decided at an early age that she was going to be famous, and that it was her voice that would make it happen. She worked hard, cleaning studios in exchange for dance lessons, holding three after-school jobs to pay for a voice coach, training for hours. In interviews, my mother claims to never have smoked or drunk alcohol in her life, and I believe it. Nothing was going to get in the way of her success.

And when she did make it big, she worked her ass off to stay there. No missed performances for Lolly Fletcher. The unofficial motto in our household was "Why bother if you're not going to give it your all?"

My mother still gives it her all every damn day.

Her first two shows were mounted by the Greene Brothers, one of the prime producing duos of the day. Stuart Greene was the in-your-face, larger-than-life publicity man. Gareth Greene was the pale, unflappable bean counter. Both were instantly smitten with young Lolly, and most people thought she would choose the PR guy. Instead, she picked the accountant twenty years her senior.

Many years later, Stuart married a chorus girl and had Marnie.

Three years after that, my parents had me.

I was a late-in-life baby. My mother was forty-one, which always made me suspect my birth was a distraction. Something to keep her busy during a career lull in which she was too old to be playing Eliza Doolittle or Maria von Trapp but still a few years away from Mrs. Lovett and Mama Rose.

But motherhood was less interesting to her than performing. Within six months, she was back to work in a revival of *The King and I* while I, quite literally, became a Broadway baby. My crib was in her dressing room, and I took my first steps on the stage, practically basking in the glow of the ghost light.

Because of this, my mother assumed I'd follow in her footsteps. In fact, she demanded it. I made my stage debut playing young Cosette when she did *Les Misérables* for six months in London. I got the part not because I could sing or dance or was even remotely talented but because Lolly Fletcher's contract stipulated it. I was replaced after two weeks because I kept insisting I was too sick to go on. My mother was furious.

That leads us to Step Two: rebellion.

After the *Les Mis* fiasco, my level-headed father shielded me from my mother's star-making schemes. Then he died when I was fourteen and I rebelled, which to a rich kid living in Manhattan meant drugs. And going to the clubs where you took them. And the after parties, where you took more.

I smoked.

I snorted.

I placed candy-colored pills on my tongue and let them dissolve until I could no longer feel the inside of my mouth.

And it worked. For a few blissful hours, I didn't mind that my father was dead and that my mother cared more about her career than me and that all the people around me were only there because I paid for the drugs and that I had no real friends other than Marnie. But then I'd be jerked back to reality by waking up in a stranger's apartment I never remembered entering. Or in the back of a cab, dawn peeking through the buildings along the East River. Or in a subway car with a homeless man asleep in the seat across from me and vomit on my too-short skirt.

My mother tried her best to deal with me. I'll grant her that. It's just that her best consisted of simply throwing money at the problem. She did all the things rich parents try with troubled girls. Boarding school and rehab and therapy sessions in which I gnawed at my cuticles instead of talking about my feelings.

Then a miracle happened.

I got better.

Well, I got bored, which led to betterment. By the time I hit nineteen, I'd been making a mess of things for so long that it grew tiresome. I wanted to try something new. I wanted to try *not* being a trainwreck. I quit the drugs, the clubs, the "friends" I'd made along the way. I even went to NYU for a semester.

While there, Step Three—another miracle—occurred.

I got into acting.

It was never my intention to follow in my mother's footsteps. After growing up around showbiz, I wanted nothing to do with it. But here's the thing: It was the only world I knew. So when a college friend introduced me to her movie-director father, who then asked me if I wanted to play a small part in his next feature, I said, "Why not?"

The movie was good. It made a lot of money, and I made a name for myself. Not Casey Greene, which is my real name. I insisted on being billed as Casey Fletcher because, honestly, if you've got the kind of heritage I do, you'd be foolish not to flaunt it.

I got another part in another movie. Then more after that. Much to my mother's delight and my surprise, I became my worst fear: a working actress.

But here's another thing: I'm pretty good at it.

Certainly not legendary, like my mother, who truly is great at her craft. But I take direction well, have decent presence, and can put a fresh spin on the most tired of dialogue. Because I'm not classically beautiful enough for leading lady status, I often play the supportive best friend, the no-nonsense sister, the sympathetic coworker. I'm never going to become the star my mother is, which isn't my goal. But I am a *name*. People know me. Directors like me. Casting agents put me in big parts in small movies and small parts in big movies and as the lead in a sitcom that lasted only thirteen episodes.

It's not the size of the role I care about. It's the character itself. I want complicated, interesting parts into which I can disappear.

When I'm acting, I want to become someone else entirely.

That's why my main love is theater. Ironic, I know. I guess growing up in the wings really did rub off on me. The parts are better, that's for damn sure. The last movie offer I got was playing the mother of an actor six years younger than me in a *Transformers* reboot. The character had fourteen lines. The last theater offer was the lead role in a Broadway thriller, with dialogue on every page.

I said no to the movie, yes to the play. I prefer the palpable spark between performer and audience that exists only in theater. I feel it every time I step onstage. We share the same space, breathe the same air, share the same emotional journey. And then it's gone. The whole experience as transitory as smoke.

Kind of like my career, which is all but over, no matter what Marnie says.

Speaking of things that don't last, welcome to Step Four: Marry a screenwriter who is also a name but not one big enough to eclipse yours.

In my case, Len. Known professionally as Leonard Bradley, who helped pen a few movies you've definitely seen and quite a lot that you haven't. We met at a party first, then on the set of a movie on which he did some uncredited script polishing. Both times, I thought he was cute and funny and maybe secretly sexy under his gray hoodie and Knicks cap. I didn't think of him as boyfriend material until our third meeting, when we found ourselves boarding the same flight back to New York.

"We need to stop meeting like this," he said.

"You're right," I replied. "You know how this town talks."

We finagled our way into adjacent seats and spent the entire flight deep in conversation. By the time the plane touched down, we'd made plans to meet for dinner. Standing in JFK's baggage claim area, both of us flushed from flirtation and reluctant to part, I said, "My car is waiting outside. I should go."

"Of course." Len paused, suddenly shy. "Can I get a kiss first?"

I obliged, my head spinning like one of the luggage carousels piled high with Samsonite suitcases.

Six months later, we got married at city hall, with Marnie and my mother as witnesses. Len didn't have any family of his own. At least none that he wanted to invite to his impromptu wedding. His mother was thirty years younger than his father, pregnant and eighteen when they wed and twenty-three when she abandoned them. His father took it out on Len. Not long into our relationship, Len told me how his father broke his arm when he was six. He spent the next twelve years in foster care. The last time Len spoke to his father, now long dead, was right before he left for UCLA on a full scholarship.

Because of his past, Len was determined not to make the same mistakes as his parents. He never got angry and was rarely sad. When he laughed, it was with his whole body, as if there was too much happiness within him to be contained. He was a great cook, an even better listener, and loved long, hot baths, preferably with me in the tub with him. Our marriage was a combination of gestures both big—like when he rented an entire movie theater on my birthday so the two of us could have a private screening of *Rear Window*—and small. He always held the door for me. And ordered pizza with extra cheese without asking because he knew that's how I liked it. And appreciated the contented silence when the two of us were in the same room but doing different things.

As a result, our marriage was a five-year period in which I was almost deliriously happy.

The happiness part is important.

Without it, you'd have nothing to miss when everything inevitably turns to shit.

Which brings us to Step Five: Spend a summer at Lake Greene.

The lake house has always been a special place for my family. Conceived by my great-great-grandfather as an escape from New York's steaming, stinking summers, it was once the only residence on this unassuming slash of water. That's how the lake got its name. Originally called Lake Otshee by the indigenous tribe that once lived in the area, it was renamed Lake Greene in honor of the first white man intrepid enough to build here because, well, America.

My father spent every summer at the lake that bore his family name. As did his father before him. As did I. Growing up, I loved life on the lake.

It was a much-needed reprieve from my mother's theatrics. Some of my fondest memories are of endless days spent catching fireflies, roasting marshmallows, swimming in the sun until I was as tanned as leather.

Going to the lake for a summer was Len's idea, proposed after a frigid, slushy winter during which we barely saw each other. I was busy with the Broadway thriller I'd chosen over the *Transformers* movie, and Len kept having to return to LA to bang out another draft of a superhero screenplay he'd taken on because he mistakenly thought it would be easy money.

"We need a break," he said during Easter brunch. "Let's take the summer off and spend it at Lake Greene."

"The whole summer?"

"Yeah. I think it'll be good for us." Len smiled at me over the Bloody Mary he'd been drinking. "I know I sure as hell need a break."

I did, too. So we took it. I left the play for four months, Len finally finished the screenplay, and we set off for Vermont for the summer. It was wonderful. During the day, we whiled away the hours reading, napping, making love. In the evenings, we cooked long dinners and sat on the porch sipping strong cocktails and listening to the ghostly call of loons echoing across the lake.

One afternoon in late July, Len and I filled a picnic basket with wine, cheese, and fresh fruit bought that morning at a nearby farmers' market. We hiked to the southern end of the lake, where the forest gives way to a craggy bluff. After stumbling our way to the top, we spread the food out on a checkered blanket and spent the afternoon snacking, drinking wine, and staring at the water far below.

At one point, Len turned to me and said, "Let's stay here forever, Cee." Cee.

That was his nickname for me, created after he had deemed *Case* too hard-boiled for a term of endearment.

"It makes me think of a private detective," he said. "Or, worse, a lawyer."

"Or maybe I don't need a nickname," I said. "It's not like my name's that unwieldy."

"I can't be the only one of us with a nickname. That would make me incredibly selfish, don't you think?"

We'd been officially dating two weeks by then, both of us sensing things were getting very serious very quickly but neither of us ready to admit it. It's why Len was trying too hard that night. He wanted to dazzle me with wit. And even though the wit might have been strained, I was indeed dazzled.

I remained that way most of our marriage.

"Define *forever*," I said that July afternoon, hypnotized by the sunlight sparking off the lake and the summer breeze in my hair.

"Never leaving. Just like Old Stubborn there."

Len pointed to a petrified tree stump that jutted from the water about fifty yards from the shore below. It was legendary on Lake Greene, mostly because no one knew how this sun-bleached piece of wood came to be poking twenty feet out of the water or how much more of it stretched from the surface to the lake's bottom. We all called it Old Stubborn because Eli, who researched such things, claimed it had been there for hundreds of years and would remain long after the rest of us were gone.

"Is that even possible?" I said.

"Sure, we'd still have to go to the city and LA a lot for work, but there's no law saying we must live in Manhattan. We could live here full-time. Make this place our home base."

Home.

I liked the sound of that.

It didn't matter that the lake house technically belonged to my aunt and mother. Or that eastern Vermont was quite a hike from Manhattan, not to mention a world away from LA, where Len had been spending so much time. The idea was still appealing. Like Len, I longed for a life removed from our bicoastal grind.

"Let me think about it," I said.

I never got the chance. A week later, Len was dead.

That's Step Six, by the way.

Have your husband die while on vacation.

The morning it happened, I was tugged out of bed by the sound of Eli knocking on the front door. Before opening it, I checked the clock in the foyer. Seven a.m. Way too early for him to be paying a neighborly visit.

Something was wrong.

"Your boat got loose," Eli announced. "Woke up and saw it drifting on the lake. Guess you didn't tie it up right."

"Is it still out there?" I said.

"Nah. I towed it back to my dock. I can take you over to get it." Eli looked me over, noticing my nightgown, hastily-thrown-on robe, out-of-control bedhead. "Or I can take Len."

Len.

He wasn't in bed when I woke up. Nor was he anywhere in the house. Eli and I searched the place from top to bottom, calling out his name. There was no sign of him. He was gone.

"Do you think he could be out for a morning run or something?"

"Len's not a runner," I said. "He swims."

Both of us looked to the lake, shimmering beyond the tall windows in the living room. The water was calm. And empty. I couldn't help but picture our boat out there, unmoored, drifting aimlessly. Also empty.

Eli pictured it, too, because the next thing he said was, "Do you know if Len had any reason to take the boat out this morning?"

"Some—" I paused to swallow the lump of worry that had suddenly caught in my throat. "Some mornings he goes fishing."

Eli knew this. He'd seen Len out on the water, wearing that silly fisherman's hat and smoking his disgusting cigars, which he claimed kept the mosquitoes away. Sometimes the two of them even went fishing together.

"Did you see him go out this morning?" Eli took another look at my bedclothes and puffy eyes, rightfully concluding that he was the reason I got out of bed. "Or hear him?"

I answered with a short, scared head shake.

"And he didn't tell you last night that he was thinking about going fishing?"

"No," I said. "But he doesn't always tell me. Especially if he thinks I won't be up for a few hours. Sometimes he just goes."

Eli's gaze drifted back to the empty lake. When he spoke again, his voice was halting, cautious. "When I fetched your boat, I saw a rod and tackle box inside. Len doesn't always keep them there, does he?"

"No," I said. "He keeps them—"

In the basement. That's what I intended to say. Instead, I went there, down the rickety steps to what's technically the first level of the lake house but is treated like a cellar because it's built into the steep hillside that slopes to the water. Eli followed me. Past the room with the furnace and hot-water heater. Past the Ping-Pong table that had last been used in the nineties. Past the skis on the wall and the ice skates in the corner. Stopping only when I stopped.

The mudroom.

The place where Len and I entered and exited after swimming and boating, using the old blue door that had been part of the house since the very beginning. There's an old sink there, and a long wooden rack on which hung jackets and hoodies and hats.

Except one.

Len's fishing hat—floppy and foul smelling, colored army green—was missing.

Also, the shelf that should have held his tackle box and fishing rod was empty, and the creaky blue door that led outside was open just a crack.

I let out a choked sob, prompting Eli to spin me away from the door, as if it were a mutilated corpse. He gripped my shoulders, looked me in the eyes, and said, "I think we might want to call the police."

Eli did the calling. He did everything, to be honest. Rounding up the Fitzgeralds on his side of the lake and the Mitchells, who lived on mine, to form a search party.

And he's the one who eventually found Len, just after ten that morning.

Eli discovered his hat first, floating like a lily pad a few yards from shore. He waded out to fetch it, and when he turned to head back to dry land he spotted Len a hundred yards away, washed ashore like the victim of a shipwreck.

I don't know any other details. Neither Eli nor the police told me exactly where my husband had been found, and I didn't ask. I was better off not knowing. Besides, it didn't really matter. Len was still dead.

After asking me a few questions, the police pieced everything together pretty quickly. Len, always an early riser when at the lake, woke up, made coffee, and decided to go fishing.

At some point, he fell overboard, although authorities couldn't tell me how or why or when. An autopsy found alcohol in his system—we had been drinking the night before—and a large amount of the antihistamine Len took for his allergies, suggesting he had double-dosed before going out that morning. All the medical examiner knew was that he had dropped into the water and drowned, leaving behind a boat, a tackle box and fishing rod, and a thermos of still-warm coffee.

I was also left behind.

At age thirty-five, I had become a widow.

After that happens, there's just one final step.

Unlucky Number Seven.

Fall apart.

My unraveling happened rather slowly, thanks to the many people who cared for me. Eli stayed by my side until Ricardo was able to drive up from Manhattan with my mother and Marnie in tow. We spent a sleepless night packing up my things and left early the next morning.

For the next six months, I did as well as one can under such circumstances. I mourned, both publicly and in private. I dutifully attended two memorial services, one in New York and the other in Los Angeles, before returning to Lake Greene for an afternoon when, watched by a small gathering of friends and family, I poured Len's ashes into the water.

It wasn't until the second six months that it all went downhill. Before then, I'd been surrounded by people. My mother visited daily or sent Ricardo when she was working. Marnie and other friends and colleagues made sure to call, to stop by, to reach out and see how I was coping. But an outpouring of kindness like that can only last for so long. People move on. They must.

Eventually it was just me, left with a thousand emotions and no way of softening them without some form of assistance. When I was fourteen and mourning my father, I turned to drugs. Rather than repeat myself, I decided booze was the answer on this go-round.

Bourbon, mostly. But also gin. And vodka. And wine of any color. And once, when I'd forgotten to stock up before a snowstorm, pear brandy chugged straight from the bottle. It didn't make the pain completely go away, but it sure as hell eased it. Drinking made the circumstances of my widowhood feel distant, like it was a vaguely remembered nightmare I'd woken from long ago.

And I was determined to keep drinking until no memory of this particular nightmare remained.

In May, I was asked if I wanted to return to the Broadway play I'd left before going to Vermont. *Shred of Doubt*, it was called. About a woman who suspects her husband is trying to kill her. Spoiler alert: He is.

Marnie recommended I say no, suggesting the producers merely wanted to boost ticket sales by capitalizing on my tragedy. My mother told me to say yes, advising that work was the best thing for me.

I said yes.

Mother knows best, right?

The irony is that my performance had improved greatly. "Trauma has unlocked something in you," the director told me, as if my husband's death was a creative choice I'd made. I thanked him for the compliment and walked straight to the bar across the street.

By that point, I knew I was drinking too much. But I managed. I'd have two drinks in my dressing room before a performance, just to keep me loose, followed by however many I wanted after the evening show.

Within a few months, my two drinks before curtain had become three and my postshow drinking sometimes lasted all night. But I was discreet about it. I didn't let it affect my work.

Until I showed up to the theater already drunk.

For a Wednesday matinee.

The stage manager confronted me in my dressing room, where I was applying my makeup with wildly unsteady hands.

"I can't let you go on like this," she said.

"Like what?" I said, pretending to be insulted. It was the best acting I'd do all day.

"Drunk off your ass."

"I've played this role literally a hundred times," I said. "I can fucking do it."

I couldn't fucking do it.

That was clear the moment I stepped onstage. Well, *stepped* isn't the right word. I *lurched* onto the stage, swaying as if hit by hurricane winds. Then I blanked on my entrance line. Then stumbled into the nearest chair. Then slid off the chair and collapsed onto the floor in a drunken heap, which is how I stayed until two costars dragged me into the wings.

The show was halted, my understudy was brought in, and I was fired from *Shred of Doubt* as soon as the producers thought me sober enough to comprehend what they were telling me.

Hence the tabloids and the paparazzi and the being whisked away to a remote lake where I won't publicly embarrass myself and where my mother can check in daily.

"You're really not drinking, right?" my mother says.

"I'm really not drinking." I turn to the moose on the wall, a finger to my lips, as if we're sharing a secret. "But would you blame me if I were?"

Silence from my mother. She knows me well enough to understand that's as much of a yes as she's going to get.

"Where did you get it?" she finally says. "From Ricardo? I specifically told him not to—"

"It wasn't Ricardo," I say, leaving out how on the drive from Manhattan I had indeed begged him to stop at a liquor store. For cigarettes, I told him, even though I don't smoke. He didn't fall for it. "It was already here. Len and I stocked up last summer."

It's the truth. Sort of. We did bring a lot of booze along with us, although most of those bottles had long been emptied by the time Len died. But I'm certainly not going to tell my mother how I really got my hands on the alcohol.

She sighs. All her hopes and dreams for me dying in one long, languid exhalation.

"I don't understand," she says, "why you continue to do this to yourself. I know you miss Len. We all do. We loved him, too, you know."

I do know. Len was endlessly charming, and had Lolly Fletcher cooing in the palm of his hand five minutes after they met. Marnie was the same way. They were crazy about him, and although I know his death devastated them as well, their grief is nothing compared with mine.

"It's not the same," I say. "You're not being punished for grieving."

"You were so out of control that I had to do *something*."

"So you sent me here," I say. "Here. Where it all happened. Did you ever stop to consider that maybe it would fuck me up even more?"

"I thought it would help you," my mother says.

"How?"

"By making you finally confront what happened. Because until you do, you won't be able to move on."

"Here's the thing, Mom," I say. "I don't want to move on."

I slam the phone onto the receiver and yank the cord out of the jack in the wall. No more landline for her. After shoving the phone into the drawer of an unused sideboard, I catch a glimpse of myself in the gilt-edged mirror hanging above it.

My clothes are damp, my hair hangs in strings, and beads of water still stick to my face like warts. Seeing myself like this—a mess in every conceivable way—sends me back to the porch and the glass of bourbon waiting there. The ice has melted, leaving two inches of amber liquid swirling at the bottom of the glass.

I tip it back and swallow every drop.

By five thirty, I'm showered, dressed in dry clothes, and back on the porch watching the sun dip behind the distant mountains on the other side of the lake. Next to me is a fresh bourbon.

My fourth for the day.

Or fifth.

I take a sip and look out at the lake. Directly across from me, the Royce house is lit like a stage set, every room aglow. Inside, two figures move about, although I'm not able to see them clearly. The lake is about a quarter mile wide here. Close enough to get a gist of what's going on inside, but too far away to glean any details.

Watching their blurry, distant activity, I wonder if Tom and Katherine feel as exposed as I did when I was inside that house. Maybe it doesn't bother them. Being a former model, Katherine is probably used to being watched. One could argue that someone who buys a house that's half glass knows being seen is part of the deal. It might even be the reason they bought it.

That's bullshit, and I know it. The view afforded to residents of Lake Greene is one of the reasons the houses here are so expensive. The other is privacy. That's likely the real reason Tom and Katherine Royce bought the house across the lake.

But when I see the binoculars sitting a few feet away, right where I'd dropped them earlier, I can't help but pick them up. I tell myself it's to clean them off. But I know it'll only be a matter of time before I lift them to my eyes and peer at the opposite shore, too curious to resist a glimpse of the inner lives of a former supermodel and her tech titan husband.

The binoculars belonged to Len, who bought them during a short-lived bird-watching phase, spending a small fortune in the process. In his post-purchase speech justifying the expense, he talked about their insane magnification, wide field of vision, image stabilization, and top-of-the-line clarity.

"These binoculars rock," he said. "They're so good that if you look up at a full moon, you can see craters."

"But this is for birds," I replied. "Who wants to see birds that up close?"

When I inevitably do lift them to my eyes, I'm not impressed. The focus is off, and for a few jarring seconds, everything is skewed. Nothing but woozy views of the water and the tops of trees. I keep adjusting the binoculars until the image sharpens. The trees snap into focus. The lake's surface smooths into clarity.

Now I understand why Len was so excited.

These binoculars do indeed rock.

The image isn't super close. Definitely not an extreme close-up. But the detail at such a distance is startling. It feels like I'm standing on the other side of a street rather than the opposite shore of the lake. What was fuzzy to the naked eye is now crystal clear.

Including the inside of Tom and Katherine Royce's glass house.

I take in the first floor, where details of the living room are visible through the massive windows. Off-white walls. Mid-century modern furniture in neutral tones. Splashes of color provided by massive abstract paintings. It's an interior designer's dream, and a far cry from my family's rustic lake house. Here, the hardwood floor is scratched and the furniture threadbare. Adorning the walls are landscape paintings, crisscrossed snowshoes, and old advertisements for maple syrup. And the moose in the den, of course.

In the much more refined Royce living room, I spy Katherine reclining on a white sofa, flipping through a magazine. Now dry and fully dressed, she looks far more familiar than she did in the boat. Every inch the model she used to be. Her hair shines. Her skin glows. Even her clothes—a yellow silk blouse and dark capri pants—have a sheen to them.

I check her left hand. Her wedding band is back on, along with an engagement ring adorned with a diamond that looks ridiculously huge even through the binoculars. It makes my own ring finger do an involuntary flex. Both of my rings from Len are in a jewelry box in Manhattan. I stopped wearing them three days after his death. Keeping them on was too painful.

I tilt the binoculars to the second floor and the master bedroom. It's dimmer than the rest of the house—lit only by a bedside lamp. But I can still make out a cavernous space with vaulted ceilings and décor that looks plucked from a high-end hotel suite. It puts my master bedroom, with its creaking bed frame and antique dresser of drawers that stick more often than not, to shame.

To the left of the bedroom is what appears to be an exercise room. I see a flat-screen TV on the wall, the handlebars of a Peloton bike in front of it, and the top of a rack holding free weights. After that is a room with bookshelves, a desk and lamp, and a printer. Likely a home office, inside of which is Tom Royce. He's seated at the desk, frowning at the screen of a laptop open in front of him.

He closes the laptop and stands, finally giving me a full look at him. My first impression of Tom is that he looks like someone who'd marry a supermodel. It makes sense why Katherine was drawn to him. He's handsome, of course. But it's a lived-in handsomeness, reminding me of Harrison Ford just a year past his prime. About ten years older than Katherine, Tom exudes confidence, even when alone. He stands ramrod straight, dressed like he's just stepped off the pages of a catalogue. Dark jeans and a gray T-shirt under a cream-colored cardigan, all of it impeccably fitted. His hair is dark brown and on the longish side. I can only imagine how much product it takes to get it to swoop back from his head like that.

Tom leaves the office and appears a few seconds later in the bedroom.

A few seconds after that, he disappears through another door in the room. The master bath, from the looks of it. I get a glimpse of white wall, the edge of a mirror, the angelic glow of perfect bathroom lighting.

The door closes.

Directly below, Katherine continues to read.

Because I'm unwilling to admit to myself that I picked up the binoculars just to spy on the Royces, I swing them toward Eli's house, the cluster of rocks and evergreens between the two homes passing in a blur.

I catch Eli in the act of coming home from running errands—an all-day affair in this part of Vermont. Lake Greene sits fifteen minutes from the nearest town, reached by a highway that cuts southwest through the forest. The highway itself is a mile away and accessed via a ragged gravel road that circles the lake. That's where Eli is when I spot him, turning his trusty red pickup off the road and into his driveway.

I watch him get out of the truck and carry groceries up the side porch and through the door that leads to the kitchen. Inside the house, a light flicks on in one of the back windows. Through the glass, I can see into the dining room, with its brass light fixture and giant old hutch. I can even make out the rarely used collection of patterned china that sits on the hutch's top shelf.

Outside, Eli returns to the pickup, this time removing a cardboard box from the back. Provisions for me that I assume he'll be bringing over sooner rather than later.

I direct the binoculars back to the Royces'. Katherine's at the living room window now. A surprise. Her unexpected presence by the glass hits me with a guilty jolt, and for a moment, I wonder if she can see me.

The answer is no.

Not when she's inside like that, with the lights on. Maybe, if she squinted, she could make out the red plaid of my flannel shirt as I sit tucked back in the shadow of the porch. But there's no way she can tell I'm watching her.

She stands inches from the glass, staring out at the lake, her face a gorgeous blank page. After a few more seconds at the window, Katherine moves deeper into the living room, heading toward a sideboard bar next to the fireplace. She drops some ice into a glass and fills it halfway with something poured from a crystal decanter.

I raise my own glass in a silent toast and time my sip to hers.

Above her, Tom Royce is out of the bathroom. He sits on the edge of the bed, examining his fingernails.

Boring.

I return to Katherine, who's back at the window, her drink in one hand, her phone in the other. Before dialing, she tilts her head toward the ceiling, as if listening to hear if her husband is coming.

He's not. A quick uptilt of the binoculars shows him still preoccupied with his nails, using one to dig a smidge of dirt out from under another.

Below, Katherine correctly assumes the coast is clear, taps her phone, and holds it to her ear.

I let my gaze drift back to the bedroom, where Tom is now standing in the middle of the room, listening for his wife downstairs.

Only Katherine isn't talking. Holding her phone and tapping one foot, she's waiting for whoever she just called to answer.

Upstairs, Tom tiptoes across the bedroom and peeks out the open door, of which I can see only a sliver. He disappears through it, leaving the bedroom empty and me moving the binoculars to try to catch his reappearance elsewhere on the second floor. I swing them past the exercise room to the office.

Tom isn't in either of them.

I return my gaze to the living room, where Katherine is now speaking into the phone. It's not a conversation, though. She doesn't pause to let the other person talk, making me think she's leaving a message. An urgent one, from the looks of it. Katherine's hunched slightly, a hand cupped to her mouth as she talks, her eyes darting back and forth.

On the other side of the house, movement catches my attention.

Tom.

Now on the first floor.

Moving out of the kitchen and into the dining room.

Slowly.

With caution.

His long, quiet strides make me think it's an effort not to be heard. With his lips flattened together and his chin jutting forward, his expression is unreadable. He could be curious. He could be concerned.

Tom makes his way to the other side of the dining room and he and Katherine finally appear together in the binoculars' lenses. She's still talking, apparently oblivious to her husband watching from the next room. It's not until Tom takes another step that Katherine becomes aware of his presence. She taps the phone, hides it behind her back, whirls around to face him.

Unlike her husband's, Katherine's expression is easily read.

She's startled.

Especially as Tom comes toward her. Not angry, exactly. It's different from that. He looks, to use Marnie's description, intense.

He says something to Katherine. She says something back. She slips the phone into her back pocket before raising her hands—a gesture of innocence.

"Enjoying the view?"

The sound of another person's voice—at this hour, in this place—startles me so much I almost drop the binoculars for a second time that day. I manage to keep hold of them as I yank them away from my face and, still rattled, look for the source of the voice.

It's a man unfamiliar to me.

A very good-looking man.

In his mid-thirties, he stands to the right of the porch in a patch of weedy grass that serves as a buffer between the house and rambling forest situated next to it. Appropriate, seeing how he's dressed like a lumberjack. The pinup-calendar version. Tight jeans, work boots, flannel shirt wrapped around his narrow waist, broad chest pushing against a white T-shirt. The light of magic hour reflecting off the lake gives his skin a golden glow. It's sexy and preposterous in equal measure.

Making the situation even weirder is that I'm dressed almost exactly the same way. Adidas sneakers instead of boots, and my jeans don't look painted on. But it's enough for me to realize how frumpily I always dress when I'm at the lake.

"Sorry?" I say.

"The view," he says, gesturing to the binoculars still gripped in my hands. "See anything good?"

Suddenly—and rightfully—feeling guilty, I set the binoculars on the wobbly table beside the rocking chair. "Just trees."

The man nods. "The foliage is beautiful this time of year."

I stand, make my way to the end of the porch, and look down at him. He's come closer to the house and now gazes up at me with a glint in his eyes, as if he knows exactly what I've been doing.

"I don't mean to sound rude," I say, "but who are you and where did you come from?"

The man takes a half step back. "Are you *sure* you didn't mean to sound rude?"

"Maybe I did," I say. "And you still haven't answered my question."

"I'm Boone. Boone Conrad."

I barely stop myself from rolling my eyes. That cannot be his real name.

"And I came from over there."

He jerks his head in the direction of the woods and the house slightly visible two hundred yards behind the thinning trees. The Mitchell place. An A-frame cabin built in the seventies, it sits tucked within a small bend of the lakeshore. In the summer, the only part of it visible from my family's house is the long dock that juts into the lake.

"You're a guest of the Mitchells?" I say.

"More like their temporary handyman," Boone says. "Mr. and Mrs. Mitchell said I could stay for a couple of months if I did some work on the place while I'm here. Since we're neighbors, I thought I'd stop by and introduce myself. I would have done it earlier, but I was too busy stuck inside refinishing their dining room floor."

"Nice to meet you, Boone. Thanks for stopping by."

He pauses a beat. "You're not going to introduce yourself, Casey Fletcher?"

I'm not surprised he knows who I am. More people than not recognize me, even though sometimes they're not sure how. "You just did it for me."

"Sorry," Boone says. "The Mitchells told me your family owned the house next door. I just didn't think you'd be here."

"Neither did I."

"How long are you staying?"

"That's up to my mother," I say.

A sly grin plays across Boone's lips. "Do you do everything your mother tells you to?"

"Everything except not doing this." I lift my glass. "How long will you be staying?"

"Another few weeks, I suspect. I've been here since August."

"I didn't know the Mitchells needed so much work done on their house."

"Honestly, they don't," Boone says. "They're just doing me a favor after I found myself in a bit of a lurch."

An intriguing response. It makes me wonder what his deal is. I don't see a wedding ring—apparently a new obsession of mine—so he's not married. Not now, at least. I peg him as recently divorced. The wife got the house. He needed a place to live. In step David and Hope Mitchell, a friendly but dull pair of retirees who made their money in pharmaceuticals.

"How do you like life on the lake?"

"It's quiet," Boone says after thinking it over for a few seconds. "Don't get me wrong. I like the quiet. But nothing much seems to happen here."

Spoken like a man whose spouse wasn't found dead on the lakeshore fourteen months ago.

"It takes some getting used to," I say.

"Are you also here by yourself?"

"I am."

"Don't you get lonely?"

"Sometimes."

"Well, if you ever get bored or need some company, you know where to find me."

I note his tone, pitched somewhere between friendly and flirtatious. Hearing it is surprising, but not unwelcome to someone like me who's watched way too many Hallmark Channel Christmas movies. This is how they always begin. Jaded big-city professional woman meets rugged local man. Sparks fly. Hearts melt. Both live happily ever after.

The only differences here are that Boone isn't a local, my heart's too shattered to melt, and there's no such thing as happily ever after. There's only happy for a short period of time before everything falls apart.

Also, Boone is more attractive than the blandly handsome men of the Hallmark Channel. He's unpolished in the best of ways. The stubble on his chin is a tad unruly and the muscles evident under his clothes are a bit too big. When he follows up his offer of company with a sleepy, sexy grin, I realize that Boone could be trouble.

Or maybe I'm simply looking for trouble. The no-strings kind. Hell, I think I've earned it. I've been intimate with only one man since Len's death, a bearded stagehand named Morris who worked on *Shred of Doubt*. We were postshow drinking buddies for a time, until suddenly we were more. It wasn't romance. Neither of us was interested in each other that way. He was, quite simply, yet another means to chase away the darkness. I was the same thing for him. I haven't heard from Morris since I got fired. I doubt I ever will.

Now here's Boone Conrad—quite an upgrade from Morris and his dad bod.

I gesture to the pair of rocking chairs behind me. "You're welcome to join me for a drink right now."

"I'd love to," Boone says. "Unfortunately, I don't think my sponsor would be too happy about that."

"Oh." My heart sinks past my spleen. "You're—"

Boone interrupts me with a solemn nod. "Yeah."

"How long have you been sober?"

"A year."

"Good for you," I manage. I feel like a horrible person for asking an alcoholic if he'd like a drink, even though there's no way I could have known he had a problem. But Boone definitely knows about mine. I can tell from the way he looks at me with squinty-eyed concern.

"It's hard," he says. "Every day is a challenge. But I'm living proof it's possible to go through life without a drink in your hand."

I tighten my grip around the bourbon glass. "Not my life."

After that, there's not a whole lot else to say. Boone gives me his little twelve-step pitch, which I suspect is the real reason he stopped by. I express my distinct lack of interest. Now there's nothing left to do but go our separate ways.

"I guess I should get going then." Boone offers a little wave and turns back to the woods. Before stepping into them, he gives me an over-the-shoulder glance and adds, "My offer still stands, by the way. If you're ever feeling lonely, stop on by. There might not be any liquor in the house, but I can make a mean hot chocolate and the place is well stocked with board games. I need to warn you, though, I show no mercy at Monopoly."

"I'll keep that in mind," I say, meaning thanks but no thanks. Despite Boone's looks, that doesn't sound like a good time. I suck at Monopoly, and I prefer my drinks stronger than Swiss Miss.

Boone waves again and trudges through the trees on his way back to the Mitchell place. Watching him go, I don't feel a bit of remorse. Sure, I might be missing out on a few nights in the sack with a guy way out of my league. If that was even his intention. But I'm not willing to accept what goes along with it—chiefly being reminded that I drink too much.

I do.

But with good reason.

I once read a biography of Joan Crawford in which she was quoted as saying, "Alcoholism is an occupational hazard of being an actor, of being a widow, and of being alone. And I'm all three."

Ditto, Joan.

But I'm not an alcoholic. I can quit at any time. I just don't want to.

To prove it to myself, I set the bourbon down, keeping my hand close to the glass but not touching it. Then I wait, seeing how long I last before taking a sip.

The seconds tick by, me counting each one in my head the same way I did when I was a girl and Marnie wanted me to time how long she could stay underwater before coming up for air.

One Mississippi. Two Mississippi. Three Mississippi.

I make it to exactly forty-six Mississippis before sighing, grabbing the glass, and taking a gulp. As I swallow, I'm struck by a thought. One of those insights I usually drink to avoid.

Maybe I'm not looking for trouble.

Maybe I *am* the trouble.

The sun has slipped beneath the horizon by the time Eli makes his way over. Through the binoculars, which I picked up again soon after Boone departed, I watch him return to his truck carrying a bag of groceries before going back to his house for the cardboard box. When he climbs into the truck, I follow the glow of headlights as he drives the road circling the lake.

I put the binoculars down when the headlights enter the section of the road not visible from the back porch and walk to the front of the house. I get there just in time to see Eli pull into the driveway and emerge from the truck.

Back when he was on the bestseller lists, Eli cut a dashing figure in tweed jackets and dark jeans. For the past three decades, though, he's been in Hemingway mode. Cable-knit sweaters, corduroy, and a bushy white beard. Grabbing the cardboard box from the back of the truck, he resembles a rustic Santa Claus bearing gifts.

"As requested," he says, placing the box in my arms.

Inside, clanging together like tangled wind chimes, are a dozen bottles of various colors. The deep crimson of pinot noir. The honey brown of bourbon. The pristine clarity of dry gin.

"Pace yourself," Eli says. "I won't be making another trip until next week. And if you breathe a word of this to your mother, I'm cutting you off. The last thing I need is an angry phone call from Lolly Fletcher telling me I'm a bad influence."

"But you are a bad influence."

Eli smiles in spite of himself. "It takes one to know one."

Know me he does. During my childhood, Eli was an unofficial summer uncle, always in my life between Memorial Day and Labor Day, mostly forgotten the rest of the year. That didn't change much in adulthood, when I visited Lake Greene less frequently. Sometimes years would pass between visits, but whenever I returned, Eli would still be here, quick with a warm smile, a tight hug, and whatever favor I needed. Back then, it was showing me how to build a campfire and properly roast a marshmallow. Now it's illicit trips to the liquor store.

We retreat into the house, me burdened with the box of bottles and Eli carrying the grocery bag. In the kitchen, we unpack everything and prepare to make dinner. It's part of the deal we made my first night back here: I cook dinner anytime he brings me booze.

I like the arrangement, and not just because of the alcohol. Eli is good company, and it's nice to have someone else to cook for. When it's just me, I make whatever's fast and easy. Tonight's dinner, on the other hand, is salmon, roasted acorn squash, and wild rice. Once everything's unpacked and two glasses of wine have been poured, I preheat the oven and get to cooking.

"I met the next-door neighbor," I say as I grab the largest, sharpest blade from the wooden knife block on the countertop and start cutting the acorn squash. "Why didn't you tell me there was someone staying at the Mitchell place?"

"I didn't think you'd care."

"Of course I care. There are only two houses on this side of the lake. If someone else is in one of them—especially a stranger—I'd like to be aware of it. Is there someone staying at the Fitzgerald house I need to know about?"

"The Fitzgerald place is empty, as far as I know," Eli says. "As for Boone, I thought it would be best if the two of you didn't meet."

"Why?"

I think I already know the answer. Eli met Boone, learned he was a recovering alcoholic, and decided it was wise to keep me away from him.

"Because his wife died," Eli says instead.

Surprise stills the knife, stuck deep within the squash. "When?"

"A year and a half ago."

Because Boone told me he's been sober a year, I assume the six months after his wife's death were a self-destructive blur. Not quite the same situation as mine, but close enough to make me feel like shit for the way I behaved earlier.

"How?" I say.

"I didn't ask and he didn't volunteer the information," Eli says. "But I guess I thought it would be best if you two didn't cross paths. I was afraid it would dredge up bad memories. For both of you."

"Bad memories are already here," I say. "They're everywhere I look."

"Then maybe—" Eli pauses. It's brief. Like the tentative halt a firewalker makes just before stepping onto pulsing-hot coals. "Maybe I thought you wouldn't be the best influence on him."

There it is. The ugly truth at last. Even though I suspected it, it doesn't mean I like hearing it.

"Says the man who just brought me a case of booze," I say.

"Because you asked me to," Eli says, bristling. "I'm not judging you, Casey. You're a grown woman. The choices you make are none of my business. But Boone Conrad has been sober a year. You—"

"Haven't been," I say, mostly so Eli doesn't have to.

He nods, both in agreement and in thanks. "Exactly. So maybe it's best if you keep away from each other. For both of your sakes."

Despite being rankled by what he said, I'm inclined to agree with Eli. I have my reasons for drinking, and Boone has his for not. Whatever they are, I'm sure they're not compatible with mine.

"Deal," I say. "Now give me a hand. Dinner isn't going to cook itself."

The rest of the evening passes in a blur of small talk and hurt feelings left unexpressed.

We finish cooking.

"How was the summer?" I ask while plating the fish.

"Quiet," Eli says. "Nothing to report. Here or elsewhere in the area. Although they still haven't found that girl who drowned in Lake Morey last summer. No sign of the one who went missing two years ago, either."

I empty my glass of wine and pour another.

"That storm's probably heading this way," Eli says as we eat.

"What storm?"

"That hurricane that hit North Carolina. Don't you watch the news?"

I don't. Not lately.

"A hurricane? Here?"

The last time something like that happened here was Hurricane Sandy's long, slow march through the Northeast. Lake Greene was without power for two weeks.

"Trish," Eli says. "That's what they're calling it."

"That's a perky name for a hurricane."

"It's just a tropical storm now, but still plenty strong. Looks like it'll reach us by the end of the week."

Eli has another glass of wine.

I have two.

After dinner, we retreat to the porch and plop into rocking chairs while sipping from steaming mugs of coffee. Night has fully fallen over the lake, turning the water into a blue-black surface shimmering with starlight.

"God, that's lovely," I say, my voice dreamy because I'm slightly drunk. Just one step past tipsy. The sweet spot between numbness and being able to function.

Getting there is easy. Remaining that way requires planning and determination.

It begins around noon, with my first real drink of the day. Mornings are reserved for coffee, which sweeps away the cobwebs of the previous night, and water. Hydration is important.

For the day's inaugural drink, I like two large shots of vodka, downed quickly. A strong double punch to dull the senses.

The rest of the afternoon is devoted to bourbon, sipped over ice in a steady dose. Dinnertime brings wine. A glass or two or three. It leaves me feeling mellow and fuzzy—on the precipice of full-tilt intoxication. That's when coffee reenters the picture. A strong cup of joe pulls me back from the brink without completely dulling my buzz. Finally, before bed, it's another hard hit of whatever strikes my fancy.

Two, if I can't fall asleep immediately.

Three, if I can't sleep at all.

Even as Eli sits next to me, I think about what I'll drink once he leaves.

Across the lake, a light flicks on at the back door of the Royce house, flooding the patio in a warm white glow. I lean forward and squint, seeing two people emerge from the house and make their way to the property's dock. Soon after, there's another light, this time in the form of a spotlight at the front of their boat. The low rumble of an outboard motor echoes off the trees.

"I think you're about to have more guests," Eli says.

He might be right. The spotlight grows larger as the boat cuts straight across the water toward our side of the lake.

I put down my coffee. "The more the merrier," I say.

The Royces arrive in a vintage mahogany-paneled powerboat that's both sporty and elegant. The kind of boat I'm certain George Clooney rides around in when staying at his palazzo in Lake Como. Watching it approach my family's scuffed and faded motorboat feels like sitting at a stoplight and having a Bentley Continental pull up next to your Ford Pinto.

Which the Royces also have. A Bentley, not a Pinto. Eli told me all about it at dinner.

I greet them at the dock, tipsier than I initially thought. To keep myself from swaying, I plant both feet on the dock and straighten my spine. When I wave, it's a little too emphatic.

"What a nice surprise!" I call out once Tom cuts the boat's motor and glides it toward the dock.

"I brought your blanket!" Katherine calls back.

Her husband holds up two bottles of wine. "And I brought Pauillac Bordeaux from 2005!"

That means nothing to me except that it sounds expensive and that I will definitely *not* be waiting until Eli leaves to drink more.

Katherine hops out of the boat as her husband ties it to the dock. She presents the blanket like it's a satin pillow with a tiara on top. "Washed and dried," she says as she presses it into my hands. "Thanks for letting me keep it earlier."

I tuck the blanket under one arm and try to shake Katherine's hand with the other. She surprises me with a hug, capping it with a kiss on both cheeks, like we're old friends and not two people who met in the middle of the lake a few hours ago. The warm greeting brings with it a twinge of guilt for spying on them.

As Tom comes toward me, I can't help but think about how he looked when eavesdropping on his wife.

And that *is* what he was doing.

Eavesdropping. Listening in. Spying on her as blatantly as I was spying on him. All with that unreadable expression on his face.

"Sorry for dropping by unannounced," he says, not sounding sorry at all.

Unlike his wife, he settles for a handshake. His grip is too firm, too eager. When he pumps my hand, it almost knocks me off-balance. Now I know what Marnie meant by *intense*. Instead of friendly, the handshake comes off like an unnecessary show of strength. He stares at me as he does it, his eyes so dark they're almost black.

I wonder how I look to him in my slightly drunken state. Glassy-eyed, probably. Face flushed. Sweat forming along my hairline.

"Thank you for coming to Katherine's rescue today." Tom's voice is deep, which might be why his words sound insincere. A baritone like that doesn't leave much room for nuance. "I hate to think what would have happened if you hadn't been there to save her."

I glance up at the porch, where Eli stands at the railing. He arches his brows, silently chastising me for failing to mention that over dinner.

"It was nothing," I say. "Katherine pretty much saved herself. I just provided the boat that took her home."

"Liar." Katherine wraps an arm around my waist and walks me up the dock, as though I'm the sudden guest in this situation. Over her shoulder, she tells her husband, "Casey's being modest. She did all the rescuing."

"I told her not to swim in the lake," Tom says. "It's too dangerous. People have drowned in there."

Katherine gives me a look of utter mortification. "I'm so sorry," she tells me before turning to her husband. "God, Tom, must you always say the wrong thing?"

It takes him another second to understand what she's talking about. The realization, when it dawns, drains the color from his face.

"Shit," he says. "I'm an idiot, Casey. Truly. I wasn't thinking."

"It's fine," I say, forcing a smile. "You didn't say anything that's not true."

"Thank you for being so understanding," Katherine says. "Tom would be devastated if you were mad at him. He's such a fan."

"I really am," he says. "We saw you in *Shred of Doubt*. You were amazing. Just fantastic."

We reach the porch steps, Katherine and me climbing them in tandem, Tom at our backs. He's so close his breath hits the nape of my neck. Again, I think of him creeping across the first floor of their house. I sneak a glance at Katherine, recalling the way she looked when she spotted her husband lurking at the edge of the dining room.

Startled, then scared.

She doesn't seem scared now, which makes me start to doubt she was then. It's more likely she was merely surprised and that I'd misread the situation entirely. It wouldn't be the first time.

On the porch, Eli greets the Royces with the familiarity of neighbors who've spent an entire summer next to each other.

"Didn't think I'd see you again until next summer," he says.

"This was an impromptu trip," Tom tells him. "Katie missed the lake and I wanted to see the foliage."

"How long do you plan on staying?"

"The plan was to wing it. A week. Maybe two. But that was before Trish decided to come our way."

"I still think we should stay," Katherine says. "How bad could it really get?"

Eli runs a hand through his snowy beard. "Worse than you think. The lake looks peaceful now, but looks can be deceiving. Especially in a storm."

Their small talk makes me feel like an outsider, even though my family has been coming to Lake Greene the longest. I think about what might have been if Len hadn't died and we'd ended up living here full-time.

Maybe there'd be many impromptu gatherings like this.

Maybe I wouldn't be eyeing the wine bottles in Tom's hand with such thirst.

"I'll grab glasses and a corkscrew," I say.

I move into the house, finding the corkscrew still sitting on the dining room table. I then go to the liquor cabinet and grab four fresh wineglasses.

Out on the porch, the small talk continues, with Eli asking them, "How's the house been treating you?"

"We adore it," Tom says. "It's perfect. We spent the past few summers in the area. A different rental on a different lake every year. When we finally decided to buy, we couldn't believe our luck when our Realtor told us there was a property for sale on Lake Greene."

I return to the porch, corkscrew and wineglasses in hand. I give a glass to everyone but Eli, who declines with a shake of his head and a pointed look that suggests I shouldn't have any, either.

I pretend I don't see it.

"You also have a place in the city, though, right?" I ask Katherine.

"An apartment on the Upper West Side."

"Corner of Central Park West and 83rd Street," Tom adds, which elicits an eyeroll from his wife.

"Tom's a stickler about status," she says as the binoculars sitting next to a chair catch her eye. "Oh, wow. I used to have a pair just like those."

63

"You did?" Tom says as twin furrows form across his otherwise smooth forehead. "When?"

"A while ago." Katherine turns back to me. "Are you a birder?"

"Are *you*?" Tom asks his wife.

"I used to be. Before we met. A lifetime ago."

"You never told me you like birds," Tom says.

Katherine turns to face the water. "I've always liked them. You just never noticed."

From the other side of the porch, Eli gives me another look. He's noticed the tension between them, too. It's impossible to miss. Tom and Katherine seem so at odds that it sucks all energy from the area, making the porch seem stuffy and crowded. Or maybe it's just me, overheated by inebriation. Either way, I feel the need to be out in the open.

"I've got an idea," I say. "Let's have our wine by a fire."

Eli rubs his hands together and says, "An excellent suggestion."

We leave the porch, descending the steps to ground level and the small courtyard nestled between the lakeshore and the inward corner of the house. In the center is a firepit surrounded by Adirondack chairs where I'd spent many a childhood summer night. Eli, no stranger to this area, collects a few logs from the woodpile stacked against the house and starts building the fire.

Armed with the corkscrew, I reach for the wine bottles that are still in Tom's grip.

"Allow me, please," he says.

"I think Casey knows how to open a bottle of wine," Katherine says.

"Not a five-thousand-dollar bottle."

Katherine shakes her head, gives me another apologetic look, and says, "See? Status."

"I don't mind," I say, no longer wanting the bottles now that I know how crazy expensive they are. "Or we could open one of mine. You should keep those for a special occasion."

"You saved my wife's life," Tom says. "To me, that makes this a very special occasion."

He moves to the porch steps, using them as a makeshift bar. With his back toward us, he says, "You have to pour it just so. Allow it to breathe."

Behind us, Eli has gotten a fire going. Small flames crawl across the logs before leaping into bigger ones. Soon the wood is emitting that satisfying campfire crackle as sparks swirl into the night sky. It all brings a rush of memory. Me and Len the night before he died. Drinking wine by the fire and talking about the future, not realizing there was no future.

Not for us.

Definitely not for Len.

"Casey?"

It's Tom, handing me a glass of five-thousand-dollar wine. Under normal circumstances, I'd be nervous about taking a single sip. But gripped by a sorrowful memory, I gulp down half the glass.

"You have to sniff it first," Tom says, sounding both annoyed and insulted. "Swirl it around in the glass, get your nose in close, then sniff. Smelling it prepares your brain for what you're about to taste."

I do as I'm told, holding the glass to my nose and inhaling deeply.

It smells like every other glass of wine I've had. Nothing special.

Tom hands a glass to Katherine and instructs us both to take a small sip and savor it. I give it a try, assuming the wine's taste will live up to its price tag. It's good, but not five-thousand-dollars good.

Rather than sniff and savor, Katherine brings the glass to her lips and empties it in a single swallow.

"Oops," she says. "I guess I need to start over."

Tom considers saying something in response, thinks better of it, takes her glass. Through clenched teeth, he says, "Of course, darling."

He returns to the steps, his back toward us, one elbow flexing as he tilts the bottle, his other hand digging into his pocket. He brings Katherine a generous pour, swirling the wine in the glass so she doesn't have to.

"Savor, remember," he tells her. "In other words, pace yourself."

"I'm fine."

"Your tilt says otherwise."

I look at Katherine, who is indeed listing slightly to the left.

"Tell me more about what happened today in the lake," Eli says.

Katherine sighs and lowers herself into an Adirondack chair, her legs curled beneath her. "I'm still not sure. I know the water is cold this time of year, but it's nothing I can't handle. And I know I can swim across the lake and back because I did it all summer. But today, halfway across, everything just froze. It was like my entire body stopped working."

"Was it a cramp?"

"Maybe? All I know is that I would have drowned out there if Casey hadn't spotted me. Like that girl that vanished in Lake Morey last summer. What was her name again?"

"Sue Ellen," Eli says solemnly. "Sue Ellen Stryker."

"Tom and I were renting a place there that summer," Katherine says. "It was all so awful. Did they ever find her?"

Eli shakes his head. "No."

I take a sip of wine and close my eyes as it flows down my throat, listening as Katherine once again says, "So awful."

"Only swim at night," Eli intones. "That's what my mother told me."

And it's what Eli told me and Marnie every summer when we were kids. Advice we ignored as we splashed and swam for hours under the full weight of the sun. It was only after the sun set that the lake frightened us, its black depths made even darker by the shroud of night.

"She heard it from her own mother," Eli continues. "My grandmother was a very superstitious woman. She grew up in Eastern Europe. Believed in ghosts and curses. The dead terrified her."

I slide into the chair next to him, feeling light-headed from both the wine and the topic of conversation. "Eli, please. After what happened to Katherine today, I'm not sure anyone wants to hear about that right now."

"I don't mind," Katherine says. "I actually like telling ghost stories around the fire. It reminds me of summer camp. I was a Camp Nightingale girl."

"And I'm curious why swimming at night is better than daytime," Tom says.

Eli jerks his head toward the lake. "At night, you can't see your reflection on the water. Centuries ago, before people knew any better, it was a common belief that reflective surfaces could trap the souls of the dead."

I stare into my glass and see that Eli's wrong. Even though it's night, my reflection is clearly visible, wobbling on the wine's surface. To make it go away, I empty the glass. Savoring be damned.

Tom doesn't notice, too intrigued by what Eli just said. "I read about that. In the Victorian era, people used to cover all the mirrors after someone died."

"They did," Eli says. "But it wasn't just mirrors they were worried about. Any reflective surface was capable of capturing a soul."

"Like a lake?" Katherine says, a smile in her voice.

Eli touches the tip of his nose. "Exactly."

I think about Len and get a full-body shudder. Suddenly restless, I stand, go to the wine bottle on the porch steps, and pour myself another glass.

I empty it in three gulps.

"And it wasn't just the Victorians and their superstitious relatives in Eastern Europe who thought this way," Eli says.

I reach for the bottle again. It's empty, the last few dregs of wine falling into my glass like drops of blood.

Behind me, Eli keeps talking. "The tribes that lived in this area long before any European settlers arrived—"

I grab the second bottle of wine, still uncorked, which annoys me almost as much as what Eli's saying.

"—believed that those trapped souls could overtake the souls of the living—"

Instead of asking Tom to do it, I pick up the corkscrew, prepared to jam it into a five-thousand-dollar bottle of wine I have no business touching.

"—and that if you saw your own reflection in this very lake after someone had recently died in it—"

The corkscrew falls from my grip, slipping between steps into a patch of weeds behind the staircase.

"—it meant you were allowing yourself to be possessed."

I slam the bottle down and the porch steps rattle. "Will you shut the fuck up about the lake?"

I don't mean to sound so angry. In fact, I don't mean to speak at all. The words simply roar out of me, fueled by a fiery blend of alcohol and unease. In their wake, everyone else is silent. All I can hear are the steady crackle of the fire and an owl hooting in the trees somewhere along the lakeshore.

"I'm sorry," Eli says gently, aware of his rare lack of tact. "You were right. No one is interested in this nonsense."

"It's not that. It's just—"

I stop talking, unsure of what it is I'm trying to say.

It dawns on me that I'm drunk. *Drunk* drunk. Tipsy is now just a memory. I've started to tilt like Katherine, the lake going sideways. I try to stop it with a too-tight grip on the porch steps.

"I don't feel too good."

At first, I think I'm the one who says it. Another unprompted outburst, even though I'm not conscious of my mouth opening, my lips moving, my tongue curling.

But then more words arrive—"Not good at all"—and I realize they're coming not from me but from Katherine.

"What's wrong?" Tom says.

"I'm dizzy."

Katherine stands, swaying like a wind-bent pine.

"So dizzy."

She stumbles away from the firepit, toward the lake.

The wineglass falls from her hand and hits the ground, shattering.

"Oh," she says absently.

Then, suddenly and without warning, she collapses into the grass.

Midnight.

I'm alone on the porch, wrapped in the same blanket Katherine had returned earlier. I'm mostly sober, which is why there's a beer in my hand. I need something to ease me into sleep; otherwise it'll never happen. Even with a few drinks, I rarely sleep a full night.

Not here.

Not since Len died.

Boone was right when he said the lake was too quiet. It is. Especially at this hour, when the only things breaking the steady nighttime silence are the occasional loon call or a nocturnal animal scurrying through the underbrush along the shore.

Caught in that quiet, I stare at the lake.

I take a sip of beer.

I try not to think about my dead husband, although that's difficult after what happened earlier.

It's been hours since everyone left, the party breaking up immediately after Katherine passed out in the grass. The Royces were the first to go, Tom mumbling apologies as he led a woozy Katherine down the dock. Even though she regained consciousness after only a few seconds, I was still concerned. I suggested letting her rest and giving her some coffee, but Tom insisted on taking Katherine home immediately.

"This time you've really embarrassed yourself," he hissed at her before starting the powerboat and zipping away.

Hearing that side comment made me feel sorry for Katherine, who'd clearly been more drunk than I thought. I then felt guilty for feeling sorry, because it meant I was pitying her, which is a by-product of judging someone. And I had no right to judge Katherine Royce for drinking a little too much.

On the bright side, Tom left in such a rush that he forgot his other five-thousand-dollar bottle of wine. I found it on the porch steps and put it in the liquor cabinet. Finders keepers, I guess.

Eli lingered a little longer, dousing the fire and plucking shards of broken wineglass out of the grass.

"Just leave it," I told him. "I'll get the rest tomorrow when the sun's out."

"Are you going to be okay?" Eli asked as I walked him around the house to his truck.

"I'll be fine," I said. "I'm doing a lot better than Katherine right now."

"I meant about the other stuff." He paused, looking at the gravel driveway under his feet. "I'm sorry for talking about the lake like that. I was just trying to entertain them. I didn't mean to upset you."

I gave Eli a hug. "You did, but it was only temporary."

I believed it then. Not so much now, as thoughts of Len glide through my head as smoothly as the loons out on the lake. When my mother banished me here, I didn't protest. She was right. I do need to lie low for a few weeks. Besides, I thought I'd be able to handle it. I'd spent more than a year living in the apartment I'd shared with Len. I didn't think the lake house could be any worse.

But it is.

Because this is the place where Len died.

It's where I became a widow, and everything about it—the house, the lake, the damn moose head in the den—reminds me of that fact. And it will continue to do so for as long as I'm alive.

Or sober.

I take another sip of beer and scan the shoreline on the other side of the lake. From the Fitzgerald place to the Royces' to Eli's house, all is dark. A thick mist rises from the lake itself, rolling languidly toward land in billowy waves. Each one skims onto shore and surrounds the support beams below the porch in a swirl of fog like seafoam crashing against the pylons of a pier.

I'm watching the mist, hypnotized, when a sound breaks the night's silence.

A door creaking open, followed by footsteps on wood.

They're coming from my right, which means the Mitchell place.

After a few more seconds, Boone Conrad appears—a slim silhouette making its way toward the end of the Mitchells' dock.

The binoculars still sit on the table next to my chair. I lift them to my eyes and get a closer view of Boone. He's reached the edge of the dock and stands there in nothing but a towel, confirming my first impression of him.

Boone Conrad is fit as hell.

Even though Eli suggested I keep clear of Boone, which I completely understand, he said nothing about not being allowed to look at him. Which I do, feeling only a twinge of guilt as I keep watching him through the binoculars.

That twinge becomes a pang—and something more—when Boone loosens the towel and lets it fall to the dock, revealing that he's not wearing anything underneath.

I lower the binoculars.

I raise them again.

I consider the morality of watching someone without his knowledge or consent. Especially someone naked.

This is wrong, I think as I continue to stare. *So very wrong.*

Boone remains on the dock, basking in the moonlight, which makes his pale body look like it's glowing. He then glances over his shoulder, almost as if he's checking to see if I'm watching. I still am, but he can't know that. He's too far away and all the lights are off here, leaving me hidden in darkness. Yet a smirk crosses Boone's lips anyway, one that's arousing and shame inducing in equal measure.

Then, satisfied that whoever might be watching got a good show, he dives into the water. Although freezing, the lake probably feels like bath-water compared with the cold night air. Even if it doesn't, Boone pays it no mind. His head pops out of the water about ten feet from the dock. He shakes it, flinging water from his shaggy hair, and begins to swim. Not with purpose, like I imagine Katherine was doing when she ran out of steam in the middle of the lake. Boone swims the way I used to do when I was a kid. Playful. Moving willy-nilly through the water. He ducks under again and emerges floating on his back, eyes on the starlit sky.

He looks, if not happy, then at least at peace.

Lucky him, I think as I lift the beer bottle to my lips and take a big swallow.

In the water, something catches Boone's attention. His head snaps to the opposite shore, where a light has flicked on in the Royce house.

First floor.

The kitchen.

I swing the binoculars away from Boone in time to see Katherine dressed in satin pajamas and staggering into the kitchen like she has no idea where she is.

I know the feeling well.

Hands running along walls, floors spinning, reaching for chairs that are only two feet away but feel like twenty.

Watching Katherine throw open kitchen cupboards, searching for something, I'm overwhelmed by a sense of familiarity. This is me on many, many nights. Different person. Different kitchen. Same drunken reeling.

Katherine finds what she's looking for—a glass tumbler—and drifts to the sink. I nod, pleased to see she also knows the importance of hydration after a night of drinking.

She fills the glass, barely taking a sip before her attention drifts to the window at the sink. Katherine stares straight ahead, and for a sliver of a second, I think she's looking right at me, even though that's impossible. Like Boone, she can't see me. Not from the other side of the lake.

Yet Katherine keeps her gaze fixed in my direction. It's not until she touches her face, sliding her fingers from cheek to chin, that I understand.

She's not looking at me.

She's examining her reflection in the window.

Katherine stays that way a moment, drunkenly fascinated by what she sees, before returning to the glass of water. Tipping it back, she empties the glass and refills it. After a few more thirsty gulps, she sets the glass down and leaves the kitchen, her gait noticeably more assured.

The kitchen light goes out.

I turn once more to the Mitchells' dock, hoping for another glimpse of Boone. To my disappointment, he's no longer there. While I was busy watching Katherine, he got out of the water, grabbed his towel, and went back inside.

Bummer.

Now it's just me and the darkness and the bad thoughts rolling like the mist off the lake.

I tighten the blanket around my shoulders, finish my beer, and get up to fetch another one.

The worst part about drinking too much—other than, you know, drinking too much—is the morning after, when everything you gulped down the night before comes back to haunt you.

The steady drumbeat of a headache.

The churning stomach.

The bladder close to bursting.

I wake with all three, plus a sensitivity to sunlight that borders on the vampiric. It doesn't matter that the long row of bedroom windows faces west, ignored by the sun until early afternoon. The brightness pouring through them is still enough to make me wince the second I open my eyes.

Rolling over, I squint at the alarm clock on the nightstand.

Nine a.m.

Late for lake life. Early for me.

I want to go back to sleep, but the headache and roiling stomach and gargantuan urge to pee pull me out of bed, into the bathroom, then downstairs to the kitchen. While coffee brews, I wash down an Advil with a glass of tap water and check my phone. There's a joke text from Marnie—that atrocious poster of a kitten dangling from a tree branch that reads, *Hang in there!*

I reply with a vomit emoji.

There's also another text, this one from an unknown number. I open it, surprised to see it's from Katherine Royce.

Sorry about last night.—K.

So she remembers what happened by the fire. I wonder if she also recalls stumbling into the kitchen at midnight. Probably not.

No worries, I text back. *Who among us hasn't passed out in a stranger's yard?*

Her reply arrives instantly. *It was my first time.*

Welcome to the club.

On my phone, three dots appear, vanish, reappear. The telltale sign of someone debating what to text next. Katherine's reply, when it finally arrives, is succinct: *I feel like shit.* To drive home that point, she includes a poop emoji.

Need some coffee? I text back.

The suggestion earns a heart-eyed emoji and an all-caps *YES!!!!!*

Come on over.

Katherine arrives in the wood-paneled powerboat, looking like a fifties movie star at the Venice Film Festival as she pulls up to the dock. Cornflower blue sundress. Red sunglasses. Yellow silk scarf tied under her chin. I get a pang of envy as I help her out of the boat and onto the dock. Katherine Royce feeling like shit still looks better than I do on my very best day.

Before I can get too jealous, though, she takes off the sunglasses, and I have to stop myself from flinching. She looks *rough*. Her eyes are bloodshot. Beneath them, dark purple circles hang like garlands.

"I know," she says. "It was a bad night."

"Been there, done that, had the pictures printed in a tabloid."

She takes my arm, and we stroll up the dock, past the firepit, and up the steps to the back porch. Katherine eases into a rocking chair while I step inside to fetch us two mugs of coffee.

"How do you take it?" I ask through the open French doors.

"Normally with cream and sugar," Katherine calls back. "But today I think I'll take it black. The stronger, the better."

I bring out the coffee and sit in the rocking chair next to hers.

"Bless you," Katherine says before taking a sip, wincing at its bitterness.

"Too strong?"

"Just right." She takes another sip, smacks her lips. "Anyway, I'm sorry again about last night."

"Which part?"

"All of it? I mean, Tom is Tom. He's constantly putting his foot in his mouth. The thing is, he never means to. He's just missing that filter the rest of us have. He says what's on his mind, even if it makes things awkward. As for me—" Katherine jerks her head toward the ground below, where she'd dropped like a sack of flour twelve hours before. "I don't know what happened."

"I think it's called drinking too much, too fast," I say. "I'm an expert at it."

"It wasn't the drinking, no matter what Tom thinks. If anything, he's the one who drinks too much." She pauses and looks across the lake to her own house, its glass walls made opaque by the reflection of the morning sky. "I'm just not myself lately. I haven't felt right for days. I feel weird. Weak. That exhaustion I felt while swimming yesterday? That wasn't the first time it's happened. It always feels like what happened last night. My heart starts beating fast. Like, illegal-diet-drug fast. It just overwhelms me. And before I know it, I'm passed out in the grass."

"Do you remember getting home?"

"Vaguely. I remember feeling sick in the boat and Tom putting me to bed and then waking up on the living room couch."

No mention of fumbling around in the kitchen. Guess I was right about her having no memory of it.

"You didn't embarrass yourself, if that's what you're worried about," I say. "And I'm not upset at Tom, either. I meant what I said last night. My husband died in the lake. It's something that happened, and I see no point in pretending it didn't."

I leave out the part about me spending most of my days doing exactly that. Trying to forget has become my full-time job.

Katherine says nothing after that, and I don't need her to. I'm content to simply be in her company, the two of us sipping coffee as we rock back and forth, the chairs creaking dryly beneath us. It helps that it's a glorious autumn morning, full of sunshine and leaves blazing with color. There's a chill to the air, which isn't unwelcome. It balances everything out. A refreshing bite against the golden light.

Len had a name for days like this: Vermont perfect. When the land and water and sky conspire to take your breath away.

"It's got to be hard always seeing this lake," Katherine eventually says. "Are you okay staying here by yourself?"

I'm taken aback by the question, mostly because no one else has thought to ask it. My mother never even considered it when she banished me to the lake house. That it occurred to Katherine, who barely knows me, says a lot about both women.

"I am," I say. "Mostly."

"But doesn't being here bother you?"

"Not as much as I thought it would."

It's as honest an answer as I can give. The first thing I did after Ricardo drove away, leaving me all but stranded here, was come out to this porch and look at the lake. I thought I'd experience a pileup of emotions. Grief and fear and rage. Instead, all I felt was grim resignation.

Something bad happened in that water.

I can't change it, no matter how much I want to.

All I can do is try to forget it.

Hence all my time spent staring across the water. My theory is that if I look long enough, the bad memories associated with Lake Greene will eventually grow dull and fade away.

"Maybe because it's so pretty," Katherine suggests. "It was Tom's idea to buy here. I was content to rent a different place every summer. Tom was adamant about owning. If you couldn't already tell, my husband loves possessing things. But in this case, he's right. The lake is gorgeous. So is the house. It's funny, when I'm not here, I don't miss the place very much. But when I am here, I don't ever want to leave. I suppose all vacation homes are like that."

I think of Len and our late-July picnic. *Let's stay here forever, Cee.*

"Should I expect you here for more than just a week or two, then?"

Katherine shrugs. "Maybe. We'll see. Tom's getting worried about the weather, but I think it might be fun to be here during a storm. Romantic, even."

"Wait until your sixth day without power. Romance will be the furthest thing from your mind."

"I don't mind roughing it." Noticing my look of surprise, Katherine adds, "I don't! I'm tougher than I look. Once, three model friends and I spent a week rafting in the Grand Canyon. No electricity. Definitely no cell service. We ran the rapids during the day, and at night we slept in tents, cooked over an open fire, and peed in the weeds. It was heavenly."

"I didn't know models were that close."

"The idea of bitchiness and backstage catfights is mostly just a myth. When there are twelve girls sharing a dressing room, you're kind of forced to get along."

"Are you still friends with any of them?"

Katherine gives a slow, sad shake of her head. "They're all still in the game, and I'm not. Makes it hard to keep in touch. Most of my friends I only talk to through Instagram. That's the weird thing about being famous. Everyone knows who you are—"

"But sometimes you feel completely alone."

"Yeah," Katherine says. "That."

She looks away, as if embarrassed to be understood so clearly. Her gaze lands on the binoculars, which rest on the small table between our rocking chairs. Drumming her fingers over them, she says, "Ever see anything interesting with these?"

"Not really," I lie, holding back a guilty blush as I think about watching Boone last night, how good he looked naked in the moonlight, how a bolder, more confident me might have joined him in the lake.

"So you haven't watched my house?"

"Never."

Another lie. Because it's Katherine I'm lying to—right to her face, no less—the guilt that comes with it cuts deeper.

"Oh, I'd totally watch my house. Those huge windows? How could anyone resist?" Katherine picks up the binoculars and peers through them at her house on the opposite shore. "God, it's so ostentatious. Like, who needs a house that big? As a vacation home, no less."

"If you can afford it, there's no reason not to enjoy it."

"That's the thing," Katherine says as she lowers the binoculars. "We *can't* afford it. Well, Tom can't. I pay for everything. The house. The apartment. The five-thousand-dollar wine and the Bentley, which *is* pretty sweet. We should take it out sometime, just you and me."

"Tom has no money of his own?"

"All of Tom's money is tied up in Mixer, which still hasn't turned a profit and probably never will. The joys of being married to a so-called tech titan. He looks the part and acts it exceptionally well, but in reality—" Katherine stops her rant with a gulp of coffee, followed by an apologetic "You must think I'm insufferable. Here I am, complaining about my husband, when you—"

"It's fine," I say, cutting off the rest of her sentence before she can utter it. "Most marriages have their difficulties."

"Most? Was your marriage always perfect?"

"It wasn't," I say, looking at the lake, at how the morning light seems to dance across the water's surface. "But it felt that way. Right up until the end."

A pause.

"Then again, we weren't married long enough for Len to get sick of me and initiate our inevitable divorce."

Katherine turns my way, those large eyes of hers searching my face to see if I'm being serious. "Do you always do that?" she asks.

"Do what?"

"Make a joke to avoid talking about your true feelings?"

"Only ninety percent of the time," I say.

"You just did it again."

I shift uneasily in my chair. Katherine's right, of course. She's pinpointed one of my worst traits. The only person besides Marnie and my mother to do so. Not even Len, who bore the brunt of it, ever called me out on it.

"I make jokes," I say, "because it's easier to pretend I'm not feeling what I'm feeling than to actually feel it."

Katherine nods, turns away, looks again to her glass house at the water's edge. The side that faces the lake is still reflecting sky, although the sun has entered the picture now. A glowing circle right where her bedroom is located. So bright it could blind you if you stared at it long enough.

"Maybe I should try that," she says. "Does it really help?"

"Yes. Especially if you drink enough."

Katherine responds with a dry chuckle. "Now that I *have* tried."

I stare deeply into my coffee mug, regretting that I didn't add a splash of bourbon. I think about getting up to add some. I think about asking Katherine if she also wants some. I'm about to do just that when I spot a gray-clad figure stepping onto the patio outside Katherine's house.

She sees it, too, and says, "That's Tom wondering where I am."

"You didn't tell him you were coming over?"

"I like to keep him guessing." She rises, does a little stretch, then comes in for her second surprise hug in two days. "Thanks for the coffee. We should do it again tomorrow."

"My place or yours?" I say, aiming for a Mae West impersonation but ending up sounding more like Bea Arthur.

"Here, definitely. There's only decaf at our place. Tom says caffeine blunts the body's natural energy. That right there is grounds for divorce." She pauses, no doubt taking in the look of surprise on my face. "It was a joke, Casey. To cover up how I truly feel."

"Is it working for you?"

Katherine thinks it over. "Maybe. I still prefer honesty. And in this case, the truth is that Tom needs me too much to agree to a divorce. He'd kill me before letting me leave."

She gives me a wiggle-fingered wave and skips down the steps. I stay at the porch railing, watching her cross the dock, hop into the boat, and start the short crossing to the other side of the lake.

When she's about halfway there, something on the ground below catches my eye. A spot of brightness in a swath of tall grass near the stone wall running along the shoreline.

Glass.

Reflecting the sun as brightly as Katherine's house.

I descend the steps and pick it up, discovering it's a shard of the wineglass she'd broken last night. When I hold it to the light, I can see drops of wine dried on its surface, along with a light film that resembles dried salt.

I scan the ground for similar chunks of glass. Seeing none, I go back inside and drop the shard into the kitchen trash. By the time it's clinked to the bottom of the bin, a thought occurs to me.

Not about the broken wineglass.

About Katherine.

She texted me this morning, but I have no idea how she got my number.

The rest of the day passes on its regularly scheduled course.

Vodka. Neat.

Another vodka. Also neat.

Cry in the shower.

Grilled cheese sandwich for lunch.

Bourbon.

Bourbon.

Bourbon.

My mother calls at her regularly scheduled time, using my cell and not the landline still stuffed into a drawer in the den. I let it go to voicemail and delete her message without listening to it.

Then I have another bourbon.

Dinner is steak with a side salad so I can pretend my body isn't a complete nutritional wasteland.

And wine.

Coffee to sober up a tad.

Ice cream, just because.

It's now a few minutes after midnight and I'm sipping cheap whiskey poured from an unopened bottle I found stuffed in the back of the liquor cabinet. It's probably been there for decades. But it does the trick, smoothing the peaks and valleys of intoxication I've experienced over the course of the day. Now I'm enveloped in a dreamy calmness that makes all of it worthwhile.

I'm on the porch, snug in a heavy sweater, the blanket from the boat once again wrapped over my shoulders. It's not as foggy as last night. Lake Greene and its environs sit encased in a silvery crispness that provides a clear view across the water. I take in each house there.

The Fitzgeralds'. Dark and empty.

The Royces'. Not empty, but dark all the same.

Eli's. A single light aglow on the third floor.

I turn to my side of the lake. The Mitchell house, also dark, can barely be glimpsed through the trees. I assume that means no midnight swim for Boone.

Pity.

I'm contemplating going to bed myself when a light appears at the Royces'. Seeing it makes me immediately reach for the binoculars, but I stop myself before my fingers can snag them.

I shouldn't be doing this.

I don't *need* to do this.

What I should do is drink some water, go to bed, and ignore what my neighbors are up to. Not a difficult task. Yet that rectangle of brightness on the other side of the lake tugs at me like a rope around my waist.

I try to resist, hovering my hand over the binoculars while counting Mississippis just like I did yesterday with my bourbon. This time, I fall well short of forty-six before grabbing them. In fact, I barely make it to eleven.

Because resistance also has its drawbacks. It makes me want something— watching the Royces, knocking back a drink—even more. I know how denial works. You withhold and withhold and withhold until that mental dam breaks and all those bad urges come spilling out, often causing harm in the process.

Not that this behavior is hurting anyone. No one will ever know but me.

Binoculars in hand, I zero in on the window glowing in the otherwise dark night. It's on the second floor, coming from the home office where I saw Tom yesterday. Now, though, it's Katherine who sits at the desk by the window, staring at the laptop.

Wrapped in a white robe, she looks worse than she did this morning. A pale imitation of her usual self. Not helping is the glow from the laptop, which gives her face a sickly blue tinge.

I watch as Katherine types something, then squints at the laptop's screen. The squint grows more pronounced as she leans forward, engrossed in whatever she's looking at.

Then something surprises her.

It's clear even from this distance.

Her lower jaw drops and a hand flies to her bottom lip. Her eyes, released from their squint, grow wide. Katherine blinks. Rapidly. A full two seconds of fluttering eyelids.

She pauses.

She exhales.

She turns her head slowly toward the office door, which is completely open.

She listens, head cocked, on alert.

Then, seemingly satisfied she won't be interrupted, Katherine turns back to the laptop in a flurry of activity. Keys are tapped. The cursor is moved. All while she keeps sneaking occasional glances back to the open door.

I do the same, jerking the binoculars to the right, where the master bedroom is located.

It's completely dark.

I return my gaze to the office, where Katherine spends the next minute typing, then reading, then typing some more. The surprise on her face has dulled slightly, morphing into something that to my eye looks like determination.

She's searching for something. I don't know how I know it, but I do. It's not the expression of someone casually scrolling through emails in the middle of the night. It's the look of someone on a mission.

On the other side of the house, another light appears.

The bedroom.

Sheer white curtains cover the tall windows. Through them, I see the diffuse glow of a bedside lamp and the silhouette of Tom Royce sitting up in bed. He slides out from under the covers and, wearing only a pair of pajama bottoms, takes a few stiff-jointed steps across the room.

At the slice of door that's visible, Tom pauses, just like he did in the dining room when I watched them yesterday.

He's listening again, wondering what his wife is up to.

Two rooms away, Katherine continues to type, read, type. I move back and forth between the two of them, like someone watching a tennis match.

Tom still listening at the bedroom door.

Katherine's face lit by the laptop's glow.

Tom slipping out of the room.

Katherine leaning forward slightly, getting a better look at the computer screen.

Tom reappearing in the doorway behind her.

He says something, alerting Katherine to his presence.

She jolts at the sound of his voice, slams the laptop shut, whirls around to face him. Although I can only see the back of her head, it's clear she's speaking. Her gestures are big, demonstrative. A pantomime of innocence.

Tom says something back, chuckles, scratches the back of his neck. He doesn't appear angry or even suspicious, which means Katherine must have said the right thing.

She stands and kisses Tom the same way a sitcom wife would. Perched on tiptoes for a quick peck, one leg bent back in a flirty kick. Tom hits the light switch by the door, and the office becomes a rectangle of blackness.

Two seconds later, they're back in the bedroom. Tom climbs into bed and rolls onto his side, his back to the window. Katherine disappears into the bathroom. There's another flash of perfect lighting, followed by the door closing.

In the bed, Tom rolls over. The last thing I see is him reaching for the bedside lamp. He turns it off and the house is plunged into darkness.

I lower the binoculars, unnerved by what I just saw, although I can't articulate why. I want to think it stems from getting another unfiltered glimpse of someone else's life. Or maybe it's simply guilt over convincing myself it was okay to yet again watch something I was never supposed to see. As a result, I'm turning what I saw into something bigger than it really is. The proverbial mountain out of a molehill.

Yet I can't shake the way Katherine reacted the moment she realized Tom had entered the room.

Lifted out of her chair.

Panic writ large on her face.

The more I think about it, the more certain I am that she'd been caught looking at something she didn't want Tom to see. The way she slammed the laptop shut made that abundantly clear, followed up with the too-cutesy kiss.

It all leads me to one conclusion.

Tom Royce has a secret.

And I think Katherine just discovered what it is.

One a.m.

Porch, rocking chair, booze, etc.

I'm half asleep in the chair, doing that dozing-until-your-head-droops-and-wakes-you-up thing my father used to do when I was a kid. I'd watch it happen as the two of us sat in front of the TV, waiting for my mother to get home from a performance. First the eyes would slide shut. Then came stillness and maybe some growl-like snoring. Finally his head would tilt forward, startling him awake. I'd chuckle, he'd mumble something, and the whole process would begin again.

Now it's me doing it, the traits of the father passed on to his daughter. After another bob-and-wake, I tell myself it's time to go to bed.

But then a light blinks on at the Royce house on the other side of the lake.

The kitchen.

Suddenly wide-awake, I fumble for the binoculars, not even thinking about resisting this time. I simply grab them, lift them to my eyes, and see Katherine march into the kitchen. The robe she'd been wearing earlier is gone, replaced by jeans and a bulky white sweater.

Tom's right behind her, still in pajama bottoms, talking.

No.

Shouting.

His mouth is wide open, an angry oval that expands and contracts as he keeps yelling at his wife in the middle of the kitchen. She whirls around, shouts something back.

I lean forward, ridiculously, as if I'll hear what they're saying if I get just a little bit closer. But the Royce house is like a silent movie playing just for me. No voices. No music. No sound at all save for the ambient noise of the wind in the leaves and the lapping of water along the shore.

Katherine enters the darkened dining room, nothing but a faint shadow passing the floor-to-ceiling windows. Tom trails a few paces behind her, following her as she disappears into the living room.

For a moment, there's nothing. Just the steady glow of the kitchen light, illuminating an empty room. Then a living room lamp is turned on. Tom's doing. I see him on the white sofa, one hand retracting from the freshly lit lamp. Katherine stands at the window, back turned to her husband, looking directly across the lake to my house.

Like she knows I'm watching.

Like she's certain of it.

I slide deeper into the rocking chair. Again, ridiculous.

She can't see me.

Of course she can't.

If anything, I suspect she's watching her husband's reflection in the glass. On the edge of the couch, he slumps forward, head in his hands. He looks up, seemingly pleading with her. His gestures are desperate, almost frantic. By focusing on his lips, I can almost make out what he's saying.

How? Or maybe *Who?*

Katherine doesn't reply. At least not that I can see. Away from the couch and backlit by the lamp, the front of her is cast in shadow. She's not moving, though. That much I can tell. She stands mannequin-like in front of the window, arms at her sides.

Behind her, Tom rises from the couch. The pleading morphs into shouting again as he takes a halting step toward her. When Katherine refuses to respond, he grabs her arm and jerks her away from the glass.

For a second, her gaze stays fixed on the window, even as the rest of her is being pulled away from it.

That's when our eyes lock.

Somehow.

Even though she can't see me and my eyes are hidden behind binoculars and we're a quarter mile apart, our gazes find each other.

Just for a moment.

But in that tiny slice of time, I can see the fear and confusion in her eyes.

Less than a second later, Katherine's head turns with the rest of her body. She whirls around to face her husband, who continues to drag her toward the couch. Her free arm rises, fingers curling into a fist that, once formed, connects with Tom's jaw.

The blow is hard.

So hard I think I hear it from the other side of the lake, although more likely the sound is me letting out a half gasp of shock.

Tom, looking more surprised than hurt, releases Katherine's arm and stumbles backwards onto the couch. She seems to say something. Finally. No yelling from her. No pleading, either. Just a sentence uttered with what looks like commanding calmness.

She leaves the room. Tom remains.

I nudge the binoculars upward to the second floor, which remains dark. If that's where Katherine went, I can't see her.

I return my gaze to the living room, where Tom has pulled himself back onto the sofa. Watching him hunched forward, head in his hands, makes me think I should call the police and report a domestic dispute.

While I can't begin to know the context of what I saw, there's no mistake that some form of spousal abuse occurred. Although Katherine was the one to strike, it was only after Tom had grabbed her. And when our eyes briefly locked, it wasn't malice or vengeance I saw.

It was fear.

Obvious, all-consuming fear.

In my mind, Tom had it coming.

It makes me wonder how many times something like this has happened before.

It makes me worry it'll happen again.

The only thing I'm certain of is that I regret ever picking up these binoculars and watching the Royces. I knew it was wrong. Just like I knew that if I kept watching, I was eventually going to see something I didn't want to see.

Because I wasn't spying on just one person.

I was watching a married couple, which is far more complex and unwieldy.

What is marriage but a series of mutual deceptions?

That's a line from *Shred of Doubt*. Before I was fired, I spoke it eight times a week, always getting an uneasy laugh from audience members who recognized the truth behind it. No marriage is completely honest. Each one is built on some type of deception, even if it's something small and harmless. The husband pretending to like the sofa his wife picked out. The wife who watches her husband's favorite show even though she quietly despises it.

And sometimes it's bigger.

Cheating. Addiction. Secrets.

Those can't stay hidden forever. At some point, the truth comes out and all those carefully arranged deceptions topple like dominoes. Is that what I just saw in the Royce house? A marriage under pressure finally imploding?

In the living room, Tom stands and crosses to the sideboard bar. He grabs a bottle of honey-colored liquid and splashes some into a glass.

Above him, a light goes on in the master bedroom, revealing Katherine moving behind the gauzy curtains. I grab my phone when I see her, not thinking about what I'll say. I simply call.

Katherine answers with a hushed, husky "Hello?"

"It's Casey," I say. "Is everything okay over there?"

There's nothing on Katherine's end. Not a breath. Not a rustle. Just a blip of silence before she says, "Why wouldn't things be okay?"

"I thought I—"

I barely manage to stop the word about to career off my tongue.

Saw.

"I thought I heard something at your house," I say. "And I just wanted to know if you're okay."

"I'm fine. See."

My body goes numb.

Katherine knows I've been watching.

I guess I shouldn't be this surprised. She's been in this very same rocking chair, looking at her house through the same pair of binoculars now sitting next to me.

I'd totally watch my house, she said, subtly indicating she knew I was watching, too.

But there's nothing subtle about this. Now she's outright telling me to look.

The sheer curtains in the master bedroom part, and I scramble for the binoculars. At the window, Katherine waves. Because she's mostly cloaked in shadow, I can't see her face.

Or if she's smiling.

Or if the fear I noticed earlier is still in her eyes.

All I can see is her still-waving silhouette until that, too, stops. Katherine's hand drops to her side, and after standing at the window for another second, she backs away and leaves the room, hitting the light switch on her way out.

Directly below that, Tom has finished his drink. He stands there a moment, staring into the empty glass, looking like he's considering having another.

Then his arm rears back and he flings the glass.

It hits the wall and shatters.

Tom storms back to the sofa, reaches for the lamp, and, with a flick of his fingers, an uneasy darkness returns to the house across the lake.

I'm startled awake by a sound streaking across the lake. With my eyes still closed, I catch only the last breath of it. An echo of an echo fading fast as it whooshes deeper into the woods behind my house.

I remain frozen in place for half a minute, waiting for the sound to return. But it's gone now, whatever it was. The lake sits in silence as thick as a wool blanket and just as suffocating.

I fully open my eyes to a gray-pink sky and a lake just beginning to sparkle with daylight.

I spent the whole night on the porch.

Jesus.

My head pounds with pain and my body crackles with it. When I sit up, my joints creak louder than the rocking chair beneath me. As soon as I'm upright, the dizziness hits. A diabolical spinning that makes the world feel like it's tilting off its axis and forces me to grip the arms of the chair for balance.

I look down, hoping it will steady me. At my feet, rocking slightly on the porch floor, is the whiskey bottle, now mostly empty.

Jesus.

Seeing it brings a rush of nausea so strong it eclipses my pain and confusion and dizziness. I stand—somehow—and rush inside, heading for the small powder room just off the foyer.

I make it to the powder room, but not the toilet. All the poison churning in my stomach comes out in a rush over the sink. I turn the tap on full blast to wash it down and stumble out of the room, toward the staircase on the other side of the living room. I can only reach the top floor by crawling up the steps. Once there, I continue down the hall on my hands and knees until I'm in the master bedroom, where I manage to pull myself into bed.

I flop onto my back, my eyes closing of their own accord. I have no say in the matter. The last thought I have before spiraling into unconsciousness is a memory of the sound that woke me up. With it comes recognition.

I now know what I heard.

It was a scream.

Tell me what you did to Katherine," I say again, twisting the towel that had just been in his mouth. It's damp with saliva. An icky, warm wetness that makes me drop the towel to the floor. "Tell me and this will all be over."

He doesn't, of course.

There's no reason he would.

Not to me.

Not after everything I've done. And what I'm still doing.

Holding him captive.

Lying to Wilma.

I'll have a lot of explaining to do later. Right now, though, my only goal is saving Katherine. If that's even possible. I have no way of knowing until he tells me.

"What happened to her?" I say after a minute passes and the only sound I hear is rain pounding the roof.

He tilts his head to the side, unbearably smug. "You're assuming I know."

I mirror his expression, right down to the thin-lipped smile that conveys anything but friendliness. "It's not an assumption. Now tell me what you did with her."

"No."

"But you *did* do something?"

"I want to ask *you* a question," he says. "Why are you so concerned about Katherine? You barely knew her."

His use of the past tense sends a streak of fear down my back. I'm certain that was his intent.

"That doesn't matter," I say. "Tell me where she is."

"A place where you'll never find her."

The fear remains. Joining it is something new: anger. It bubbles in my chest, as hot and turbulent as boiling water. I leave the room and march downstairs as the lights perform another unnerving flicker.

In the kitchen, I go to the knife block on the counter and grab the biggest blade. Then it's back upstairs, back into the room, back to the bed where I'd slept as a child. It's hard to fathom that that little girl is the same person now buzzed on bourbon and wielding a knife. If I hadn't personally experienced the years between those two points, I wouldn't believe it myself.

With trembling hands, I touch the knife's tip to his side. A poke of warning.

"Tell me where she is."

Rather than cower in fear, he laughs. An actual, honest-to-God laugh. It scares me even more that he finds this situation so amusing.

"You have absolutely no idea what you're doing," he says.

I say nothing.

Because he's right.

I don't.

But that's not going to stop me from doing it anyway.

BEFORE

I wake again just after nine, my head still pounding but the spinning and nausea blessedly gone. Still, I feel like death. Smell like it, too. And I'm certain I look like it.

My mother would be appalled.

I *am* appalled.

As I sit up in a tangle of blankets, the first thing I notice is the muted rush of running water coming from downstairs.

The sink in the powder room.

I never turned it off.

I leap out of bed, hobble down the steps, find the tap still running at full blast. Two-thirds of the basin is filled with water, and I suspect excellent plumbing is the only thing that prevented it from overflowing. I cut the water as memories of last night come back in stark flashes.

The whiskey.

The binoculars.

The fight and the phone call and Katherine's wave at the window.

And the scream.

The last thing I remember but the most important. And the most suspect. Did I really hear a scream at the break of dawn? Or was it just part of a drunken dream I had while passed out on the porch?

While I hope it was the latter, I suspect it was the former. I assume that in a dream, I would have heard a scream more clearly. A vivid cry filling my skull. But what I heard this morning was something else.

The aftermath of a scream.

A sound both vague and elusive.

But if the scream *did* happen—which is the theory working its way through my hungover brain—it sounded like Katherine. Well, it sounded like a woman. And as far as I know, she's the only other woman staying at the lake right now.

I spend the next few minutes hunting my phone, eventually finding it still on the porch, sitting on the table next to the binoculars. After an entire night spent outside, there's only a wisp of battery life left. Before taking it inside to charge, I check to see if I got any calls or texts from Katherine.

I didn't.

I decide to text her, carefully wording my message while a strong mug of coffee zaps me to life and the charger does the same to my phone.

I just made coffee. Come over if you want some. I think we should talk about last night.

I hit send before I can even consider deleting it.

While waiting for a response, I sip my coffee and think about the scream.

If that's what it really was.

I've spent half my life on this lake. I know it could have been something else. Many animals arrive at night to prowl the lakeshore or even the water itself. Screeching owls and loud waterfowl. Once, when Marnie and I were kids, a fox somewhere along the shore, defending its turf from another animal, screamed for the better part of the night. Literally screamed. Hearing its cries echo over the water was bone-chilling, even after Eli explained to us in detail what was happening.

But I'm used to those noises, and am able to sleep right through them. Especially after a night spent drinking. This was something different enough to startle me awake, even with most of a bottle of whiskey under my belt.

Right now, I'm seventy-five percent sure that what I heard was a woman screaming. While that's far from certain, it's enough to keep concern humming through me as I check my phone again.

Still nothing from Katherine.

Rather than continue to wait for a return text, I decide to call her. The phone rings three times before going to voicemail.

"Hi, you've reached Katherine. I'm not available to take your call right now. Or maybe I'm just ignoring you. If you leave your name and number, you'll find out which one it is if I call you back."

I wait for the beep and leave a message.

"Hey, it's Casey." I pause, thinking of how to phrase this. "I just wanted to see if you're all right. I know you said you were last night, but early this morning, I thought I heard—"

I pause again, hesitant to come right out and say what it is I think I heard. I don't want to sound overly dramatic or, worse, downright delusional.

"Anyway, call me back. Or feel free to just come over. It'll be nice to chat."

I end the call, shove my phone back into my pocket, and go about my day.

Vodka. Neat.

Another vodka. Also neat.

Shower, minus the crying but with a new, unwelcome anxiety.

A grilled cheese sandwich for lunch.

When the grandfather clock in the living room strikes one and Katherine still hasn't replied, I call again, once more getting her voicemail.

"Hi, you've reached Katherine."

I hang up without leaving a message, pour a bourbon, and carry it to the porch. The whiskey bottle from last night is still there, a mouthful of liquid still sloshing inside. I kick it out of the way, sink into a rocking chair, and check my phone ten times in three minutes.

Still nothing.

I pick up the binoculars and peer at the Royce house, hoping for a sign of Katherine but seeing nothing in return. It's that hour when the sun starts glinting off the glass walls and the reflection of the sky hides what's behind them like a pair of closed eyelids.

While watching the house, I think about the unusual nature of what I saw last night. Something big went down inside that house. Something that's none of my business yet, oddly, still my concern. Even though I haven't known her very long at all, I consider Katherine a friend. Or, at the very least, someone who could become a friend. And new friends aren't easy to come by once you hit your thirties.

Out on the lake, a familiar boat floats in the distance. I swing the binoculars toward it and see Eli sitting at the bow, fishing rod in hand. If anyone else on the lake heard the same sound I did, it would be him. I know he likes to rise with the sun, so there's a chance he was awake then. And if he did hear it, he might be able to clarify what it was and put my simmering worry to rest.

I call his cell, assuming he has it on him.

While the phone rings, I continue to watch him through the binoculars. An annoyed look crosses his face as he pats a front pocket of his fishing vest—a sign he's definitely carrying his phone. After propping his fishing rod against the side of the boat, he looks at his phone, then at the lake house. Seeing me on the porch, my phone in hand, he gives me a wave and answers.

"If you're calling to see if I've caught anything, the answer is no."

"I have a different question," I say, adding a warning. "An unusual one. Did you happen to hear a strange noise outside this morning?"

"What time?"

"Dawn."

"I wasn't awake then," Eli says. "Decided to sleep in a little. I'm assuming you heard something?"

"I think so. I'm not sure. I was hoping you could back me up on that."

Eli doesn't ask me why I was awake at dawn. I suspect he already knows.

"What kind of noise are you talking about?"

"A scream."

Saying it out loud, I realize how unlikely it sounds. The odds of someone, let alone Katherine Royce, screaming at the break of dawn are slim, although not impossible.

Bad things can happen on this lake.

I know that from experience.

"A scream?" Eli says. "You sure it wasn't a fox or something?"

Am I sure? Not really. Even during this conversation, my certainty level has lowered from seventy-five percent to about fifty.

"It sounded like a person to me," I say.

"Why would someone be screaming at that hour?"

"Why does anyone scream, Eli? Because she was in danger."

"She? You think it was Katherine Royce you heard?"

"I can't think of anyone else it could have been," I say. "Have you seen any sign of her today?"

"No," Eli says. "Then again, I haven't exactly been looking. You worried something happened to her?"

I tell him no, when the opposite is true. Katherine's lack of a response to my text and calls has me feeling unnerved, even though in all likelihood there's a perfectly good reason for it. She could still be sleeping, her phone silenced or in another room.

"I'm sure everything's fine," I say, more to convince myself than Eli.

"Do you want me to stop over there and check?"

Because he's the lake's one-man neighborhood watch, I know Eli would be happy to do it. But this is my worry, not his. It's time to pay the Royces a visit, and hopefully all my concerns will be put to rest.

"I'll go," I say. "It'll be good to get out of the house."

Tom Royce is on the dock by the time I reach it. Clearly, he saw me coming because he stands like a man expecting company. He's even dressed for casual visitors. Black jeans. White sneakers. Cashmere sweater the same color as the pricey wine he brought over two nights ago. He offers an exaggeratedly friendly wave as I moor the boat and join him on the dock.

"Howdy, neighbor. What brings you by this afternoon?"

"I came by to see if Katherine wanted to come over for some girl talk and an afternoon cocktail on the porch."

I prepared the excuse on the trip from my dock to his, hoping it would make it look like I'm not overreacting. Which I suspect I totally am. Katherine's fine and I'm just worried because of something I saw and something I heard and something that happened to my husband more than a year ago. All of which are completely unrelated.

"I'm afraid she's not here," Tom says.

"When will she be back?"

"Probably not until next summer."

The answer's as unexpected as a door slammed in my face.

"She's gone?"

"She went back to our apartment in the city," Tom says. "Left early this morning."

I take a few more steps closer to him, noticing a red patch on his left cheek where Katherine had punched him. Considering that, maybe her departure shouldn't be a surprise after all. I can even picture the events leading up to her decision.

First the fight, ending with a haymaker to Tom's face.

Then my phone call, likely made after she'd already decided to leave. Thinking about her brief appearance at the bedroom window, I now see that strange wave in a different light. It's entirely possible it was a wave goodbye.

After that there could have been some frantic packing in the darkness of their bedroom. Finally, just as she was about to leave, the fight flared up again. Both of them trying to get in their last licks. During that final showdown, Katherine screamed. It might have been from frustration. Or from rage. Or simply just a release of all the emotions she'd had pent up inside her.

Or, I think with a shudder, maybe Tom did something that made her scream.

"What time this morning?" I say as I eye him with suspicion.

"Early. She called me a little while ago to say she arrived safely."

So far, that tracks with my theory about when Katherine left. What doesn't track is Tom's Bentley, which sits beneath the portico that juts from the side of the house. It's slate gray, as sleek and shiny as a wet seal.

"How'd she get there?"

"Car service, of course."

That doesn't explain why Katherine hasn't called or texted me back. After last night—and after making casual plans to meet again for coffee this morning—it seems unusual she hasn't told me herself that she went back to New York.

"I've tried reaching her several times today," I say. "She's not answering her phone."

"She doesn't check her phone when traveling. She keeps it in her purse, silenced."

Tom's response, like all of them so far, makes perfect sense and, if you

107

think about it too much, no sense at all. Six days ago, as Ricardo drove me to the lake house, sheer boredom kept me fixated on my phone. Then again, most of that time was spent Googling to see if any liquor stores in the area delivered.

"But you just said she called you from the apartment."

"I think she wants to be left alone," Tom says.

I take that to mean *he* wants to be left alone. I'm not ready to do that just yet. The more he talks, the more suspicious I get. I zero in on the red mark on Tom's cheek, picturing the exact moment he got it.

Him jerking Katherine away from the window.

Her lashing out, punching back.

Was that the first time something like that happened? Or had it occurred multiple times before? If so, maybe it's possible that Tom took it one step further just as dawn was breaking over the lake.

"*Why* did Katherine leave?" I say, being purposefully nosy in the hope he'll reveal more than he's told me so far.

Tom squints, scratches the back of his neck, and then folds his arms tight across his chest. "She said she didn't want to be here when Hurricane Trish passed through. She was worried. Big house. Strong winds. All this glass."

That's the opposite of what Katherine told me yesterday. According to her, it was Tom who was concerned about the storm. Still, it's certainly possible me talking about being without power for days made her change her mind. Just like it's also possible she's not into roughing it as much as she claimed.

But then why is she gone while Tom remains?

"Why didn't you go with her?" I ask.

"Because I'm *not* worried about the storm," Tom says. "Besides, I thought it best to stick around in case something happens to the place."

A rational answer. One that *almost* sounds like the truth. I'd be inclined to believe it if not for two things.

Number one: Tom and Katherine fought last night. That almost certainly has something to do with why she left so suddenly.

Number two: It doesn't explain what I heard this morning. And since Tom isn't going to mention it, it's up to me.

"I thought I heard a noise this morning," I say. "Coming from this side of the lake."

"A noise?"

"Yes. A scream."

I pause, waiting to see how Tom reacts. He doesn't. His face remains still as a mask until he says, "What time?"

"Just before dawn."

"I was asleep long past dawn," Tom says.

"But I thought that's when Katherine left?"

He stands frozen for a second, and at first I think I've caught him in a lie. But he recovers quickly, saying, "I said she left early. Not at dawn. And I don't appreciate you insinuating that I'm lying."

"And I wouldn't need to insinuate that if you just told me a time."

"Eight."

Even though Tom throws out the number like he's just thought of it, the timeline fits. It takes a little under five hours to get from here to Manhattan, making it more than conceivable that Katherine would be there by now, even with a lengthy pit stop.

Tom lifts a hand to his cheek, rubbing the spot where it connected with his wife's fist. "I don't understand why you're so curious about Katherine. I didn't know the two of you were friends."

"We were friendly," I say.

"I'm friendly with lots of people. That doesn't make it okay to interrogate their spouses if they went somewhere without telling me."

Ah, the old minimize-a-woman's-concern-by-making-her-think-she's-obsessed-and-slightly-hysterical bit. I expected something more original from Tom.

"I'm simply concerned," I say.

Realizing he's still rubbing his cheek, Tom drops his hand and says, "You shouldn't be. Because Katherine's not concerned about you. That's the thing you need to understand about my wife. She gets bored very easily.

One minute, she wants to leave the city and drive up here to the lake for two weeks. A couple of days after that, she decides she wants to go back to the city. It's the same with people. They're like clothes to her. Something she can try on and wear for a while before moving on to the newest look."

Katherine never gave off that vibe. She—and the brief connection we had—seemed genuine, which makes me think even more that Tom is lying.

Not just about this.

About everything.

And I decide to call his bluff.

"I talked to Katherine last night," I say. "It was after one in the morning. She told me you two had a fight."

A lie of my own. A little one. But Tom doesn't need to know that. At first, I think he's going to tell another lie in response. There's something at work behind his eyes. Wheels turning, seeking an excuse. Finding none, he finally says, "Yes, we fought. It got heated. Both of us did and said things we shouldn't have. When I woke up this morning, Katherine was gone. *That's* why I was being vague about everything. Happy now? Or are there even more personal questions about our marriage you'd like to ask?"

At last, Tom seems to be telling the truth. Of course that's likely what happened. They had a fight, Katherine left, and she's now in New York, probably calling the most expensive divorce lawyer money can buy.

It's also none of my business, a fact I never seriously considered until this moment. Now that I have, I find myself caught between vindication and shame. Tom was wrong to imply I was being obsessive and hysterical. I was worse: a nosy neighbor. A part I've never played before, either on-stage or onscreen. In real life, it's not a good fit. In fact, it's downright hypocritical. I, of all people, know what it feels like to have private problems dragged out for public scrutiny. Just because it had been done to me doesn't mean it's okay for me to do it to Tom Royce.

"No," I say. "I'm really sorry to have bothered you."

I slink back down the dock and step into the boat, already making a to-do list for when I get back to the lake house.

First, toss Len's binoculars into the trash.

Second, find a way to occupy myself that doesn't involve spying on the neighbors.

Third, leave Tom alone and forget about Katherine Royce.

That turns out to be easier planned than done. Because as I push the boat away from the dock, I catch a glimpse of Tom watching me leave. He stands in a slash of sunlight that makes the mark on his face stand out even more. He touches it again, his fingers moving in a circle over the angry red reminder that Katherine had once been here but is now gone.

Seeing it prompts a memory of something Katherine said about him yesterday.

Tom needs me too much to agree to a divorce. He'd kill me before letting me leave.

I text Katherine again as soon as I get back to the lake house.

Heard you're back in the Big Apple. Had I known you were plotting an escape, I would have hitched a ride.

I then plant myself on the porch and stare at my phone, as if doing it long enough will conjure up a response. So far, it's not working. The only call I receive is my mother's daily check-in, which I let go straight to voicemail before heading inside to pour a glass of bourbon.

My second of the day.

Maybe third.

I take a hearty sip, return to the porch, and check the previous texts I sent Katherine. None of them have been read.

Worrisome.

If Katherine called Tom after arriving home in New York, then she certainly would have seen that I had called and texted.

Unless Tom was indeed lying about that.

Yes, he told the truth about their fight, but only after I prodded. And on another matter—the scream I'm still fifty percent sure I heard—he remained frustratingly vague. Tom only said he was asleep past dawn. He never actually denied hearing a scream.

Then there are those two sentences—easy to dismiss at the time, increasingly ominous in hindsight—Katherine spoke while sitting in the very same rocking chair I occupy now. They refuse to leave my head, repeating in the back of my skull like lines I've spent too much time rehearsing.

Tom needs me too much to agree to a divorce. He'd kill me before letting me leave.

Ordinarily, I'd assume it was a joke. That's my go-to defense mechanism, after all. Using humor as a shield, pretending my pain doesn't hurt at all. Which is why I suspect there was a ring of truth to what she said. Especially after what she told me yesterday about all of Tom's money being tied up in Mixer and how she pays for everything.

Then there's the fight itself, which could have been over money but I suspect was about more than that. Seared into my memory is the way Tom pleaded with Katherine, repeating that word I couldn't quite read on his lips. *How? Who?* All of it climaxing with him wrenching her away from the window and her striking back.

Just before that, though, was the surreal moment when Katherine and I locked eyes. I know from the phone call afterwards that she somehow knew I was watching. Now I wonder if, in that brief instant when her gaze met mine, Katherine was trying to tell me something.

Maybe she was begging for help.

Despite my vow to drop the binoculars in the trash, here they are, sitting right next to my glass of bourbon. I pick them up and look across the lake to the Royce house. Although Tom's no longer outside, the presence of the Bentley lets me know he's still there.

Everything he told me mostly adds up, signaling I should believe him. Those few loose threads prevent me from doing so. I won't be able to fully trust Tom until Katherine gets back to me—or I get proof from another source.

It occurs to me that Tom mentioned exactly where they live in the city. A fancy building not too far from mine, although theirs borders Central Park. I know it well. Upper West Side. A few blocks north of where the Bartholomew once stood.

Since I can't go there myself, I enlist the next best person for the job.

"You want me to do *what?*" Marnie says when I call to make my request.

"Go to their building and ask to see Katherine Royce."

"Katherine? I thought she was at Lake Greene."

"Not anymore."

I give her a recap of the past few days. Katherine unhappy. Tom acting strange. Me watching it all through the binoculars. The fight and the scream and Katherine's sudden departure.

To Marnie's credit, she waits until I'm finished before asking, "Why have you been spying on them?"

I don't have a suitable answer. I was curious, bored, nosy, all of the above.

"*I* think it's because you're sad and lonely," Marnie offers. "Which is understandable, considering everything you've been through. And you want a break from feeling all of that."

"Can you blame me?"

"No. But this isn't the way to take your mind off things. Now you've become obsessed with the supermodel living on the other side of the lake."

"I'm not obsessed."

"Then what are you?"

"Worried," I say. "Naturally worried about someone whose life I just saved. You know that saying. Save a person's life and you're responsible for them forever."

"One, I've never heard that saying. Two, that is, like, the definition of being obsessed."

"Maybe so," I say. "That's not what's important right now."

"I beg to differ. This isn't healthy behavior, Casey. It's not *moral* behavior."

I let out an annoyed huff so loud it sounds like rustling wind hitting my phone. "If I wanted a lecture, I would have called my mother."

"Call her," Marnie says. "*Please.* She's been bothering me instead, saying that you're ignoring her."

"Which I am. If you go check to see if Katherine is there, I'll call my mother and get her off your back."

Marnie pretends to think it over, even though I already know it's a done deal.

"Fine," she says. "But before I go, one last question. Have you checked social media?"

"I'm not on social media."

"And thank God for that," Marnie says. "But I assume Katherine is. Find some of her accounts. Twitter. Instagram. The one her husband literally invented and owns. Surely she's on that. Maybe it'll give you an idea of where she is and what she's up to."

It's such a good idea I'm pissed I didn't think of it on my own. After all, following someone on social media is just a more acceptable form of spying.

"I'll do that. While you go check to see if Katherine's home. Right now."

After a few muttered curse words and a promise that she's leaving this second, Marnie ends the call. While waiting to hear back, I do what she says and check Katherine's social media.

First up is Instagram, where Katherine has more than four million followers.

Of course she does.

The pictures she's posted are an eye-pleasing mix of sun-flooded interiors, throwbacks to her modeling days, and candid selfies of her slathered in face cream or eating candy bars. Interspersed are gentle, earnest urgings to support the charities she works with.

Even though it's all carefully curated, Katherine still comes off as a sharp-witted woman who wants to be known as more than just a pretty face. An accurate representation of the Katherine I've come to know. There's even a recent photo taken at Lake Greene, showing her reclining on the edge of their dock in that teal bathing suit, the water behind her and, beyond that, the very porch I'm now sitting on.

I look at the date and see it was posted two days ago.

Right before she almost drowned in the lake.

Her most recent photo is a view of a pristine, all-white kitchen with a stainless steel teakettle on the stove, a Piet Mondrian calendar on the wall, and lilies in a vase by the window. Outside, Central Park spreads out below in all its pastoral splendor. The caption is short and sweet: *There's no place like home.*

I check when it was posted.

An hour ago.

So Tom wasn't lying after all. Katherine did indeed return to their apartment, a fact that seems to have surprised her famous friends who've left comments.

Ur back in the city?! YAY!! one of them wrote.

Another replied, *That was quick!*

Tom himself even weighed in: *Keep the home fires burning, babe!*

I exhale, breathing out all the tension I didn't know I was holding in.

Katherine is fine.

Good.

Yet my relief is tempered by a slight stab of rejection. Maybe that was another of Tom's truths—that Katherine gets bored quickly. Now that I know with certainty that she's been on her phone, it's clear Katherine didn't miss my calls or texts. She's avoiding me, just like I'm avoiding my mother. I realize I'm the kind of person Katherine gently chided in her voicemail message. The ones who are being ignored.

After last night, I can't really blame her. She knows I've been watching her house. Marnie was right when she said that's not healthy behavior. In fact, it's downright unnerving. Who spends so much time spying on their neighbors? Losers, that's who. Lonely losers who drink too much and have nothing better to do.

Okay, maybe Marnie's correct and I *am* a little obsessed with Katherine. Yes, some of that obsession is valid. Since I saved Katherine's life, it's only natural to be concerned with her well-being. But the truth is harsher than that. I became fixated on Katherine to avoid facing my own problems, of which there are many.

Annoyed—at Katherine, at Marnie, at myself—I grab the binoculars, carry them inside, and drop them into the trash. Something I should have done days ago.

I return to the porch and my go-to security blanket of bourbon, which I sip until Marnie calls back a half hour later, the familiar sounds of Manhattan traffic honking in the background.

"I already know what you're going to say," I tell her. "Katherine's there. You were right and I was stupid."

"That's not what their doorman just told me," Marnie says.

"You talked to him?"

"I told him I was an old friend of Katherine's who just happened to be in the neighborhood and wondered if she wanted to grab lunch. I don't think he believed me, but it doesn't matter because he still told me that the Royces are currently at their vacation home in Vermont."

"And those were his exact words?" I say. "The Royces. Not just Mr. Royce."

"Plural. I even did the whole oh-I-thought-I-saw-Katherine-across-the-street-yesterday routine. He told me I was mistaken and that Mrs. Royce hasn't been at the apartment for several days."

A fierce chill grips me. It feels like I've just been thrown into the lake and am now lost in the water's frigid darkness.

I was right.

Tom *was* lying.

"Now I'm really worried," I say. "Why would Tom lie to me like that?"

"Because whatever's going on is none of your business," Marnie says. "You said yourself that Katherine seemed unhappy. Maybe she is. And so she left him. For all you know, there's a Dear John letter sitting on the kitchen counter right now."

"It still doesn't add up. I did what you suggested and looked at her Instagram. She just posted a picture from inside her apartment."

Marnie chews on that a minute. "How do you know it's her apartment?"

"I don't," I say. I only assumed it was because Katherine said so in the caption and because it had a view of Central Park and looked to be roughly where the Royces' apartment is located.

"See?" Marnie says. "Maybe Katherine told Tom she was going to the apartment but really went to stay with a friend or a family member. He might not have any clue where she is and was too embarrassed to admit that."

It would be a sound theory if I hadn't seen Tom's comment on the picture.

Keep the home fires burning, babe!

"That means it really is their apartment," I tell Marnie after explaining what I saw.

"Fine," Marnie says. "Let's say it *is* their apartment. That either means Katherine's there and the doorman lied, or it means she posted a photo that was saved on her phone to hide the fact from her husband that she's not really at their apartment. Either way, none of this points to Katherine being in danger."

"But I heard Katherine scream early this morning," I say.

"Are you certain that's what you heard?"

"It wasn't an animal."

"I'm not suggesting it was," Marnie says. "I'm merely saying that maybe you didn't hear it at all."

"You think I imagined it?"

The delicate pause I get in return warns me that Marnie's about to drop a truth bomb.

A big one.

Atomic.

"How much did you have to drink last night?" she says.

My gaze is drawn to the mostly empty whiskey bottle still overturned on the porch floor. "A lot."

"How much is a lot?"

I think it through, counting the drinks on my fingers. The ones I can remember, at least.

"Seven. Maybe eight."

Marnie lets out a small cough to hide her surprise. "And you don't think that's too much?"

I bristle at her too-earnest tone. She sounds like my mother.

"This isn't about my drinking. You have to believe me. Something about this situation isn't right."

"That might be true." Marnie's voice remains annoyingly calm. Like someone talking to a kindergartener throwing a tantrum. "It still doesn't mean Tom Royce murdered his wife."

"I didn't say he did."

"But that's what you think, isn't it?"

Not quite, but close enough. While it's absolutely crossed my mind that Tom did something to hurt Katherine, I'm not yet ready to make the mental leap to murder.

"Be honest," Marnie says. "What do you *think* happened to her?"

"I'm not sure anything happened," I say. "But something's not right about the situation. Katherine was here, and suddenly she's not. And I'm not sure her husband is telling the truth."

"Or he told you what he *believes* to be the truth."

"I don't buy that. When I talked to him, he gave me a very simple explanation to something that, at least from what I saw, looked like a complex situation."

"What you saw?" Marnie repeats, my words sounding undeniably stalker-y. "Is this how you spend all your time? Watching them?"

"Only because I sensed trouble the minute I started watching."

"I wish you could hear yourself right now," Marnie says, her calm tone replaced by something even worse. Sadness. "Admitting that you're spying on your neighbors and talking about Tom Royce hiding something—"

"You'd think it, too, if you saw the things I have."

"That's the point. You shouldn't be seeing it. None of what's going on in that house is any of your business."

I can't argue with Marnie on that point. It's true that I had no right watching them the way I have been. Yet, in doing so, if I stumbled upon a potentially dangerous situation, isn't it my responsibility to try to do something about it?

"I just want to help Katherine," I say.

"I know you do. But if Katherine Royce wanted your help, she would have asked for it," Marnie says.

"I think she did. Late last night, when I saw them fighting."

Marnie lets slip a sad little sigh. I ignore it.

"Our eyes met. Just for a second. She was looking at me and I was looking at her. And I think, in that moment, she was trying to tell me something."

Marnie sighs again, this one louder and sadder. "I know you're going through a hard time right now. I know you're struggling. But please don't drag other people into it."

"Like you?" I shoot back.

"Yes, like me. And Tom and Katherine Royce. And anyone else at the lake right now."

Although Marnie sounds nothing but sympathetic, I know the deal. She, too, has officially grown tired of my bullshit. The only surprise, really, is that it took her this long. Unless I want to lose her completely—which I don't—I can't push any further.

"You're right," I say, trying to sound appropriately contrite. "I'm sorry."

"I don't need you to be sorry," she says. "I need you to get better."

Marnie ends the call before I can say anything else—an unspoken warning that, while all is forgiven, it's certainly not forgotten. And when it comes to Katherine and Tom Royce, I'll need to leave her out of it.

Which is fine. Maybe she's right and nothing's really going on except the unraveling of the Royces' marriage. I sincerely hope that's the worst of it. Unfortunately, my gut tells me it's not that simple.

I return to Katherine's Instagram and examine that picture of her apartment, thinking about Marnie's theory that she posted an old photo to deceive her husband. The idea makes sense, especially when I take another look at the view of Central Park outside the apartment window. The leaves there are still green—a far cry from the blazing reds and oranges of the trees surrounding Lake Greene.

I zoom in until the picture fills my phone's screen. Scanning the grainy blur, I focus on the Mondrian calendar on the wall. There, printed right below an image of the artist's most famous work—*Composition with Red Blue and Yellow*—is the month it represents.

September.

Marnie was right. Katherine really did post an old photo. Faced with proof that she's being deceitful, most likely to fool her husband, I realize I can stop worrying—and, yes, obsessing—over where Katherine is or what happened to her.

It's none of my business.

It's time to accept that.

I swipe my phone, shrinking the photo down to its original size.

That's when I see it.

The teakettle on the stove, polished to a mirrorlike shine. It glistens so much that the photographer can be seen reflected in its surface.

Curious, I zoom in again, making the kettle as big as possible without entirely blowing out the image. Although the photographer's reflection is blurred by the amplification and distorted by the kettle's curve, I can still make out who it is.

Tom Royce.

There's no mistaking it. Dark hair, longish in the back, too much product in the front.

Katherine never took this photo.

Which means it was saved not on her phone but on her husband's.

The only explanation I can think of is that Marnie was right about the deception, wrong about who is doing it and why.

Tom posted this photo on his wife's Instagram account.

And the person being deceived is me.

T he hardest part about doing *Shred of Doubt* eight times a week was the first act, in which my character had to walk a fine line between being too worried and not suspicious enough. I spent weeks of rehearsal trying to find the perfect balance between the two, and I never did get it completely right.

Until now.

Now I'm perched precisely between those two modes, wondering which one I should lean into. It's easy now that I'm living it. No acting required.

I want to call Marnie for guidance, but I know what she'd say. That Katherine is fine. That I should leave it alone. That it's none of my business.

All of that might be true. And all of it could be dead wrong. I can't be sure until I have a better grasp on the situation. So it's back to social media I go, leaving Instagram behind and diving into Tom Royce's brainchild, Mixer.

First, I have to download the app to my phone and create a profile. It's a brazenly invasive process requiring my full name, date of birth, cell phone number, and location, which is determined through geotracking. I make several attempts to do an end run around it, entering Manhattan as my location instead. The app changes it to Lake Greene every time.

And I thought *I* was being nosy.

Only after my profile is created am I allowed to enter Mixer. I have to give Tom and his development team credit. It's a well-designed app. Clean, good-looking, easy to use. Within seconds, I learn there are several ways to find contacts, including by company, by location, and by entering your favorite bars and restaurants and seeing who else has listed them.

I choose a location search, which lets me see every user within a one-mile radius. Right now, four other users are currently at Lake Greene, each one marked with a red triangle on a satellite view of the area.

The first is Tom Royce.

No surprise there.

Eli and Boone Conrad also have profiles, which would be a surprise if I didn't suspect both joined as a courtesy to their neighbor. Like me, neither has filled out his profile beyond the required information. Eli hasn't listed any favorites or recently visited locations, and the only place on Boone's profile is a juice bar two towns away.

The real surprise is the fourth person listed as currently being at Lake Greene.

Katherine Royce.

I stare at the triangle pinpointing her location.

Just on the other side of the lake.

Directly across from my own red triangle.

Seeing it sends my heart skittering. While I have no idea about the app's accuracy, I assume it's pretty good. Since I wasn't able to change my location despite multiple attempts, it's likely Katherine can't, either.

If that's the case, it means she either left Lake Greene without taking her phone—or that she never left at all.

I stand, shove my phone in my pocket, and go inside, heading straight for the kitchen. There, I dig the binoculars out of the trash, blow stray crumbs from my lunch off the lenses, and carry them out to the porch. Standing at the railing, I peer at the Royces' glass house, wondering if Katherine is there after all. It's impossible to tell. Although the sun is close to slipping behind the mountains on that side of the lake, the shimmering reflection of the water masks whatever might be going on inside.

Still, I scan the areas where I know each room to be located, hoping a light on inside will improve my view. There's nothing. Everything beyond the dim windows is invisible.

Next, I examine the house's surroundings, starting with the side facing Eli's place before leading my gaze across the back patio, down to the dock, and then to the side facing the Fitzgeralds' house. Nothing to see there, either. Not even Tom's sleek Bentley.

Once again, I realize I'm currently watching the Royce house with a pair of binoculars powerful enough to view craters on the moon. It's extreme.

And obsessive.

And just plain weird.

I lower the binoculars, flushed with shame that maybe I'm being ridiculous about all of this. Marnie would tell me there's no maybe about it. I'd feel the same way if it weren't for the one thing that put me on edge in the first place.

The scream.

Without it, I wouldn't be this worried.

Even if it was just my imagination, I can't stop thinking about it.

I slump in the rocking chair, imitating the ache-inducing condition I woke up in. Eyes closed tight, I try to recall the exact sound I heard, hoping it will spark some revelation of memory. Although I bristled when she mentioned it, Marnie was right to say I drank too much last night. I did, with good reason, just like every night. But in my drunken stupor, it's entirely possible I imagined that scream. After all, if Eli didn't hear it and Tom didn't hear it, then it stands to reason I didn't really hear it, either.

Then again, just because no one else claims to have heard it doesn't mean it didn't happen. When a tree falls in a forest, to use that hoary cliché, it still makes a sound. And as Mixer reminds me when I check my phone for the umpteenth time, there's another person on this lake who I haven't yet asked. I can see his little red triangle on my screen right now, located a few hundred yards from my own.

Yes, I know I promised Eli that I would stay away from him. But sometimes, such as now, a promise needs to be broken.

Especially when Boone Conrad might have the answer to what's currently my most pressing question.

I stand, put away my phone, and hop down the porch steps. Rather than go to the front of the house and make the trek from driveway to driveway, I choose the same path Boone used the other day and cut through the woods between us. It's a pretty route, especially with the setting sun casting its golden shine on this side of the lake. It's so bright I have to squint as I walk. A welcome feeling that reminds me of being onstage, caught in the spotlight, warmed by its glow.

I loved that sensation.

I miss it.

If Marnie were here, she'd tell me it's only a matter of time before I'm back treading the boards. I sincerely doubt it.

Up ahead, visible through the thinning trees, sits the hulking A-frame of the Mitchell house. Like the Royces', it has large windows overlooking the lake, which now reflects the flaming hues of the sunset. That, coupled with the house's shape, reminds me of a child's drawing of a campfire. An orange triangle sitting atop a stack of wood.

As I push through the tree line into the Mitchells' small, leaf-studded yard, I spot Boone on the back deck. Dressed in jeans and a white T-shirt, he stands facing the lake, a hand shielding his eyes from the setting sun. Immediately, I understand that he, too, is watching the Royce house.

Boone seems to know why I'm here, because when he sees me crossing the lawn, a strange look passes over his face. One part confusion, two parts concern, with just a dash of relief for good measure.

"You heard it, too, didn't you?" he says before I can get a word out.

"Heard what?"

"The scream." He turns his head until he's once again facing the Royce house. "From over there."

H ave you seen anything else?" Boone says.

"Only what I already told you."

The two of us are on the back porch of my family's lake house, me watching Boone watch the Royce house through the binoculars. He's at the porch railing, leaning so far forward I worry he'll break right through it and tumble to the ground below. He's certainly big enough, which I realized only when we were standing face-to-face. Because I was above him during our first meeting, I couldn't quite tell how tall he is. Now I know. So tall he towers over me as I stand next to him.

"You told me you've been here since August," I say. "Did you ever meet Tom and Katherine?"

"Once or twice. I don't know them very well."

"Did you notice anything strange about them?"

"No," Boone says. "Then again, I wasn't watching them through these."

He pulls the binoculars away from his eyes long enough to give me a grin, telling me he's joking. But I detect a hint of judgment in the remark, suggesting he's not totally okay with what I've been doing.

I'm not, either, now that I'm a foot away from the man I spied on while he was naked. At no point has Boone voiced suspicion that I had watched him skinny-dip the other night. In turn, I give no hints that I was indeed watching. It makes for an awkward silence in which I wonder if he's think-ing that I'm thinking about it.

On the other side of the lake, the Royce house remains dark, even though the cottony grayness of dusk has descended. Tom still hasn't re-turned, as evidenced by the empty space under the portico where his Bent-ley should be.

"Do you think he's going to come back?" I say. "Or did he get the hell out of Dodge?"

Boone returns to the binoculars. "I think he'll be back. There's still furniture on the patio. If he was leaving for the winter, he would have taken all of it inside."

"Unless he had to leave in a hurry."

Boone hands me the binoculars and lowers himself into a rocking chair, which creaks under his weight. "I'm not ready to think the worst."

I felt the same way an hour ago, when I wasn't sure the scream was real and there were logical reasons as to why Katherine wasn't where Tom says she was. Now that Boone has confirmed what I heard and Katherine's Mixer location marker remains parked at her house while her husband's has long disappeared, I'm ready to let my suspicions run free.

"Where were you when you heard the scream?" I ask Boone.

"In the kitchen, making coffee."

"Are you always such an early riser?"

"More like a very light sleeper." Boone shrugs, and in that sad little lift of his broad shoulders, I sense a weary acceptance common among people haunted by something. *It sucks*, it seems to say, *but what can you do?* "The door to the deck was open. I like to hear the birds on the lake."

"Because it's too quiet otherwise."

"Exactly," Boone says, pleased I remember something from our first conversation. "I was just about to pour the coffee when I heard it. It sounded to me like it came from the other side of the lake."

"How could you tell?"

"Because it would have sounded different on this side. Louder. I knew as soon as I heard it that it came from over there." Boone points to the opposite shore, his finger landing between Eli's house and the Royces'. "There was just enough distance for me to catch the echo."

"Did you see anything?" I say.

Boone shakes his head. "I went out to look, but there was nothing to see. The lake was calm. The far shore appeared to be empty. It was like any typical morning out here."

"Only with a scream," I say. "You agree with me that it sounded like a woman, right?"

"Even more, I agree that it sounded like Katherine Royce."

I leave the railing and drop into the rocking chair next to Boone. "Do you think we should call the police?"

"And tell them what?"

"That our neighbor is missing and we're worried about her."

On the table between us sit two glasses of ginger ale. Not my first choice of drink, but I would have felt bad nursing a bourbon in front of Boone. The ginger ale, which has been sitting in the fridge since the last time I stayed here, is flat as a map. Boone doesn't seem to mind as he takes a sip and says, "We don't want to do that just yet. First of all, we don't know that Katherine is definitely missing. If we go to the police, the first thing they're going to do is talk to Tom—"

"Who might be the reason Katherine is missing."

"Maybe," Boone says. "Maybe not. But when the police talk to him, he'll likely tell them the same thing he told you and point to that Instagram post you showed me to prove it. That will make the cops back off. Not forever. Especially not if more people who know Katherine come forward to say they haven't heard from her. But long enough to give Tom ample time to run."

I glance to the far side of the lake and the empty spot where Tom's car used to be parked. "If he hasn't already started running."

Boone lets out a grunt of agreement. "And that's the big unknown right now. I think we should wait and see if he returns."

"And if he doesn't?"

"I know someone we can call. She's a detective with the state police, which is who'll be investigating it anyway. If there even is something to investigate. We'll tell her what the deal is and get her opinion. Right now, it's best to be as discreet as possible. Trust me, Casey, we don't want to make an accusation, get police and rescue involved, and then find out we were wrong the whole time. Cops frown upon that kind of thing."

"How do you know so much about cops?"

"I used to be one."

I'm caught by surprise, even though I shouldn't be. Boone possesses a familiar kind-but-weary cop flintiness. And muscles. Lots of muscles. I don't ask why he stopped being a cop and he doesn't elaborate. Knowing that he's now in AA, I can connect the dots myself.

"Then we'll wait," I say.

Which we do, sitting in relative silence as nightfall covers the valley.

"Don't you wish I'd brought my Monopoly board?" Boone says when the clock strikes seven.

"Is it rude to say no?"

Boone lets out a rueful chuckle. "Very. But your honesty is refreshing."

At seven thirty, after hearing Boone's stomach rumble one time too many, I head inside and make us sandwiches. My hands tremble as I spread mayonnaise on the bread. Withdrawal shakes. My body wants to be drinking wine right now and not fizzless ginger ale. I glance at the liquor cabinet in the adjoining dining room, and my body seizes up with longing. A tightness forms in my chest—an internal itch that's driving me crazy because it can't be scratched. I take a deep breath, finish the sandwiches, and carry them outside.

On the porch, Boone has the binoculars in hand again, even though no lights can be seen inside Tom and Katherine's place. The house wouldn't be visible at all if not for the moonlight shimmering over the lake.

"Did he come back?" I say.

"Not yet." Boone sets the binoculars down and accepts the paper plate filled with turkey on white bread and a side of potato chips. Not my finest culinary moment. "I was just admiring how good these things are."

"My husband bought them. For birding."

Boone's voice grows hushed. "I'm sorry about what happened to him, by the way. I should have told you that the other day."

"And I heard about your wife."

"I guess Eli told you."

"He did. I'm sorry you had to go through that."

"Likewise." He pauses before adding, "I'm here, if you ever want to talk about it."

"I don't."

Boone nods. "I get that. I didn't, either. Not for a long time. But one of the things I've learned in the past year is that it helps to talk about things. Makes it easier to deal with."

"I'll keep that in mind."

"She fell down the stairs." Boone pauses, letting the information settle in. "That's how my wife died. In case you were wondering."

I was, but I didn't have the courage to ask outright. Despite my current habit of spying on my neighbors, I mostly still have respect for others' privacy. But Boone seems to be in the mood to divulge information, so I nod and let him continue.

"No one quite knows how it happened. I was at work. Got home from my shift, walked in the door, and found her crumpled at the bottom of the stairs. I did all the things you're supposed to do. Call nine one one. Try CPR. But I knew as soon as I saw her that she was gone. The ME said she had been dead for most of the day. It must have happened right after I left for work. She either tripped or lost her balance. A freak accident." Boone pauses to look at the food on his plate, still untouched. "Sometimes I think it's the suddenness of it that makes it hard to deal with. She was there one minute, gone the next. And I never got to say goodbye. She simply vanished. Like in that TV show."

"*The Leftovers*," I say, not bothering to mention I had been offered a part on the show but turned it down because I found the subject matter too depressing.

"Right. That's the one. When it's so sudden like that, it makes you regret all those times you took for granted. I can't remember the last thing I said to her, and that kills me. Sometimes, even now, I stay awake at night trying to think of what it was and hoping it was something nice." Boone looks up at me. "Do you remember the last thing you said to your husband?"

"No," I say.

I put my plate down, excuse myself, and go inside. Seconds later, I'm in the dining room, kneeling at the liquor cabinet, a bottle of bourbon gripped in my fist. As my final words to Len storm through my head—unforgettable no matter how much I try—I tip the bottle back and swallow several blessed gulps.

There.

That's much better.

Back outside, I see that Boone's taken a few bites from his sandwich. That makes one of us who feels like eating.

"I'm not really hungry," I say, wondering if he can smell the bourbon on my breath. "If you want, you can have the rest of mine."

Boone starts to reply but stops when something on the other side of the lake catches his attention. I look where he's looking and see a pair of headlights pulling into the driveway of the Royce house.

Tom has returned.

I reach for the binoculars and watch him bring the Bentley to a stop beneath the portico on the side of the house before cutting the headlights. He gets out of the car, carrying a large plastic bag from the only hardware store in a fifteen-mile radius.

Boone taps my shoulder. "Let me look."

I hand him the binoculars, and he peers through them as Tom enters the house. On the first floor, the kitchen lights flick on. They're soon followed by the dining room lights as Tom makes his way deeper into the house.

"What's he doing?" I ask Boone.

"Opening the bag."

"What's in it?"

Boone sighs, getting annoyed. "I don't know yet."

That ignorance lasts only a second longer before Boone lets out a low whistle. Handing the binoculars back to me, he says, "You need to see this."

I lift the binoculars to my eyes and see Tom Royce standing at the dining room table. Spread out before him is everything he bought from the hardware store.

A plastic tarp folded into a tidy rectangle.

A coil of rope.

And a hacksaw with teeth so sharp they glint in the light of the dining room.

"I think," Boone says, "it might be time to call my detective friend."

Detective Wilma Anson isn't even close to what I expected. In my mind, I pictured someone similar to the detective I played in a three-episode arc of *Law & Order: SVU*. Tough. No-nonsense. Dressed in the same type of function-over-style pantsuit my character wore. The woman at my door, however, wears purple yoga pants, a bulky sweatshirt, and a pink headband taming her black curls. A yellow scrunchie circles her right wrist. Wilma catches me looking at it as I shake her hand and says, "It's my daughter's. She's at karate class right now. I have exactly twenty minutes until I need to go pick her up."

At least the no-nonsense part meets my expectations.

Wilma's demeanor is softer to Boone, but only by a degree. She manages a quick hug before spotting the liquor cabinet two rooms away.

"You okay with that around?" she asks him.

"I'm fine, Wilma."

"You sure?"

"Certain."

"I believe you," Wilma says. "But you better call me if you so much as think of touching one of those bottles."

In that moment, I get a glimpse of their relationship. Former colleagues, most likely, who know each other's strengths and weaknesses. He's an alcoholic. She's support. And I'm just the bad influence thrown into the mix because of something suspicious taking place on the other side of the lake.

"Show me the house," Wilma says.

Boone and I lead her to the porch, where she stands at the railing and takes in the dark sky and even darker lake with curious appraisal. Directly across from us, the Royce house has lights on in the kitchen and master bedroom, but from this distance and without the binoculars, it's impossible to pinpoint Tom's location inside.

Wilma gestures to the house and says, "That's where your friend lives?"

"Yes," I say. "Tom and Katherine Royce."

"I know who the Royces are," Wilma says. "Just like I know who you are."

From her tone, I gather Wilma's seen the terrible-but-true tabloid headlines about me. It's also clear she disapproves.

"Tell me why you think Mrs. Royce is in danger."

I pause, unsure just where to begin, even though I should have known the question was coming. Of course a police detective is going to ask me why I think my neighbor did something to his missing wife. I become aware of Wilma Anson's stare. Annoyance clouds her features, and I worry she'll just up and leave if I don't say something in the next two seconds.

"We heard a scream this morning," Boone says, coming to my rescue. "A woman's scream. It came from their side of the lake."

"And I saw things," I add. "Worrisome things."

"At their house?"

"Yes."

"How often are you there?"

"I haven't been inside since they bought the place."

Wilma turns back to the lake. Squinting, she says, "You noticed worrisome things all the way from over here?"

I nod to the binoculars sitting on the table between the rocking chairs, like they have been for days. Wilma, looking back and forth between me and the table, says, "I see. May I borrow these?"

"Knock yourself out."

The detective lifts the binoculars to her eyes, fiddles with the focus, scans the lake's opposite shore. When she lowers the binoculars, it's to give me a stern look.

"There are laws against spying on people, you know."

"I wasn't spying," I say. "I was observing. Casually."

"Right," Wilma says, not even bothering to pretend she thinks I'm telling the truth. "How well do each of you know them?"

"Not well," Boone says. "I met them a couple of times out and about on the lake."

"I only met Tom Royce twice," I say. "But Katherine and I have crossed paths a few times. She's been over here twice, and we talked after I saved her from drowning in the lake."

I know it's wrong, but I'm pleased that last part of my sentence seems to surprise the otherwise unflappable Wilma Anson. "When was this?" she says.

"Day before yesterday," I say, although it feels longer than that. Time seems to have stretched since I returned to the lake, fueled by drunken days and endless, sleepless nights.

"This incident in the lake—do you have any reason to believe her husband had something to do with it?"

"None. Katherine told me she was swimming, the water was too cold, and she cramped up."

"When you talked to her, did Katherine ever give any indication she thought her husband was trying to do her harm? Did she say she was scared?"

"She hinted that she was unhappy."

Wilma stops me with a raised hand. "That's different than fear."

"She also told me there were financial issues. She said she pays for everything and that Tom would never agree to a divorce because he needed her money too much. She told me he'd probably kill her before letting her leave."

"Do you think she was being serious?" Wilma asks.

"Not really. At the time, I thought it was a joke."

"Would *you* joke about a thing like that?"

"No," Boone says.

"Yes," I say.

Wilma brings the binoculars to her eyes again, and I can tell she's ze-roed in on the lit windows of the Royce house. "Have you seen anything suspicious inside? You know, while casually observing?"

"I saw them fighting. Late last night. He grabbed her by the arm and she hit him."

"Then maybe it's for the best that they're currently apart," Wilma says.

"I agree," I say. "But the big question is where Katherine went. Her husband says she's back at their apartment. I called a friend in the city, who went there and checked. The doorman said she hasn't been there for days. One of them is lying, and I don't think it's the doorman."

"Or maybe it's your friend who lied," Wilma says. "Maybe she didn't talk to the doorman at all."

I shake my head. Marnie wouldn't do that, no matter how fed up she is with me.

"There's also this." I show Wilma my phone, Instagram already open and visible. "Katherine allegedly posted this from their apartment today. But this picture wasn't taken today. Look at the leaves in the trees and the calendar on the wall. This was likely taken weeks ago."

"Just because someone posts an old photo doesn't mean they're not where they say they are," Wilma says.

"You're right. But Katherine didn't even take that picture. Her husband did. If you look closely, you can see his reflection in the teakettle."

I let Wilma peer at the picture a moment before switching from Insta-gram to Mixer. I point to Katherine's red triangle, nestled right next to the one belonging to her husband. "Why would Katherine post an old photo she didn't even take? Especially when, according to the location-tracking software on her husband's app, her phone is still inside that house."

Wilma takes my phone and studies the map dotted with red triangles. "This is like a thousand privacy invasions in one."

"Probably," I say. "But don't you think it's weird Katherine would leave and not take her phone?"

"Weird, yes. Unheard of, no. It doesn't mean Tom Royce did something to his wife."

"But he's covering up where she is!" I realize my voice is a bit too loud, a tad too emphatic. Faced with Wilma's skepticism, I've become the impatient one. It also doesn't help that I snuck two more gulps of bourbon while Boone used the powder room before Wilma arrived. "If Katherine's not here, but her phone is, that means Tom posted that photo, most likely trying to make people think Katherine is someplace she's not."

"He also bought rope, a tarp, and a hacksaw," Boone adds.

"That's not illegal," Wilma says.

"But it *is* suspicious if your wife has suddenly disappeared," I say.

"Not if she left of her own accord after getting into a heated argument with her husband."

I give Wilma a curious look. "Are you married, Detective?"

"Seventeen years strong."

"And have you ever gotten into a heated argument with your husband?"

"Too many to count," she says. "He's as stubborn as a mule."

"After those arguments, have you ever gone out and bought things you could use to hide his body?"

Wilma pushes off the railing and drifts to the rocking chairs, handing me the binoculars in the process. She sits, twisting the scrunchie around her wrist in a compulsive way that makes me think it doesn't belong to her daughter at all.

"You seriously think Tom Royce is over there right now chopping up his wife?" she says.

"Maybe," I say, slightly horrified that not only am I thinking it, but I now consider it a more likely scenario than Katherine running away after an argument with her husband.

Wilma sighs. "I'm not sure what you want me to do here."

"Confirm that Tom Royce is lying," I say.

"It's not that simple."

"You're with the state police. Can't you trace Katherine's phone to check and see if she's called someone today? Or look at her bank and credit card records?"

Impatience thins Wilma's voice as she says, "We could do all of those things—if Katherine is reported missing to the local authorities. But I'm going to be straight with you here, if you do it, they're not going to believe you. People are usually reported missing by someone closer to them. Like a spouse. Unless Katherine has other family members you might know about who are also worried about her."

Boone looks to me and shakes his head, confirming that both of us are clueless about Katherine's next of kin.

"That's what I thought," Wilma says.

"I guess searching the house is out of the question," I say.

"It most definitely is," Wilma says. "We'd need a warrant, and to get that we'd need a clear indication of foul play, which doesn't exist. Tom Royce buying rope and a hacksaw isn't the smoking gun you think it is."

"But what about the scream?" Boone says. "Both of us heard it."

"Have you considered that maybe Katherine had an accident?" Wilma looks to me. "You told me she almost drowned the other day. Maybe it happened again."

"Then why hasn't Tom reported it yet?" I say.

"When your husband went missing, why didn't you report it?"

I had assumed Wilma knew all about that. She might even have been one of the cops I talked to afterwards, although I have no memory of her. What I *do* know is that, by bringing it up now, she can be a stone-cold bitch when she wants to be.

"His body was found before I got the chance," I say through a jaw so clenched my teeth ache. "Because people immediately went looking for him. Unlike Tom Royce. Which makes me think he's not concerned about Katherine because he knows where she is and what happened to her."

Wilma holds my gaze, and the look in her large hazel eyes is both apologetic and admiring. I think I earned her respect. And, possibly, her trust, because she breaks eye contact and says, "That's a valid point."

"Damn right it is," I say.

This earns me another look from Wilma, although this time her eyes seem to say, *Let's not get too cocky.*

"Here's what I'm going to do." She stands, stretches, gives the scrunchie on her wrist one last twirl. "I'll do a little digging and see if anyone else has heard from Katherine. Hopefully someone has and this is all just a big misunderstanding."

"What should we do?" I say.

"Nothing. That's what you should do. Just sit tight and wait to hear from me." Wilma starts to leave the porch, gesturing to the binoculars as she goes. "And for God's sake, stop spying on your neighbors. Go watch TV or something."

After Wilma leaves, taking Boone with her, I try to follow the detective's advice and watch TV. In the den, sitting in the shadow of the moose head on the wall, I watch the Weather Channel map the storm's progress. Trish, despite no longer being a hurricane, is still wreaking havoc in the Northeast. Right now, she's over Pennsylvania and about to bring her strong winds and record rains into New York.

Vermont is next.

The day after tomorrow.

Yet another thing to worry about.

I change the channel and am confronted by an unexpected sight.

Me.

Seventeen years ago.

Strolling across a college campus strewn with autumn leaves and casting sly glances at the blindingly handsome guy next to me.

My film debut.

The movie was a vaguely autobiographical dramedy about a Harvard senior figuring out what he wants to do with his life. I played a sassy co-ed who makes him consider leaving his long-term girlfriend. The role was small but meaty, and refreshingly free of any scheming bad-girl clichés. My character was presented as simply an appealing alternative the hero could choose.

Watching the movie for the first time in more than a decade, I remember everything about making it with dizzying clarity. How intimidated I was by the logistics of shooting on location. How nervous I was about hitting my marks, remembering my lines, accidentally looking directly into the camera. How, when the director first called action, I completely froze, forcing him to pull me aside and gently—so gently—say, "Be yourself."

That's what I did.

Or what I thought I did. Watching the performance now, though, I know I must have been acting, even if it didn't feel like it at the time. In real life, I've never been that charming, that bold, that *vivid*.

Unable to watch my younger self a second longer, I turn off the TV. Reflected in the dark screen is present me—a jarring transformation. So far removed from the vibrant young thing I'd just been watching that we might as well be strangers.

Be yourself.

I don't even know who that is anymore.

I'm not sure I'd like her if I did.

Leaving the den, I go to the kitchen and pour myself a bourbon. A double, to make up for what I missed while Boone was here. I take it out to the porch, where I rock and drink and watch the house on the other side of the water like I'm Jay Gatsby pining for Daisy Buchanan. In my case, there's no green light at the end of the dock. There's no light at all, in fact. The windows were dark by the time I returned to the porch, although a quick look through the binoculars at Tom's Bentley tells me he's still there.

I keep watching, hoping he'll turn on a light somewhere and provide a clearer idea of what he might be up to. That's what Wilma wants, after all. Something solid onto which we can pin our suspicions. Even though I want that, too, I get queasy thinking about what, exactly, that something solid would be. Blood dripping from Tom's newly purchased hacksaw? Katherine's body washed ashore like Len's?

There I go again, thinking Katherine is dead. I hate that my mind keeps veering in that direction. I'd prefer to be like Wilma, certain there's a logical explanation behind all of it and that everything will turn out right in the end. My brain just doesn't work that way. Because if what happened with Len has taught me anything, it's to expect the worst.

I take another sip of bourbon and bring the binoculars to my eyes. Instead of focusing on the still frustratingly dark Royce house, I scan the area in general, taking in the dense forests, the rocky slope of mountain behind them, the jagged shore on the far edges of the lake.

So many places to bury unwanted things.

So many places to disappear.

And don't even get me started on the lake. When we were kids, Marnie would tease me about Lake Greene's depth, usually when both of us were neck-deep in the water, my toes stretched as much as possible to retain the faintest bit of contact with the lake bed.

"The lake is darker than a coffin with the lid shut," she'd say. "And as deep as the ocean. If you sink under, you'll never come back up again. You'll be trapped forever."

While that's not technically true—Len's fate proved that—it's easy to imagine parts of Lake Greene so deep that something could be forever lost there.

Even a person.

That thought takes more than a gulp of bourbon to chase from my brain. It takes the whole damn glass, downed in a few heavy swallows. I get up and wobble into the kitchen, where I pour another double before returning to my post on the porch. Even though I've now got a hearty buzz going, I can't stop wondering, if Katherine really is dead, why Tom would do such a thing.

Money is my guess.

That was the motive in *Shred of Doubt*. The character I played had inherited a fortune, her husband had grown up dirt poor—and he wanted what she had. Snippets of things Katherine said to me float through my bourbon-soaked brain.

I pay for everything.

Tom needs me too much to agree to a divorce.

He'd kill me before letting me leave.

I head inside, grab my laptop from the charging station in the den, say hi to the moose head, and go upstairs. Snuggled in bed under a quilt, I fire up the laptop and Google Tom Royce, hoping it'll bring up information incriminating enough to persuade Wilma that something is amiss.

One of the first things I see is a *Bloomberg Businessweek* article from last month reporting that Mixer has been courting venture capital firms, seeking a cash influx of thirty million dollars to keep things afloat. Based on what Katherine told me about the app's lack of profitability, I'm not surprised.

"We're not desperate," the article quotes Tom as saying. "Mixer continues to perform above even our loftiest expectations. To take it to the next level as quickly and as efficiently as possible, we need a like-minded partner."

Translation: He's absolutely desperate.

The lack of a follow-up article suggests Tom hasn't yet been able to lure any investors with deep pockets. Maybe that's because, as I read in a separate *Forbes* piece on popular apps, Mixer is reportedly losing members while most others are steadily gaining them.

More words from Katherine nudge into my thoughts.

All of Tom's money is tied up in Mixer, which still hasn't turned a profit and probably never will.

I decide to switch gears. Instead of looking for information about Tom, I do a search of Katherine Royce's net worth. Turns out it's surprisingly easy. There are entire websites devoted to listing how much celebrities make. According to one of them, Katherine's net worth is thirty-five million dollars. More than enough to meet Mixer's needs.

That word lodges itself in my skull.

Need.

Contrary to Tom's quote, the word smacks of desperation. *Want* implies a desire that, if not met, won't change things too much in the long run. *Need* implies something necessary to survive.

We need a like-minded partner.

Tom needs me too much to agree to a divorce.

He'd kill me before letting me leave.

Perhaps Katherine was being completely serious when she said that. She even might have been hinting.

That Tom was planning something.

That she knew she might be in danger.

That she wanted someone else to know it, too. Just in case.

I close the laptop, half sick from worry and half sick from too much bourbon downed way too quickly. When the room begins to spin, I assume either one of those things is to blame. Probably both.

The room continues to rotate, like a carousel steadily gaining speed. I close my eyes to make it stop and collapse onto my pillow. A dark numbness envelopes me, and I'm not sure if I'm falling asleep or passing out. As I plummet into unconsciousness, I'm greeted with a dream of Katherine Royce.

Instead of the Katherine I met in real life, Dream Katherine looks the same way she did in that Times Square billboard all those years ago.

Begowned and bejeweled.

Shoes kicked off.

Running through the dewy grass, trying desperately to escape the man she was going to marry.

Katherine is still sprinting through my dreams when I awake sometime after three a.m., slightly confused by, well, everything. All the bedroom lights are on and I'm still fully dressed, sneakers and jacket included. The laptop sits on the side of the bed that used to be Len's, reminding me that I'd been drunk Googling earlier.

I slide out of bed and change into pajamas before heading to the bathroom. There I pee, brush my teeth, which had grown filmy, and gargle with mouthwash to clear away my bourbon breath. Back in the bedroom, I'm switching off all the lamps I had left on when I spot something through the tall windows that overlook the lake.

A light on the opposite shore.

Not at the Royce house but in the copse of trees to the left of it, near the water's edge.

From where I'm standing, I don't need the binoculars to know it's the beam of a flashlight bobbing through the trees. The big unknown is who's carrying that flashlight and why they're roaming the lakeside at this hour.

I rush out of the bedroom and down the hallway, passing empty bedrooms along the way, their doors open and their beds neatly made, as if waiting for others to arrive. But there's only me, all alone in this big, dark house, now descending the stairs to the main floor and heading to the porch where I spend most of my time. Once outside, I grab the binoculars.

It turns out I'm too late.

The light is gone.

Everything is dark once more.

But as I return inside and head back upstairs, I suspect I already know who it was and why he was out so late.

Tom Royce.

Putting the rope, tarp, and saw he'd purchased earlier in the day to good use.

I wake again at eight, dry-mouthed and nauseated. Nothing new there. What *is* new is a gut punch of unease about Katherine's fate, summed up by the thoughts that hit me as soon as I gain consciousness.

She's dead.

Tom killed her.

And now she's either in the ground somewhere on the other side of the lake or in the water itself, sunk so deep she may never be found.

This leaves me so rattled my legs tremble when I go downstairs to the kitchen and my hands shake as I pour a cup of coffee. While drinking it, I use my phone to confirm that, no, Katherine hasn't posted another photo to Instagram since yesterday and, yes, her location on Mixer remains directly across the lake from me.

Neither of those is a good sign.

Later, after forcing down a bowl of oatmeal and taking a shower, I'm back on the porch with my phone, in case Wilma Anson calls, and the binoculars, in case Tom Royce makes an appearance. For an hour, both go unused. When my phone does eventually ring, I'm disappointed to hear not Wilma's voice, but my mother's.

"I talked to Marnie and I'm concerned," she says, cutting right to the chase.

"Concerned that I talk to her more than I talk to you?"

"Concerned that you've been spying on your neighbors and now seem to think your new model friend was murdered by her husband."

Goddamn Marnie. Her betrayal feels as pointed and painful as a bee sting. What's worse is knowing it'll get even more irritating now that my mother is involved.

"This has nothing to do with you," I tell her. "Or Marnie, for that matter. Please just leave me alone."

My mother gives a haughty sniff. "Since you haven't denied it yet, I assume it's true."

There are two ways to play this. One is to issue the denial my mother so desperately craves. Just like my drinking, she'll be doubtful but will eventually fool herself into thinking it's true because it's easier that way. The other is to simply admit it in the hope she gets as exasperated as Marnie did and leaves me alone.

I go with the latter.

"Yes, I'm worried the man across the lake murdered his wife."

"Jesus, Casey. What has gotten into you?"

She shouldn't sound so scandalized. Banishing me to the lake house was her idea. Of all people, my own mother should have realized I'd get up to no good after being left alone here to my own devices. Though in my mind, finding out what happened to Katherine is a good thing.

"She's missing and I want to help her."

"I'm sure everything's fine."

"It's not," I snap. "Something very wrong is going on here."

"If this is about Len—"

"He has nothing to do with this," I say, even though this has everything to do with Len. What happened to him is the sole reason I'm willing to believe something bad also could have befallen Katherine. If it happened once, it could easily happen again.

"Even so," my mother says, "it's best if you stay out of it."

"That's no longer an option. A guy staying at the Mitchells' place thinks the same way I do. We already told a detective friend of his."

"You got the police involved?" My mother sounds like she's about to get the vapors or drop the phone or pass out from shock. Maybe all three. "This—this isn't good, Casey. I sent you there so you'd be out of the public eye."

"Which I am."

"Not when there are cops around." My mother's voice lowers to a whispered plea. "Please don't get involved any further. Just walk away."

But I can't do that, even if I wanted to. Because as my mother talks, something catches my eye on the other side of the lake.

Tom Royce.

As he crosses the patio on the way to his Bentley, I raise the binoculars and my mother's voice fades into background noise. I focus solely on Tom, searching for ways in which he could seem suspicious. Is his slow, easygoing walk to the car all an act because he knows he's being watched? Is that grim look on his face because his wife left him? Or is it because he's thinking about how he refused to let her leave?

My mother keeps talking, sounding like she's a thousand miles away. "Casey? Are you listening to me?"

I continue to stare across the water as Tom slides behind the wheel of the Bentley and backs it out from under the portico. When the car turns left, heading toward town, I say, "Mom, I need to go."

"Casey, wait—"

I hang up before she can finish. Staring at the now-empty Royce house, I think about the last birthday I celebrated with Len. The Big Three-Five. To celebrate, he rented an entire movie theater so I could finally fulfill my dream of watching *Rear Window* on the big screen.

If my mother were still on the line, she'd tell me what I'm doing is playing pretend. Role-playing Jimmy Stewart in his wheelchair because I have nothing else going on in my sad little life. While that's probably truer than I'd care to admit, this isn't just playacting.

It's real. It's happening. And I'm a part of it.

That doesn't mean I can't take a cue from good old Jimmy. In the movie, he had Grace Kelly search his suspicious neighbor's apartment, finding the wedding ring that proved he had murdered his wife. While times have changed and I don't know if Katherine's wedding ring will be enough proof for Wilma Anson, maybe something else in that house will do the trick.

By the time Tom's Bentley vanishes from view, the phone is stuffed back in my pocket, the binoculars are taking my place in the rocking chair, and I'm marching off the porch.

While he's away, I plan on doing more than just watch the Royces' house.

I'm going to search the place.

Rather than take the boat across the lake—the quickest and easiest option—I choose to walk the gravel road that circles Lake Greene. It's completely quiet and less conspicuous than the boat, which could be seen and heard by Tom if, God forbid, he returns while I'm still there and I have to make a quick getaway.

Also, walking gives me a chance to clear my head, gather my thoughts, and, if I'm being completely honest, change my mind. The road, so narrow and tree-lined in spots that it could pass for a path, invites contemplation. And as I walk, the lake glistening through the trees on my left and the thick forest rising to my right, what I'm thinking is that breaking into the Royce house is a bad idea.

Very bad.

The worst.

I pause when I reach the northernmost corner of the lake, smack in the middle of the horseshoe curve separating Eli's house from the Mitchells', where Boone is staying. I wonder what both men would say if they knew what I'm planning. That it's illegal, probably. That breaking and entering is a crime, even if my intentions are pure. Boone, ex-cop that he is, would likely list more than a dozen ways in which I'll be charged if I get caught. And Eli wouldn't hesitate to mention that what I'm about to attempt is also dangerous. Tom Royce *will* come back at some point.

Far across the water, all the way at the lake's southern tip, I can spot the rocky bluff where Len and I had our afternoon picnic a week before he died. In the water below, Old Stubborn pokes from the surface. Because of the way it's situated, the ancient tree can't be seen from any of the houses on Lake Greene, which is probably why it's attained such mythical status.

The guardian of the lake, according to Eli.

Even if he's right and Old Stubborn *is* keeping watch over Lake Greene, there are limits to what it can do. It can't, for instance, break into the Royce house and search for clues.

That leaves me to do the job.

Not because I want to.

Because I have to.

Especially if finding something incriminating inside is the only way I'm going to convince Wilma that Tom is lying about Katherine.

I resume walking, faster than before, not slowing until I've passed Eli's place and the Royces' house comes into view. The front is far different from the back. No floor-to-ceiling glass here. Just a modern block of steel and stone with narrow slats for windows on both the upper and lower floors.

The front door, made of oak and big enough for a castle, is locked, forcing me to go around the side of the house and try the patio door in the back. I had wanted to avoid the possibility of being seen from my side of the lake. Hopefully Boone is busy working inside the Mitchells' house and not sitting on the dock, watching this place as fervently as I've been.

I cross the patio quickly, making a beeline to the sliding door that leads into the house. I give it a tug and the unlocked door opens just a crack.

Seeing that two-inch gap between the door and its frame gives me pause. While I'm not up to speed on Vermont's penal code, I don't need Boone to tell me what I'm about to do is against the law. It's not quite breaking and entering, thanks to the unlocked door. And I'm certainly not intending to steal anything, so it's not burglary. But it *is* trespassing, which will result in at least a fine and some more horrible headlines if I'm caught.

But then I think about Katherine. And how Tom has lied—blatantly lied—about her whereabouts. And how if I don't do anything about it now, no one will. Not until it's too late. If it isn't too late already.

So I pull the door open a little wider, slip inside, and quickly close it behind me.

Inside the Royce house, the first thing that catches my eye is the view from the wall-sized windows overlooking the lake. Specifically the way my family's charmingly ramshackle lake house appears from here. It's so small, so distant. Thanks to the shadows of the trees surrounding it, I can barely make out the row of windows at the master bedroom or anything on the back porch beyond the railing. No rocking chairs. No table between them. Certainly no binoculars. Someone could be sitting there right now, watching me from across the lake, and I'd have no idea.

Yet Katherine knew I was watching. The last night I saw her, right before Tom jerked her away from this very spot, she looked directly at that porch, knowing I was there, watching the whole thing happen. My hope is that it comforted her. My fear is that it left her as unnerved as I feel right now. Like I'm in a fishbowl, my every move exposed. It brings a sense of vulnerability I neither expected nor enjoy.

And guilt. A whole lot of that.

Because today isn't the first time I've entered the Royces' house.

With my near-constant spying, in a way I've been doing it for days.

And although I'm certain, down to my core, that no one would have known Katherine was in trouble without me watching them, shame warms my cheeks harder than the sun slanting through the windows.

My face continues to burn as I decide where to search first. Thanks to that long-ago visit and my recent hours of spying, I'm well acquainted with the layout of the house. The open-plan living room takes up one whole side of the first floor, from front to back. Since it strikes me as the least likely place to find anything incriminating, I cross the dining room and head into the kitchen.

Like the rest of the house, it's got a mid-century modern/Scandinavian-sparse vibe that's all the rage on the HGTV shows I sometimes watch when

I'm drunk and can't sleep in the middle of the night. Stainless steel appliances. White everywhere else. Subway tile out the ass.

Unlike on those design shows, the Royce kitchen shows signs of frequent, messy use. Multicolored drops of food spatter the countertops. A tray on the center island holds a bowl and spoon crusted with dried oatmeal. On the stovetop is a pot with soup dregs at the bottom. From the milky film coating it, my guess is cream of mushroom, reheated last night. I assume Katherine was the cook of the marriage and Tom has been reduced to eating like a frat boy. I can't help but judge him as I peek into the trash can and see boxes that once held microwave Mexican and Lean Cuisines. Even at my drunkest and laziest, I would never resort to frozen burritos.

What I don't see—in the trash or anywhere else in the kitchen—are signs something bad happened here. No drops of blood among the food spatter. No sharp knife or hacksaw or weapon of any kind drying in the dishwasher. There's not even a Dear John letter from Katherine, which is what Marnie had predicted.

Satisfied there's nothing else to see here, I do a quick tour of the rest of the first floor—tasteful sun-room off the kitchen, guest powder room that smells like lavender, entrance foyer—before heading upstairs.

My first stop on the second floor is the only room not visible through the expansive windows at the back of the house—a guest room. It's luxurious, boasting a king bed, sitting area, and en suite bathroom that looks like something out of a spa. It's all crisp, clean, and completely boring.

The same goes for the exercise room, although I do examine the rack of free weights for dried blood in case any of them had been used as a weapon. They're clean, which makes me feel both relieved and slightly troubled that I'd thought to check them in the first place.

After that, it's on to the master bedroom, where the sight of my own house through the massive windows brings another guilt-inducing reminder that I watched Katherine and Tom in this most private of spaces. It's made worse by the fact that I'm now *inside* their inner sanctum, casing it the way a burglar would.

I see nothing immediately amiss in the bedroom itself, other than an unmade bed, a pair of Tom's boxer shorts discarded on the floor, and an empty rocks glass on his nightstand. I can't decide which is worse—that my spying has already taught me which side of the bed is Tom's or that a single sniff of the rocks glass instantly tells me he was drinking whiskey.

When I round the bed and check Katherine's nightstand, I encounter the first sign of something suspicious. A small bowl the color of a Tiffany's box sits next to her bedside lamp. Resting at its bottom are two pieces of jewelry.

An engagement ring and a wedding band.

It immediately reminds me of *Rear Window* and Grace Kelly as seen through Jimmy Stewart's telephoto lens, flashing dead Mrs. Thorwald's wedding ring. In 1954, that was proof of guilt. Today, however, it proves nothing. That's what Wilma Anson would tell me.

In this case, I'm inclined to agree. If Katherine did indeed leave Tom, wouldn't it be natural for her to leave her rings behind? The marriage is over. She wants a fresh start. She doesn't need to keep the jewelry that symbolized their unhappy union. Also, I know from our first, dramatic meeting that Katherine doesn't always wear her wedding band.

Still, it's suspicious enough for me to pull my phone from my pocket and snap a few pictures of the rings sitting in the bowl's gentle curve. I keep the phone out as I peek into the bathroom, which is even bigger and more spa-like than the one in the guest room. Like everywhere else, the only thing it points to is that Tom Royce is a slob when left on his own. Exhibit A is the towel bunched next to the sink. Exhibit B is yet another pair of boxer shorts on the floor. This time, I don't judge. Someone prowling my bedroom right now would see yesterday's clothes in a heap at the foot of my bed and a bra tossed across the back of the easy chair in the corner.

I move from bathroom to walk-in closet. It's large and tidy, the walls covered by an elaborate grid of shelves, hanging rods, and drawers. Nothing appears to be missing, a realization that brings a renewed sense of worry. While roaming the house, I'd been slowly coming around to the idea that maybe Katherine really did just up and leave Tom without giving him a clue about where she went. All these clothes, bearing labels from Gucci, Stella McCartney, and, in a refreshing bit of normalcy, H&M, suggest otherwise. As does a matching set of luggage tucked in the corner that I would have assumed belonged to Tom if the tags dangling from the handles didn't bear Katherine's name.

While I can understand leaving her engagement ring and wedding band behind, Katherine surely would have taken clothes with her. Yet the closet is filled with her things, to the point where I can spot only one empty hanger and one blank space on the shelves.

When Katherine left—*if* she left—she took only the clothes on her back.

I start opening drawers, seeing neatly folded sweaters, T-shirts and sweats, underwear in a rainbow of colors.

And a phone.

It's stuffed into the back of Katherine's underwear drawer, almost hidden behind a pair of Victoria's Secret panties. Seeing it makes me think of Mixer and Katherine's red triangle pinpointing her location.

I use my own phone to take a picture of it, then swipe through my call log until I find Katherine's number. The second I hit the call button, the phone in the drawer starts to ring. I brush aside the panties until I can see my number lit up across its screen. Below it is the last time I called her.

Yesterday. One p.m.

I let the phone keep ringing until her voicemail message kicks in.

"Hi, you've reached Katherine."

More worry pulses through me. Everything Katherine brought with her—her phone, her clothes, her jewelry—is still here.

The only thing missing is Katherine herself.

I pick up her phone, using a pair of panties to keep my fingerprints from smudging the screen. Thank you, guest arc on *Law & Order*.

The phone itself is locked, of course. The only information it provides is what's available on the lock screen. Time, date, and how much juice is left in the battery. Very little, it turns out. Katherine's phone is near death, which tells me it hasn't been charged for at least a day, maybe longer.

I put the phone back where I found it, just in case Tom is keeping tabs on it. No need to alert him to my presence. I close the drawer and am about to leave the closet when Katherine's phone begins to ring again, the sound muffled inside the drawer.

I return to the drawer, yank it open, see a phone number glowing white against the black screen. Just like me, whoever's calling hasn't been deemed familiar enough by Katherine to have their number saved in her phone.

But they have called before.

Along with the number is a reminder of the last time they did it.

This morning.

Because I can't answer, I whip out my own phone and snap a picture of the number glowing on Katherine's screen before the caller can hang up. It might be a good idea to call them later. Maybe they're looking for Katherine, too. Maybe they're as worried as I am.

I pocket my phone, close the drawer, leave the closet. After that, I move out of the bedroom and into the second-floor hallway, on my way to the only room yet to be searched.

The home office. Very much Tom's domain. The furnishings have a more masculine feel. Dark woods and glass and a distinct lack of personality. There's a shelf of antique barware befitting the name of his app and a bookcase filled with business-y titles heavy on aspiration. Sitting atop the shelf, in a silver frame, is the same wedding photo of Tom and Katherine I'd seen years before in *People* magazine.

By the window is a glass-topped desk upon which sits Tom Royce's laptop. It's closed now, as flat and compact as a picture book. I glide toward it, remembering the night I watched Katherine at that desk, using that very computer. I can't forget how surprised she had looked. So shocked it was clear even through the binoculars and a quarter mile of distance. I also recall how startled she seemed when Tom appeared in the doorway, barely managing to hide it.

My hand hovers over the laptop as I debate opening it up and seeing what I can find. Unlike Katherine's phone, there's no way to use it without getting my fingerprints all over it. Yes, I could use my shirt to wipe it down when I'm done, but that would get rid of Tom's and Katherine's prints as well. That might look like tampering with evidence, which courts tend to frown upon. Another thing I picked up from *Law & Order*.

On the flip side, this laptop could be the key we need to unlock the truth about what happened to Katherine. Showing Wilma Anson pictures of Katherine's phone and discarded rings might not be enough to get a search warrant. In the meantime, it would be so easy for Tom to make sure no one else sees what's on the laptop. All it would take is a single toss into Lake Greene.

That thought—of the laptop sinking to the lake's dark, muddy floor—makes me decide to open it. If I don't look—right now—there's a chance no one ever will.

I crack the laptop open, and its screen springs to life, revealing a home page of a lake in full summer splendor. Trees a shade of green that only exists in July. Sunlight twinkling like pixie dust on the water. A sky so blue it looks like CGI.

Lake Greene.

I'd recognize it anywhere.

I tap the space bar and the lake is replaced by a desktop strewn with tabs, icons, and file folders. I let out a relieved breath. I'd been worried the laptop was as locked down as Katherine's phone.

But now that I have access, I can't decide what to search first. Most of the folders look Mixer specific, with names like Q2 data, Ad roster, Mockups2.0. I click on a few of them, seeing spreadsheets, saved memos and reports using so much business-speak they might as well be written in Sanskrit.

Only one of the spreadsheets catches my eye. Dated three months ago, it consists of a column of numbers, all of them red. I take a picture of the laptop screen despite not knowing if the figures are dollars or subscribers or something else. Just because I can't understand it doesn't mean it won't come in handy later.

I close the folder and start looking for ones that seem unrelated to Tom Royce's app. I choose one marked with a telling name.

Kat.

Inside are more folders, labeled by year and going back half a decade. I peek inside each one, seeing not only photos of Katherine from her modeling days but more spreadsheets. One per year. Atop each is the same heading: *earnings.* I scan a few of them, noting there's not a red number to be found. Even though she's no longer a model, Katherine's been making an obscene amount of money. Far more than that net worth website estimated and far more than Mixer.

I take photos of spreadsheets for the past three years and move on to the laptop's web browser. Two seconds and one click later, I find myself staring at the browsing history.

Jackpot.

Immediately, I see that Tom hasn't done any obvious web surfing in the past two days. There are no instantly suspicious searches for ways to dispose of a body or the best hacksaws for cutting through bone. Either Tom hasn't touched the laptop since Katherine disappeared or he cleared the browsing history for the past forty-eight hours.

Three days ago, however, brings up a bonanza of visited sites. Some, including the same *Bloomberg Businessweek* article about Mixer I'd found, strike me as the work of Tom Royce. Others, such as the *New York Times* fashion section and *Vanity Fair,* suggest Katherine's doing. As does an interesting Google search.

Causes of drowning in lakes.

I click the link and see a brief list of reasons, including swimming alone, intoxication, and boating without a life jacket. That last one makes me think of Len. It also makes me want to clomp downstairs and pour myself something strong from the living room bar.

Trying to rid myself of both the thought and the urge, I do a little shimmy and move on. I go to Google and check the most recent topics searched on the laptop, finding more about drowning and water.

Swimming at night.

Ghosts in reflections.

Haunted lakes.

A sigh escapes my lips. Eli's campfire tale sent either Tom or Katherine running to Google. One of them, in fact, did a lot of searching a few days ago. In addition to lake-related topics, I find searches for World Series scores, the weather forecast, paella recipes.

One topic, however, stops me cold.

Missing women in Vermont.

Why on earth was Tom or Katherine interested in *this*?

Shocked, I move to click on the link when I spot a name just beneath it. Mine.

Seeing my name in the browser history isn't a surprise. I'm sure I've been Googled by plenty of complete strangers in the past year. It makes sense my new neighbors would do it, too. I even know what the top hit will be before I click it. Sure enough, there's a picture of me guzzling down a double old-fashioned and the headline that will likely dog me for the rest of my life.

"Casey's Booze Binge."

Below it are articles about my firing from *Shred of Doubt*, my IMDb page, Len's obituary in the *LA Times*. All of the links had been clicked, making it clear that either Tom or Katherine had been researching me.

What's not so clear is which one it was.

And why.

When I return to the browser history to try to find out, I notice another familiar name had been entered into Google.

Boone Conrad.

The search brought up an article about his wife's death. Reading it over, I learn two surprising facts. The first is that Boone is indeed his real name. The second is that he was a cop in the police department closest to Lake Greene. Everything else in the article is exactly what he'd told me yesterday. He came home from work, found his wife at the bottom of the stairs, and called paramedics, who declared her dead. The chief of police—Boone's boss—is quoted as saying it was a tragic accident. End of story.

I move on, seeing that it's not just people on the lake who have been

Googled by one of the Royces. I also spot a search for someone I've never heard of: Harvey Brewer.

Clicking on it brings up a staggering number of hits. I choose the first one—a year-old article from a Pennsylvania newspaper with a ghoulish headline.

"Man Admits to Slowly Poisoning His Wife."

I read the article, each sentence making my heart thump faster. It turns out that Harvey Brewer was a fifty-something mail carrier from East Stroudsburg whose forty-something wife, Ruth, suddenly dropped dead of a heart attack inside a Walmart.

Although she was a healthy type—"Fit as a fiddle," a friend said—Ruth's death wasn't a complete surprise. Her siblings told police she had been complaining about sudden weakness and dizzy spells in the weeks leading up to her death. "She said she wasn't feeling quite like herself," one of her sisters said.

Because Harvey was set to receive a healthy sum of money after her death, Ruth's family suspected foul play. They were right. An autopsy discovered trace amounts of brimladine, a common ingredient in rat poison, in Ruth's system. Brimladine, a stimulant that some experts have called "the cocaine of poisons," works by increasing the heart rate. In rodents, death is instantaneous. In humans, it takes a good deal longer.

When the police questioned Harvey, he caved immediately and confessed to giving his wife microdoses of brimladine for weeks. The poison, doled out daily in her food and drink, weakened Ruth's heart to the point of failure. Harvey claimed to have gotten the idea from a Broadway play the two of them had seen on a recent trip to New York.

Shred of Doubt.

Holy.

Shit.

Harvey Brewer had been in the audience of my play. He'd seen me onstage, playing a woman who comes to realize her husband is slowly poisoning her. He'd sat in that darkened theater, wondering if such a thing could be done in real life. Turns out, it could. And he almost got away with it.

By the time I reach the end of the article, different moments with Katherine are gliding through my thoughts like a slide show.

Floating in the lake, motionless, her lips an icy blue.

It was like my entire body stopped working, was how she later described it.

Slumped in a rocking chair, gripped by a hangover.

I'm just not myself lately.

Woozy from only two glasses of wine.

I don't feel too good.

It's that night by the fire I latch on to the hardest, as details that seemed small at the time suddenly loom large with meaning.

Tom telling me how fantastic he thought I was in *Shred of Doubt*.

Him insisting on pouring the wine, doing it with his back to us, so we couldn't see what he was doing.

Him carefully handing each of us our own glass, as if they'd been specifically assigned.

Katherine downing hers in a mighty gulp, getting a refill from her husband.

For a second, I'm dumb struck. The realization is like an old-timey flashbulb going off in my face. White-hot and blinding. Dizzy from the shock of it all, I close my eyes and wonder if what happened to Ruth Brewer also happened to Katherine.

It makes sense in the same way a jigsaw puzzle does once all the pieces have been snapped into place. Tom saw *Shred of Doubt* and, like Harvey, got to thinking. Or maybe he stumbled upon Harvey Brewer's crime first and decided to see the play for himself. There's no way to know the how, the why, or the when. Not that it matters. Tom decided to imitate both Harvey and the play, slipping Katherine tiny doses of poison when he could, weakening her until, one day, everything just stopped.

And Katherine found out, most likely by doing what I'm doing now and simply seeing it in her husband's browsing history.

That's what she saw the night before she vanished.

That's why she looked simultaneously shocked and curious as I watched her from the porch. Sitting in this very chair. Staring at this very laptop. As stunned as I am now.

And it's why she and Tom fought later that night. She told him she knew what he was doing. He denied it, maybe demanded to know where such an idea came from. *How? Who?*

By dawn, Katherine was gone. Tom either killed her or she ran, leaving everything behind. Now she could be buried in the woods or resting at the bottom of the lake or in hiding. Those are the only options I can think of.

I need to find out which one it is.

And convince Detective Wilma Anson to help me do it.

I grab my phone again and take a picture of the laptop screen, the article about Harvey Brewer unreadable but the headline crystal clear. I'm about to take another when I hear an unwelcome sound arrive outside the house.

Tires crunching gravel.

To my right is a window that provides a view from the southwestern side of the house. I go to it and see Tom Royce's Bentley vanishing under the portico.

Shit.

I run out of the office, only to stop and turn back around when I realize the laptop is still open. I rush back to the desk, slam the laptop shut, speed out of the office again. I pause in the second-floor hall, unsure where to go next. Within seconds, Tom will be inside. If I run down the stairs now, it's likely he'll spot me. It might be wiser to stay on this floor and hide in a place he probably won't enter. The guest room seems to be the best bet. I could crawl under the bed and wait until I'm certain I can escape unseen.

Which could be hours.

Meanwhile, Tom still hasn't come into the house. Maybe he's doing something outside. Maybe there *is* enough time for me to fly down the stairs and zoom out the front door.

I decide to risk it, mostly because hiding here—possibly for a long time—is no guarantee Tom won't find me anyway. The safest thing to do is leave the house.

Right now.

With no thoughts in my head other than getting out of here as fast as possible, I sprint for the stairs.

Then down the stairs.

Then toward the front door.

I grab the handle and pull.

The door is locked, which I already knew but had forgotten because, one, there are other things on my mind and, two, I've never done this before.

As I reach for the lock, I hear another door being pushed open.

The sliding glass door in back of the house.

Tom is coming inside—and I'm a second away from being caught. The front door is just off the living room. If he goes anywhere but the dining room or kitchen, I'll be spotted. Even if he doesn't, the click of the lock and sound of the door opening will alert him to my presence.

I spin around, ready to face him, my mind whirling to come up with a vaguely logical excuse as to why I'm inside his house. I can't. My brain is blank with panic.

As a second passes, then another, I realize I haven't heard the sliding door close or Tom's footsteps inside the house. What I *do* hear, drifting on the autumn breeze coming through that still-open door, is water lapping on the shore, the sound of a boat arriving at the Royces' dock, and a familiar voice calling Tom's name.

Boone.

I remain by the door, waiting for verification that Tom's still outside. I get it when I hear Boone, now on the back patio, ask him if he needs any work done on the house.

"I figured I'd check, since I'm pretty much done with the Mitchells' place."

"I'm good," Tom replies. "Everything seems to be in—"

I don't pay attention to the rest because I'm too busy unlocking the door and yanking it open. As soon as I'm outside, I do the only reasonable thing.

Run.

Thanks to his boat, Boone beats me back to our side of the lake. Even though I'd stopped running as soon as I passed Eli's house, I'm still out of breath when I see him standing in the road ahead, his arms folded across his chest like an angry parent.

"That was a stupid and dangerous thing you did back there," Boone says as I approach him. "Tom would have caught you if I hadn't jumped in my boat and stopped him."

"How did you know I was there?"

The answer, I realize, is gripped in Boone's right hand.

The binoculars.

Handing them to me, he says, "I borrowed them after I saw you walking past the house. I knew what you were up to and ran onto your porch to keep watch."

"Why didn't you stop me from going?"

"Because I was thinking about doing it myself."

"But you just told me it was stupid and dangerous."

"It was," Boone says. "That doesn't mean it wasn't necessary. Did you find anything?"

"Plenty."

We resume walking, making our way past where Boone is staying on the way to my place. Strolling side by side as leaves the color of a campfire swirl around us, it would be a lovely walk—almost romantic—if not for the grim subject matter at hand. I tell Boone about how Katherine's rings, phone, and clothes are still in her bedroom before getting into what I found on Tom's laptop, including Harvey Brewer.

"Tom was slowly poisoning her," I say. "Just like what this guy did to his wife. I'm certain of it. Katherine told me she hadn't been feeling well. She kept getting suddenly weak and tired."

"So you think she's dead?"

"I think she found out about it. Hopefully, she ran. But there's a chance . . ."

Boone gives me a somber nod, no doubt thinking about the tarp, the rope, the hacksaw. "Tom got to her before she could."

"But we have proof now." I grab my phone and start swiping through the photos I took. "See? That's the article about Harvey Brewer, right on Tom's own laptop."

"It's not enough, Casey."

I stop in the middle of the leaf-strewn road, letting Boone walk several paces ahead before he realizes I'm no longer at his side.

"What do you mean it's not enough? I have pictures of Katherine's phone and clothes, not to mention proof her husband was reading about a man who murdered his wife."

"What I mean," Boone says, "is that it's not legal. You got all that stuff by breaking into their house. A crime that's worse than spying."

"You know what's even worse?" I say, unable to keep an impatient edge out of my voice. "Planning to kill your wife."

I still haven't budged, forcing Boone to come back and wrap one of his big arms around my shoulders to get me moving again.

"I agree with you," he says. "But that's how the law works. You can't prove someone committed a crime by committing another crime. In order to really nail him, we need some kind of evidence—*not* gained illegally— that could point to foul play."

What he doesn't say—but what I infer anyway—is that, so far, Tom Royce has been very good at covering his tracks. That Instagram photo he posted on Katherine's account is proof of that. Therefore it's unlikely he left some damning piece of evidence within legal reach.

I stop again, this time stilled by the realization that there *is* a piece of evidence in my possession.

But it wasn't left by Tom.

This was all Katherine's doing.

I start off down the road again, the motion as abrupt as when I'd stopped. Rather than walk, I return to running, trotting far ahead of Boone on the way to the lake house.

"What are you doing?" he calls.

I don't slow as I shout my reply. "Getting evidence. Legally!"

Back at the house, I head straight for the kitchen and the trash can that should have been emptied a day ago but thankfully wasn't. A rare win for laziness. I sort through the garbage, my fingers squishing into soggy paper towels and clammy wads of oatmeal. By the time Boone reaches me, I've overturned the can and dumped its contents onto the floor. After another minute of searching, I find what I'm looking for.

A piece of broken wineglass.

Triumphantly, I hold it to the light. The glass is dirtier now than when I found it glinting in the yard. Crumbs dust the surface, and there's a white splotch that might be salad dressing. Hopefully that won't matter because the saltlike film I'd seen the other day remains.

If Tom Royce really did slip something into Katherine's wine that night, hopefully this piece of glass will be able to prove it.

When Wilma Anson arrives, the glass shard has been safely tucked inside a Ziploc bag. She studies it through the clear plastic, the tilt of her head signaling either curiosity or exasperation. With her, it's hard to tell.

"Where'd you get this again?"

"The yard," I say. "The glass broke when Katherine passed out in the grass while holding it."

"Because she'd allegedly been drugged?" Wilma says.

"Poisoned," I say, correcting her.

"The lab results might say otherwise."

Boone and I agreed it wasn't a good idea to tell Wilma just how, exactly, I came to suspect Tom of trying to poison his wife. Instead, we told her I had suddenly remembered Katherine mentioning the name Harvey Brewer, which led me to the internet and my theory that Tom might have tried the same thing Brewer had done to his wife. It was enough to get Wilma to come over. Now that she's here, the big question is if she'll do anything about it.

"That means you're going to test it, right?" I say.

"Yes," Wilma says, the word melting into a sigh. "Although it'll take a few days to get the results back."

"But Tom could be gone by then," I say. "Can't you at least question him?"

"I plan to."

"When?"

"When the time is right."

"Isn't *now* the right time?" I start to sway back and forth, put into motion by the impatience fizzing inside me. All the things I want to tell Wilma are the same things I *can't* tell her. Revealing that I know Katherine's phone, clothes, and rings remain in her bedroom would also be admitting that I broke into the Royces' house. So I keep it in, feeling like a shaken champagne bottle, hoping I don't explode under the pressure. "Don't you believe us?"

"I think it's a valid theory," Wilma says. "One of several."

"Then investigate it," I say. "Go over there and question him."

"And ask him if he killed his wife?"

"Yes, for starters."

Wilma moves into the adjoining dining room without invitation. Dressed in a black suit, white shirt, and sensible shoes, she finally resembles the TV detective of my imagination. The only similarity to her outfit from last night is a scrunchie around her wrist. Green instead of yellow and clearly not her daughter's. Slung over Wilma's shoulder is a black messenger bag, which she drops onto the table. When she sits, her jacket flares open, offering a glimpse of the gun holstered beneath it.

"This isn't as simple as you think," she says. "There might be something else going on here. Something bigger than what happened to Katherine Royce."

"Bigger how?" Boone says.

"You ever do a trust exercise? You know, one of those things where a person falls backwards, hoping he'll be caught by the people behind him?" Wilma demonstrates by raising her index finger and slowly tilting it sideways. "What I'm about to tell you is a lot like that. I'm going to trust you with classified information. And you're going to reward that trust by doing nothing and saying nothing and just letting me do my job. Deal?"

"What kind of information?" I say.

"Details of an active investigation. If you tell anyone I showed them to you, I could get in trouble and you could get your asses put in jail."

I wait for Wilma to reveal she's exaggerating with a just-kidding smile. It doesn't happen. Her expression is as severe as a tombstone as she gives the scrunchie on her wrist a twirl and says, "Swear you will tell no one."

"You know I'm good," Boone says.

"It's not you I'm worried about."

"I swear," I say, even though Wilma's seriousness makes me wonder if I *want* to hear what she's about to say. What I've discovered already today has me sparking with anxiety.

Wilma hesitates, just for a moment, before grabbing her bag. "When did the Royces buy that house?"

"Last winter," I say.

"This was their first summer here," Boone adds.

Wilma unzips the messenger bag. "Did Tom Royce ever mention coming to the area before they bought it?"

"Yeah," I say. "He told me they spent several summers at different rental properties."

"He told me the same thing," Boone says. "Said he was glad to finally find a place of their own."

Wilma motions for us to sit. After we do, Boone and me sitting side by side, she pulls a file folder out of her bag and places it on the table in front of us.

"Are either of you familiar with the name Megan Keene?"

"She's that girl who disappeared two years ago, right?" Boone says.

"Correct."

Wilma opens the folder, pulls out a sheet of paper, and slides it toward us. On the page is a snapshot, a name, and a single word that brings a shiver to my spine.

Missing.

I stare at the photo of Megan Keene. She's as pretty as a model in a shampoo commercial. All honey-blonde hair and rosy cheeks and blue eyes. The embodiment of Miss American Pie.

"Megan was eighteen when she vanished," Wilma says. "She was a local. Her family owns the general store in the next town. Two years ago, she told her parents she had a date and left, kissing her mother on the cheek on her way out. It was the last time anyone saw her. Her car was found where she always left it—parked behind her parents' store. No signs of foul play or struggle. And nothing to suggest she never planned to come back to it."

Wilma slides another page toward us. It's the same format as the first.

Picture—a dark beauty with lips painted cherry red and her face framed by black hair.

Name—Toni Burnett.

Also missing.

"Toni disappeared two months after Megan. She was basically a drifter. Born and raised in Maine but kicked out of the house by her very religious parents after one too many arguments about her behavior. Eventually, she ended up in Caledonia County, staying at a motel that rents rooms by the week. When her week was up and she didn't check out, the manager thought she'd skipped town. But when he entered her room, all her belongings still seemed to be there. Toni Burnett, though, wasn't. The manager didn't immediately call the police, thinking she'd return in a day or two."

"I guess that never happened," Boone says.

"No," Wilma says. "It definitely did not."

She pulls a third page from the folder.

Sue Ellen Stryker.

Shy, as evidenced by the startled smile on her face, as if she'd just realized someone was taking her picture.

Missing, just like the others.

And the same girl Katherine had mentioned while we sat around the fire the other night.

"Sue Ellen was nineteen," Wilma says. "She went missing last summer. She was a college student spending the season working at a lakeside resort in Fairlee. Left work one night and never came back. Like the others, there was nothing to suggest she packed up and ran away. She was simply . . . gone."

"I thought she drowned," Boone says.

"That was one theory, although there's nothing concrete to suggest that's what really happened."

"But you do think she's dead," Boone says. "The others, too."

"Honestly? Yes."

"And that their deaths are related?"

"I do," Wilma says. "Recently, we've come to believe they're all victims of the same person. Someone who's been in the area on a regular basis for at least two years."

Boone sucks in a breath. "A serial killer."

The words hang in the stuffy air of the dining room, lingering like a foul stench. I stare at the pictures spread across the table, my gut clenched with both sadness and anger.

Three women.

Girls, really.

Still young, still innocent.

Taken in their prime.

Now lost.

Studying each photograph, I'm struck by how their personalities leap off the page. Megan Keene's effervescence. Toni Burnett's mystery. Sue Ellen Stryker's innocence.

I think of their families and friends and how much they must miss them.

I think of their goals, their dreams, their disappointments and hopes and sorrows.

I think of how they must have felt right before they were killed. Scared and alone, probably. Two of the worst feelings in the world.

A sob rises in my chest, and for a stricken moment, I fear it's going to burst out of me. But I swallow it down, keep it together, ask the question that needs to be asked.

"What does this have to do with Katherine Royce?"

Wilma removes one more item from the folder. It's a color photocopy of a postcard. An aerial view of a jagged lake surrounded by forests and mountains. I've seen the image a hundred times on racks in local stores and know what it is without needing to read the name printed at the bottom of the card.

Lake Greene.

"Last month, someone sent this postcard to the local police department." Wilma looks to Boone. "Your old stomping grounds. They passed it on to us. Because of this."

She flips the page, revealing the photocopied back of the postcard. On the left side, written in all-caps handwriting so shaky it looks like the work of a child, is the address of Boone's former workplace, located about fifteen minutes from here. On the right side, in that same childlike scrawl, are three names.

Megan Keene.

Toni Burnett.

Sue Ellen Stryker.

Beneath the names are four words.

I think they're here.

"Holy shit," Boone says.

I say nothing, too stunned to speak.

"There's no way to trace who sent it," Wilma says. "This exact postcard has been sold all over the county for years. As you can see, there's no return address."

"Fingerprints?" Boone says.

"Plenty. That card passed through more than a dozen hands before coming to the state police. The stamp was self-stick, so there's no DNA on the back. A handwriting analysis concluded it was written by someone right-handed using their left hand. That's why it's barely legible. Whoever sent it did a very good job of covering their tracks. The only clue we have, really, is the postmark, which tells us it had been dropped into a mailbox on Manhattan's Upper West Side. That, incidentally, is where Tom and

Katherine Royce's apartment is located. It could be a coincidence, but I doubt it."

Boone rubs a hand through his stubble, contemplating all this information. "You think one of them sent that postcard?"

"Yes," Wilma says. "Katherine, in particular. The handwriting analysis suggests it was written by a female."

"Why would she do that?"

"Why do you think?"

It takes less than a second for it to sink in, with Boone's expression shifting as he moves from thought to theory to realization. "You really think Tom killed those girls?" he says. "And that Katherine knew about it? Or at least suspected it?"

"That's one theory," Wilma says. "That's why we're being very careful here. If Katherine sent that postcard as a way to tip off the police about her husband, then it's also possible she ran away and is in hiding somewhere."

"Or that Tom found out and silenced her," Boone says.

"That's also a possibility, yes. But if she *has* gone into hiding as a way to protect herself, we want to find her before her husband does. Either way, both of you deserve some credit for this. If you hadn't called me about Katherine, we never would have thought to tie her and Tom to this postcard. So thank you."

"What's the next step?" Boone asks, beaming with pride. Once a cop, always a cop, I guess.

Wilma gathers up the pages and stuffs them back into the folder. As she does, I get one last glimpse at the faces of those missing girls. Megan and Toni and Sue Ellen. Each one squeezes my heart so tight that I almost wince. Then Wilma closes the folder and the three of them vanish all over again.

"Right now, we're looking into all the places Tom rented in Vermont in the past two years. Where he stayed. How long he was there. If Katherine was with him." Wilma drops the folder into her messenger bag and looks my way. "If the dates match up to these disappearances, then *that* will be the right time to talk to Tom Royce."

Another shiver hits me. One of those full-body ones that rattle you like a cocktail shaker.

The police think Tom is a serial killer.

Although Wilma didn't say it outright, the implication is clear.

They think he did it.

And the situation is all so much worse than I first thought.

I grip the knife tighter, hoping it will mask the way my hand is still shaking. He looks at it with feigned disinterest and says, "Am I supposed to feel threatened by that? Because I don't."

"I honestly don't care how you feel."

It's the truth, although slightly overstated. I *do* care. I *do* want him to feel threatened. But I also know it doesn't really matter. The most important thing is getting him to talk, and if matching him in indifference will do the trick, then I'm willing to go there.

I return to the other bed in the room, putting down the knife and picking up the glass of bourbon on the nightstand.

"I thought you were going to make coffee," he says.

"Changed my mind." I hold out the glass. "Want some?"

He shakes his head. "I don't think that's a good idea. I want to keep my mind clear."

I take a sip. "More for me then."

"You might also want to think about keeping a clear head," he says. "You'll need it during this battle of wits you seem to think we're playing."

"It's not a battle." I take one more drink, smacking my lips to let him know how much I'm enjoying it. "And we're not playing anything. You're going to tell me what I want to know. Eventually."

"And what will you do if I don't?"

I gesture toward the knife sitting next to me on the bed.

He smiles again. "You don't have it in you."

"You say that," I tell him, "but I don't think you fully believe it."

Just like that, the smile disappears.

Good.

Outside, the wind remains at full howl as rain continues to pummel the roof. The storm is supposed to end by dawn. According to the clock between the beds, it's not quite midnight. Even though there's a lot of time between then and now, it might not be enough. What I plan on doing can't be done in broad daylight, and I don't think I can remain in this situation until tomorrow night. I might go mad by then. Even if I don't, I suspect Wilma Anson will be coming around again first thing in the morning.

I need to get him talking now.

"Since you refuse to talk about Katherine," I say, "tell me about the girls instead."

"What girls?"

"The ones you murdered."

"Ah, yes," he says. "*Them.*"

The smile returns, this time so twisted and cruel that I want to grab the knife and plunge it right into his heart.

"Why—" I stop, take a deep breath, try to gain control over my emotions, which hover somewhere between rage and revulsion. "Why did you do it?"

He appears to think it over, even though there's not a single reason he could offer that would justify what he's done. He seems to realize this and gives up. Instead, with that twisted smile still intact, he simply says, "Because I enjoyed it."

BEFORE

When she leaves, Wilma Anson takes the piece of broken wine-glass with her. The way she carries it to her car, holding the baggie at arm's length like there's a moldy sandwich inside, tells me she already thinks it won't lead to anything. I'd be annoyed if I weren't so caught off guard by what we've just been told.

She thinks Tom Royce is a serial killer.

She thinks Katherine thought that, too.

And that now Katherine is dead or in hiding because of it.

Wilma was right. This is a lot bigger than Katherine's disappearance. And I have no idea what to do now. I know what Marnie and my mother would say. They'd tell me to protect myself, stay out of the way, not make myself a target. I agree, in theory. But the reality is that I'm already a part of this, whether I want to be or not.

And I'm scared.

That's the brutal truth of it.

After watching Wilma drive away, I return to the dining room, looking for Boone. I find him on the porch instead, gripping the binoculars and staring at the Royce house on the other side of the lake.

"The bird-watching is amazing this time of year," I say. "All that plumage."

"So I hear," Boone says, indulging me and my weak attempt at a joke.

I settle into the rocking chair beside him. "Any sign of Tom?"

"None. But his car is still outside, so I know he's there." Boone pauses. "You think Wilma's right? About Tom being a serial killer?"

I shrug, even though Boone can't see me because he's still looking through the binoculars. Watching him observe the Royce house so intently gives me an idea of how I've looked the past few days. Parked on this porch. Binoculars pressed to my face. Focused on nothing else. It isn't a great look, even on someone as absurdly handsome as Boone.

"I think she could be onto something," he says. "Tom's been in the area a lot, something I never understood. He's rich. His wife's a supermodel. They could go anywhere. Hell, they could probably buy their own private island. Yet they always chose here, the backwoods of Vermont, where it's quiet and he's less likely to be disturbed. Then there's the fact that I always got a weird vibe from him. He seems so . . ."

"Intense?" I say, echoing Marnie's description of Tom Royce.

"Yeah. But it's a quiet intensity. Like there's something simmering just below the surface. Those are the kind of people you need to watch out for. Thank God you were doing just that, Casey. If you hadn't been watching, no one might have noticed any of this. Which means we can't let up now. We need to keep watching him."

I turn toward the lake, focused not on the Royce house but the water itself. Now streaked with afternoon sunlight, it looks peaceful, even inviting. You'd never guess how deep it is or how dark the water can get. So dark you can't tell what's down there.

Maybe Megan Keene.

And Toni Burnett.

And Sue Ellen Stryker.

Maybe even Katherine Royce.

Thinking about multiple women resting among the silt and seaweed makes me so woozy I grip the rocking chair's armrests and look away from the water.

"I don't think Wilma would like that," I say. "You heard what she said. She wants us to stay out of the way and let the police handle it."

"You're forgetting she also said they wouldn't have made the connection between Katherine and that postcard without us. Maybe we can find something else that will be of use to them."

"What if we do? Will they actually be able to use it?"

I think about everything I saw in the Royce house. Katherine's phone and clothes and the treasure trove of information on that laptop. It's maddening that none of it can be used against Tom, even though all of it points to him being guilty of *something*.

"This is different than you breaking into their house. That was illegal. What I'm talking about isn't."

Boone lowers the binoculars and gives me a look bright with restless excitement. The opposite of how I'm feeling. Even though I have no idea what he's planning, I don't think I'm going to like it. Especially because it sounds like Boone has more in mind than just watching Tom's house.

"Or we could do what Wilma told us to do," I say. "Which is nothing."

That suggestion does little to douse the fire in Boone's eyes. In fact, he looks even more determined as he says, "Or we could stop by the store Megan Keene's parents own. Maybe look around, ask a few innocent questions. I'm not saying we'll crack this case wide open. Hell, most likely it'll lead to nothing. But it's better than sitting here, waiting and watching."

He jerks his head toward the other side of the lake. There's frustration in the gesture, telling me this isn't just about Tom Royce. I suspect it's really about Boone, having once been a cop, now longing to be part of the action again. I understand the feeling. I get fidgety every time I watch a really good movie or see a great performance on TV, my body longing to again get onstage or be in front of the camera.

But that part of my life is over now. Just as being a cop is for Boone. And playing detective isn't going to change that.

"It could be exciting," he says, nudging my arm with one of his formidable elbows. "And it'll be good to get out of the house for a bit. When was the last time you left this place?"

"This morning." Now it's my turn to gesture to the Royce house. "Being in there was enough excitement for one day."

"Suit yourself," Boone says. "But I'm going with you or without you."

I almost tell him it'll be without me. I have no desire to get wrapped up in this more than I already am. But when I consider the alternative—being alone here, waiting for something to happen, trying not to watch when I know I will—I realize it's best to stick with the hot former cop.

Besides, he's right. It will do me some good to get away, and not just from the house. I need a break from Lake Greene itself. I've spent too much time gazing at the water and the home on the opposite shore. Which is exactly what I'll be doing if Boone leaves alone. The idea of me sitting here, staring at the sun-speckled water, thinking about all the people who might be resting at the bottom, is so depressing I have no choice but to agree.

"Fine," I say. "But you're buying me an ice cream on the way home."

A grin spreads across Boone's face, one so big you'd think I just agreed to a game of Monopoly.

"Deal," he says. "I'll even spring for extra sprinkles."

The store Megan Keene's family runs is part supermarket, part tourist trap. Outside, facing the road in an attempt to lure passing motorists, is a chainsaw sculpture of a moose. Draped over the front door is a banner telling everyone they sell maple syrup, as if that's a rarity in syrup-drenched Vermont.

It's the same inside. A mix of blandly functional and effusively homey. The aforementioned maple syrup sits in an antique bookcase right by the door, lined up in sizes ranging from shot glass to gallon jug. Next to it is a bourbon barrel filled with plush moose and bears, and a wire rack of postcards. I give it a rickety spin and spot the same card Wilma Anson showed us. I recoil at the sight of it, nearly bumping into yet another wood-carved moose, this one with knit hats placed on its antlers.

The store becomes more utilitarian the farther back we go. There are several aisles bearing canned goods, boxed pasta, toothpaste, and toilet paper, most of it cleared out in anticipation of the approaching storm. There's a deli counter, a frozen food section, and a checkout area bursting with the convenience store staples of lottery tickets and cigarettes.

When I see the girl manning the cash register, my heart skips two beats.

It's Megan Keene.

Even though her face is in profile as she stares out the window at the front of the store, I recognize that fresh-scrubbed prettiness from the photo I'd seen an hour ago. For a moment, shock holds me in its grip.

Megan isn't dead.

Which means maybe none of them are.

This was all some big, horrible misunderstanding.

I'm about to grab Boone and tell him all of this when the girl behind the cash register turns to face me and I realize I'm wrong.

She's not Megan.

But she is definitely related to her. She has the same blue eyes and picture-perfect smile. My guess is a younger sister who blossomed into the girl-next-door sweetheart Megan seemed to be.

"Can I help you?" she says.

I don't know how to respond, partly because the shock of seeing who I'd thought was Megan is slow to leave me and partly because Boone and I never discussed what to do or say when we reached the store. Luckily, he answers for me.

"We're just browsing," he says as he approaches her. "Saw the moose outside and decided to stop in. It's a nice store."

The girl looks around, clearly unimpressed by the shelves and souvenirs she sees every day.

"I guess," she says. "My parents try their best."

So she *is* Megan's sister. I'm proud of myself for guessing that, even though the resemblance is so uncanny that most people would.

"You get a lot of business on the weekends, I bet," Boone says.

"Sometimes. It's been a good fall. Lots of people have come up to see the leaves."

I notice something interesting as the girl talks. She isn't looking at Boone, which is where I'd be looking if I were her. Instead, she keeps glancing my way.

"Are you on Mixer?" Boone asks as he takes out his phone.

"I don't think so. What's that?"

"An app. People link to their favorite businesses so their friends can see." He taps his phone and shows it to the girl. "You should be on it. Might be a way to bring in some extra business."

The girl looks at Boone's phone for only a second before glancing at me again. It's clear she recognizes me but isn't sure from where. I get that a lot. I only hope it's from my film and television work and not one of the tabloids filling the magazine rack within eyeshot of the register.

"I'll ask my parents," the girl says as she turns back to Boone's phone.

"It's a great app. The guy who invented it lives nearby. He's got a house on Lake Greene."

Until now, I'd been wondering why Boone was steering the conversation toward Mixer. But when he taps his phone again and brings up Tom Royce's profile, I understand exactly what he's doing.

"His name is Tom," Boone says as he shows off Tom's picture. "You ever see him come into the store?"

The girl studies Boone's phone. "I'm not sure. Maybe?"

"He's very memorable," Boone says, prodding. "I mean, it's not every day a tech millionaire comes to your store."

"I'm only here after school and on weekends," the girl says.

"You should ask your parents then."

She gives a nervous nod before looking at me again, only this time I think she's seeking someone to rescue her from the conversation. She seems so vulnerable—so goddamn young and in need of protection—that I'm overcome with the urge to hop the counter, pull her into a tight hug, and whisper how sorry I am for her loss. Instead, I approach the register and nudge Boone aside.

"You'll have to excuse my boyfriend," I say, the word slipping out before I can think of a better alternative. "He's trying to distract you from the reason we really came inside."

"What's that?" the girl says.

Boone drops his phone back into his pocket. "I'm curious about that myself."

A second ticks by while I come up with a good excuse for entering the store. "I wanted to know if there are any good ice cream places in the area."

"Hillier's," the girl says. "It's the best."

She's not wrong. Len and I went to Hillier's, a quaint little dairy farm a mile down the road, several times last summer. We'd get our favorites and eat them on the wooden bench out front. Pistachio in a waffle cone for me. A cup of rum raisin for him. I can't remember the last time we were there, which seems like a thing someone would want to remember. The last ice cream cone with your husband before he died.

I look at Megan's sister and wonder if she has a similar problem. Unable to remember so many last moments because she was blithely unaware of their finality. Last sisterly chat. Last sibling spat. Last ice cream cone and family dinner and wave goodbye.

Thinking about it makes my heart ache. As does wondering if Toni Burnett and Sue Ellen Stryker also have sisters who miss them and mourn them and wish, deep down in dark parts of their hearts they don't tell anyone about, that someone would just find their bodies and put them out of their misery.

"Thanks," I say, giving her a smile that in all likelihood looks more sad than grateful.

"I'm not sure they're open right now, though. It's the off-season."

"Do *you* sell ice cream?"

Megan's sister points to the frozen food section. "We have gallon containers, quarts, and a couple of individual novelty cones."

"That'll do just fine."

I grab Boone by the elbow and pull him to the ice cream case. As we look at our options, he leans in and whispers, "Boyfriend, huh?"

Warmth spreads across my cheeks. I pull open one of the freezer doors, hoping a blast of frigid air will cool them down, and snag a red, white, and blue Bomb Pop. "Sorry. It's all I could come up with on short notice."

"Interesting," Boone says as he picks out a chocolate-covered Drumstick. "And just so you know, there's no need to be sorry. But I do think we're going to have to keep up the ruse until we're out of the store."

With a wink, he takes my hand, his palm hot against mine. It feels strange to have something so cold in one hand and so warmly alive in the other. As we return to the cash register, my body doesn't know if it should sweat or shiver.

Megan's sister rings up our order, and Boone releases my hand just long enough to pull out his wallet and pay. As soon as the wallet's back in his pocket, he reaches for my hand again. I grasp it and let myself be led out of the store.

"Thanks for your help," Boone says over his shoulder to Megan's sister.

"Anytime," she says. "Have a nice day."

Before stepping outside, I take one last look at the girl at the register. She's got her elbow on the counter and her head resting dreamily in a cupped hand. She watches as we go out the door, looking past us to the road and the trees and the mountains in the distance. Even though she might be focused on any of those things, I can't help but think that she's really gazing beyond them, eyes on some distant, unseen place where her sister might have run off to and is still, waiting for the right moment to come home.

We eat the ice cream in the back of Boone's pickup truck, our legs dangling from the lowered tailgate. I regret choosing the Bomb Pop the moment it touches my lips. It's far too sweet and artificial tasting, and it colors my tongue a garish red. I lower the popsicle and say, "So this was all for nothing."

Boone chomps down on his Drumstick, the chocolate shell on top breaking with a loud crunch. "I don't see it that way."

"You heard what she said. Tom Royce never came to the store."

"That she knows of. Which doesn't surprise me. If we're right about this, Tom came to the store while Megan was working. Not her sister. It probably happened several times. He came in, chatted with her, flirted, maybe asked her out on a date. Then he killed her."

"You sound pretty certain."

"That's because I am. I've still got a cop's instinct."

"Then why did you quit?"

Boone gives me a sidelong glance. "Who said I quit?"

"You did," I say. "You told me that you *used* to be a cop, which I took to mean you quit."

"Or it meant I was suspended without pay for six months and never returned when my punishment was up."

"Oh, shit."

"That about sums it up," Boone says before taking another bite.

I look at my popsicle. It's starting to melt a little. Rainbow-colored drips spatter the ground like blood in a horror movie.

"What happened?" I say.

"A few months after my wife died, I was drunk on duty," Boone says. "Not the worst thing a cop's done, obviously. But bad. Especially when I responded to a call. Suspected burglary. Turns out it was just a neighbor using the spare key to borrow the owner's lawn mower. But I didn't know that until after I discharged my weapon, barely missing the guy and getting my drunk ass put on leave."

"Is that why you decided to get sober?"

Boone looks up from his ice cream. "Isn't that enough of a reason?"

It is, which I should have realized before asking.

"Now that you're sober, why don't you go back to being a cop?"

"It's just no longer a good fit," Boone says. "You know that saying, 'Old habits die hard'? It's true. Especially when everyone you know still has those habits. Being a cop is a stressful job. It takes a lot to unwind after a shift. Beers after work. Drinks during weekend barbecues. I just needed to get away from all of that. Otherwise I would have had one of those cartoon devils always sitting on my shoulder, whispering in my ear that it's fine, it's just one drink, nothing bad will happen. I knew I couldn't live like that, so I got away. Now I scrape by doing odd jobs, and I'm happier now, believe it or not. I wasn't happy for a very long time. It just took hitting rock bottom for me to realize it."

I give the popsicle a halfhearted lick and wonder if I've already reached rock bottom or if I still have some distance left to fall. Worse, I consider the possibility that getting fired from *Shred of Doubt* was the bottom, and now I'm somewhere below that, burrowing down to a sublevel from which I'll never emerge.

"Maybe things would have been different if we'd had kids," Boone says. "I probably wouldn't have hit the bottle so hard after my wife died. Having someone else to take care of forces you to be less selfish. I mean, we wanted kids. And we certainly tried. It just never happened."

"Len and I never talked about it," I say, which is true. But I suspect he wanted kids, and that it was part of his plan to live at the lake house full-time. I also suspect he knew I didn't want them, mostly because I didn't want to inflict the same kind of psychological damage my mother had caused me.

It ended up being for the best. While I'd like to think I would have kept my shit together after Len was gone if a child had been in the picture, I doubt it. I might not have fallen apart so quickly and so spectacularly. A long, slow unraveling instead of my very public implosion. Either way, I have a feeling I would have ended up exactly where I am now.

"Do you miss it?" I say.

Boone takes a bite of his ice cream, stalling. He knows I'm no longer talking about being a cop.

"Not anymore," he eventually says. "At first I did. A lot. Those first few months, man. They're *hard*. Like, it's the only thing you can think about. But then a day passes, and then a week, and then a month, and you start to miss it less and less. Soon you don't even think about it because you're too distracted by the life you could have been living all this time but weren't."

"I don't think it's that easy."

Boone lowers his Drumstick and shoots me a look. "Really? You're doing it right now. When was the last time you had a drink?"

I'm shocked I need to think about it—and not because I've been drinking so much that I've forgotten. At first, I'm certain I had something to drink today. But then it hits me that my most recent drink was a double dose of bourbon last night before Googling Tom and Katherine Royce on my laptop.

"Last night," I say, suddenly and furiously craving a drink. I suck on my Bomb Pop, hoping it will quench my thirst. It doesn't. It's too cloying and missing that much-needed kick. The ice pop version of a Shirley Temple.

Boone notices my obvious distaste. Holding out his half-eaten Drumstick, he says, "You don't seem to like yours. Want to try some of mine?"

I shake my head. "I'm good."

"I don't mind. I'm pretty sure you don't have cooties."

I lean in and take a small bite from the side, getting half ice cream, half cone.

"I loved those as a kid," I say.

"Me, too." Boone looks at me again. "You have some ice cream on your face."

I touch my lips, feeling for it. "Where? Here?"

"Other side," he says with sigh. "Here, let me get it."

Boone touches an index finger to the corner of my mouth and slowly runs it over the curve of my bottom lip.

"Got it," he says.

At least, I think that's what he says. My heart's beating too fast and too loudly in my ears to know for sure. Even as everything gets fluttery, I know this was all a move on Boone's part. A smooth one. But a move all the same. So much more calculated than Len's shy honesty that day at the airport.

Can I get a kiss first?

I was willing to go there then. Not so much now. Not yet.

"Thanks," I say, scooting to the side to put a few more inches between us. "And thank you for earlier today. For distracting Tom long enough to let me slip out of the house."

"It was nothing."

"And thank you for not telling Wilma about that. I imagine you wanted to. The two of you seem close."

"We are, yeah."

"Did you work together?"

"We did, but I knew Wilma long before that," Boone says. "We went to school together, both high school and the police academy. She's helped me out a lot over the years. She was one of the people who convinced me to quit drinking. She made me realize I was hurting others and not just myself. And now that I'm sober, she still keeps an eye out for me. She's the one who introduced me to the Mitchells. She knew they needed work done on their house and that I needed a place to crash for a few months. So you can blame her for saddling you with me as a neighbor."

He pops the last nub of ice cream cone into his mouth before glancing at my popsicle, which is too much of a melted mess to resume eating.

"You done with that?" he says.

"I guess so."

I hop down from the tailgate to let Boone slam it back into place. After throwing my half-eaten popsicle into a nearby trash can, I get back into the truck. As I strap the seat belt across my chest, a thought hits me: Boone and I aren't the only people at the lake with Tom. He also has a neighbor, who to my knowledge has no idea about any of this.

"Do you think we should tell Eli?" I say.

"About Tom?"

"He lives right next door. He deserves to know what's going on."

"I don't think you should worry," Boone says. "Eli can take care of himself. Besides, it's not like Tom is preying on seventy-year-old men. The less Eli knows, the better."

He starts the truck and pulls out of the parking lot. In the side mirror, I get a glimpse of a battered Toyota Camry parked in a gravel area behind the store. Seeing it makes me wonder if it's Megan Keene's car, now being driven by her sister.

And if her sister is walloped with grief every time she gets behind the wheel.

And how long the car was parked there before Megan's parents realized something was wrong.

And if, when they see it parked there now, they think for a brief, cruel moment that their long-lost daughter has returned.

Those thoughts continue to churn through my mind long after the car and the store it's parked behind recede in the side mirror, leaving me to wish I was like Eli and didn't know anything about what's going on.

But it's too late for that.

Now I'm afraid I know far too much.

I nstead of taking the spur of the road leading to our respective houses, Boone drives a little bit farther to the one that accesses the other side of the lake. He doesn't explain why, nor does he need to. I know that circling the entire lake will bring us past the Royce house so we can see if Tom's still there.

It turns out that he is.

And he's not alone.

When the Royce driveway comes into view, we see Wilma Anson's car parked close to the portico on the side of the house, effectively blocking Tom's Bentley. The two of them are outside, having what appears to be a friendly conversation.

Well, as friendly as Detective Anson can get. She doesn't smile as she talks, but she also doesn't look too concerned to be conversing with a man she suspects is a serial killer.

Tom, on the other hand, is all charm. Standing at ease in the front yard, he chuckles at something Wilma just said. His eyes sparkle and his teeth shine a bright white behind parted lips.

It's all an act.

I know because when Boone and I drive by in the truck, Tom gives me a look so cold it could refreeze the popsicle I'd only recently dropped into a parking lot trash can. I try to look away—to Boone, to the road ahead, to the slice of lake glimpsed through the trees—but can't. Pinned down by Tom's stare, I can only endure it as it follows me in the passing truck.

His head slowly turning.

His eyes locked on mine.

The smile that had been there only seconds before now completely gone.

When Boone drops me off at the lake house, there's an awkward few seconds of silence as he waits for me to invite him in and I debate whether that's something I want. Every conversation or bit of contact brings us slightly closer, like two shy teenagers sitting on the same bench, sliding inexorably together. And right now, that might not be the best thing for either of us.

I experienced no such hesitation with Morris, the drinking-buddy-turned-fuck-buddy stagehand from *Shred of Doubt*. He and I had the same idea: get drunk and screw.

But Boone isn't Morris. He's sober, for one thing. And just as damaged as I am. As for what he wants, I assume—and hope—it involves his naked body entwined with mine. But to what end? That's the question that sticks in my head like a Taylor Swift song. Not knowing his end game makes me unwilling to play at all.

Also, I really need a drink.

That thirst I immediately got when reminded I haven't had one all day hasn't left me. Sure, it faded a bit when Boone swiped a finger across my bottom lip and when Tom stared at me as we passed his house. Now, though, it's an itch that needs to be scratched.

One I can't touch while Boone is around.

"Good night," I say, talking louder than usual to be heard over the truck's idling engine. "Thanks for the ice cream."

Boone responds with a meme-worthy blink, as if he's surprised to be rejected. Looking the way he does, I suspect it doesn't happen often.

"No problem," he says. "Have a good night, I guess."

I get out of the truck and go inside. Dusk has descended over the valley, turning the interior of the lake house gloomy and gray. I go from room to room, switching on lights and chasing away the shadows. When I reach the dining room, I head straight for the liquor cabinet and grab the closest bottle within reach.

Bourbon.

But after opening the bottle, something Boone said earlier stops me from bringing it to my lips.

I was hurting others and not just myself.

Am *I* hurting others with my drinking?

Yes. There's no doubt about that. I'm hurting Marnie. I'm hurting my friends and colleagues. I cringe thinking about how fucking rude I was toward the cast and crew of *Shred of Doubt*. Showing up drunk was the ultimate sign of disrespect for their hard work and preparation. Not a single one of them came to my defense after I was fired, and I can't blame them.

As for my mother, I am absolutely drinking to hurt her, even though she'd insist I'm only punishing myself. Not true. If I truly wanted to be punished, I'd deny myself one of the few things that bring me pleasure.

And I like drinking.

A lot.

I like the way I feel after three or four or five drinks. Limp and floating. A jellyfish drifting in a calm sea. Even though I know it won't last—that at some point hours in the future I might be dry-mouthed and headachy and heaving it all back up—that temporary weightlessness is worth it.

But none of those things are the reason why I haven't been sober for a single day in the past nine months.

I don't drink to hurt or punish or feel good.

I drink to forget.

Which is why I tilt the bottle and bring it to my parched, parted lips. When the bourbon hits my tongue and the back of my throat, all the tension in my mind and muscles suddenly eases. I unclench, like a flower bud spreading open into full bloom.

That's much, much better.

I take another two gulps from the bottle before filling a rocks glass—minus the rocks—and carrying it out to the porch. Twilight has turned the lake quicksilver gray, and a light breeze blowing across the water wrinkles the surface. On the other side of the lake, the Royce house sits in darkness. Its glass walls reflect the moving water, making it look like the house itself is undulating.

The optical illusion hurts my eyes.

I close them and take a few more blind sips.

I stay that way for God knows how long. Minutes? A half hour? I don't keep track because I don't really care. I'm content to simply sit in the rocking chair, eyes shut tight as the warmth of the bourbon counteracts the chill of the evening breeze.

The wind has picked up enough to whip the lake into unruliness. Trish, announcing her impending arrival. The water rolls toward the shoreline, slapping the stone retaining wall just beyond the porch. It sounds unnervingly like someone stomping through the water, and I can't help but imagine the fish-pecked bodies of Megan Keene, Toni Burnett, and Sue Ellen Stryker rising from the depths and stepping onto shore.

Even worse is when I picture Katherine doing the same thing.

And worse still is imagining Len there as well, a mental image so potent I swear I can feel his presence. It doesn't matter that, unlike the others, his body was found and cremated, the ashes sprinkled into this very lake. I still think he's there, a few yards from shore, standing in the darkness as water laps past his knees.

You know the lake is haunted, right?

No, Marnie, it isn't.

Memories, though, are a different matter. They're filled with ghosts.

I drink more to chase them away.

Two—or three—glasses of bourbon later, the ghosts are gone but I'm still here, beyond buzzed and sliding inexorably into utter drunkenness. Tom's still here, too, safe in his house that's now bright as a bonfire.

Apparently Wilma didn't want to haul him in for further questioning, or Tom somehow told enough lies to avoid it for now. Either way, it's not a good sign. Katherine's still missing, and Tom's still walking free as if nothing is wrong.

Holding the binoculars with hands that are numb and unsteady from too much bourbon, I watch him through the kitchen window. He stands at the stove with a dish towel thrown over his shoulder like he's a professional chef and not just a coddled millionaire struggling to reheat soup. Another bottle of five-thousand-dollar wine sits on the counter. He pours himself a glass and takes a lip-smacking sip. Seeing Tom so carefree while his wife remains unaccounted for makes me reach for the rocks glass and empty it.

When I stand to go inside and pour another, the porch, the lake, and the Royce house start listing like the *Titanic*. Under my feet, it feels like the earth is shifting, as if I've stumbled into some stupid disaster movie Len would have written. Instead of walking back to the kitchen, I stagger.

Okay, so I'm not nearing drunkenness.

I've already arrived.

Which means another drink won't hurt, right?

Right.

I splash more bourbon into the glass and take it back outside, moving with caution. One foot slowly in front of the other like a tightrope walker. Soon I'm in the rocking chair, plopping into it with a giggle. After another sip of bourbon, I trade my glass for the binoculars and peer at the Royce house again, focusing on the kitchen.

Tom's no longer there, although the soup remains. The pot sits on the counter next to the wine, wisps of steam still coiling in the air.

My gaze slides to the dining room, also empty, and then the large living room. Tom's not there, either.

I tilt the binoculars slightly upward, tracing with my vision the same path I took in person earlier.

Exercise room.

Empty.

Master bedroom.

Empty.

Office.

Empty.

A worrisome thought pokes through my inebriation: What if Tom suddenly took off? Maybe he got spooked by his conversation with Wilma Anson. Or maybe she called him right as he was about to eat his soup, saying she wanted him to come in for formal questioning, which sent him running for his keys. It's entirely possible he's driving away this very second, speeding for the Canadian border.

I swing the binoculars away from the second floor toward the side of the house, looking for his Bentley. It's still there, parked beneath the portico.

As I bring my gaze back toward the house, sliding it past the back patio strewn with dead leaves and the bare trees on the lakeshore that they've fallen from, I notice something on the Royces' dock.

A person.

But not just any person.

Tom.

He stands at the end of the dock, spine as straight as a steel beam. In his hands are a pair of binoculars, aimed at this side of the lake.

And at me.

I duck, trying to hide behind the porch railing, which even in my drunken state I understand to be ridiculous on so many levels. First, it's a railing, not a brick wall. I'm still visible between the whitewashed slats. Second, Tom saw me. He knows, like Katherine did, that I've been watching them.

Now he's watching me back. Even though I've lowered the binoculars, I can still see him, a night-shrouded figure on the edge of the dock. He stays that way another minute before turning suddenly and walking up the dock.

It's only after Tom crosses the patio and heads back into the house that I risk bringing the binoculars to my eyes again. Inside, I see him pass through the dining room into the kitchen, where he pauses to snatch something from the counter. Then he's on the move again, pushing back outside through the side door off the kitchen.

He slides into his Bentley. Two seconds later, the headlights spring to life—twin beams that shoot straight across the lake.

As Tom backs the car out from under the portico, I at first think he's finally running away. He knows I'm onto him and has decided to flee, maybe for good. I yank my phone from my pocket, ready to call Wilma Anson and alert her. The phone springs like a leaping frog from my bourbon-dulled fingers. I lunge for it, miss, and watch helplessly as it hits the porch, slips under the railing, and drops to the weedy ground below.

Across the water, the Bentley has reached the end of the driveway. It turns right, onto the road that circles the lake. Seeing it brings another sobering thought. If Tom were running away, he would have turned left, toward the main road.

Instead, he's driving in the opposite direction.

Around the lake.

Right toward me.

Still kneeling on the porch, I watch the Bentley's headlights carve a path through the darkness, marking its progress past Eli's house, then out of sight as it reaches the lake's northern curve.

Finally, I start to move.

Stumbling into the house.

Slamming the French doors behind me.

Fumbling with the lock because I'm drunk and scared and I've never had to use it before. Most nights, there's no reason to lock any of the doors.

Tonight, I have one.

Inside the house, I veer from room to room, switching off all the lights I'd turned on earlier.

Dining room and kitchen. Living room and den. Library and foyer.

Soon the whole house has been returned to the darkness I'd walked into when I arrived. I push aside the curtain at the small window beside the front door and peek outside. Tom has reached this side of the lake and is coming my way. I see the headlights first, plowing through the darkness, clearing a path for the Bentley itself, which slows as it draws closer to the house.

My foolish hope is that, even though he knows I'm here, Tom will see the place in utter darkness and keep driving.

He doesn't.

Despite the dark house, Tom steers the car into the driveway. The headlights shine through the beveled panes of the front door's window, casting a rectangular glow on the foyer wall. I duck out of its reach, crawl to the door, and engage the lock.

Then I wait.

Hunched on the floor.

Back against the door.

Listening as Tom gets out of the car, crunches up the driveway toward the house, steps onto the front porch.

When he pounds on the door, it shimmies beneath my back. I clamp both hands over my nose and mouth, praying he can't hear me breathing.

"I know you're in there, Casey!" Tom's voice is like cannon fire. Booming. Angry. "Just like I know you were inside my house. You forgot to lock the front door when you left."

I cringe at my stupidity. Even though I had to leave in a hurry, I should have known to lock the door behind me. Little details like that can trip you up when you've got something to hide.

"Maybe I should have told your detective friend about *that* instead of answering all her questions. What have I been doing? Have I heard from my wife? Where have I stayed every summer for the past two years? I know you sent her, Casey. I know you've been spying on me."

He pauses, maybe expecting I'll respond in some way, even if it's to deny what's clearly the truth. I remain silent, taking short, frantic breaths through interlaced fingers, worrying about what Tom will do next. The glow of the headlights through the door's window are an unwelcome reminder of the house's many vulnerabilities. Tom could break in easily if he wanted to. A smashed window or a powerful push on one of the doors is all it would take.

Instead, he pounds the door again, hitting it so hard I really do think he's about to break it down. A startled yelp squeaks out from beneath my cupped hands. I press them tighter against my mouth, but it doesn't matter. The noise escaped. Tom heard it.

When he resumes talking, his mouth is at the keyhole, his voice a whisper in my ear.

"You should learn to mind your own business, Casey. And you should learn to keep your mouth shut. Because whatever you think is happening, you've got it all wrong. You have no idea what's going on. Just leave us the fuck alone."

I remain slumped against the door as Tom leaves. I listen to his footsteps moving away from the house, the car door opening and closing. I watch the headlights fade on the foyer wall and hear the hum of the car growing distant in the October night.

Yet I stay where I am, weighed down with worry.

That Tom will return at any second.

That, if he does, I'll suddenly vanish like Katherine.

Too scared and spent—and, let's be honest, too drunk—to move, I close my eyes and listen to the grandfather clock in the living room tick off the seconds in my head. The sound soon fades. As do my thoughts. As does consciousness.

When there's another knock on the door, I'm only vaguely aware of it. It sounds distant and not quite real. Like a noise in a daydream or a TV left on while you sleep.

A voice accompanies it.

Maybe.

"Casey?" A pause. "Are you there?"

I mumble something. I think it's "No."

The voice on the other side of the door says, "I saw Tom drive by and got worried he was coming to see you. Are you okay?"

I say "No" again, although this time I'm unsure if the word is spoken and not simply thought. My consciousness is fading again. Beyond my closed eyelids, the foyer spins like a Tilt-A-Whirl, and I move with it, spiraling toward a dark pit of nothingness.

Before I reach it, I'm aware of two things. The first is a sound coming from below, in the basement I refuse to enter. The second is the chilling feeling that I'm no longer alone, that someone else is inside the house with me.

I sense a door opening.

Footsteps coming toward me.

Another person in the foyer.

Startled out of my shit-faced state for just a second, my eyes fly open and I see Boone standing over me, his head cocked in what's either curiosity or pity.

My eyes fall shut again as he scoops me up and I finally pass out.

I wake with a pounding head and a roiling stomach in a bed I have no memory of getting into. When I open my eyes, the light coming through the tall windows makes me squint, even though the morning sky is slate gray. Through that heavy-lidded gaze, I see the time—quarter past nine—and a mostly full glass of water on the nightstand. I take several greedy gulps before collapsing back onto the bed. Splayed across the mattress, the sheets tangled around my legs, I struggle to recall the night before.

I remember drinking on the porch.

And ducking stupidly behind the railing when I realized Tom was watching me.

And Tom at the door, yelling and knocking, although most of what he said is lost in a bourbon haze. So is everything that happened after that, which is why I'm startled when I notice the scent of something cooking rising from downstairs.

Someone else is here.

I spring out of bed, accidentally kicking a trash can that's been left beside it, and hobble out of the bedroom, my body stiff and sore. In the hallway, the cooking smells are stronger, more recognizable. Coffee and bacon. At the top of the stairs, I call down to whoever's in the kitchen.

"Hello?" I say, my voice ragged from both uncertainty and a killer hangover.

"Good morning, sleepyhead. I thought you'd never wake up."

Hearing Boone's voice brings another flash of memory. Him coming to the door not long after Tom left, me trying to answer but uncertain if I actually did, then him being inside, even though I'm pretty sure I never opened the door.

"Have you been here all night?"

"I sure have," Boone says.

His answer only prompts more questions. How? Why? What did we do all night? Although the realization that I'm still in the same jeans and sweatshirt I wore yesterday suggests we didn't do anything.

"I'll, uh, be right down," I say before hurrying back to the bedroom. There, I check the mirror over the dresser. The reflection staring back at me is alarming. Red-eyed and wild-haired, I look like a woman still reeling from drinking too much the night before, which is exactly what I am.

The next five minutes are spent stumbling and fumbling in the bathroom. I set what has to be a record for the world's fastest shower, followed by the necessary brushing of teeth and hair. One gargle with mouthwash and a change into a different, less smelly pair of jeans and sweatshirt later, I look presentable.

Mostly.

The upside to that flurry of activity is that it made me forget just how hungover I really am. The downside is that it all comes roaring back as soon as I try to descend the steps. Looking down the steep slope of the stairwell makes me so dizzy I think I might be sick. I suck in air until the feeling passes and take the stairs slowly, one hand on the banister, the other flat-palmed against the wall, both feet touching each step.

At the bottom, I take a few more deep breaths before heading into the kitchen. Boone is at the stove, making pancakes and looking like a sexy celebrity chef in tight jeans, a tighter T-shirt, and an apron that literally says *Kiss the Cook*. I catch him in the middle of flipping a pancake. With a flick of his wrist, it leaps from the pan like a gymnast before somersaulting back into place.

"Take a seat," he says. "Breakfast is almost ready."

He turns away from the stove long enough to hand me a steaming mug of coffee. I take a grateful sip and sit at the kitchen counter. Despite my clanging headache and not knowing any details about the previous night, there's a coziness to the situation that prompts both comfort and no small amount of guilt. This is exactly how Len and I spent our weekend mornings here, with me savoring coffee while he made breakfast in the same apron Boone now wears. Doing it with someone else feels like cheating, which surprises me. I felt no such guilt when having sex with a stagehand from *Shred of Doubt*. I guess because, in that instance, I knew the score. What this is, I have no idea.

Boone slides a plate piled with pancakes and bacon on the side, and my stomach gives off a painful twinge.

"Truth be told, I'm not very hungry," I say.

Boone joins me with his own plate heaped with food. "Eating will do you some good. Feed a hangover, starve a fever. Isn't that how the saying goes?"

"No."

"Close enough," he says as he tops his pancakes with two pats of butter. "Now eat."

I nibble a piece of bacon, nervous it might send me running to the bathroom with nausea. To my surprise, it makes me feel better. As does a bite of pancake. Soon I'm shoveling the food into my mouth, washing it down with more coffee.

"We should have picked up some maple syrup at the store yesterday," Boone says casually, as if we have breakfast together all the time.

I lower my fork. "Can we talk about last night?"

"Sure. If you can remember it."

Boone immediately takes a sip of coffee, as if that will somehow soften the judgment in his voice. I pretend to ignore it.

"I was hoping you could fill in the blanks a bit."

"I was just about to go up to bed when I saw Tom's Bentley drive by the house," Boone says. "Since there's no reason for him to be driving on this side of the lake, I assumed he was coming to see one of us. And since he didn't stop at my place, I figured he had to be going to see you. And I didn't think that was a good thing."

"He caught me watching the house," I say. "Apparently he picked up his own pair of binoculars while at the hardware store."

"Was he mad?"

"That's putting it mildly."

"What happened while he was here?"

I eat two more bites of pancake, take a long sip of coffee, and try to bring my blurry memories of Tom's visit into focus. A few do, snapping into clarity right when I need them to.

"I turned off all the lights and hid by the door," I say, remembering the feel of the door against my back as it rattled under Tom's knocking. "But he knew I was here, so he yelled some stuff."

Boone looks up from his plate. "What kind of *stuff*?"

"This is where it starts to get foggy. I think I remember the gist of what he said, but not his exact words."

"Then paraphrase."

"He said he knew that I've been spying on him and that it was me who told Wilma about Katherine. Oh, and that he knew I'd broken into his house."

"Did he threaten you?" Boone says.

"Not exactly. I mean, it was scary. But no, there were no threats. He just told me to leave him alone and left. Then you came to the door."

I pause, signaling that I can't remember anything else and that I'm hoping Boone can tell me the rest. He does, although he looks slightly annoyed at having to remind me of something I should have been sober enough to recall on my own.

"I heard you inside after I knocked," he says. "You were mumbling and sounded dazed. I thought you were hurt and not—"

Boone stops talking, as if the word *drunk* is contagious and he'll become one again if he dares to utter it.

"You came inside to check on me," I say, hit with the image of him looming over me, swathed in shadow.

"I did."

"How?"

"The ground floor."

Boone's referring to the door to the basement. The one with faded blue paint and a persistent squeak that leads directly to the backyard beneath the porch. I didn't know it was unlocked because I haven't been down there since the morning I woke up and Len was gone.

"I found your phone out there, by the way," he says, gesturing to the dining room table, where the phone now sits.

"Then what happened?"

"I picked you up and carried you to bed."

"And?"

"I made you drink some water, put a garbage can by the bed in case you got sick, and left you alone to sleep it off."

"Where'd you sleep?"

"Bedroom down the hall," Boone says. "The one with the twin beds and slanted ceiling."

My childhood bedroom, shared with Marnie, who I imagine would be both amused and mortified by my completely unromantic night with the hot ex-cop next door.

"Thank you," I say. "You didn't need to go to all that trouble."

"Considering the state you were in, I kind of think I did."

I say nothing after that, knowing it's pointless to make excuses for getting so blitzed in such a short amount of time. I focus on finishing my breakfast, surprised when the plate is empty. When the mug of coffee is also drained, I get up and pour myself another.

"Maybe we should call Wilma and let her know what happened," Boone says.

"Nothing happened," I say. "Besides, it'll require too much explanation."

If we tell Wilma Anson about Tom coming to my door, we'll also have to reveal *why*. And I'm not too keen on admitting to a member of the state police that I've illegally entered a person's home. Tom's the one I want in jail. Not me.

"Fine," Boone says. "But don't think for a second I'm leaving you here by yourself while he's still around."

"*Is* he still around?"

"His car is there," Boone says with a nod toward the French doors and its view of the opposite shore. "Which I take to mean he's still there, too."

I look out the door and across the lake, curious as to why Tom still hasn't made a break for it. When I mention this to Boone, he says, "Because it'll make him look guilty. And right now, he's betting that the cops won't be able to pin anything on him."

"But he can't keep up this charade forever," I say. "Someone else is going to realize Katherine is missing."

I move to the dining room and grab my phone, which shows damage from its fall from the porch. The bottom right corner has caved in, and a crack as jagged as a lightning bolt slices from one side to the other. But it still works, which is all that matters.

I go straight to Katherine's Instagram, which has remained unchanged since the morning she disappeared. I can't be the only one to realize the photo of that pristine kitchen wasn't posted by Katherine. Surely others, especially people who know her better than I do, will notice the wrong month on the calendar and Tom's reflection in the teakettle.

In fact, it's possible one of them already has.

I close Instagram and go to the photos stored on my phone. Boone watches me from the kitchen counter, his mug of coffee paused mid-sip.

"What are you doing?"

"When I was searching Tom and Katherine's house, I found her phone."

"I know," Boone says. "Which would be amazing evidence if not for that whole, you know, being-obtained-illegally thing."

I note his sarcasm but am too busy swiping through photos to care. I pass the picture of the article about Harvey Brewer, looking grainy on the laptop's screen, and photos of Katherine's financial records and Mixer's quarterly data.

"While I was there, someone called Katherine," I say as I reach the photos taken inside the master bedroom. "I took a picture of the number that popped up on the screen."

"Which will help how?"

"If we call them and it's someone worried about Katherine—especially a family member—maybe it will be enough for Wilma and the state police to declare her missing and officially question Tom."

I scan the photos on my phone.

Katherine's rings.

Katherine's clothes.

And, finally, Katherine's phone, both blank and lit up with an incoming call.

I stare at the screen inside my screen. A strange feeling. Like looking at a photograph of a photograph.

There's no name. Just a number, leading me to think it's probably someone Katherine didn't know well. If she even knew them at all. There's the very real possibility it was a telemarketer or a vague acquaintance or simply a wrong number. I remember my own number appearing on the screen when I called to confirm the phone belonged to Katherine. Although those ten digits made it clear Katherine hadn't added me to her contacts, it doesn't make me less concerned about where she could be or what might have happened to her. It might be the same for this other caller. They could be just as worried as I am.

I call them without a second thought, toggling between the photo and my phone's keypad until the number is typed in completely.

I hold my breath.

I hit the call button.

At the kitchen counter, Boone's phone begins to ring.

NOW

W hat did you do with the girls after you killed them?" I say. "Are they here, in the lake?"

He lolls his head to the side and faces the wall. At first, I think he's giving me the silent treatment again.

Rain slaps the window.

Just beyond it, something snaps.

A tree branch succumbing to the wind.

On the bed, he speaks, his voice only one step louder than the storm raging outside.

"Yes."

The answer shouldn't be a surprise. I think about the postcard, that bird's-eye view of Lake Greene, the four words shakily written beneath three names.

I think they're here.

Nevertheless, I'm hit with a tiny tremor of shock. I inhale. A rattling half gasp prompted by the confirmation that Megan Keene, Toni Burnett, and Sue Ellen Stryker have been at the bottom of the lake all this time. More than two years, in Megan's case. A horrible way to be buried.

Only they weren't buried here.

They were dumped.

Disposed of like pieces of trash.

Just thinking about it makes me so sad that I instantly have another sip of bourbon. When I swallow, the alcohol burns rather than soothes.

"Do you remember where?"

"Yes."

He rolls his head my way again. As we lock eyes, I wonder what he sees in mine. I hope it's what I'm trying to project and not my emotional reality. Steely reserve instead of fear, determination instead of unfathomable grief for three women I've never met. I suspect, however, that he can see right through me. He knows I act for a living.

"Then tell me," I say. "Tell me where they can be found."

He squints, curious. "Why?"

Because then the truth will be known. Not just that he killed Megan, Toni, and Sue Ellen, but what happened to them, where they were when they died, where they now rest. Then their families and friends, who have gone too long without answers, will be able to grieve and—hopefully, eventually—be at peace.

I don't tell him this because I don't think he cares. If anything, it might make him less willing to talk.

"Is this about finding them?" he says. "Or finding out what happened to Katherine?"

"Both."

"What if only one of those things is possible?"

I slide a hand across the mattress until I'm touching the handle of the knife. "I think everything's on the table, don't you?"

He responds with an eye roll and a sigh, as if bored by the idea of me actually using the knife.

"Look at you acting all tough," he says. "I have to admit, even this weak attempt at threatening me is a surprise. I might have underestimated you a little."

I wrap my fingers around the knife. "More than a little."

"There's just one problem," he says. "Some unfinished business I'm not sure you've thought of yet."

In all likelihood, he's right. There's a lot I haven't thought of. None of this was planned. I'm working without a script now, improvising wildly and hoping I don't fuck it all up.

"I'm not going anywhere." He moves his arms as far as they can go, the ropes binding them to the bedposts stretched taut. "And you're clearly staying. Which leaves me curious about one thing."

"What's that?"

"What you plan on doing with Tom Royce."

BEFORE

I let the phone keep ringing, too stunned to end the call. For his part, Boone doesn't bother to answer it. He knows who's calling.

Me.

Trying to reach the same person who had called Katherine Royce.

"I can explain," he says at the same time the call transfers to his voice-mail recording, bringing two versions of Boone to my ears. They wind around each other, performing a surreal duet.

"Hi, I'm not available to take your call. Please—"

"—listen to me, Casey. I know what—"

"—your name and number, and I'll—"

"—thinking, and I can assure—"

"—you back."

I tap my phone, cutting off the recorded Boone as the real one gets up from the kitchen counter and takes a step toward me.

"Don't," I warn.

Boone raises his hands, palms up, in a gesture of innocence. "Please just hear me out."

"Why were you calling her?"

"Because I was worried," Boone says. "I'd called her the day before, not getting any answer. And when I saw you break into the house, I called one last time, hoping that we were wrong and she was there avoiding me and that you barging in like that would force her to answer the phone and tell me she was okay."

"Avoiding you? You told me you barely knew her. That you'd only met once or twice. You said the same thing to Wilma. That seems like a lot of concern for someone you claimed not to know very well."

Boone sits back down at the counter, a smug look on his face. "You have no right to judge. You hardly knew Katherine."

I can't argue with that. Katherine and I were barely past the acquaintance stage when she disappeared.

"At least I didn't lie about it," I say.

"You're right. I lied. There, I admitted it. I did know Katherine. We were friends."

"Then why didn't you say that? Why lie to me? To Wilma?"

"Because it was complicated," Boone says.

"Complicated how?"

I think back to the afternoon I spotted Katherine in the water. There was one thing about that moment that should have bothered me then but ended up getting lost in the shuffle of everything else that's happened.

Why hadn't I seen her earlier?

I was there all afternoon, sitting on the porch, facing her house and dock. Even though it was far away and I hadn't yet hauled out the binoculars—and even though I wasn't paying much attention to the water—I would have noticed someone on the other side of the lake coming outside, strolling down their dock, diving in, and starting to swim.

But I saw nothing. Not until Katherine was in the middle of the lake.

Which meant she'd been swimming not from her side of the lake, but from mine. Specifically, the area of the Mitchell house, where the lake bends inward, partially hiding the shore.

"She was with you, wasn't she?" I say. "The day she almost drowned?"

Boone doesn't blink. "Yes."

"Why?" Jealousy seeps into my voice, unintended yet also unavoidable. "Were you two having an affair?"

"No," Boone says. "It was all very innocent. We met the night I arrived in August. She and Tom came over to introduce themselves and told me they were here until Labor Day and that I shouldn't be a stranger. The next day, Katherine swam across the lake to my dock and asked me if I wanted to join her."

"Do you think she was trying to seduce you?"

"I think she was just lonely. If she did have sex in mind, I didn't pick up on it. She's a supermodel, for Christ's sake. She could have any man she wanted. No way did I suspect she was interested in me."

All this aw-shucks modesty is an act. Boone knows exactly how good-looking he is. I picture him naked on the dock, bathed in moonlight, as beguilingly beautiful as Katherine herself. Now more than ever, I'm convinced he knew I was watching that night.

"So you went swimming together," I say.

"A few times, yeah. But nothing more. Afterwards, we'd hang out on the deck and talk. She was really unhappy, that much was clear. She never said it outright. Just strongly hinted that things were bad between her and Tom."

Katherine had done the same with me, dropping arch comments about the state of her marriage. Like Boone, I'd assumed she was sad, lonely, and looking for a friend. Which is why I had no reason to lie about the extent of our relationship.

"If it was all so innocent, why didn't you come clean earlier?"

"Because it stopped being that way. Well, it almost did." He slumps on the stool, as if telling the truth has made him exhausted. If it weren't for his elbows on the counter propping him up, I assume he'd drop straight onto the floor. "The day after Labor Day, before she and Tom went back to New York, I kissed her."

I picture a scenario similar to the two of us yesterday. Boone and Katherine sitting together, closer than they should be, the heat of attraction radiating from their bodies. I imagine Boone running a finger across her lower lip, leaning in, kissing the spot he'd just touched. Another smooth move.

"Katherine freaked out, left, went back to her fancy life with her billionaire husband." Boone's voice has turned hard—a tone I've never heard from him before. There's an echo of anger and bitterness in it. "I never thought I'd see her again. Then, a few days ago, there she was, back in that house with Tom. She never told me they'd returned. Never stopped by to see me. I called her a few times, just to see how she was doing. She ignored them. And me."

"Not completely, remember," I say. "Since she was with you the day I rescued her from the lake."

"She swam over, unannounced, just like the first time she did it," Boone says. "When I saw her, I thought that maybe nothing had changed and that we'd pick up where we left off. Katherine made it clear that wasn't going to happen. She told me she only came over to demand that I stop calling her. She said Tom had noticed and was asking a lot of questions."

"What did you say?"

"That she was free to leave. So she did. Which is why I was surprised when she called me later that afternoon."

"Why?"

"I don't know," Boone says with a shrug. "I didn't answer and I deleted her message without listening to it."

I get a sudden flashback to me on the porch, spying on the Royces for the very first time. I'll never forget the way Tom crept through the dining room as Katherine, in the living room, made a phone call, waited for someone to pick up, whispered a message. I now know who that message was for.

"You were on your way over here when she called," I say. "Was she the reason you came by to introduce yourself? Since Katherine rejected you, you decided you'd try your luck with the woman next door?"

Boone flinches, hurt. "I introduced myself because I was lonely and thought you might be lonely, too. And that if we hung out a little, both of us wouldn't feel that way. And I don't regret that. Because I *like* you, Casey. You're funny and smart and interesting. And you remind me exactly of how I used to be. I look at you, and I just want to—"

"Fix me?"

"Help you," Boone says. "Because you need help, Casey."

But he wanted more than that when he introduced himself that day. I remember the charm, the swagger, the flirtation I'd found both tiresome and tantalizing.

Thinking back to that afternoon prompts an unsavory realization. Boone had mentioned spending the day working on the Mitchells' dining room floor. If he was there the whole time, within earshot of the activity on the lake, why didn't he do anything when Katherine was drowning and I was calling for help?

That question leads to another. One so disturbing I'm barely able to ask it.

"When Katherine came over that day, did you give her anything to drink?"

"Lemonade. Why do you—" Boone stands again, suddenly understanding. "I didn't do what you're thinking."

I wish I could believe him. But the facts warn me not to. Katherine claimed to have grown suddenly weary while swimming.

It was like my entire body stopped working.

All this time, I thought Tom was the one who'd caused it. Imitating Harvey Brewer and slipping small doses of poison into his wife's drinks. But it also could have been Boone. Angry, jealous, rejected Boone, mixing a large dose into Katherine's lemonade.

"Casey," he says. "You know me. You know I would never do something like that."

But I *don't* know him. I thought I did, but only because I believed everything he told me. Now I'm forced to doubt all of it.

Including, I realize, what he said about the scream the morning Katherine vanished. Because I was still drunk, I didn't quite know where the sound had originated. Boone's the one who concluded it had come from the other side of the lake, citing an echo I'm now not sure existed.

It's possible he was lying. That the scream came not from across the lake, but this side.

His side.

Which means there's also a chance Boone's the person who *caused* Katherine to scream.

"Stay away from me," I say as Boone starts to approach. The way he moves—slowly, methodically—is more intimidating than if he were in a hurry. It gives me ample time to notice how big he is, how strong, how it would take him no effort at all to overpower me.

"You've got it all wrong," he says. "I didn't do anything to Katherine."

He keeps walking toward me, and I look around for the nearest escape route. Right behind me are the French doors leading to the porch, still locked. I might be able to unlock them and run outside, but doing so would take up precious seconds I'm not sure I can spare.

When Boone's almost within reach, I skirt sideways and bolt into the heart of the kitchen. Although not an escape, it at least gives me access to things with which I can defend myself. I pick one—the largest blade from the knife block on the counter—and thrust it in front of me, daring Boone to come closer.

"Leave my house," I say. "And don't ever come back."

Boone's mouth drops open, as if he's about to make another denial—or switch to threatening me. Apparently deciding silence is the best policy, he closes his mouth, lifts his hands in defeat, and leaves the house without another word.

I move from door to door, making sure all of them are locked. The front door is secured minutes after Boone passes through it, and the doors to the porch remain locked from the night before. That leaves one more—the creaky blue door in the basement.

The last place I want to go.

I know there's nothing physically dangerous down there. It's nothing but junk, once frequently used, now forgotten. It's the memories of the day Len died that I'd like to avoid. No good can come from reliving that morning. But since the basement door is how Boone got inside last night, I need to lock it to keep him from doing it again.

Even though it's only mid-morning, I have a shot of vodka before heading down to the basement. A little liquid courage never hurts.

Nor does a second helping.

And a third.

I'm feeling much better when I finally start down the basement steps. I barely hesitate at the bottom one, pausing only a second before placing both feet onto the concrete floor. But the front of the basement is the easy part. Here lie the happy memories. Playing Ping-Pong with my father. Marnie and me during a Christmas vacation, putting on hats and parkas before bounding out onto the frozen lake.

The bad memories are toward the back, in the mudroom. As I enter it, I regret not having a fourth shot of vodka.

I speed toward the door and twist the handle. It's locked. Boone did what I'd overlooked yesterday at the Royces'. Maybe that's the house he should have broken into instead of mine.

Knowing the blue door is also secure, I turn back to the rest of the mudroom, facing a wall paneled in flat, horizontal boards that have been painted gray. The nails keeping them in place are visible, giving off a rustic vibe that's trendy now but was merely utilitarian when the house was built. One of the boards is missing two nails, revealing a slight gap between it and the wall. It reminds me again of how old the house is, how fragile, how easy it would be for someone to get inside even with all the doors locked.

Trying to shake away that grim but honest assessment, I push out of the mudroom, through the basement and up the stairs to the dining room, where I snatch the vodka from the liquor cabinet and have one more shot. Properly fortified, I pull my phone from my pocket, ready to call Eli and tell him everything that's happened the past few days.

He'll know what to do.

But when I check my phone, I see that Eli actually called me while I was still asleep. The voicemail is short and sweet and slightly unnerving.

"Just got done watching the news. This storm's looking like it's going to be worse than they thought. Heading out for supplies. Call me in the next half hour if you need anything."

That was three hours ago.

I try calling Eli back anyway. When the call goes straight to voicemail, I hang up without leaving a message, grab my laptop, and carry it to the living room. There I do something I should have done days ago: a Google search of Boone Conrad.

The first thing that comes up is an article about his wife's death, which I expected. Completely unexpected is the nature of the article, made clear in the headline.

"Cop Probed in Wife's Death."

I stare wide-eyed at the headline, my nerves becoming jumpy. It only gets worse when I read the article and learn that members of Boone's own department noticed discrepancies in his story about the day his wife died. He'd told them—as he told me—that she was still alive when he left for work that morning. What Boone neglected to mention was how the medical examiner had narrowed the time of death to a two-hour window, including a half hour in which he still could have been home.

But the suspicion didn't stop there. It turned out Boone's wife—Maria was her name—had gone to see a divorce attorney a week before her death. And although he swore he didn't know Maria was considering divorce, Boone's colleagues had no choice but to recuse themselves from the case and let the state police conduct a formal investigation.

I keep searching, finding another article dated a week later, this one announcing that Boone wouldn't be charged in Maria Conrad's death. The article points out that there was nothing to prove Boone hadn't killed her. There simply wasn't any evidence to show that he had.

Included with the article are two photos. One of Boone, the other of his wife. Boone's picture is an official police department photo. It should come as no surprise that he looks ridiculously good in uniform. The real shock is that Maria was equally as gorgeous. With bright eyes, a big smile, and great bone structure, she looks like she could have walked the runway right alongside Katherine Royce.

Imagining the two of them on the catwalk reminds me that I'm not the only person on the lake curious about what happened to Maria Conrad. One of the Royces had also taken an interest. Boone was one of the many searches I found on Tom's laptop.

Maybe it was Katherine.

Maybe that's the thing that so shocked her in Tom's office as I watched from the other side of the lake.

Maybe she confronted Boone about it the next morning.

And maybe he felt the need to silence her.

While all of this is just wild conjecture, it's important enough to tell Wilma Anson, which is why I dig out my phone and immediately give her a call.

"Anson," she answers before the first ring is finished.

"Hi, Wilma. It's Casey Fletcher. From Lake—"

She cuts me off. "I know who you are, Casey. What's going on? Did something happen with Tom Royce?"

Actually, something *did* happen, but the drama from last night feels distant after the events of this morning.

"I'm calling about Boone."

"What about him?"

"How well do you know him?"

"As well as I know my own brother," Wilma says. "Why are you asking?"

"I was doing some investigating."

"Which is my job," Wilma replies without a hint of humor. "But go on."

"And I learned—well, Boone told me, actually—that he and Katherine Royce did know each other. They were friends. Maybe more than friends."

"I know," Wilma says.

I pause, more confused than surprised. "You do?"

"Boone called a half hour ago and told me everything."

"So he's now a suspect, right?"

"Why would he be?"

"Because he lied," I say. "About a lot of things. Then there's what happened to his wife."

"That has nothing to do with this," Wilma says with sudden sharpness.

"But it does. Katherine knew about it. She—at least I think it was her—Googled an article about it on Tom's laptop."

I realize my mistake the second the words are out. Like a car sailing over a cliff, they can't be taken back. The only option is to wait and see how hard they land.

"How do you know that?" Wilma asks.

At first, I say nothing. When I do speak, it's with a guilty hush. "I was inside their house."

"Please tell me Tom let you in and that you didn't just barge in when he wasn't home."

"I didn't barge in," I say. "I snuck in."

The long silence from Wilma that follows feels like a lit fuse slowly snaking its way toward a pile of dynamite. Any second now, there's going to be an explosion. When it arrives, it's both louder and fiercer than I expect.

"Give me one reason why I shouldn't come over and arrest your sorry ass right now," Wilma says, her voice booming in my ear. "Do you know how stupid that was, Casey? You might have just fucked up my entire investigation."

"But I found things," I say.

"I don't want to know."

"Important things. Incriminating things."

Wilma's voice gets louder. Somehow. I'd assumed she had already reached peak volume.

"Unless you found Katherine Royce herself, *I don't want to know.* You understand me? The more shit you say and do means the less I'll be able to legally present to a judge and prosecutor. That laptop you looked at is evidence. Those rooms you walked through might be a crime scene. And you just tainted all of it. Not only that, your presence in that house—and the possibility that you could have planted something incriminating inside it—gives Tom an easy way to explain away every single thing we might find in there."

"I didn't plant—"

"*Stop talking,*" Wilma commands. "Stop snooping. Stop everything."

"I'm sorry." It comes out as a squeak. "Really, I was just trying to help."

"I don't need you to be sorry and I don't need your help," Wilma says. "I need you to stay the fuck away from Tom Royce. And from Boone."

"But you have to admit Boone's suspicious, right? First his wife died, and then Katherine goes missing."

I glance at the laptop, still open to the article about Boone not being charged in Maria's death. I scan it, hoping to find a snippet that supports my argument. Instead, I see a quote at the tail end of the article.

"As far as the state police are concerned, Officer Conrad is completely innocent and all accusations against him are completely baseless."

I go cold when I see who provided the quote.

Detective Wilma Anson.

"I told you—"

I end the call, cutting off Wilma mid-sentence. When she calls me back seconds later, I let the phone ring. When she tries again, I silence the phone. There's no point in answering. It's clear she thinks Boone is capable of doing no wrong. Nothing I say is going to change that.

I can no longer trust Wilma.

And I certainly can't trust Boone.

I am, I realize, completely on my own.

I don't step outside of the house until night has fallen, and even then I only go as far as the porch. There's a heaviness to the air that's unnerving. Thick with humidity and turmoil. Last night's wind is gone, replaced by eerie stillness.

The calm immediately before the storm.

Slouched in a rocking chair, I take a drink of bourbon.

My fourth or fifth or sixth.

It's impossible to keep count when I'm drinking straight from the bottle.

During the afternoon and early evening, I was either in bed, trying in vain to get some rest; in the kitchen, chowing down on whatever food took the least time to prepare; or roaming the rest of the house like a bird trapped in a cage. As I walked—from library to den to living room—I thought about what, if anything, I can do now.

It didn't take long to suss out the answer.

Nothing.

That's what Wilma wants, after all.

So I picked up my old friend bourbon—the only thing I can trust at the moment. Now I'm buzzed and careening toward drunkenness. All it will take to push me over the edge is one or two more swigs from the bottle.

A tantalizing option.

Because I want everything to go away.

My concern about Katherine, my suspicion of both Tom and Boone, my loneliness and guilt and grief. I want all of it gone, never to return. And if that requires drinking myself into oblivion, so be it.

Gripping the bottle's neck, I tip it back, ready to empty the damn thing.

Before I can do that, though, I notice a light brightening the kitchen window of the Royce house. Like a moth, I'm drawn to it. I can't help it. I put down the bottle and pick up the binoculars, telling myself that it's fine if I watch the house one last time. According to Wilma, I've already ruined everything. Spying on Tom now isn't going to make things any worse.

He's at the stove again, heating up another can of soup. When he gives a disinterested glance out the window, I don't fear that he'll again catch me watching. The porch, like the rest of the house, is pitch-black. As are the lake and the surrounding shore.

Other than the kitchen at the Royce house, the only other light around is a large rectangular glow on the lake's rippling surface to my right. The Mitchell place. Although I can't get a good look at the house from where I'm sitting, the bright patch tells me everything I need to know.

Boone is home.

I've got a possible wife-killer on one side of me and another possible wife-killer directly across the lake.

Not a comforting thought.

I swing the binoculars toward Eli's house. It's completely dark. Of course the sole person on this lake I can trust is the only one *not* home. I call his cell, hoping he'll answer, say he's on his way back from gathering supplies and will swing by before heading to his house. Instead, the call again goes instantly to his voicemail.

I leave a message, straining to sound both sober and nonchalant. I fail at both.

"Eli, hi. It's Casey. I, um, I hope you're coming home soon. Like, right now. There have been things going on around the lake that you don't know about. Dangerous things. And, well, I'm scared. And I could really use a friend right now. So if you're around, please come over."

I'm crying by the time I end the call. The tears are a surprise, and as much as I'd like to chalk them up to stress and bourbon, I know it goes deeper than that. I'm crying because the fourteen months since Len died have been hard as hell. Yes, I had Marnie, my mother, and plenty of others willing to offer comfort. None of them—not even Beloved Lolly Fletcher—could truly understand how I felt.

So I drank.

It was easier that way.

Alcohol doesn't judge.

And it never, ever disappoints.

But if you drink too much, for too long, all those well-meaning people in your life who try to understand but can't eventually give up and drift away.

That's the realization that came over me as I rambled on the phone even though no one was listening. The story of my life. Right now, I have nothing and no one. Eli's gone, Boone can't be trusted, and Marnie wants nothing to do with this. I am completely alone, and it makes me utterly, unbearably sad.

I wipe my eyes, sigh, pick up the binoculars again because, hey, I have literally nothing else to do. I zero in on the Royces' kitchen, where Tom has finished reheating the soup. Instead of a bowl, he pours it into a large thermos and screws on the lid.

Curious.

Thermos in hand, he opens a drawer and pulls out a flashlight.

Curiouser.

Soon he's outside, the flashlight's beam slicing through the darkness. Seeing it brings back a memory of the other night, when I noticed Tom do the same thing from the bedroom window. Although I couldn't tell where he was going to or coming from then, I certainly do now.

The Fitzgeralds' house.

In an instant, I go from buzzed to hyperalert, suddenly aware of everything. The clouds scudding in front of the moon. A loon hooting a lonely call in an unseen nook of the lake. The flashlight moving through the trees, bobbing and winking like a giant firefly. Another memory returns, pried loose by the sight.

Me against the door, Tom on the other side, shouting things I'd been too drunk and scared to comprehend.

You have no idea what's going on, he said. *Just leave us the fuck alone.*

Us.

Meaning not just him.

Meaning someone else is a part of all this.

My chest expands. A bubble of hope, pushing against my rib cage.

Katherine could still be alive.

I wait to make my move until Tom completes the return trip to his house. It happens fifteen minutes later, the flashlight's beam appearing outside the Fitzgerald place and moving in the opposite direction of its earlier path. I follow it with the binoculars all the way to the Royce house, where Tom turns off the flashlight just before going inside.

I put down the binoculars and spring into action.

Down the porch steps.

Across the yard.

Onto the dock.

It's started to rain—fat drops that land hard on my face, my hair, the planks of the dock as I make my way to the boat moored to its end.

The wind has picked up, too, turning the lake choppy. The boat bobs and sways, making it difficult to step into and forcing me to do an awkward half leap from the dock. Once inside, I instantly regret the drinks I've had as the boat rides the ever-growing swells of the water.

I close my eyes, lift my face to the wind, and let the rain spatter my skin. It's definitely not a cure-all. My stomach keeps churning and my head continues to ache. But the rain is cold enough to sober me up and painful enough to make me focus on what I need to do next.

Get across the lake.

I untie the boat from the dock, not daring to use the motor. I know how sound travels on this lake, even in a storm, and don't want to risk getting caught. Instead, I paddle, using slow, measured strokes to counteract the roughness of the water. It's exhausting—far more taxing than I expected—and I need to pause in the center of the lake to catch my breath.

As the boat continues to rise and fall, I swivel in my seat and look at every house on Lake Greene's shore. My family's house and the Fitzgerald place are so dark they almost blend in with the night. The same goes for Eli's house, telling me he still hasn't returned.

In contrast, the entire first floor of the Mitchells' house is aglow, making me picture Boone pacing from room to room, angry at me. Then there's the Royce place, dark on the first floor and only the window of the master bedroom lit on the second. Maybe Tom, finished with whatever needed to be done at the house next door, is going to bed, even though it's only eight o'clock.

To the west, a rolling wall of pitch-black clouds blocks out the stars, the moon, most of the sky itself. It looks like a wave. One about to crash onto the valley and drown everything in its path.

The storm has arrived.

I resume rowing, now more worried about being out on the lake in worsening conditions than facing what awaits me on the other side. Already, the rain is falling harder, the wind is blowing stronger, and the water is churning faster. It takes three strokes of the paddle to go the distance of one in normal conditions. When I do eventually reach the other side of the lake, my shoulders are tight and aching, and my arms feel like jelly. I barely have the strength to moor the boat as it bucks in the wind, its side continually slamming against the Fitzgeralds' dock.

Getting out of the boat requires another precarious leap, this time onto the dock. I then hurry to land, exhausted, nervous, and soaked to the bone. Overhead, thunder begins to rumble across the sky. Flashes of lightning illuminate the ground ahead as I swish across the yard to the French doors at the back of the Fitzgerald house.

Locked.

Of course.

It's the same with both the front door and the side one that leads to the kitchen. Standing in the downpour and jiggling the handle, I realize that Tom is able to get inside because the Fitzgeralds likely gave him a set of keys in case something was wrong with the house. It's common among the homeowners here on the lake. The Fitzgeralds have keys to my family's house, as does Eli. And somewhere in the lake house is probably a key that would grant me entry to this very door.

Out of door-shaped options, I try the windows, striking gold on my third try. The sitting room window. Even better, it's on the side of the house that doesn't face the Royces', giving me ample time and cover to lift the window, pop out the screen, climb through.

I tumble inside and shut the window to keep rain from blowing in. The silence of the house is a jarring contrast with the storm outside, making it seem extra quiet.

And extra unnerving.

I have no idea what—or who—waits for me here, a fact that makes my heart rumble as hard as the thunder echoing through the sky outside. The stillness and silence are so heavy it makes me want to turn around and crawl right back out the window. But Tom came here for a reason. The urge to learn what that reason is keeps me moving, even though I can barely see. I make it two steps before slamming into a sideboard crowded with framed photos and a Tiffany lamp.

Damn Mrs. Fitzgerald and her antiques.

The house is stuffed to the gills with them. Ornate chests, love seats draped with tapestries, rococo floor lamps with crystals dangling from their shades. Each one is an obstacle I have to sidestep around as I move through the gloom.

"Hello?" I say in a voice that's more whisper than word. "Katherine? Are you in here?"

I stop between the kitchen and the dining room, listening for any sound that might suggest she is. At first, I hear nothing but the steadily increasing rain on the roof and more bursts of thunder. But soon a noise—distant and muted—reaches my ears.

A creak.

I hear it a second time, rising from below, as wispy as smoke.

The basement.

I move to a door in a short hall just off the kitchen, secured by an old-fashioned chain lock that's currently slid into place. Because a large hutch sits next to it, I'd normally think the door would lead to a pantry or a broom closet. The chain says otherwise, especially when I look closer. It's screwed into two short chunks of wood that have been nailed to both the door and the wall next to it, as if it's just a temporary fix. A recent one. The wood gives off a fresh-cut scent, making me think of the hacksaw Tom Royce recently bought.

This is his handiwork.

And inside is something—or someone—he doesn't want anyone else to know about.

My hand shakes as I fumble with the chain, sliding it free of the lock. Holding my breath, I pull the door open to reveal a set of steps leading down into a pool of blackness.

"Hello?" I call, alarmed by how the gloom consumes my voice, snuffing it out like a candle. But coming from within that darkness is another creak, beckoning me to venture down those stairs.

A light switch sits just beyond the door. I flip it, and a dull orange glow appears far below, bringing with it another creak and, I think, a murmur.

The sound pulls me forward, onto the top step, where I pause and listen closely.

There's nothing.

If there's someone down there, they've gone completely silent.

I take another step.

Then another, which creaks under my weight, the sound startling me.

It's followed by another creak.

Not from me.

From somewhere deeper in the basement.

I hurry down the remaining steps, into the basement, which is lit by a single exposed bulb dangling from the ceiling. The basement is bare-bones. Cement floor. Concrete walls. The steps I'd just descended nothing more than a skeleton of wood.

I take another step, my field of vision expanding, revealing junk crowded at the edges of the basement. Castoffs from Mrs. Fitzgerald's antique business. Chipped dressers and chairs missing legs and boxes stacked upon boxes.

Pushed against the wall is an old-fashioned brass bed that has something on top of it.

No.

Not something.

Someone.

I creep closer and see—

Oh, God.

Katherine.

Her clothes are the same ones I saw her wearing the night she vanished. Jeans and a white sweater, now stained in spots. Her shoes are gone, revealing bare feet made dirty by the trek from her house to this one. A line of soup, still wet, drips from a corner of her mouth onto her neck.

But it's her arms that unnerve me the most.

They've been lifted above her and connected to the brass bed's corners by rope knotted around her wrists. I see more rope at her ankles, keeping her spread-eagled atop a plastic tarp that's been laid over the mattress.

I choke out a gasp.

Katherine hears it and her eyes flutter open. She looks up at me, at first utterly confused, then full-blown panicked.

"Who—"

She stops herself, still looking, her large, frightened eyes softening into recognition.

"Casey?" Her voice is weird. Hoarse and slightly wet, as if there's water in the back of her throat. It doesn't sound like her at all. "Is it really you?"

"It's me. It's me and I'm going to help you."

I rush to her, putting a hand on her forehead. Her skin is cold and clammy with sweat. And pale. So startlingly pale. Her lips have become cracked with dryness. She parts them and croaks, "Help me. Please."

I reach for the rope knotted around her right wrist. It's been tied tight. The skin under it has been rubbed raw, and dried blood flakes off the rope.

"How long have you been down here?" I say. "Why did Tom do this to you?"

I give up on untying the rope around her wrists and instead move to the end lashed to the brass railing. It, too, is knotted tight, and I tug at it helplessly.

But there's a noise.

Near the stairs.

An unnaturally loud creak as someone pushes off the bottom step.

Tom.

Soaked by the storm.

His expression is a mix of surprise and disappointment and fear.

"Get away from her," he says as he barrels toward me. "You shouldn't have looked for her, Casey. You really, *really* should have left us alone."

I continue fumbling with the rope, as if sheer determination will loosen it. I'm still tugging when Tom wraps an arm around my waist and drags me away. I flail in his grip, kicking and swatting. It's no use. He's shockingly strong, and soon I find myself shoved against the stairs. The bottom step hits my calves and I fall backwards until I'm sitting down against my will.

"What the fuck are you doing to her?"

"Protecting her," Tom says.

"From what?"

"Herself."

I look to the brass bed, where Katherine has gone still. But her eyes remain open, watching us. To my surprise, she looks not distressed but slightly amused.

"I don't understand. What's wrong with your wife?"

"That is *not* my wife."

"It sure as hell looks like Katherine."

"It looks like her," Tom says. "But it's not."

I cast another glance at the bed. Katherine remains motionless, content to watch us talk. Maybe it's merely Tom's words getting under my skin, but something about her seems off. Katherine's energy feels different from what I'm used to.

"Then who is it?"

"Someone else," Tom says.

My head is spinning. I have no idea what he's talking about. Nor do I understand what's going on. All I know is that the situation is far weirder than I ever imagined—and that it's up to me to defuse it.

"Tom." I take a step toward him, hands raised to show I mean him no harm. "I need you to tell me what's going on."

He shakes his head. "You're going to think I'm crazy. And maybe I am. I've considered that possibility a lot in the past few days. It would be easier to deal with than *this*."

Tom gestures Katherine's way, and although I'm not certain, I think what he's just said pleases her. The corners of her mouth lift ever so slightly into a quarter smile.

"I won't think that," I say. "I promise."

Desperation fills Tom's gaze as it darts between me and the woman he says isn't his wife, although it clearly is. "You won't understand."

"I will if you explain it to me." I take another step toward him. Calm. Careful. "Please."

"That stuff Eli told us the other night?" Tom says in a scared, guilty murmur. "About the lake and people believing spirits are trapped in the water?"

"I remember."

"I think—I think it's *true*. I think something was in that lake. A ghost. A soul. Whatever. And it was waiting there. In the water. And whatever it was entered Katherine when she almost drowned and now—now it's taken over."

I'm unsure how to respond.

What can one say when faced with something so absurd?

The only thought going through my head is that Tom is right. He *has* gone insane.

"I know you think I'm lying," he says. "That I'm spouting bullshit. I'd feel the same way if I hadn't lived through it. But it's true. I swear to you, Casey. All of it is true."

I push past Tom, who no longer tries to stop me from approaching the bed. I stand at the foot of it, gripping the brass railing, and stare down at Katherine. The hint of a smile grows at my presence, blooming into a full-on grin that makes me queasy.

"If you're not Katherine," I say, "then who are you?"

"You know who I am." Her voice has deepened slightly, changing into one that's chillingly familiar. "It's me—Len."

A jolt of shock rushes through me, so fast and buzzing it feels like the bed frame has been electrified. I let go of it and, swaying slightly, stare at the person tied to the bed. A person who is definitely Katherine Royce. It's the same coltish body, long hair, and billboard-ready smile.

Yet I seem to be the only person here who understands that fact, making me unsure who to be worried about more. Katherine, for making such an outlandish claim, or her husband, for believing it.

"I told you so," Tom says.

From the bed, Katherine adds, "I know how weird this seems, Casey. And I know what you're thinking."

That's not possible. I've just been told my husband, dead for more than a year, is inside the body of a woman I had thought was missing for days. No one else can fully comprehend the chaos of my thoughts.

At least now I understand all of Tom's secrecy, not to mention his lies. He believed he couldn't keep Katherine around, pretending everything was normal, when to him, nothing about the situation was normal. So he whisked her to the house next door, away from their glass palace and my prying eyes. He hid her cell phone, posted that sham picture on Instagram, tried as much as he could to keep what he believed to be the truth from getting out.

Because who would have believed him?

I sure as hell don't.

The idea is more than crazy.

It's batshit insane.

"This is real, Casey," Tom says, easily reading my thoughts.

"I believe you think that." My words are calm and careful—a clear indicator that I've made up my mind. Right now, Tom is the more dangerous of the two. "When did you start to think it was happening?"

"Not as early as I should have." Tom looks askance at his wife's form, as if he can't bring himself to completely face her. "I knew something was wrong the day you fished her out of the lake. She was acting weird. Not quite herself."

It's exactly the way Katherine described what she thought was happening to her. The sudden weakness. The coughing fits. The fainting. It occurs to me that this could be a form of simultaneous delusion, with one of them influencing the other. Maybe Katherine's symptoms prompted Tom to start thinking she was possessed, which in turn made Katherine believe it herself. Or vice versa.

"It just kept getting worse and worse," Tom continues. "Until, one night, it was like Katherine was no longer there. She didn't act like herself or sound like herself. She'd even started to move differently. I confronted her about it—"

"And I told him the truth," Katherine says.

I don't ask when this happened because I already know.

The night before Katherine disappeared.

If I close my eyes, I'll be able to picture the scene with cinematic clarity. Tom pleading with Katherine as she stood by the window.

Who.

That's the word I'd struggled to identify.

Who was she?

Len, apparently. An idea preposterous to everyone but the two other people in this basement. Stuck between them, their madness coming at me from both sides, I know I need to get them away from each other. Even though it's clear Tom's been feeding Katherine, he's neglected everything else. A foul odor rises from the bed, indicating she hasn't been bathed in days. An even worse smell wafts from a bucket in a corner of the basement.

"Tom," I say, trying not to let my horror at the situation seep into my voice. "Could you leave us alone? Just for a minute?"

He finally looks at the bed and the person he thinks is someone other than his wife. "I don't think that's a good idea, Casey."

"I just want to talk to her," I say.

Tom continues to hesitate, even though his entire body appears eager to leave. His legs are parted, as if gearing up for a sprint, and he leans slightly toward the basement stairs.

"I won't be long," I say. "Katherine's not going to go anywhere."

"Don't untie her."

"I won't," I say, even though it's one of the first things I plan on doing.

"She'll ask you to. She's . . . tricky."

"I'm prepared for that." I put both hands on his shoulders and turn him until we're eye to eye. Knowing that placating him is the only way I'll get him to leave, I say, "Listen, I know I've caused you a world of trouble the past few days. The spying and the police. I'm truly sorry. I didn't know what was going on, so I thought the worst. And I promise to make it up to you as much as I can. But right now, please, if this is my husband, I want to talk to him. Alone."

Tom considers it, closing his eyes and pressing his fingers to his temples as if he's a clairvoyant trying to summon the future. "Fine," he says. "I'll give you five minutes."

Mind made up, he grudgingly starts up the steps. At the halfway point, he turns to give me one last look of concern.

"I'm serious, Casey," he says. "Don't do a single thing she asks."

I let that sink in as he clomps up the remaining steps. When he reaches the top, I hear the door close behind him and, unnervingly, the chain being slid back into place.

The only thing keeping me from panicking that I'm now also trapped down here is the person on the bed. At this moment, Katherine is enough to worry about.

"Why are you doing this, Katherine?"

"You know that's not who I am."

"It's who you look like," I say, although it's no longer entirely true. Katherine's appearance seems to subtly be changing, turning harder and colder. Like a layer of ice forming over still water.

"Looks can be deceiving."

They can. I know that all too well. But I don't for a second believe my dead husband is inhabiting Katherine's body. Outside of it being completely beyond all laws of science and logic, there's the simple fact that people's brains are capable of strange things. They split and mutate and create all kinds of trouble. Katherine could have a brain tumor that's causing her to act out of character, or she's suffering from an undiagnosed multiple personality disorder that's only now manifested itself. She knows who Len was. She knows what happened to him. After almost meeting the same fate he did, she might have convinced herself that she's become him. All of that makes more sense than this possessed-by-a-spirit-in-the-lake bullshit.

Yet now that it's just the two of us, I can't shake the feeling that Len is somewhere in this basement. His presence fills the room just like it did when he was alive. Whether in our apartment or at the lake house, I always knew when he was around, even if he was out of sight in a distant room. I get that same sensation now.

But he can't be *here*.

It's just not possible.

"You need help," I tell Katherine. "A hospital. Doctors. Medication."

"That won't do me any good."

"It's better than being held captive here."

"About that, I agree."

"Then let me help you, Katherine."

"You need to start using my real name."

I fold my arms across my chest and huff. "If you're Len, tell me something only the two of us would know. Prove to me you're really him."

"You sure you want that, Cee?"

I gasp.

Cee was Len's nickname for me. No one outside of close friends and family knew he called me that. Katherine certainly didn't, unless I let it slip at some point. It's possible I could have casually mentioned it when we were drinking coffee on the porch or chatting in the boat after I pulled her from the lake, although I have no memory of doing so.

"How do you know about that?"

"Because I came up with it, remember? I even used it the last time we talked, hoping you'd get the hint."

My heart hopscotches in my chest as I think back to that late-night phone call and Katherine's enigmatic wave from the window.

I'm fine. See.

Now I understand what she really said.

I'm fine, Cee.

But I also understand it was Katherine who said it. There's no other person it could have been. Which means I had to have mentioned Len's nickname at some point. Katherine remembered it and made it just another brick in her vast wall of delusion.

"That's not enough," I say. "I'll need more proof than that."

"How about this?" Katherine grins, the smile spreading like an oil slick across her face. "I haven't forgotten that you killed me."

NOW

Y ou still haven't answered my question," he says after I let a minute pass without speaking. "What about Tom?"

"He's fine," I say. "Right now, the least of my concerns is your husband."

I freeze, noticing my mistake.

Until now, I've been good about not thinking I'm talking to Katherine. But it's easy to slip up when she's the person I see tied up and spread wide across the bed like this is some controversy-courting fashion shoot from her modeling days. Although the clothes are different, Katherine looks eerily similar to when I pulled her from the lake. Lips pale from the cold. Wet hair clinging to her face in dripping tendrils. Bright eyes open wide.

Yet I also know that Katherine is no longer present. She's now just a vessel for someone else. Someone worse. I suppose what's happening is a lot like demonic possession. Innocence subsumed by evil. I think of Linda Blair, spinning heads, pea soup.

"It's you I'm worried about," I say.

"Nice to see you still care."

"That's not why I'm worried."

I'm concerned he'll break loose, escape, run free to resume all the horrible things he'd done when he was alive.

He murdered Megan Keene, Toni Burnett, and Sue Ellen Stryker.

He took them, then killed them, then dumped their bodies into the pitch-black depths of Lake Greene.

And although right now he might *look* like Katherine Royce, inhabiting her body, speaking through her mouth, seeing through her eyes, I know who he really is.

Leonard Bradley.

Len.

The man I married.

And the man I thought I had removed from the face of this earth for good.

BEFORE

W hen I joked with that editor acquaintance of mine about naming her proposed memoir *How to Become Tabloid Fodder in Seven Easy Steps*, I should have included one more in the title. A secret step, tucked like a bookmark between Five and Six.

Discover your husband is a serial killer.

Which I did the summer we spent at Lake Greene.

It was by accident, of course. I wasn't prying into Len's life, searching for any dark secrets, because I'd foolishly assumed he didn't have any. Our marriage had felt like an open book. I told him everything and thought he had been doing the same.

Until the night I realized he wasn't.

It was less than a week after our picnic on the bluff at Lake Greene's southern tip. Since that afternoon, I'd given a lot of thought to Len's suggestion that we become like Old Stubborn poking from the water and stay here forever. I'd decided it was a fine idea, and that we should try it for a year and see how it went.

I thought it would be nice to tell him all of this at night as we drank wine outside by the fire. Complicating my plan was the fact that, thanks to a morning drizzle that had soaked the ridiculously long fireplace matches we'd left out overnight, there was no way to start said fire.

"There's a lighter in my tackle box," Len said. "I use it to light my cigars."

I made a gagging noise. He knew I hated the cigars he sometimes smoked while fishing. The stench lingered long after he was done with them.

"Want me to get it?" he said.

Since Len was busy opening a bottle of wine and slicing some cheese to pair with it, I told him I'd go to the basement and fetch the lighter. A split-second decision that changed everything, although I didn't know it at the time.

To the basement I went. There was no hesitation back then. Just a quick clomping down the stairs followed by a straight shot to the mudroom and the long wall rack filled with our outdoor gear. Above it was the shelf on which Len kept his tackle box. It was a stretch to reach it. Standing on my tiptoes with my arms extended, I grabbed it with both hands. Everything inside the box rattled together as I lowered it to the floor, and when I opened it, I saw a tangle of rubbery lures colored like candy but bearing barbed hooks sharp enough to draw blood.

A warning, I know now. One I instantly ignored.

I found the lighter at the bottom of the tackle box, along with a couple of those blasted cigars. Beneath them, tucked in a back corner, was a red handkerchief folded into a lumpy rectangle.

At first, I thought it was weed. Although I hadn't used marijuana since my drug-fueled teenage years, I knew Len still occasionally did. I assumed it was something else he smoked while fishing when he wasn't in the mood for a cigar.

But instead of a baggie full of dried leaves, when I unfolded the handkerchief I found three driver's licenses. A lock of hair was paper-clipped to each one, colored the same shade as the hair of the woman pictured on it.

I flipped through the licenses a dozen times, the names and faces shuffling like a slide show from hell.

Megan Keene.

Toni Burnett.

Sue Ellen Stryker.

My first thought, born of naïveté and denial, was that they had been placed there by someone else. It didn't matter that the tackle box belonged to Len and that few people came to the lake house. My mother's visits had grown less frequent as she got older, and Marnie and my aunt had stopped coming entirely years earlier. Unless there was some renter I didn't know about, that left Len.

The second thought, once that initial hopefulness had worn off, was that Len had been fucking around. Until then, I'd never given infidelity much thought. I wasn't a jealous wife. I never questioned my husband's faithfulness. In a business full of philanderers, he didn't seem like the cheating kind. And even as I held three strangers' IDs in my hand, I continued to give Len the benefit of the doubt.

I told myself there had to be a rational explanation. That these licenses, all of which were current, and strands of hair were simply props kept from a film he'd worked on. Or research for a future project. Or that the licenses had been sent to him by crazed fans. As someone who'd once been met at the stage door by a man trying to give me a live chicken he'd named after me, I knew all about weird fan gifts.

But then I took another look at the licenses and realized two of the names were vaguely familiar. Leaning against the mudroom's ancient sink, I pulled out my phone and Googled them.

Megan Keene, the first familiar name, had gone missing the previous summer and was assumed to be the victim of foul play. I'd heard about her because Eli told us all about the case when Len and I had spent a week at the lake the summer she disappeared.

Sue Ellen Stryker, the other name I recognized, had been all over the news a few weeks earlier. She disappeared and was thought to have drowned in a different lake several miles south of here. As far as I knew, police were still trying to recover her body.

I found nothing on Toni Burnett except a Facebook page started by friends of hers seeking information about where she might be. The last time anyone saw her was two months after Megan Keene vanished.

Instantly, I became ill.

Not nauseated.

Feverish.

Sweat formed on my skin even as my body shook with chills.

Still, a part of me refused to believe the worst. This was all some horrible mistake. Or sick joke. Or strange coincidence. It certainly didn't mean Len had made those three women disappear. He simply wasn't capable of something like that. Not my sweet, funny, gentle, sensitive Len.

But when I checked the calendar app we both used to keep track of our schedules, I noticed an unnerving trend—on the days each woman went missing, we weren't together.

Sue Ellen Stryker vanished during a weekend in which I had returned to New York to do voice-over work for a commercial. Len had stayed here at the lake house.

Megan Keene and Toni Burnett both disappeared when Len had been in Los Angeles, working on the superhero script that had bedeviled him for months.

That should have been a relief.

It wasn't.

Because I had no proof he truly was in LA both of those times. We traveled for work so much—both together and separately—that I never stopped to wonder if Len's stated destination was where he had actually gone. According to the calendar, those two LA trips were weekenders. Fly out Friday, come back Monday. And even though I was certain Len had called me from the airport each time before taking off and after landing, it dawned on me that he also could have made those calls from a rental car heading to and from Vermont.

On the day Megan Keene disappeared, Len had stayed at the Chateau Marmont. At least, that's what the calendar app claimed. But when I called the hotel and asked if Leonard Bradley had checked in that weekend, I was told no.

"A reservation was made," the desk clerk informed me. "But he never showed. Because he didn't cancel, we had to charge his credit card. I'm assuming that's what this is about."

I hung up and called the hotel he'd allegedly stayed at the weekend Toni Burnett had vanished. The answer was the same. Reservation made, room never canceled, Len never arrived, weekend charged to the credit card.

That's when I knew.

Len—*my* Len—had done something horrible to those girls. And the locks of hair and the licenses in his tackle box were mementos. Sick souvenirs kept so he could remember his kills.

In the span of minutes, I experienced every terrible emotion you can think of. Fear and sadness and shock and confusion and despair, all colliding in a single, devastating moment.

I cried. Hot tears that, because I was trembling so hard, shook from my cheeks like raindrops off a windblown tree.

I moaned, shoving my fist into my mouth to keep it from being heard by Len upstairs.

The anger, hurt, and betrayal were so overwhelming I honestly thought they would kill me. Not a horrible prospect, all things considered. It certainly would have put me out of my misery, not to mention saved me from facing the dilemma about what to do next. Going to the police was a given. I had to turn Len in. But when? And how?

I decided to tell Len that I couldn't find his lighter and that I needed to run to the store to buy more matches. Then I'd drive straight to the nearest police department and tell them everything.

I told myself it was possible. I was an actress, after all. For a few minutes, I could fake not being sick and terrified and veering between wanting to kill myself and wanting to kill Len. I shoved the licenses and locks of hair in my pocket and headed upstairs, prepared to lie to Len and run to the police.

He was still in the kitchen, looking as nerdy-sexy as always in his silly *Kiss the Cook* apron. He had poured two glasses of wine and arranged the cheese on a platter. It was the very picture of domestic contentedness.

Except for the knife in his hand.

Len was using it innocently enough, slicing a salami to join the platter of cheese. But the way he gripped it, with a smile on his face and his hand so tight his knuckles had turned pale, made my own hands shake. I couldn't help but wonder if he'd killed those three girls with that same knife, using that same tight grip, sporting that same contented grin.

"That took forever," Len said, oblivious to the fact that everything had changed since we last saw each other. That my entire existence had just turned to ash like I was a character in one of those fucking superhero movies he was supposed to be working on while he was really here, ending the lives of three people.

He continued to slice, the blade thwacking against the cutting board. As I listened to it, all those horrible emotions I'd been feeling went away.

Except for one.

Fury.

It vibrated through me, like I was a water glass struck with a hammer. I felt just as brittle. Just as ready to shatter. And as it coursed through me, I started to come up with reasons why I *shouldn't* go to the police. At least, not alone.

The first thing I thought about was my career. God help me, it was. A fact that I still hate myself for. But I knew instantly that this was going to end it. No one would hire me after this. I'd become a pariah. One of those people involved in something so shameful it taints their reputation forever. As soon as word got out that Len was a murderer, people would judge me—and very few would give me the benefit of the doubt. I was certain most people would question how I failed to notice there was a serial killer right under my nose, living in my apartment, sleeping in my bed.

I knew because I was asking those very same things. How did I not suspect anything? How did I miss the signs? *How did I not know?*

Even worse would be the people who assumed I *did* know about it. There'd be plenty of speculation, wondering if I was a killer myself. Or at least an accomplice.

No, the only way I could do this and keep my reputation and career intact was if Len went with me. If he confessed—to me, then to the police—then maybe I'd emerge from the situation unscathed. An innocent victim.

"Sorry," I said, shocked I was able to speak at all. "Marnie texted me about something."

Len stopped slicing, the knife hovering over the cutting board. "Texted? I thought I heard you talking to someone."

"I ended up calling her. You know how much she likes to chat."

"What about the lighter?"

I gulped, uneasy. "What about it?"

"Did you find it?"

"Yes."

With that one word, I started to prepare for what would surely be the worst night of my life. I handed Len the lighter and asked if he could start the fire while I went upstairs to change clothes. In the bedroom, I shoved the licenses in the back of a dresser drawer before slipping into a pair of jeans and a floral blouse Len always said made me look extra sexy. In the bathroom, I grabbed several tablets of the antihistamine he used to ward off allergies. In the kitchen, I dropped one of them into a glass of wine and took it outside to Len. My goal was twofold—get him relaxed enough to confess while also keeping him drunk and drugged enough so that he wouldn't become violent or dangerous.

Len drank the wine quickly. When he was finished, I brought the glass inside, added another antihistamine, filled it up.

Then I did it a third time.

For the rest of the night, I smiled and chatted and laughed and sighed contentedly and pretended to be perfectly happy.

It was the greatest performance I ever gave.

"Let's go out on the water," I said as midnight drew near.

"In the boat?" Len said, his voice already a slurred murmur. The pills were working.

"Yes, in the boat."

He stood, swayed, dropped like a sack back into his chair. "Whoa. I'm really tired."

"You're just drunk," I said.

"Which is why I don't want to take the boat out."

"But the water's calm and the moon is so bright." I leaned in close, pressing my breasts against him and bringing my lips to his ear. "It'll be romantic."

Len's expression brightened the way it always did when he thought he was about to get laid. Seeing it then made me wonder if he looked exactly like this while he killed Megan, Toni, and Sue Ellen. That horrible thought stuck with me as I led him into the boat.

"No motor?" he said when I pushed off from the dock.

"I don't want to wake the neighbors."

I rowed to the center of the lake and dropped the anchor into the water. By this time, Len was as high as the moon.

Now was the time.

"I found them," I said. "The driver's licenses in your tackle box. The locks of hair. I found it all."

Len made a little noise. A low half chuckle of realization. "Oh," he said.

"You killed those women, didn't you?"

Len said nothing.

"Answer me. Tell me you killed them."

"What are you going to do if I say yes?"

"Call the police," I said. "Then I'm going to make sure you go to jail and never, ever get out."

Len suddenly began to cry. Not out of guilt or remorse. These were selfish tears, bursting forth because he'd been caught and now had to face his punishment. Bawling like a child, he leaned toward me, arms outstretched, as if seeking comfort.

"Please don't tell on me, Cee," he said. "Please. I couldn't control myself. I tried. I really did. But I'll be better. I swear."

Something overcame me as I watched my husband cry for mercy after showing none for others. An internal realignment that left me feeling as hollow and ablaze as a jack-o'-lantern.

It was hatred.

The seething, unquenchable kind.

I hated Len—for what he'd done, for deceiving me so thoroughly.

I hated him for destroying the life we had built together, erasing five wonderful years and replacing them with this moment of him weeping and begging and grasping for me even as I recoiled.

I hated him for hurting me.

But I wasn't the only victim. Three others suffered far worse than me. Knowing this made me hope they had at least tried to fight back and, in the process, brought Len some amount of pain. And if they hadn't, well, I was now able to do it on their behalf.

Because someone needed to make Len pay.

As his angry, deceived, now-ruined wife, I was suddenly in a position to do just that.

"I'm so sorry, Cee," Len said. "Please, please forgive me. Please don't turn me in."

Finally, I relented and pulled him into an embrace. Len seemed to melt as I wrapped my arms around him. He put his head to my chest, still sobbing, as a thousand memories of our marriage passed through my thoughts.

"I love you so much," Len said. "Do you love me?"

"Not anymore," I said.

Then I pushed him over the side of the boat and watched him vanish into the dark water.

You killed me," Katherine says again, as if I didn't hear her the first time.

I did, but barely. My whole body is vibrating with shock. An internal hum that gets louder and louder, building from a whisper to a scream.

That's what I want to do.

Scream.

Maybe I am screaming and just don't know it, the noise still rising inside me so loud it eclipses all outside sound.

I bring a hand to my mouth and check. It's shut tight, my lips flattened together, my tongue still and useless. The inside of my mouth is dry—so parched and numb from surprise, fear, and confusion that I begin to wonder if I'll ever be able to speak again.

Because there's no way Katherine could know what I'd done to Len.

No one knows.

No one but me.

And him.

Which means Tom is right about Eli's campfire tale being true. Even though it's utterly preposterous, it's literally the only explanation for what I'm experiencing right now. Len's soul or spirit or whatever the fuck was left of him after life fled his body remained in Lake Greene, waiting in the dark water, biding its time until it could take the place of the next person to die there.

Who happened to be Katherine.

She was dead the afternoon I went out to rescue her. I'm certain of that now. I hadn't reached her in time, a fact the state she was in—that lifeless body, those dead eyes, her blue lips and ice-cold flesh—made clear.

And I'd believed she was dead.

Until, suddenly, she wasn't.

When Katherine sprang back to life, jolting and coughing and spitting up water, it was like some kind of miracle had occurred.

A dark one.

One that only the people Eli talked about seemed to believe.

Somehow, Len had entered Katherine, bringing her back to life. In the process, he'd resurrected himself, albeit in a different body. Where Katherine—the real Katherine and everything that makes her *her*—is now, I have no idea.

"Len—"

I stop, surprised by how easy it is to use his name when it's not him I'm seeing.

It's Katherine. Her body. Her face. Everything is hers except for the voice, which sounds more like Len's with each passing word, and her attitude.

That's all Len. So much so that my brain flips like a switch, making me think of her as him.

"Now you get it," he says. "I bet you thought you'd never see me again."

I don't know which one of them he's referring to. Maybe both. It's true on either count.

"I didn't," I say.

"You don't look happy."

"I'm not."

Because this is the stuff of night terrors. My worst fear made real. My guilt manifested into physical form. It takes all the strength I have not to faint. Even then, specks of blue buzz like flies across my vision.

I literally can't believe this is happening.

It shouldn't be happening.

How the fuck is this happening?

A hundred possibilities run through my shock-addled brain, trying to land on something remotely logical. That it happened because Len's ashes had been scattered in Lake Greene. That there was a combination of minerals in the water that kept his soul alive. That because he died before his time, he was forced to roam the depths. That the lake, quite simply, is as cursed and haunted as Eli and Marnie say it is.

But none of those are possible.

It can't be real.

Which means it isn't. There's no way it could be.

Relief starts to seep into both my body and brain as I realize that this is all a dream. Nothing but a bourbon-induced nightmare. There's a very real possibility that I'm still on the porch, passed out in a rocking chair, at the mercy of my subconscious.

I run a hand along my cheek, wondering if I should slap myself awake. I fear it will only lead to disappointment. Because this doesn't feel like a nightmare. Everything is too vivid, too *real*, from the mismatched antiques crowding the corners of the room like bystanders to the creak of the bed to the twin smells of body odor rising off Len and piss wafting from the nearby bucket.

A different thought occurs to me.

That instead of dreaming, maybe I'm actually dead and am only now realizing it. God knows how it happened. Alcohol poisoning. A heart attack. Maybe I drowned in the lake and that's why I'm seeing Len in Katherine's body. It's my personal limbo, where my good and bad deeds are now colliding.

But it doesn't explain Tom's presence. Or why my heart is still beating. Or why sweat pops from my skin in the stifling basement. Or how the storm continues to rage outside.

"After what you did to me, of course you wouldn't be happy," Len says. "But don't worry. I didn't tell Tom about that."

I've said exactly five words to my long-dead husband, which is five too many. Yet I can't resist adding two more to the tally.

"Why not?"

"Because our secrets are as wedded together as we are. I did a bad thing, which caused you to do a bad thing."

"Yours was far worse than mine, Len."

"Murder is still murder," he says.

"I didn't murder you. You drowned."

"Semantics," Len says. "You're the reason I'm dead."

That part is true, but it's only half the story. The rest—memories I never want to think about but am always thinking about—crashes over me like a thousand waves. All those details I'd try to chase away with whatever liquor I could get my hands on. They're back.

Every.

Single.

One.

And I'm drowning in them.

I remember leaning over the edge of the boat, watching Len splash and sputter for what was probably minutes but felt like hours, thinking the whole time that it wasn't too late, that I could dive in, save him, take him ashore and call the police, but also realizing I had no desire to do that.

Because he'd done terrible things and deserved to be punished.

Because I had loved him and trusted him and adored him and now hated him for not being the man I thought he was.

So I stopped myself from diving in. From saving him. From taking him ashore. From calling the police.

I stopped myself and watched him drown.

Then, when I was certain he was dead, I hauled up the anchor and rowed the boat back to shore. Inside the house, the first thing I did was pour a bourbon, beginning a pattern that continues to this day. I took it to the porch and sat in one of the rocking chairs, drinking and watching the water, fearful that Len hadn't really drowned and I'd see him swimming to the dock at any second.

After an hour had passed and the ice in my empty glass had melted to shards, I decided I needed to call someone and confess.

I chose Marnie. She had a level head. She'd know what to do. But I couldn't bring my finger to tap the phone and make the call. Not for my sake. For Marnie's. I didn't want to drag her into my dirty deeds, make her complicit in something she had nothing to do with. But there's another reason I didn't call her, one I only realized in hindsight.

I didn't want her to turn me in.

Which she would have done. Marnie is a good person, far better than me, and she wouldn't have hesitated to get the police involved. Not to punish me. Because it was the right thing to do.

And I, who had definitely *not* done the right thing, didn't want to risk it.

Because this wasn't a cut-and-dried case of self-defense. Len didn't try to physically hurt me. Maybe he would have without that potent cocktail of alcohol and antihistamine churning in his system. But he was drunk and drugged and I had plenty of ways to get away.

Even if I did claim self-defense, the police wouldn't see it that way. They would only see a woman who drugged her husband, took him out on the lake, shoved him overboard, and watched him drown. It didn't matter that he was a serial killer. Or that those locks of hair and stolen IDs were proof of his crimes. The police would still charge me with murder, even though I hadn't killed my husband.

He drowned.

I just chose not to save him.

But the police would make me pay for it anyway. And I didn't want to be punished for punishing Len.

He deserved it.

I didn't.

So I covered my tracks.

First I removed the hair and licenses from the dresser drawer, wiped them clean with the handkerchief I'd found them in, and hid everything behind the loose plank in the basement wall.

Then I brewed a pot of coffee, poured it into Len's battered thermos, and returned to the basement. There, I grabbed everything Len took with him when he went fishing. The floppy green hat, the fishing rod, the tackle box.

When I exited through the blue door, I left it open just a crack to make it look like Len had also used it. I then carried everything to the boat, which wasn't easy. It was dark and I couldn't use a flashlight because my arms were full and I feared someone on the opposite shore would notice it.

Back in the boat, I rowed to the middle of the lake. After tossing the hat into the water, I lowered myself into it and swam back to shore. Once inside the lake house, I stripped off my wet clothes, put them in the dryer, changed into a nightgown, and crawled into bed.

I didn't sleep a wink.

I spent the night wide-awake, alert to every creak of the house, every rustling leaf, every splash of waterfowl out on the lake. Each noise made me think it was either the police arriving to arrest me or Len, somehow still alive, returning home.

I knew which scenario was worse.

It was only once dawn broke over the lake that I realized the horrible thing I'd done.

Not to Len.

I don't feel guilty about that. I didn't then and I don't now.

Nor do I miss him.

I miss the person I thought he was.

My husband.

The man I loved.

That wasn't the same person I watched sink under the water. He was someone different. Someone evil. He deserved what happened to him.

Still, I'm filled with regret over what I did. Every second of every minute of every hour that I'm sober, it eats away at me. Because I was selfish. I had felt so angry, so hurt, so fucking betrayed, that I only gave a cursory thought to the women Len had killed. They're the true victims of my actions. Them and their families and the cops still struggling to find out what happened.

By killing Len instead of turning him in, I denied all of them answers. Megan Keene, Toni Burnett, and Sue Ellen Stryker are still out there, somewhere, and because of me, no one will ever know where. Their families continue to live in some horrible limbo where a small possibility exists that they'll return.

I was able to mourn Len—or at least the man I'd thought he was—at two memorial services, one on each coast. I sat through both racked with guilt that I was allowed to wallow in my sorrow, a luxury his victims' families didn't have. They weren't granted one service, let alone two. They were never allowed to fully grieve.

Closure.

That's the thing I murdered that night.

Which is why I drink until my head spins and my stomach flips and my mind goes deliciously blank. It's also why I spend all my time here sitting on that porch, staring out at the water, hoping that, if I look hard enough, at least one of those poor souls will make her presence known.

My single attempt to make amends was to slip on a pair of gloves and dig out a postcard of Lake Greene I'd bought during a visit years before, for reasons I can no longer recall. On the back, I scrawled three names and four words.

I think they're here.

When writing, I used my left hand. Wilma's handwriting analyst was spot-on about that. I slapped a self-adhesive stamp on the back of the postcard and dropped it in a random mailbox as I walked to the nearest bar. While there, I had so much to drink that I was shit-faced by the time I showed up to the theater where *Shred of Doubt* was playing.

It was one p.m. on a Wednesday.

By the time I finally sobered up, I was out of a job.

The irony is that mailing the postcard ended up being worse than useless. It confused more than clarified, convincing Wilma and Boone that Katherine Royce had sent it—and that Tom was the man who'd committed Len's crimes.

And I had to pretend I thought that, too. The only other option was to admit what I've done.

But now, as I watch a man who is definitely not my husband but also definitely is, I realize I've been granted an opportunity to right my grievous wrong.

Len is back. He can tell me what he did to his victims, and I can finally help give those who loved Megan Keene, Toni Burnett, and Sue Ellen Stryker the ending I had denied them.

I'm still not clear how or why this surreal turn of events happened. I doubt I'll ever know the forces, whether they be scientific or supernatural, behind it. If this is some sort of fucked-up miracle, I'm not going to waste my time questioning it. Instead, I'm going to make the most of it.

I take a step toward the bed, prompting an intrigued look from Len. It's strange how easily he's replaced Katherine in my mind. Even though I'm conscious that it's her I'm seeing, I can't stop myself from picturing him.

"You're planning something, Cee," he says as I draw near. "You've got that gleam in your eyes."

I'm beside the bed now, close enough to touch him. I reach out a trembling hand, place it on his right leg, retract it like I'd just bumped a hot stove.

"Don't be scared," Len says. "I would never hurt you, Cee."

"You already have."

He lets out a rueful chuckle. "Says the woman who watched me drown."

I can't disagree with him. That's exactly what I did, and in the process I'd condemned an untold number of people to a life of uncertainty. They need answers. Just as much as I need to be relieved of the guilt that's weighed me down for more than a year.

My hand returns to Len's leg, sliding over the hump of his knee and down his shin, traveling all the way to the rope around his ankle. I reach for the other end of the rope, wrapped tight around the bed frame and capped off with a large, messy knot.

"What are you doing?" Len says.

I give the knot a tug. "Getting you out of here."

It takes me a while to loosen the knot. So long that I'm surprised Tom doesn't appear before I'm finished. I do nothing to the rope around Len's ankle. Like the binds on all his limbs, I plan on using those again.

Rather than free his other leg, I move to his hands. I untie his left one first, the knot yielding faster now that I've gotten the hang of it. The moment his hand is free, Len moves it toward me, and for a panicked second I think he's going to hit me. Instead, his palm rests against my cheek, caressing it with feather-like gentleness, just like he used to do after we made love.

"Christ, I've missed you."

I pull away from his touch and start untying the rope attached to his right hand. "I can't say the same."

"You've changed," he says. "You're meaner now. Harder."

"Because of you."

I unwind the rope from the bed frame and give it a tug while quickly moving away from the bed. Len's forced to move with it, jerked partially upright like a marionette. I keep the rope taut as I cross in front of the bed and grab the one still tied around his left hand.

"You forgot my other leg," Len says.

"No, I haven't," I say. "Slide forward and let me tie your hands behind your back. If you make it easy for me, then I'll untie your other leg."

"Can I get a kiss first?"

He gives me a flirty wink. Seeing it makes me want to puke.

"I'm serious," I say. "Tom's going to come back any second now."

Len nods and I let the rope go slack. Once his hands are behind his back, I press them together and wind the rope around both wrists several times before tying the tightest knot I can manage. Satisfied that he can't get loose, I move to the foot of the bed and work on the length of rope around his left ankle.

Tom returns just as I finish untying it, the rope still falling away from the bed frame as his footfalls ring out from the stairwell.

Len slides off the bed as I search for something to fight off Tom, if it comes to that. I assume he won't let us go easily. I settle on a broken table leg leaning against a steamer trunk. Grabbing it, I realize that we have no plan. There wasn't time to come up with one. The best I can hope for is that Len is just as determined as I am to get out of this basement.

And that he won't try to hurt me in the process.

At the bottom of the stairs, Tom stops, glances at the bed, does a double take.

"What the—"

Len rushes him before he can get the rest of the sentence out, battering Tom with his shoulder like a wild ram.

Caught off guard, Tom tumbles to the floor.

Len remains upright and hustles toward the stairs, the ropes around his ankles trailing behind him. Tom reaches out, grabs one, yanks. Before he can pull hard enough to bring Len to the floor, I slam his arm with the broken table leg. Tom howls in pain and lets go of the rope, allowing Len to skitter away.

Standing between them, still brandishing the chunk of wood I've just used as a weapon so the spirit of the man whose death I caused can escape in the body of the woman I'd thought Tom had killed, one thought rings through my skull.

What the fuck am I doing?

The answer is simple: I don't know. I wasn't prepared for any of this.

How could I have been? Now that it's happening—truly, legitimately, holy shit *happening*—I'm just going on gut instinct, fueled by both the desire to locate the women Len killed and the fear that Tom will learn I'm guilty of exactly what I accused him of doing. Right now, separating them seems like the best course of action.

So I run up behind Len, give him a shove, and try to propel him up the stairs before Tom can catch us. Which he almost does. We're halfway up the steps when he come barreling after us, forcing me to swing the broken table leg at him like it's a Louisville Slugger. The wood slams against one wall of the stairwell before ricocheting into the other.

Tom staggers out of the way, trips, drops onto all fours. The whole time, he shouts at me. "Casey, stop! *Please* don't do this!"

I keep moving, catching up to Len at the top of the stairs and shoving him through the door. When both of us are out of the stairwell, I turn around and see Tom scrambling up the steps, calling out, "No! Wait!"

I slam the door, reach for the chain, slide it into place just as Tom bangs against it. The door lurches open a crack before being stopped by the chain. Tom's face fills the two-inch gap between door and frame.

"Listen to me, Casey!" he hisses. "Do not trust her!"

I push against the door, trying to shut it again as, next to me, Len starts shoving the nearby hutch. It barely moves. He grunts and pushes, forgetting he's now in the body of someone with half his former size and strength. Forced to join in, I let go of the door and start pulling the hutch. Together, we're able to nudge it an inch in front of the door before Tom rears back, ready to make another escape attempt.

He smash-kicks the door.

The chain snaps.

The door flies open a crack before bouncing off the back of the hutch.

Straining and heaving, Len and I shove the hutch against the door, forcing it shut and trapping Tom on the other side. He pounds and kicks and begs me to let him out.

I intend to.

Eventually.

Right now, though, I need to get Len to the lake house, where I can question him in peace.

We exit through the kitchen door, Tom's thumps and calls eclipsed by the storm outside. The wind roars, bending the surrounding trees so hard I'm surprised they haven't snapped. Rain falls in blinding sheets and thunder cracks overhead. There's a flash of lightning, in which I see Len start to run.

Before he can get away, I grab the ropes still around his ankles and tug them like reins. Len flops to the ground. Not knowing what else to do, I leap on top of him, holding him in place as the rain pummels us both.

Beneath me, Len grumbles, "I thought you were setting me free."

"Not even close." I slide off of him. "Get up."

He does—not an easy task with his arms still bound behind his back and me gripping the ropes around his ankles like he's an unruly dog on a leash. When he's finally on his feet, I nudge him forward.

"Head toward the dock. Slowly. The boat's there."

"Ah, the boat," Len says as he shuffles in the direction of the water. "*That* brings back memories."

Moving through the storm, I wonder just how much he remembers about the night he died. Judging by his sarcasm, I assume most of it. It makes me curious if he has any knowledge about the fourteen months between then and now. It's hard to imagine him being aware of time's passage as his spirit floated in the water. Then again, I also never imagined him shuffling down a dock in the body of a former supermodel, yet here we are.

Once again, I think: *This isn't happening. This is a nightmare. This can't be real.*

Unfortunately, it feels all too real, including the wind, the rain, the waves rising from the wind-whipped lake and crashing over the dock. If this was a dream, I wouldn't be soaking wet. Or so fucking scared. Or nervous that the lake water sloshing around my ankles might send me sliding off the dock.

Ahead of me, Len *does* slip, and I fear he's about to fall into the water.

With his hands bound behind his back, he'd surely drown. I'm not concerned about the drowning part. Clearly. It's him drowning *before* telling me where he put his victims' bodies that worries me.

Len manages to keep his balance and drop into the boat just as it crests a wave at the end of the dock. I scramble in behind him and quickly start to knot the ropes around his ankles to the legs of his seat, which is bolted to the floor.

"This is all so unnecessary," he says as I finish knotting the ropes around the seat's legs.

"I beg to differ."

With Len secured, I climb to the back of the boat and start the motor. Rowing isn't possible in water this rough. It's tough going even with the outboard motor running at full throttle. A trip that's normally two minutes ends up being closer to fifteen. When we do reach the other side of the lake, it takes three tries and two jarring slams against the dock before I'm able to tie up the boat.

I repeat the dance we just went through at the Fitzgerald place. Untie Len's legs, force him out of the boat as it bucks on the waves, and shuffle with him up the dock as water crashes around us.

By the time we reach the house, Len has become sullen and silent. He says not a word as I march him upstairs to the porch, then inside the house itself. The only sound I hear is a disgruntled sigh when I prod him to climb another set of steps, this time to the third floor.

At the top of the stairs, I choose the first bedroom I see.

My old room.

Not only does it provide quick access to the steps if things go horribly awry and I need to escape, but the twin beds inside have brass frames similar to the one in the Fitzgeralds' basement.

When it's time to tie Len to this bed, I do the reverse of what I'd done at the Fitzgeralds' house. Left ankle first, to keep him in place, followed by the left wrist.

Because the bed is pushed into a corner of the room, I'm forced to lean my entire body over his in order to secure his right wrist. Such an intimate position. One that's both familiar and foreign. The memory of long, lazy nights lying on top of Len collides with the reality of his new body and Katherine's soft skin, long hair, full breasts.

I tie his wrist in a hurry, my fingers fumbling with the rope because I fear he'll use that moment to fight me off. Instead, he stares up at me, looking as love-struck as Romeo. His lips part in a deep sigh of longing, his breath hot on my face.

It smells horrible, feels even worse.

Like an invasion.

Wincing, I finish the haphazard knot, slide off him, and move to the foot of the bed. Once his right leg is tied to the bed frame, I plop onto the opposite bed and say, "You're going to answer some questions for me."

Len remains mute, refusing to look my way. He chooses the ceiling instead, staring at it with exaggerated boredom.

"Tell me about Katherine," I say.

More silence.

"You're going to have to talk eventually."

Still nothing from Len.

"Fine." I stand, stretch, move to the door. "Since we're not going anywhere until you start talking, I guess I'll make some coffee."

I pause in the doorway, giving Len a chance to respond. After thirty more seconds of silence, I head down to the kitchen and start the coffee maker. Leaning against the kitchen counter, listening to Mr. Coffee hiss and drip, the full weight of tonight's events finally hits me.

Len is back.

Katherine is *somewhere*.

Tom is trapped in the Fitzgeralds' basement.

And me? I'm about to be sick.

The nausea arrives in a sneak attack. One second, I'm upright. The next, I'm doubled over on the floor as the kitchen spins and spins and spins. I try to stand, but my legs are suddenly too weak to support me. I'm forced to crawl to the powder room, where I retch into the toilet.

Finished, I sit propped against the wall, weeping and hyperventilating and screaming into a towel yanked from the rod beside me. I've moved from wanting to believe none of this is happening to wanting to know how to make it stop happening.

Because I won't be able to keep it together.

Not that I'm anywhere close to composed right now.

But I know it'll only get worse if Len doesn't start talking. One can only take so much stress and fear and utter fucked-upness before losing it entirely.

I haven't reached that point, although I might very soon. Until then, there's work to be done. So I stand, somewhat surprised that I can, and splash cold water onto my face. As I dry off with the towel into which I screamed, I'm struck by a small thought of consolation.

At least the situation can't get any worse.

Until it does.

B ecause I was too busy either throwing up, gasping, towel screaming, or splashing my face with water, I didn't hear the car pull into the driveway.

Or its door opening and closing as the driver got out.

Or their footfalls as they approached the house.

The first time I'm aware of someone's presence is when they knock on the door. Two raps so loud and startling they might as well be gunshots. I'm looking in the powder room mirror when I hear them, and my frozen expression is the very picture of deer-in-headlights panic. Lips parted. Eyes as big as quarters and shot through with surprise. My face, so pink and puffy a second earlier, drains of color.

Two more knocks snap me out of it. Fueled by a primal urge for self-preservation, I sprint from the powder room with the towel still in my hand, aware of what I need to do without giving it a moment's thought. I fly up the stairs and into the bedroom, startling Len, who at last tries to speak.

He doesn't get the chance.

I stuff the towel into his mouth and knot the ends behind his head.

Then it's back down the stairs, pausing halfway to catch my breath. I take the rest of the steps slowly, feeling my heartbeat move from a frantic rattle to a steady thrum. In the foyer, I say, "Who is it?"

"Wilma Anson."

My heart jumps—a single unruly spike—before settling again. I wipe the sweat from my brow, plaster on a smile big enough to reach a theater's cheap seats, and open the door. I find Wilma on the other side, shaking off the rain that drenched her on the trip between car and porch.

"Detective," I say brightly. "What brings you by in this weather?"

"I was in the neighborhood. Can I come in?"

"Sure." I open the door wide and usher her into the foyer, where Wilma spends a second staring at me, her gaze cool and probing.

"Why are you so wet?" she says.

"I was just out checking on my boat," I say, the lie appearing out of the blue. "Now I'm about to have some coffee."

"At this hour?"

"Caffeine doesn't bother me."

"Lucky you," Wilma says. "If I had a cup right now, I'd be up until dawn."

Because she's still appraising me, seeking out any sign that something's amiss, I gesture for her to follow me deeper into the house. To do otherwise would only make her more suspicious. I guide her into the kitchen, where I pour coffee into a mug before carrying it to the dining room.

Wilma follows me there. As she takes a seat at the dining room table, I look for the gun holstered under her jacket. It's there, telling me she's here on official business.

"I'm going to assume this isn't a friendly visit," I say as I sit down across from her.

"A correct assumption," Wilma says. "I think you know what this is about."

I honestly don't. So much that has happened in the past twenty-four hours could warrant a visit from the state police.

"If this is about my phone call earlier, I want you to know how sorry I am. I wasn't thinking right when I accused Boone."

"You weren't," Wilma says.

"And I don't believe he has anything to do with what's going on."

"He doesn't."

"I'm glad we agree."

"Sure," Wilma says, making it clear she doesn't give a damn if we agree or not. "Too bad I'm not here to discuss Boone Conrad."

"Then why are you here?"

I peer at her through the steam rising from my coffee mug, trying to read her thoughts. It's impossible.

"Have you watched the Royce house at all this evening?" Wilma says.

NOW

I take a sip of bourbon and stare at the person restrained to the bed, consumed with both fear and fascination that someone so evil can be contained inside someone so beautiful. Such a thing shouldn't be possible. Yet it's happening. I'm witnessing it with my very own eyes. It makes me keep the bourbon glass pressed to my lips.

This time, I take a gulp.

"I remember when you used to get tipsy after a single glass of wine," Len says as he watches me drink. "That's clearly changed. I suppose I had a little something to do with that."

I swallow. "More than a little."

"Am I allowed to say I'm worried about you?" Len says. "Because I am. This isn't like you, Cee. You're very different from the person I fell in love with."

"The feeling is mutual."

"And because of that you've decided to drink yourself to death?"

"You, of all people, have no right to judge me," I say. "I don't want your fucking concern. Because this"—I raise the glass of bourbon still clutched in my hand—"is your fault. All of it. Now, we can talk all about why I drink, but only after you tell me more about those girls you killed."

"You want to know how I did it?"

Len smiles. A sick, ghoulish grin that looks profane on Katherine's kind and lovely face. It takes every ounce of restraint I have not to slap it away.

"No," I say. "I want to know *why* you did it. There was more to it than simple enjoyment. Something compelled you to act that way."

A noise rises from outside.

A gust of wind, shrieking like a banshee across the lake.

It slams into the lake house, and the entire place shudders, sending up a communal rattle of windowpanes. The bedside lamp again starts to flicker.

This time, it doesn't stop.

"You don't really want to know, Cee," Len says. "You only think you do. Because to truly understand my actions, you'll need to confront all the things about me that you overlooked or ignored because you were too busy nursing wounds from your own shitty childhood. But you weren't abandoned by your whore mother. You didn't have a father who beat you. You didn't grow up getting passed around foster homes like an unwanted mutt."

Len wants me to feel sorry for him, and I do. No child should experience what he went through. Yet I also know that many do—and that they easily manage to go through life without hurting others.

"Those girls you killed had nothing to do with that," I say.

"I didn't care. I still wanted to hurt someone. I needed it."

And I'd needed him to be the man I thought he was. The kind, decent, charming man I wrongly assumed I'd married. That he couldn't—or wouldn't—do that fills me with a sticky combination of anger and sadness and grief.

"If you felt this way, why did you insist on dragging me into it?" There's a quiver in my voice. I'm not sure which emotion is causing it—rage or despair. "You should have left me alone. Instead, you let me fall in love with you. You let me marry you and build a life with you. A life that you knew all along you were going to destroy."

Len shakes his head. "I didn't think it would get so bad. I thought I could control it."

"Our marriage should have been enough to stop you," I say, the quiver growing to a quake. "*I should have been enough!*"

"I tried not to act on it," Len says. "The urge refused to go away, no matter how much I wanted it to. Some nights, while you were asleep, I'd lie awake and think about what it would feel like to watch the life go out of a person's eyes and know I was the cause of it. The more I thought about it, the more I resisted. And the more I resisted, the stronger the urge became."

"Until you came here and did it."

"Not at first," Len says, and my gut tightens at the thought of him killing others elsewhere. "In LA. Sometimes, when I was out there alone for work, I'd scour the streets, find a hooker, take her back to my room."

I don't flinch at the news. After knowing your husband murdered at least three women, finding out he also cheated doesn't have the sting it would under normal circumstances.

"And then one night, I didn't feel like bothering with the room. We just got in my car, parked somewhere quiet, made the necessary financial arrangements. And as it was happening, me with the front seat reclined, her kneeling in the wheel well, giving a blow job that wasn't worth the money, I thought, *It would be so easy to kill her right now.*"

I shiver, repulsed. Once again, I can't believe that this man was my husband, that most of my nights were spent sleeping by his side, that I loved him with every fiber of my being. Even worse, I can't get over how completely he had fooled me. During our time together, I never suspected—not once—he was a fraction this cruel and depraved.

"Did you?" I say, not wanting an answer but needing one all the same.

"No," Len says. "It was too risky. But I knew it was going to happen someday."

"Why here?"

"Why not here? It's quiet, secluded. Plus, I could rent a car, drive here for a weekend, come back, and pretend I was in LA. You never suspected a thing."

"I found out eventually," I say.

"Not until it was too late for Megan, Toni, and Sue Ellen."

I feel a pain in my gut, as sharp and twisting as if I'd taken the knife on the bed next to me and shoved it into my side.

"Tell me where you left their bodies."

"To atone for my sins?"

I shake my head and take another sip of bourbon. "To atone for mine."

"I see," Len says. "Then what? And don't pretend you haven't thought it through. I know exactly what you plan on doing. Once you learn where those bodies are, you're going to kill me all over again."

When he was alive, I found it uncanny how well Len could read my thoughts. Sometimes it felt like he knew my every mood, whim, and need, which I absolutely loved. What a pleasure it was to have my spouse know me so well. In hindsight, it was more curse than blessing. I suspect it's how Len was able to hide his true nature from me for so long. I'm certain it's how he knows exactly what I have planned now.

"Yes," I say, seeing no point in lying. He wouldn't believe me if I did. "That's what I intend to do."

"And what if I refuse?"

I set the glass on the nightstand, next to the lamp that continues to flicker. It's like a strobe light, plunging the room into microbursts of darkness and light as my hand once again moves toward the knife. "Then I'll kill you anyway."

"I don't think you want that much blood on your hands, Cee," Len says, pronouncing the nickname with an exaggerated hiss. "I know from experience you won't hesitate to kill me. But it's your other victim that should give you pause."

"What other victim?"

"Katherine, of course."

He doesn't need to say anything else. I now understand exactly what he means.

If I killed him, I'd also be killing Katherine Royce.

Riding on the coattails of that revelation is another bit of clarity. One that's more hopeful, if no less complicated.

"She's still there," I say.

Len doesn't get a chance to respond. He's blocked by another screaming wind outside.

Coming closer.

Swooping in.

It rams against the house and everything shakes, me included. I reach for the nightstand to steady myself. In the hallway, something falls to the floor and shatters.

The nightstand lamp stops flickering long enough for me to see the rattling bourbon glass, Len straining against the ropes, the smug grin on his face.

Then the lamp, the room, and the entire lake house go completely dark.

The plunge into darkness is so sudden and quick it makes me gasp. The sound of it slithers through the room, made louder by the all-encompassing blackness. Now *this* is darker than a coffin with the lid shut.

I remain on the bed, hoping it's just a blip and that power will return in just a few seconds. When a minute passes and the lights remain out, I resign myself to the task ahead—finding flashlights and candles and making the place as bright as possible.

While I don't trust Len in the light, I trust him even less in the dark.

I stand and leave the room, using muscle memory from a thousand nights here to navigate between the beds and out the door.

In the hallway, something crunches beneath my sneakers.

Broken glass.

A pool of it spreads across the hardwood floor. I try to step over it, accidentally nudging the source of the glass—a picture frame that fell from the wall when the house shook.

I keep moving to the stairs. Rather than walk down them, I sit and scoot step by step to the bottom. By now, my eyes have adjusted to the darkness enough for me to make my way to the den, where an emergency supply of flashlights and candles is kept. I find an LED lantern, a flashlight, and several fat candles that can burn for hours.

And I find a lighter.

One that's likely been here for ages.

At least since last summer.

And since Len was the person responsible for gathering and keeping track of the supplies, he knew of its existence.

That son of a bitch.

I turn on the lantern and carry it from room to room, lighting candles along the way. Some are from the emergency stash. Others are decorative ones in glass jars that have accumulated over the years, unlit until this very moment. Their scents mingle as I make my way through the house. Spruce and cinnamon, lavender and orange blossom. Such pretty scents for what's become a very ugly situation.

Upstairs, I light a candle in the master bedroom before returning to the room where Len remains tied up.

I place the lantern on the bed and put a candle on the nightstand. I flick the lighter and hold it to the candle's wick, which lets off a small sizzle as the flame takes hold.

"You wanted me to find those driver's licenses, didn't you?" I say. "That's why you sent me down to your tackle box and not to the lighter with the storm supplies. You wanted me to know what you did."

Len shifts on the bed, his shadow large and flickering on the wall next to him. The candlelight paints his face in shifting patterns of brightness and shadow. In each snatch of darkness, I think I get a glimpse of Len in his true form, almost as if Katherine is mutating into him. A cruel trick of the light.

"It was more of a game," he says. "I knew there was a chance you could find them, just as I knew you could completely overlook them. It was exciting trying to figure out if you did or not. I found out eventually."

"Not until it was too late for you." I lift the glass of bourbon to my lips and take a triumphant swallow. "But it's not too late for Katherine, is it? She's still present."

"She is," Len says. "Somewhere deep. I thought you understood that."

He's wrong there. I still don't understand any of it. Not just the perversion of nature that allowed the situation to happen, but how it works.

"Is she aware of what's going on?"

"You'd have to ask her," Len says.

"Is that possible?"

"Not anymore. It was back when she still mostly had control."

My thoughts drift to my few interactions with Katherine. Talking in the boat after pulling her from the lake. Downing her husband's five-grand-a-bottle wine. Drinking coffee the next morning, bemoaning the state of her marriage. That was all Katherine. Or most of it. I presume that sometimes Len broke through, like when he saw his binoculars sitting on the porch or texted me even though Katherine didn't know my phone number.

"When did you take over?" I say.

"It happened gradually," Len says. "It took me a while to get my bearings in a new form, to understand the logistics of how it worked, to learn how to control it. And, boy, did she resist. Katherine refused to go down without a fight."

Good for her, I think, before being consumed by another thought.

"Is there a way to bring her back?"

Len doesn't answer.

"There is," I say. "Otherwise you would have told me no."

"There might be a way, yes," Len says. "Not that I plan on sharing it with you."

"You can't stay like this. You're trapped. Not just here, in this room, but in another person's body."

"And what a lovely body it is. I suspect it'll make things easy for me."

Len looks down at Katherine's breasts with an exaggerated leer. Seeing him do it unleashes an anger I've probably been keeping in my entire life. Not just at him, although he's left me plenty to be angry at, but at all men who think life is somehow easier for women, especially the pretty ones.

"Easy?" I say. "You have no idea how hard it is to be a woman. Or how maddening it is to always feel at risk because that's just how our fucked-up society is. Trust me, you're not equipped to handle it. Wait until you have to walk down the street alone at night or stand on a subway platform and wonder if one—or more—of the men around you will try to harass you. Or assault you. Or kill you just like you killed those three girls who are now somewhere in that lake."

The knife is in my hand, although I have no memory of picking it up. Now that it's in my grip, I fly across the room and, seething with pent-up rage, bring the blade to Len's neck. He gulps, and the rippling of his skin scritches against the steel of the knife.

"Maybe I should do it right now," I say. "Just so you know how it feels."

"Remember what I told you," he says. "You kill me, then you also kill Katherine. Stab me, and you're stabbing her, too. My blood is her blood now."

I don't immediately remove the knife. Anger bubbling inside me like hot tar makes me keep it there another minute, the blade on the cusp of breaking skin. During those sixty seconds, I feel bright and wildly alive and finally in charge of the situation.

This, I think, *is what being a man must feel like.*

But then I catch Len looking at me, and in those gray-green eyes that once belonged to Katherine Royce but are now his, I see approval.

"I always knew we were a good match," he says as the knife blade continues to scratch his flesh.

Horrified, I recoil, drop onto the other bed, let the knife slip from my hands.

I'd *become* him.

Just for a minute.

Long enough for me to feel something inside that I'm certain wasn't part of me.

It was Len.

Curling around my organs and skittering between my ribs and tugging on my muscles and growing in my brain like a tumor.

I huff out a single, shocked breath.

"What did you just do?"

Len keeps grinning. "Tom warned you I could be tricky."

He did, but it never occurred to me that Tom meant *this*.

"How did you do that?" I say, even though I have a good idea. It happened earlier, when he'd sighed into my face as I was binding his right wrist. That foul breath had felt like an invasion because it was.

Len had planted a part of himself inside of me.

"Neat trick, right?" he says.

I scoot farther onto the bed, backing away from him until I'm pressed against the wall, more worried than ever about being too close to him. He's contagious.

"How was that possible? How is any of this possible?"

Len stares up at the spot where the wall meets the ceiling and the bit of his long shadow that crosses that divide. "When I was alive, I never gave much thought to the afterlife. I assumed that when we die, that's the end. But now I know better. Now I know that something stays behind. Our souls, I guess. When people die on land, I suspect it rides out with their final breath and eventually dissipates into the atmosphere. But when I drowned, it—"

"Went into the lake," I say.

"Exactly. I don't know if it can happen in all bodies of water or if there's something special about Lake Greene that causes it. All I know is that I was trapped there."

"What about Megan, Toni, and Sue Ellen?" I say. "Are their souls also trapped in the lake?"

"You need to die in the water for that to happen." Len pauses, knowing he just gave me a hint about what happened to them. Completely intentional, I'm sure. "So, no, I'm afraid it was just me."

While I'm not nearly as knowledgeable about Lake Greene as someone like Eli, I do know there hasn't been a drowning there since my great-great-grandfather built the earliest version of the lake house. Len had been the first since at least 1878.

Until Katherine came along.

"How were you able to enter Katherine? Or me, for that matter?"

"Because our souls—if that is indeed what it is—don't need to vanish into the ether. They're like air and liquid and shadow combined. Slippery. Weightless. Shapeless. In order to remain, all they need is a vessel. The lake was one. Katherine's body is another. I'm like water now, able to be poured from glass to glass. And what you experienced, my sweet, was a mere drop. How did it feel?"

Horrifying.

And powerful.

A realization that makes me reach for the glass of bourbon, desperate for another sip. It's empty. I hadn't realized.

Seized by both the need for a drink and the urge to get away from Len before he can slide into me again, I climb off the bed, grab the lantern, and back out of the room. In the doorway, I pause and fix him with a look of warning.

"Do that again and I *will* kill you," I say.

Downstairs, I pour a splash of bourbon into the empty glass, shuddering at how it reminds me of what Len just said.

A mere drop.

That's all it took.

I'd turned into *him*, and it's left me feeling violated, dirty, tainted.

I dump more bourbon into the glass, filling it the way Len could have filled me, emptying out of one vessel into another. I suppose that's what Lake Greene is. A vast bowl in which his evil thrived like a virus in a petri dish, waiting for the right host to come along.

Now that it has in the form of Katherine Royce, I can think of only two ways to make it stop.

The first is to kill him on land and hope his soul evaporates into the atmosphere. Not an option when he's currently inside Katherine. Len was right. I don't want any more blood on my hands.

The second way is to pour him into a different vessel.

I look to the French doors that lead to the porch. The combined light of the lantern and a candle burning in the kitchen has turned the glass into a makeshift mirror. I approach it, my reflection getting more pronounced with each step. Looking at myself, I put a hand to my heart before sliding it over my breasts and down my stomach. Then I touch my head, my face, my neck, my arms—all the places I'd briefly felt Len—making sure he's gone.

I think so.

I feel like my usual tormented, self-destructive, trainwreck self.

I move closer to the door until I'm only an inch from the glass, staring at my reflection, which in turn stares back at me. We look into each other's eyes, both of us knowing what needs to be done next.

I step away from the door, grab the lantern, and leave the kitchen, forgetting the bourbon entirely.

I climb the stairs, pausing at the top step to take a deep breath, bracing myself to face Len again before continuing. Then it's on to the landing and into the hall, where I crunch once more over the broken glass from the fallen picture frame. I then push through the doorway and into the bedroom, lit by the flickering glow of candlelight.

"If you tell me where the girls are, I'll—"

My voice withers and dies.

The bed is empty.

Where Len's arms should be, two lengths of rope dangle from the bedposts. The ropes at the foot of the bed are shorter and their ends ragged, clearly sawed apart. Their other halves are curled in the spot on the floor where the knife had been.

It, like Len himself, is now gone.

I freeze in the middle of the bedroom, listening for signs as to where Len went. While I was downstairs, I didn't hear a door open or close, which is both a pro and a con.

The pro: He hasn't left the house.

The con: He's still inside, carrying both a knife and a grudge.

I raise the lantern and rotate slowly, my gaze sliding over the entire room, seeking out places where he could be hiding. Under both beds, for starters. Those dark spaces have me expecting to see Len's hand springing out from under them, knife swinging. I jump onto the bed Len should still be in, barely able to breathe as I locate another potential hiding spot.

The closets.

There are two, both narrow spaces made for little clothes worn by little girls like Marnie and I used to be. Neither would be big enough to contain someone Len's size.

Katherine Royce is a different story.

Her willowy frame could easily fit inside.

I step to the foot of the bed, cursing the squeak of the mattress springs. Gripping the bed frame with clammy hands, I force my feet onto the floor, one at a time. I then tiptoe forward, as quick as a ballerina, toward the first closet.

Holding my breath, I reach out.

I grab the doorknob.

I give it a twist.

My heart halts when the door clicks open.

I pull it, slowly, as hinges neglected for years groan into use.

The closet is empty.

I sidestep to the other one in the room, ready to perform the dance all over again. Breath held. Doorknob grabbed and twisted. Hinges protesting. It all leads to the same outcome.

An empty closet and my mind full of thoughts.

Len has escaped to other parts of the house.

It's a big place, with so many spots to hide and wait.

Every moment I spend inside is one moment too long and I should get out.

Now.

I bolt from the bedroom, cut a hard left in the hall, and splash through the pool of broken glass on my way to the stairs. I fly down the steps so fast my feet barely touch them. I slide to a stop in the living room, which is a sea of shadows undulating in the candlelight. I skip my gaze from corner to corner, doorway to doorway, wondering if I've just stepped into a trap.

Len could be anywhere.

In a shadow-filled corner. Or that dark space by the fireplace. Or the gloom of the nook under the stairs.

It's hard to tell because everything is dark, quiet, still. The only sounds I hear are the rain outside and the grandfather clock. Each tick from it is a reminder that every second I remain in this house is one second more I've spent in danger.

I start moving again, eager to leave but unsure of the best way. The French doors lead to the porch, the steps, the dock, the water. I could take the boat and guide it over the rough water to Boone's dock, assuming he'd give me shelter. Not a guarantee after what I've accused him of.

Then there's the front door, with access to the driveway, the road, and, eventually, the highway. There, someone will surely stop to help me. Getting there won't be easy in this weather, but it might be my only option.

Mind made up, I shoot toward the foyer, ticking off each room I safely pass.

Living room.

Powder room.

Library.

Den.

As soon as I reach the foyer, power returns. Light floods the house, as sudden and startling as when it went away. The shadows that had a second ago been all around me vanish like ghosts. I halt in the unexpected brightness, aware of something behind me that had once been hidden but is now exposed.

Len.

He leaps from a corner, knife raised, hurtling forward. I drop the lantern and fall to the floor, a move fueled more by surprise than strategy. Taken off guard, Len's momentum keeps him moving long enough for me to grab one of his ankles. He's smaller as Katherine, easier to topple than his former self.

He goes down quick.

The knife comes loose.

We both lunge for it, scrambling on top of each other, our limbs tangling. I reach out, and my fingertips brush the knife's handle. Len claws at my arm, yanking it away. He's on top of me now, pressing down, Katherine's body shockingly heavy. Beneath him, I see his arm stretch past mine, reach the knife, grab hold.

Then we're rolling across the foyer floor.

I'm flipped onto my back.

Len's on top of me again, straddling my waist, raising the knife.

My entire being clenches as the knife hovers, and I wait for it to drop, hoping it won't but knowing it will. Fear pins me to the floor. Like I'm already dead, now just a corpse, heavy and motionless.

Above, Len is suddenly jerked backwards.

His arms flap.

His weight lifts.

The knife is wrenched from his grip.

As he's dragged away from me, I see the person responsible.

Eli.

Behind him, the front door hangs open, letting in a blast of night air and shivery drops of rain. Eli kicks it shut and, with Len writhing in his grip, looks down at me.

"I got your message. Are you okay?"

I remain on the floor, still as heavy as the dead, and nod.

"Good," Eli says. "Now would you mind telling me what the hell is going on here?"

I agree to start talking after Eli helps me tie Len to a chair in the living room. Since she's still Katherine in his mind, it takes some convincing. He ultimately goes along with it only because he had just seen her on top of me brandishing a knife.

But now Len is restrained with ropes knotted too tightly for him to get free like he did in the bedroom, and Eli and I are in the den, watched by the moose on the wall as we sit across from each other.

"How much have you had to drink today?" Eli asks.

"A shitload." I look him in the eyes, waiting until he blinks. "That doesn't mean any of what I'm about to tell you is a lie."

"I hope not."

I proceed to tell him everything.

I start with Len's crimes, using the driver's licenses and locks of hair pulled from behind the loose board in the basement as proof. They now sit on the coffee table between us. After taking a single glance, Eli told me he didn't want to look at them anymore, yet his gaze keeps drifting to the pictures of Megan Keene, Toni Burnett, and Sue Ellen Stryker as I recount how I learned what Len had done.

"Then I killed him," I say.

Eli, in the midst of sneaking another glance at the IDs, looks up at me, shocked.

"He drowned," he says.

"Only because I caused it."

I hold his rapt attention as I describe the events of that night, detailing every step of my crime.

"Why are you telling me this now?" Eli asks.

"Because it helps everything else make sense," I say.

The everything else is what's been going on at Lake Greene. Again, no detail is skipped and not a single bit of my bad behavior is overlooked. I hoped admitting everything would leave me feeling as cleansed as a sinner after confession. Instead, I only feel shame. I've committed too many wrongs for the blame to rest solely with Len.

Eli listens with an open mind. After getting to the part about Len taking possession of Katherine's body, I say, "You were right. Something was in the lake, waiting. I don't know if it's all bodies of water or just Lake Greene or something special about Len. But it's true, Eli. And it's happening right now."

He says nothing after that. He simply stands, leaves the den, and goes to where Len is being kept. Their voices drift in from the living room, too hushed and urgent to be heard clearly.

Ten minutes pass.

Then fifteen.

Eli ends up speaking with Len for twenty minutes. A fraction of the time I spent talking, but long enough for me to get anxious that he doesn't believe me. Or, worse, believes whatever lies Len is telling him.

I hold my breath as Eli finally returns to the den and sits down.

"I believe you," he says.

"I—" I struggle to speak, flustered by both surprise and relief. "Why? I mean, what convinced you?"

Eli cranes his neck to pass a glance into the distant living room. "She—sorry, he—admitted it."

That word—*he*—tells me Eli's serious. Knowing that he believes me would typically leave me fainting with relief if not for the last thing I need to tell him.

My plan for what's next.

Again, I go through every step, answering all of Eli's questions and addressing each of his concerns.

"It's the only way," I tell him when I'm done.

Eventually, Eli nods. "I suppose it is. When do you plan on doing it?"

I turn to the window, surprised to realize that while I was talking to Eli and he was talking to Len, the storm had moved on. No more gusts rattle the windows and no more rain thrums against the roof. In their place is the quiet stillness that always follows wild weather, as if the atmosphere, having blustered and bellowed to exhaustion, is now taking a long, restful breath. The sky, once so dark, has now thinned to a medium gray.

Dawn is on its way.

"Now," I say.

In the living room, Eli and I stand before Len, who's still trying to pretend he's bored by all of this. The old Len might have been able to get away with it. The new one, stuck with Katherine's exquisitely expressive face, can't. Curiosity peeks through his impatient facade.

"Tell me where you put those girls," I say, "and I'll let you go."

Len perks up, his feigned boredom vanishing in a snap. "Just like that? What's the catch? There has to be one."

"No catch. There's not a whole lot I can do here. I can't kill you because it would mean killing Katherine, too. And I can't keep you tied up like this forever. Like Tom Royce, I could try. Chain you up in the basement. Feed you and bathe you. But more people are going to start looking for Katherine, and it'll only be a matter of time before they find you."

"And I can go anywhere?"

"The farther, the better," I say. "You can try to live like Katherine Royce for a while, but I suspect that'll be extremely difficult. She's pretty famous. Her four million Instagram followers will easily pick you out in a crowd. My advice is to change your appearance and get away as far and as fast as you can."

Len thinks it over, no doubt considering the hurdles of starting a new life in a new place in a very recognizable body.

"And you're willing to help me?"

"I'm willing to drop you off at the Royces' dock," I say. "After that, you're on your own. What you do is none of my concern."

"It should be," Len says. "I could cause a whole lot of trouble out there on my own. Or, for that matter, a whole lot of trouble right here. You know what I'm capable of."

If his goal is to get a rise out of me, it doesn't work. I assumed he would make such a threat. To be honest, I would have been shocked if he hadn't.

"It's a risk I have to take," I say. "This isn't an ideal option. It's the *only* option. For both of us."

Len looks to Eli. "He stays here."

"I already told him that."

While I would love to have Eli by my side through all of this, I need him to go to the house next door and distract Boone. The last thing I want is for Boone to see me and someone he thinks is Katherine out on the lake.

He would definitely try to stop me.

So would Eli if he knew what I really have planned.

"It'll just be the two of us," I tell Len.

He beams. "Like I always wanted."

Before we leave, I fold Megan's, Toni's, and Sue Ellen's driver's licenses and locks of hair back into the handkerchief and force Eli to take them.

"If I don't come back, give these to Detective Wilma Anson," I say, writing down her name and phone number. "Tell her they're from me. She'll know what to do with them. And what they mean."

"You do plan on coming back, right?" Eli says.

I respond with what I hope is a believable "Of course."

With Eli's help, I release Len from the chair. Once he's standing, we force his wrists in front of him and bind them together, much to his protest.

"I thought you were letting me go."

"I am," I say. "After you show me exactly where you put those girls. Until then, the ropes stay."

Len shuts up after that, remaining mute as we walk him onto the back porch. The blanket from the boat sits heaped in one of the rocking chairs.

I pick it up and drape it over Len's shoulders. While not quite a disguise, it will hopefully make it slightly harder for Boone to see who's in the boat with me if Eli fails to distract him.

The three of us march down the porch steps, across the grass, and to the dock. Signs of the recently passed storm are everywhere. The trees have been stripped of their autumn leaves, which now litter the ground in patches of orange and brown. A large branch, snapped by the wind, lies across one of the Adirondack chairs by the firepit.

The lake itself has swollen past its banks, with water pooling in the grass along the shore and covering the dock in spots. Len splashes through it, a noticeable spring in his step. He has the appearance of a hostage who knows he's about to freed.

I look forward to the moment he realizes that's not going to happen.

"Are you sure you don't want me to come along?" Eli says.

"No," I say. "But I am sure I need to do this alone."

Eli insists on a hug before letting me get into the boat. An embrace so tight I think he might never let go. As it goes on, I whisper into his ear: "Tell Marnie and my mother anything you want about what happened. Whatever you think will be easiest for them to handle."

He pulls back and searches my face, his own features going slack as he realizes I'm not going to follow the plan I laid out for him.

"Casey, what are you going to do?"

I can't tell him. I know he'll try to talk me out of it—and that he'll likely succeed. A risk I'm unwilling to take. I've avoided paying for my sins long enough. Now it's time to atone.

"Tell them I'm sorry for putting them through my bullshit," I say. "And that I love them and hope they can forgive me."

Before Eli can protest, I give him a peck on the cheek, pull away from his embrace, and step into the boat.

The last thing I do before pushing off the dock and starting the motor is free a length of rope knotted around a cleat on the boat's rim. Still attached to the other end of the rope is the anchor.

I'll need that for later.

We set off just before sunrise, with a mist rolling over the rain-swollen lake. The fog is so thick it feels like we're in the clouds and not on the water. Overhead, the predawn gray is beginning to blush. It's all so beautiful and peaceful that I allow myself to forget what I'm about to do, just for a moment. I tilt my face skyward, feel the chill of a new day on my cheeks, and breathe in the autumn air. When I'm ready, I look at Len, seated in the front of the boat.

"Where?" I say.

He points to the southern end of the lake, and I tug the motor to life. I keep it on low—a slow glide over the water that gives me a dizzy feeling of déjà vu. This situation is just like the first time I met Katherine, right down to the blanket over her shoulders. Making it all the more surreal is knowing that nothing, not even Katherine herself, is the same.

I've changed, too.

I'm sober, for starters.

A refreshing surprise.

Then there's the fact that I'm no longer afraid. Gone is the woman so terrified of having her dark secret exposed that she couldn't sleep without a drink or three.

Or four.

The freedom of confession I'd so wanted back in the house finally arrives. With it comes a sense of inevitability.

I know what's going to happen next.

I'm ready for it.

"I'm surprised you haven't asked me yet," Len says, raising his voice to be heard over the motor's bubbling hum.

"Asked you what?"

"The question that I know has been on your mind. This entire time you've been wondering if I ever intended to kill you when I was alive. And the answer is no, Cee. I loved you too much to even consider it."

I believe him.

Which sickens me.

I hate knowing that a man like Len—a man capable of killing three women without remorse and then dumping them into the lake we now float on—loved me. Still worse is the fact that I had loved him in return. A foolish, hopeful, naive love that I refuse to subject myself to again.

"If you loved me at all," I say, "you would have killed yourself before killing someone else."

Instead, he was a coward. In many ways, he still is, using Katherine Royce as both shield and bargaining chip. He knows me well enough to assume I'll refuse to sacrifice her in order to get to him.

The reality is that he has no idea how much I'm willing to sacrifice.

As we get closer to the southern tip of the lake, Len raises his hand. "We're here," he calls.

I cut the motor and everything goes silent. The only sound I hear is lake water, whipped into waves from the boat, lapping against the hull as it settles, calms, quiets. In front of us, emerging from the mist like the mast of a ghost ship, is a dead tree poking out of Lake Greene.

Old Stubborn.

"This is it," Len says.

Of course he would choose this spot. It's one of the few places on the lake not visible from any of the houses on shore. Now the sun-bleached log juts from the surface like a tombstone, marking three women's watery graves.

"All of them are down there?" I say.

"Yes."

I lean over the side of the boat and peer into the water, naively hoping I'll be able to look beyond the surface. Instead, all I see is my own reflection staring back at me with eyes widened by fearful curiosity. I reach out and run my hand through the water, scattering my reflection, as if that will somehow chase it away for good. Before my reflection collects itself again, my ghostly features sliding into place like pieces of a jigsaw puzzle, I get a glimpse of the dark depths just beyond it.

They're down there.

Megan and Toni and Sue Ellen.

"Happy now?" Len says.

I shake my head and wipe away a tear. I'm nowhere near happy. What I am is relieved, now that I know the three of them aren't lost forever and that their loved ones will finally be able to properly mourn and move forward.

I pull out my phone, take a picture of Old Stubborn stretching out of the water, and send it to Eli.

He's expecting my text.

The last part of the plan he's aware of.

What's next is known only to me.

First, I drop my phone into a Ziploc bag I snagged from the kitchen and seal it shut. The bag goes on my vacated seat, where hopefully it will be discovered if my text to Eli doesn't go through. I then stand, sending the boat rocking slightly. It's an effort to keep my balance as I move toward Len.

"I did what you asked," he says. "Now you have to let me go."

"Of course." I pause. "Can I get a kiss first?"

I rush forward, pull him close, force my lips upon his. At first, the difference is jarring. I'd expected it to feel like kissing Len. But Katherine's lips are thinner, more feminine, delicate. This small relief makes it easier to keep kissing the man I once loved but who now repulses me.

If Len senses that repulsion, he doesn't show it.

Instead, he kisses me back.

Softly at first, then brutal in its intensity.

Burning air pushes from his mouth into mine, and I know what he's doing.

It's what I want him to do.

"Keep going," I whisper against his lips. "Don't stop. Leave her and take me instead."

I push myself into him, my arms coiling around him, holding him tight. A moan escapes Len's mouth, slides into mine, joins whatever else is pouring into me like bourbon from a bottle.

It's silky. Exactly how Len described it. Like air and water combined. Weightless and yet so heavy.

The more of it that enters me, the more sluggish I feel. Soon I'm dizzy. Then weak. Then breathless. Then—oh, God—drowning in a scary mix of water and air and Len himself, his essence filling my lungs until I'm blind and choking and dropping to the boat's floor.

For a second, everything is gone.

I feel nothing.

Finally, the full oblivion I've craved for fourteen months.

Then I come to, as startled as someone yanked back to life by CPR. My body spasms as I breathe in, then out. My eyes blink open to a sky made cotton candy pink by sunrise. Beside me, Len sits up.

Only it's no longer Len.

It's Katherine Royce.

I know because she gives me the same wide-eyed look of terror I saw when she came back to life the day we first met.

"What just happened?" she says, her voice unmistakably her own again.

"He's out of you," I say.

It's clear Katherine knows enough about the situation to understand my meaning. Touching her face, her throat, her lips, she says, "Are you sure?"

I am. Len is inside *me* now. I feel him there, as invasive as a virus. I might look fine on the outside, but inside I'm no longer fully myself.

I'm changing.

Quickly.

"Here's what I need you to do." I talk fast, afraid I won't have control over my voice for much longer. Already Len is winding his way through my system. He's done this before. He now knows where to go and what to control. "Take the boat to Boone's place. Eli will be there. Tell them you got lost in the woods. Boone might not believe you, but Eli will help convince him. The story is you and Tom got into a fight, you went for a hike and got lost, although Tom thought you'd left him."

I let out a cough as ragged as sandpaper.

"Are you okay?" Katherine says.

"I'm fine." I notice the change in my voice. It's me, but different. Like a recording that's been slightly slowed. "Tom is in the Fitzgeralds' basement. While I don't know for sure if he'll go along with your story, I think he will. Now let me untie you."

It takes a frightening amount of effort to unknot the rope around Katherine's wrists. Len's starting to fight me. My hands are awkward and numb, and sudden random thoughts push into my brain.

Don't do this, Cee.

Please don't.

I manage to loosen the rope enough for Katherine to do the rest. As she slides her hands from the restraints, I set to work creating my own. It's not easy. Not with Len getting louder.

Don't, Cee.

You promised.

My vision has blurred and my depth perception is off.

It feels, I realize, like I'm drunk.

Only this has nothing to do with alcohol. It's all Len.

With him fighting my every move, it takes me three tries to grasp the rope attached to the anchor. Knotting it around my ankle takes even longer.

"Remember—" I need to pause. Forcing out that single word has left me breathless. "Tell them you got lost. That you don't know what happened to me."

"Wait," Katherine says. "What's going to happen to you?"

"I'll be the one missing."

I pick up the anchor and, before Katherine—or Len—can try to stop me, leap into the chilly depths of Lake Greene.

Water surrounds me.
Cold. Churning. Dark.
So dark.

As dark as death as I hurtle to the lake's floor. I'd been foolish to think my descent would be gentle—a slow, inexorable drop akin to drifting off into permanent sleep. In truth, it's chaos. I twist through the black water, the anchor still hugged to my chest. Within seconds I hit bottom, the centuries of sediment collected there doing nothing to lessen the impact.

I land on my side in an eruption of silt, and the anchor jolts from my arms. I grasp for it, blind in the dark, dirty depths as my body starts to rise. Already, it wants air, and I have to fight to keep my arms from flailing, my legs from kicking.

They try anyway.

Rather, Len tries.

His presence is like a fever, both chilly and hot, coursing through my limbs, moving them against my will. I spin in the darkness, not knowing if I'm floating up or sinking down. Still blind and fumbling, my hand finds the rope stretching between my ankle and the anchor.

I grab on to it even as Len tries to pry my fingers away, his seething voice loud in my head.

Let go, Cee.

Don't make me stay down here, you fucking bitch.

I keep hold of the rope, using it to pull myself back toward the lake bed. When I reach the end of the rope, I grab the anchor, hoist it to my chest, and roll onto my back. It feels inevitable now that I'm here.

It feels right.

In the same place where Megan Keene, Toni Burnett, and Sue Ellen Stryker were laid to rest.

My limbs have turned numb, although I don't know if it's from fear or cold or Len taking over. He remains so desperate to get to the surface. My body jerks uncontrollably against the lake floor. All his doing.

But it's no use.

This time I'm stronger.

Because I'm giving Len exactly what he wanted back when he was alive.

It'll be just the two of us.

Staying here forever.

It isn't long before Len gives up. He has to, now that this body we share is winding down. My heartbeat slows. My thoughts fade.

Then, when every bit of strength has left me, I open my mouth and let the dark water pour in.

M ovement.

In the darkness.

I sense it on the distant edge of my consciousness. Two bits of motion going in separate directions. Something approaching while something else slithers away.

The motion that's stayed has moved to my ankle, the touch feathery as it unwinds the rope knotted there.

Then I'm lifted.

Up, up, up.

Soon I'm breaking the surface and my lungs start working overtime, somehow doing two things at once. Hacking out water while gulping down air. It goes on like this. Out, in, out, in. When it's over, there's no more water, only sweet, blessed air.

I feel more movement now. Something being slipped over my shoulders and tightened around my chest until I'm floating.

I open my eyes to a sky that's dazzlingly pink.

My eyes.

Not his.

My body, containing only my thoughts, my heart, my soul.

Len is gone.

I know it the same way a sick person can tell their fever has broken.

Len has poured himself from one vessel—me—into another.

Lake Greene.

The place he came from and where he'll hopefully remain.

I turn away from the sky to the person swimming beside me. Katherine beams, her smile brighter and more beautiful than any picture she's ever been in.

"Don't freak out," she says. "But I think you almost drowned."

W hat are we going to tell people?" Tom says to Katherine. "I tried to keep it a secret, but word got out you were missing. The police were involved."

He looks my way, his gaze not quite accusatory but sharp enough to know he's still annoyed, despite the fact that Katherine's only back—literally her old self—because of me. He made that clear when we returned to the Fitzgeralds' basement. At first, Tom looked ready to kill us both. But once Katherine started reciting bits of knowledge only she could know, he became overjoyed at her presence. Less so with mine.

The three of us now sit with Eli in the Royce living room. Tom and Katherine are both freshly showered and changed. I'm in a set of Versace athleisure wear borrowed from Katherine that's as comfortable as it is ridiculous.

"We tell them something as close to the truth as possible," I say. "You two fought."

Katherine turns to her husband, surprised. "We did?"

"You decked me." Tom leans in to give her a good look at the still-fading bruise under his eye. "Well, *he* did."

Len's name hasn't been uttered once since Katherine and I returned. I suspect it makes them uncomfortable acknowledging the person who, for all intents and purposes, possessed her.

I'm fine with that. I never need to hear his name again.

"The police will believe that, after the fight, Katherine left in a huff," I say. "She went for a long hike in the mountains, leaving everything behind."

"And she got lost in the woods," Tom says.

I reply with a nod. "You thought she left you, which is why you never reported her missing and posted that photo to Instagram. You were too embarrassed to admit your marriage was falling apart."

Katherine touches the bruise on her husband's face. "Poor Tom. This must have been so hard on you."

"I thought you were lost forever," he says with a quiver in his voice and tears in his eyes. "I had no idea how to bring you back."

"I tried," Katherine says. "I tried so hard to keep it from happening."

"So you knew what was going on?" Eli says.

"Sort of." Katherine hugs herself, as if chilled by the memory. "Obviously, there were the blackouts. One minute I was fine, the next I was waking up somewhere with no memory of how I got there. Then there was this weird sixth sense. I knew things I had no reason for knowing. Like your phone number, Casey. Or those binoculars on your porch. I never owned a pair. I was never into birding. But when I saw them, I suddenly had these memories of buying them, of holding them in my hands, of watching the trees across the lake right from that porch. And then they went away."

I'm chilled myself as Katherine tells us what it felt like to have someone else slowly take control. Even though I, too, experienced it, I at least knew what was happening. For Katherine, it seemed like she was losing her mind.

"I didn't fully figure out what was going on until the night I looked it up online. I felt stupid Googling articles about haunted lakes and ghosts in mirrors. But then I found stories about other people who had experienced the same thing I was going through. Strange memories of things they never experienced and sudden weakness and this sense that they were slowly losing control. That's when I knew what was happening."

It also turned out to be a moment I witnessed from the other side of the lake. Watching Katherine intently scan the computer, her shock writ large on her face.

"You should have told me," Tom says.

"You would have thought I was crazy. Which is exactly how I felt. So I kissed you on the cheek and suggested we go back to bed. I know it sounds foolish, but I hoped it was temporary. Like I would go to sleep and wake up in the morning feeling like my old self."

"Instead, the opposite happened," Eli cuts in.

"Yes," Katherine says with a grim nod. "The last thing I remember is Tom going back to bed and me going into the bathroom. I stared into the mirror, panicking as my reflection began to blur. Everything went out of focus. Then there was nothing but darkness. I have no memories after that besides waking up in the boat this morning. But the second I came to, I knew it was over and that he was gone. Thanks to you, Casey. It's like I was lost and you found me."

"Which is what we'll tell the police," I say. "I couldn't sleep, went out in the boat to see if there was any storm damage to the shore, and saw you stumbling out of the woods in a daze."

All in all, it's a good story. Not too far out of the realm of possibility, when ignoring the whole being-possessed-by-a-drowned-man thing. I think people will believe it.

Even Wilma.

With our story straight, I get ready to go to my house across the lake. I glimpse it through the giant windows of the Royces' living room, looking as warm and inviting as a nest. One I want to return to as soon as possible.

Before leaving, Tom shakes my hand and says, "I understand why you did what you did. That doesn't mean I liked being locked in that basement for twelve hours. Or having the police after me."

"Or being hit with a table leg?" I say, cringing at how unhinged I must have seemed to him at the time.

"Especially that." Tom's pissed-off look softens, as does his voice. "But it was all worth it because you brought Katherine back to me. So, thank you."

"You're forgetting that Katherine also brought me back," I say. "I think that makes us even."

Tom stays behind as Eli, Katherine, and I step onto the patio. Outside, the day is bright with promise. With the sun on my face and a breeze brushing my still-damp hair, I can't quite believe that, two hours earlier, I was at the bottom of the lake, ready to remain there.

I don't regret making that choice.

But someone else made a different choice. Katherine decided that I should live, and who am I to disagree? Especially when there's still unfinished business to take care of.

It's Eli, of course, who reminds me of that. Before walking to his house next door, he places a folded handkerchief in my hands. "You know what to do with this more than me," he says. "I hope it doesn't get you into too much trouble."

"It very well could," I say. "But I'm ready to deal with the consequences."

Eli departs with a hug, leaving me and Katherine alone to stroll to the dock and my boat tied to the end of it. She loops her arm through mine and makes sure our shoulders bump—so touchy-feely even without Len's influence.

"I need to tell you something," she says. "Those memories that I talked about? The ones that weren't mine but I had them anyway? I got some of them before he took over. Others arrived while I was unconscious and he was completely in control. But all of them are still there."

My pace quickens. I don't want to know what Len remembered.

"You made him very happy, Casey. I know that's probably not what you want to hear, but it's true. He truly did love you, and what he did—that had nothing to do with you. You can't blame yourself for any of it. He would have done it no matter what. In fact, I got the sense your presence in his life kept him from trying earlier. He thought he had too much to lose."

"Yet he still went ahead and did it anyway," I say.

Katherine stops walking and turns me until we're face-to-face. "Which is why I don't judge you for what you did to him."

Of course she knows. Len is as imprinted on Katherine as a tattoo. God help her.

"I probably would have done the same thing," she says. "It's easy to talk about justice and responsibility and taking matters into your own hands when it's not happening to you. But this did happen to you, Casey. And you did what a lot of women would have done in your shoes."

"I'm afraid that won't matter to the police."

"Maybe not," Katherine says. "But I don't plan on telling them anything about it. This will stay just between us."

I desperately wish it could, but this goes beyond me and Katherine. There are others to consider, including the friends and families of three women still submerged in the frigid darkness of Lake Greene. They're at the forefront of my thoughts as I climb into the boat and make my way across the water. I keep a grip on my phone, still in its Ziploc bag, ready to call Wilma Anson as soon as I get back to the house.

The person standing on my dock delays that plan a bit.

"Hey," Boone says, giving me a wary wave as I cut the motor and bring the boat into the dock.

"Hey yourself."

I let Boone tie up the boat because, one, he seems eager to do it and, two, I'm exhausted. Definitely far too tired to be talking to him at the moment, although it's clear that can't be avoided.

"Eli told me you found Katherine," he says, shooting a glance across the water. "Is she okay?"

"She's fine."

I give him an abridged version of the official story as we walk from the dock to the porch. I collapse into a rocking chair. Boone remains standing.

"I'm relieved to hear that she's safe and sound," he says. "Good for her. And good for Tom."

He stops talking after that, leaving me to pick up the slack. "Was that why you came by?"

"Yes. And also to tell you that I'm leaving the lake. I've done all the work I can do at the Mitchell place, so I found a nice studio apartment a few towns over. Now you no longer need to worry thinking there's a murderer living next door."

While Boone's voice retains a hint of the anger I heard the last time we talked, another mood rides on his words. It sounds like sadness.

"I'm sorry I wasn't completely honest. But it should be clear to you by now that I had nothing to do with what happened to Katherine or those other missing girls," Boone says, reminding me that he still knows nothing about Len's crime—or how I made him pay for them.

Twice.

"As for what happened to my wife," Boone says, "yes, I was investigated after her death. And, yes, there was a time when people thought I had killed her. There was no proof of that, but there also wasn't any proof that I hadn't. At least, proof that I was willing to show people."

I look up at him, surprised and suddenly insatiably curious.

"There was more to it than what you told the police?"

"My wife didn't fall down the stairs by accident." Boone stops, takes a breath. "She killed herself."

I flinch, shocked.

"I know because she left a note telling me she was sorry and that she had been unhappy for a long time—something I thought I knew but didn't. Not really. She had been more than unhappy. She'd been plunged into darkness, and I blame myself for never noticing how bad it was until it was too late."

Boone finally sits.

"I called Wilma as soon as I found the suicide note. She came over, read it, and told me I needed to go public with it. By then we both knew I looked suspicious. It was obvious. But I still couldn't do it. That kind of news would have destroyed her family. I decided that thinking it was an accident would be easier for them to deal with than knowing she'd taken her own life. They, like me, would have blamed themselves for not noticing how much pain she was in and failing to get her the help she needed. I wanted to spare them all of that. And I didn't want people judging Maria for what she did to herself. Or, worse, letting that taint their memories of her. I wanted to shield everyone from the same guilt and pain I was going through. Wilma grudgingly agreed, and together we burned the note."

No wonder Wilma had been so certain about his innocence. Unlike me, she knew the whole story. And what looked like blind trust was in reality a beautiful kind of loyalty.

"She's a good friend," I say.

"She is. She did her thing and convinced everyone we worked with that I was innocent. I hope that, eventually, you'll believe me, too."

I think I already do.

I don't know enough about his marriage to judge Boone—something I had no trouble doing when there was more bourbon than blood in my system. Right now, all I know is that, deep down, Boone seems like a good person who's struggling to tame his demons just like the rest of us. And as someone who's been terrible at demon taming, I should give him the benefit of the doubt.

"Thank you for stating your case," I say. "And I believe you."

"Really?"

"Really."

"Then I should go before you change your mind," Boone says, flashing me that killer grin one last time. Before leaving the porch, he hands me a business card. Printed on it is the name of a nearby church, a day of the week, and a specific time.

"That's the weekly AA meeting I go to," he says. "Just in case you ever feel the need to give it a try. It can be intimidating at first. And it might be easier for you if there's a familiar face present."

Boone leaves before I can respond, already assuming that my answer is no. He's right, of course. I have no intention of subjecting myself to the indignity of standing before a group of strangers and exposing my many, many flaws.

Right now.

But maybe soon.

It all depends on how what I'm about to do next goes.

Before today, I would have downed several drinks before calling Wilma Anson. Now, though, I don't hesitate, even when I know I'm about to be hit with major anger from her and a likely murder charge from her colleagues.

I've avoided it long enough.

It's well past time to come clean.

Wilma is clearly not a fan of the life vest I forced her to put on before leaving the dock. She tugs at it the way a toddler strains at a car seat, unhappy and constricted.

"This really isn't necessary," she says. "I damn well know how to swim."

"Safety first," I say from the back of the boat, where I man the motor in a matching life vest.

I refuse to allow a repeat of what happened to Katherine Royce. Lake Greene might look harmless, especially now as the reflection of sunset makes the water sparkle like pink champagne, but I know it's not.

Len is still down there.

I'm sure of it.

He left me and returned to the water. Now he lurks just beneath the surface, biding his time, waiting for someone else to come along.

Not on my watch.

Wilma also casts a wary glance at the water, although for a completely different reason. The western side of the lake, out of reach from the setting sun, has grown dark. Shadows gather on the shoreline and creep across Lake Greene's surface.

"Can't this wait until tomorrow?" she says.

"Afraid not."

I get why she's tired. It's been a long, trying day. After I called to tell her Katherine had been found, Wilma spent the afternoon interviewing all of us. Katherine and Tom went first, giving their scripted version of events. Katherine swore she got lost on a hike. Tom swore he thought she'd left him. As for where he was last night when Wilma stopped by, he told her he had been worried about the severity of the storm and decided to ride it out in the Fitzgeralds' basement.

I learned all of this from Wilma herself, when she came over to get my statement. I went through my side of the story, which lined up completely with the Royces'. If she still harbored suspicion about any of us, Wilma didn't show it. No surprise there.

"There's something else I need to tell you," I said. "But not here. On the lake."

Now we're here, the lake's surface split into two distinct halves. To the left, heavenly pink. To the right, shimmering black. I steer the boat down the middle, the wake from the motor stirring the light and the dark together.

"I talked to Boone," I say as we glide over the water. "He told me the truth about what happened to his wife."

"Oh." Wilma sounds unsurprised. I suspect she already knows. "Does it change your opinion of him?"

"Yes. And of you. I thought you were a by-the-book kind of gal."

"I am," Wilma says. "But I'm also willing to make an exception now and again. As for Boone, he's one of the good guys, Casey. Trust me on that."

We've reached Old Stubborn, which sits on the shadow side of the lake. I cut the motor, remove the handkerchief from my pocket, and hand it to Wilma. She unfolds it, and her eyes go wide with shock.

Finally, an unambiguous reaction.

"I found them in the basement," I say. "*My* basement."

Wilma doesn't take her eyes off the licenses and locks of hair. She knows what it all means.

"All three women are in the lake." I point to Old Stubborn, now a silhouette in the quickening dusk. "Right there."

"How do you know?"

"Because there's no other place my husband would have put them."

I can't tell her the truth, for oh so many reasons, the chief one being that she wouldn't believe me. My hope is that this—one wife confiding to another—might be enough to convince her.

"I'll bring in divers tomorrow and see if you're right," she says. "If you are, well, life's about to get a whole lot more complicated for you. People will know your husband was a killer—and they're going to judge you for it."

"I know."

"Do you? This is a lot more damning than a tabloid headline," Wilma says. "You're going to spend the rest of your life tied to that man. You can try to distance yourself from his actions, but it'll be hard. You might not be able to show your face in public for a very long time."

I think about that picture of me raising a glass to the paparazzi that ran on the front page of the *New York Post*. "I've already got that covered. Besides, I just want there to be justice. I want everyone who knew and loved Megan, Toni, and Sue Ellen to know what happened to them—and that the man who did it can't hurt anyone else."

Quiet settles over the boat—a moment of silence for the three women whose bodies now rest far below. When it ends, the last of the sunset has slipped behind the mountains, leaving the two of us sitting in the murkiness of early evening.

"How long have you known?" Wilma says.

"Long enough."

"Enough to have taken matters into your own hands?"

"If I did," I say, "it'll be awfully hard to prove now."

I stay motionless, too nervous to move as I wait for Wilma's response. She doesn't make it easy for me, taking almost a full minute before saying, "I suppose you're right."

Hope blooms in my chest. I think that this is maybe, hopefully, possibly one of those rare exceptions Wilma talked about earlier.

"Len was cremated, after all," I say. "There's no body to examine."

"That makes it impossible," Wilma says. "Besides, I see no reason to reopen that case, considering no foul play was ever found in the first place."

I exhale, letting go of most of the fear and tension that had been rising inside of me. Apparently it's my lucky day. I was given a second chance at life by Katherine Royce. Now here's Wilma Anson offering me a third.

I have enough self-awareness to know I don't deserve them.

But I'll accept them all the same.

All that remains is concern over one small loose end.

"What about the postcard?"

"What about it?" Wilma says. "That thing's been examined six ways to Sunday. We'll never know who sent it. In fact, it wouldn't surprise me if it just up and vanished from the evidence room. Things like that get lost all the time."

"But—"

She stops me with a look uncharacteristically readable in every way. "Are you seriously going to argue with me about this? I'm giving you an out, Casey. Take it."

I do.

Gladly.

"Thank you," I say.

"You're welcome." Two seconds pass. "Never bring it up again or I'll change my mind." Two more seconds. "Now take me back to shore. It's late, and you've just given me a shitload of paperwork to deal with."

Night has fully fallen by the time Wilma leaves. I go through the dark house turning on lights before heading to the kitchen to decide what to make for dinner. The glass of bourbon I poured last night still sits on the counter. The sight of it makes me quake with thirst.

I pick it up.

I bring the glass to my lips.

Then, thinking better of it, I take it to the sink and pour the bourbon down the drain.

I do the same with the rest of the bottle.

Then another.

Then *all* the bottles.

My mood swings like a pendulum as I rid the house of alcohol. There's the same fury one feels when clearing out a no-good lover's belongings. There's I-can't-believe-I'm-doing-this laughter. There's excitement, wild and chaotic, along with catharsis and desperation and pride. And there's sadness—a surprise. I didn't expect to be mourning a drinking life that has only brought me trouble. Yet as the contents of bottle after bottle swirl down the drain, I'm overcome with grief.

I'm losing a friend.

A horrible one, yes.

But not always.

Sometimes drinking did indeed bring me great joy, and I'll miss it.

After an hour, the doors to the liquor cabinet sit wide open, exposing only emptiness within. Filling the counter are all the bottles it had once contained, each one now drained. Some were older than a millennial; others were bought this week.

Now only one remains, a five-thousand-dollar bottle of red on the dining room table that belonged to Tom Royce. Knowing how much it cost, I couldn't bring myself to pour that one down the drain. Through the dining room window, I see the Royce house blazing in the October night. I'd return the wine now if it weren't so late and I weren't so tired.

Emptying all those bottles has left me exhausted. Or maybe that's just a symptom of withdrawal. Already, I'm dreading the myriad side effects that are surely in store.

A new Casey is on her way.

A strange feeling. I'm me—but also not. Which, come to think of it, is probably how Katherine felt before Len completely took over.

I'm just not myself lately, she told me. *I haven't felt right for days.*

The memory arrives with the force of a thunderclap. Loud. Jarring. Charged with electricity.

Because what Katherine told me that day doesn't track with everything else. When I learned that Len had returned and was controlling her like a marionette, I assumed he was the reason she'd felt so weird, so weak.

He was partly to blame, of course. I learned that myself from the short time he was inside me.

But Len wasn't the sole reason Katherine felt that way.

I know because when she confessed to not feeling quite herself, it was the morning we had coffee on the porch. One day *after* I pulled her out of the lake. But according to Katherine, she felt off earlier than that—*before* Len entered the picture.

It was like my entire body stopped working.

I turn away from the window and look at the bottle of wine sitting on the table.

Then I grab my phone and call Wilma Anson.

The call immediately goes to voicemail. After the beep, I don't leave my name or number. I simply shout what I need to say and hope Wilma hears it in time.

"That piece of wineglass I made you take? Did a report come back from the lab yet? Because I think I was right, Wilma. I think Tom Royce was— *is*—trying to murder his wife."

I end the call, rush out to the porch, and grab the binoculars. It takes me a second to adjust the zoom and the focus. The Royce house blurs and unblurs before becoming crystal clear.

I scan the house, checking each room.

The kitchen is empty.

So is the office directly above it and the master bedroom to the right.

I finally locate Katherine in the living room. She's on the sofa, propped up by throw pillows and lying under a blanket. On the coffee table beside her sits a large glass of red wine.

Still holding the binoculars to my eyes with one hand, I reach for my phone with the other. It bobbles in my hand as my thumb slides along the screen, scrolling to Katherine's number.

Across the lake, she reaches for the wine, her hand curling around the glass.

I grip the phone tighter and hit the call button.

Katherine brings the glass to her lips, about to take a sip.

The phone rings once.

She perks up at the sound, the hand holding the glass going still.

Second ring.

Katherine looks around the room, trying to locate her phone.

Third ring.

She spots it sitting on a nearby ottoman and sets the glass back down on the coffee table.

Fourth ring.

Katherine reaches for the phone, the blanket slipping from her lap. She clutches it with one hand while the other stretches for the phone.

Fifth ring.

"Hang up the phone, Casey."

I lower the binoculars and whirl around as Tom emerges from my house, joining me on the porch. The bottle of wine is in his hand, gripped by the handle like a club. He smacks the blunt end into the open palm of his free hand as he comes closer.

Katherine's voice squawks from my phone as she finally answers. "Hello?"

Tom wrenches the phone from my hand, hangs up, and flings it over the porch railing. The phone lands with a crack in the darkness below before bleating out a ring. Katherine calling me back.

"By now, I bet you wish you hadn't been so nosy," Tom says. "None of this would be happening if you had just stayed out of it. Katherine would be dead, you'd be here drinking yourself into a stupor, and I'd have enough money to save my company. But you just had to rescue her and then watch us nonstop, like our lives were a fucking reality show. And you ruined everything once you got the police involved. Now I can't just slowly poison Katherine. Now I need to be extra careful, cover my tracks, make it truly look like an accident. That's why I kept her tied up in the basement instead of killing her outright. Lucky for me, your husband had a lot of interesting things to say about that."

I flinch—a reaction I can't prevent because I'm too focused on the heavy glass of the wine bottle still slapping into Tom's palm.

"We talked a lot while he was in that basement," he says. "Chatted for hours. There wasn't much else to do once your detective friend started breathing down my neck. You want to know the most surprising thing he told me?"

He lifts the bottle, brings it down.

Slap.

"That I killed him," I say.

"Not just that. It was *how* you did it that was so fascinating."

Slap.

"A perfect murder," Tom says. "Far better than what was in that play of yours. That's where I first got the idea, but you already know that.

Poisoning my wife little by little so she dies of something else and I inherit everything."

Slap.

"But your husband—good old talkative Len—gave me a much better idea. Antihistamine in some wine. Make her good and drowsy. Drop her into the water and let her sink. The police around these parts never seem to suspect foul play when a person drowns. As you well know."

Slap.

Somewhere below, my phone stops ringing as Katherine gives up.

"She's probably taking a sip right now." Tom gestures to the binoculars still clutched in my hands. "Go ahead and watch. I know you enjoy doing that."

I raise the binoculars, needing both hands to keep them from shaking. The Royce house jitters anyway, as if an earthquake is taking place. Through the shimmying lenses, I see that Katherine has moved to the living room window. She stares outside, the glass of wine back in her hand.

She brings it to her lips and drinks.

"Katherine, no!"

I don't know if Katherine hears my scream flying across the lake because Tom is upon me in an instant. I swing the binoculars at his head. He blocks them with his arm before slamming the bottle against mine.

I drop the binoculars as pain shoots through my arm.

I cry out, stumble backwards against a rocking chair, and collapse onto the porch.

"Now you know how it feels," Tom says.

He swings the bottle again. It whooshes past my face, mere inches away.

I scramble backwards along the porch, my right arm throbbing as Tom continues to swing the bottle, slicing the air, bringing it closer.

And closer.

And closer.

"I know how to make you disappear," Tom says. "Len told me that, too. All it takes is some rope, some rocks, some deep, deep water. You'll vanish, just like those girls he killed. No one will ever know what happened to you."

He swings the bottle again, and I scoot out of the way, edging onto the top of the porch steps.

Tom swings again and I duck, trying to keep my balance. A moment of weightlessness follows—cruel in its deception that I might be able to resist the pull of gravity. It ends with a thud onto the next step.

Then I tumble, backflipping down the steps, the edge of each one feeling like a punch.

To my hip.

To my back.

To my face.

When it's over, I'm flat-backed on the ground, clanging with pain and woozy from the fall. My vision blurs. Tom drifts in and out of focus as he follows me down the steps.

Slowly.

One at a time.

The bottle again smacking into his hand.

Slap.

I try to scream, but nothing comes out. I'm too hurt, too out of breath, too scared. All I can do is try to stand, stumble toward the water, hope someone will see me.

Tom catches up to me at the lake's edge. I'm sloshing into the water when he snags my shirt, tugs me toward him, swings the bottle.

I lurch to the left, and the bottle crashes down onto my right shoulder. More screaming pain.

The blow knocks me to my knees. I splash deeper into the lake, the water now at my hips, cold as ice. The chill zaps me with just enough energy so I can twist toward Tom, wrap my arms around his knees, and pull him down with me.

We submerge as one—a seething, writhing mass of tangled arms and kicking legs. The wine bottle slips from Tom's hand, vanishing into the water just as he drags me out of it. He wraps his hands around my neck and, squeezing, dunks me back under.

I run out of air instantly. The lake is so cold and Tom's hands are so tight around my neck and I can't see anything in the dark water. Shoved to the bottom of the lake, I kick and writhe and thrash as my chest gets tighter and tighter. So tight I fear it's going to explode.

Yet all I can think about is Len.

In this very same lake.

Waiting for me to die in the dark water so he can take over once more.

I can't let that happen.

I fucking refuse.

I run a hand along the lake bed, seeking out a rock I can use to hit Tom. Maybe it'll be enough to make him stop pressing against my throat. Maybe he'll let go entirely. Maybe I'll be able to escape.

Instead of a rock, my fingernails brush glass.

The wine bottle.

I reach for it, grab it by the neck, swing.

The bottle bursts from the surface, slicing through the air before slamming into the side of Tom's skull.

His hands fall away from my neck as he grunts, sways, topples over. I rise from the water. Tom splats into it, facedown and motionless.

On the other side of the lake, police cars have started to gather in the Royces' driveway. Their lights reflect off the water in spinning streaks of red, white, and blue as officers swarm the back patio and rush inside.

Wilma got my message.

Thank God.

I try to stand, but am only able to bring myself into a kneeling position. When I attempt to yell to the cops, my cries come out a muted croak. My throat's too battered.

Next to me, Tom remains facedown in the water. Just above his left ear is a small crater where the bottle connected with his skull. Blood pours from it, mixing with the water and forming a black cloud that blooms and spreads.

I know he's dead the moment I flip him over. His eyes are as dull as old nickels and his body eerily still. I touch his neck, finding no pulse. Meanwhile, the blood continues to ooze from the dent in his head.

I finally stand, bending my legs to my will. The wine bottle, still intact, remains gripped in my hand. I take it to shore, placing it in a strip of rocks between lake and land.

Behind me, Tom jerks back to life with a watery gasp.

Not a shock.

Not in this lake.

I march back into the water and grab his arms. I try not to look at him, but it can't be avoided as I drag him ashore, making sure no part of his body is still touching the lake. He catches my eye and smiles.

"We need to stop meeting like this," he says before hissing the nickname I'm both dreading and expecting. "Cee."

"We will," I say.

I grab the bottle, smash it against the rocks, and, with a stab and a twist, drive the jagged edge into his throat until I'm certain he'll never be able to speak again.

LATER

I'm the last one awake.

Of course.

It's easy to sleep in now that the sun's path in the sky has changed with the seasons, entering the row of windows at an oblique angle that misses the bed entirely. When I do rise, the smell of coffee and the sounds of cooking are already slipping under the door. Everyone else, it seems, has been up for ages.

Downstairs, I find the kitchen abuzz with activity. Marnie and my mother huddle at the stove, debating the correct way to make French toast. I kiss them both on the cheek and let them bicker while I pour a cup of coffee.

In the dining room, Eli and Boone set the table. Six place settings in all.

"Morning, sleepyhead," Boone says. "We thought you'd never get up."

I take a sip of coffee. "I was tired. Had a long night."

"New Year's Eve will do that to you."

We all rang in the new year on the back porch, raising glasses of ginger ale in a toast at the stroke of midnight.

It was a good night.

That got even better.

"Casey could learn a thing or two from you about being an early riser," my mother tells Boone from the kitchen. "When I got up this morning, you were already awake and your bed already made."

Across the dining room, Boone gives me a sneaky look that almost makes me break out into laughter. We're still not sure if my mother hasn't yet figured out that we're together or if she realized it weeks ago and is now toying with us. Either way, it's a game we all seem to enjoy. Unlike Monopoly, which Boone beats me at every damn time.

I haven't told him the truth about what really happened to Katherine and how I knew that Len murdered three women. The same goes for Marnie and my mother. They, like most of America, still think Katherine got lost on a hike—her sense of direction addled by the small doses of poison Tom had been slipping her—and that I found the hair and driver's licenses of the three missing women while going through Len's belongings.

I plan on telling Boone, Marnie, and my mother the truth someday. I really do. I just need more time. It was hard enough admitting to Boone that I'd watched him from the porch as he stood naked on the Mitchells' dock.

He told me he had assumed that.

He also suggested I do it again as soon as the weather gets warmer.

As for everything else, that story is a little bit harder to tell, and I'm not ready for the honeymoon phase of whatever it is Boone and I are doing to end. Also, at least for the time being, I need one thing in my life not tainted by the events of October.

The day after Tom's attack, a state police search-and-rescue team swarmed the lake. The bodies of Megan Keene, Toni Burnett, and Sue Ellen Stryker were all recovered at the same time, found exactly where Len said they were.

The press lost their collective minds. I can only imagine how many editors needed smelling salts after hearing Mixer founder Tom Royce tried to poison fashion icon Katherine Royce but was stopped by Troubled Casey Fletcher, who had just learned her dead husband was a serial killer.

Talk about a headline.

It was madness at Lake Greene for more than a week. So many press vehicles rolled down the gravel road circling the lake that police had to put up barricades to keep them away. That's when the helicopters arrived, hovering just above the water, photographers leaning out the sides like they were Navy SEALs about to leap into battle. One reporter even hiked two miles in heels to ring the doorbell and ask some questions. Eli gave her a bag of ice for her sore feet and sent her packing.

Since then, I've rarely left the lake house. Unlike the Casey of old, who thought nothing of drunkenly toasting the paparazzi camped outside a bar, I know any appearance I make will only fan the media flames. Although I engendered a lot of goodwill for saving Katherine's life, Wilma Anson was right that I would be judged for Len's crimes. While most people don't think I helped him murder three young women, everyone blames me for not realizing it while he was alive. I'm okay with that for two reasons.

One, I know the truth.

Two, I also still blame myself.

When I do go out, it's incognito. I attended the funerals of all three of Len's victims—an anonymous woman in oversized sunglasses and a floppy hat sitting in the back of sparsely attended churches. Katherine wanted to go along, but I discouraged it by telling her she'd stick out too much. In truth, I wanted to be alone so that I could whisper a prayer to Megan, Toni, and Sue Ellen.

I apologized for not helping to find them sooner and I prayed that they would forgive me.

I desperately hope they heard it.

"Breakfast will be ready in five minutes," Marnie says. "Go fetch Katherine. She's out on the porch."

I grab one of the many parkas now hanging in the foyer and head to the back porch. Katherine's in one of the rocking chairs, nursing a cup of coffee and wearing a designer coat that makes it look like she just flew in from St. Moritz.

"Happy New Year," she says, beaming up at me from beneath a hood lined with fake fur.

"Likewise."

Katherine put her glass castle on the market and moved into my family's lake house the moment both of us left the hospital. Unlike mine, her reputation has only improved since the events of October. That sort of thing happens when your husband tries to kill you—and the police have a broken wineglass tainted with poison to prove it.

Also unlike me, Katherine's been out and about on a full publicity gauntlet. She landed on the cover of *People*, told her story on *Good Morning America*, wrote a personal essay for *Vanity Fair*. In all of them, she took great pains to mention how good of a friend I've been and how I went through just as much trauma as she did. Because of this—and because those daredevil photographers caught Katherine and me laughing on the porch—the media has dubbed us the Merry Widows.

I'm not going to lie. I kind of like it.

"Was it weird not to be drinking champagne at midnight?" Katherine says.

It's been ten weeks since my last real drink. Ten long, slow, white-knuckle weeks. But I'm doing better than I did last week, which was better than the week before. My urge to drink has lessened in that time. That encourages me, even though I know the urge won't permanently leave me. That thirst will haunt me like a phantom limb—missing yet keenly felt.

But I can manage.

The meetings help.

So does having a support system that now fills every bedroom of this once-empty house.

"Honestly, it was a refreshing change of pace," I say.

"Cheers to that."

We clink mugs and look out at the lake. It froze over in mid-November, and will likely remain that way until March. The valley got a foot of snow two days before Christmas, turning everything into a gleaming white oasis right out of Currier and Ives. The other day, Marnie and I slipped our feet into too-tight ice skates and slid around the lake just like we did when we were kids.

"Do you really think they're gone?" Katherine says.

I look at her, surprised. Despite everything the two of us have gone through, we've barely talked about it in private. I think it's because we're both afraid of cursing the present by mentioning the past.

This morning, though, the dawn of the new year brings a sense of hopefulness bright enough to eclipse whatever darkness talking about it might summon.

"I think they are," I say. "I *hope* they are."

"What if they're not? What if both of them are still out there, waiting?"

I've thought about that a lot, especially on nights when I'm craving a drink and end up roaming the house like a restless spirit. I look out at the water and wonder if Len somehow managed to return there, once more waiting for someone to fall victim to the lake, or if Tom has taken his place in the dark depths. Because we still have no idea how and why any of it happened, it's hard to put it to rest. Maybe the water of Lake Greene is touched by something both magical and vile. Or maybe it was Len himself, cursed by his horrible deeds.

Either way, I know there's a chance—however small—that it could happen again.

If that day comes, I'll be here.

And I'll be ready.

ACKNOWLEDGMENTS

This book would not exist without the assistance and support of many wonderful people. Chief among them are my editor, Maya Ziv, and my agent, Michelle Brower, who cheered me on from the moment I first told them the bonkers plot of this book. Without their encouragement, there'd be no Casey, no Katherine, no house across Lake Greene.

Thank you to Emily Canders, Katie Taylor, Stephanie Cooper, Lexy Cassola, Christine Ball, Ivan Held, John Parsley, and everyone at Dutton and Penguin Random House for their hard work and support. On the business side, I'm indebted to Erin Files, Arlie Johansen, Sean Daily, Shenel Ekici-Moling, Kate Mack, and Maggie Cooper.

Sarah Dutton deserves a place in the First Reader Hall of Fame for diving into uncertain waters each and every book. Her keen insights and unvarnished opinions are invaluable.

Thank you to all the family members and friends who continue to cheer me on from the sidelines. Even though we saw a lot less of each other in the past two years, you are always in my thoughts.

Finally, massive thanks go to Michael Livio, whose love and patience helped me get through writing another book during a global pandemic. I truly couldn't do this without you.

BONUS
CHAPTER

THE OTHER SIDE

I.

She jolts into consciousness, gasping in air before coughing it out along with other things. Wet, sticky things. Water and snot and slime. As she hacks it all up, she realizes she has no idea where she is. Or, at first, even her name.

Katherine, she thinks after a worrisome second. *My name is Katherine Royce.*

More thoughts follow. How she was swimming in Lake Greene. How her body suddenly seized up like a rusty car engine. How she sank under the water before everything went black. Now she's floating, not sinking, thanks to a life vest presumably provided by a woman in the water next to her. A woman she recognizes, the name arriving faster than her own.

Casey Fletcher. The actress in the house across the lake.

Katherine looks at her and says, "What just happened?"

"Don't freak out." Casey pauses. "But I think you almost drowned."

II.

Katherine reclines on the white sofa in the living room. Tom picked it out, which means it cost a fortune. So much so that she always hesitates a moment before sitting down. She feels that way about the whole house, to be honest. It's too pristine, too sterile. The kind of place that looks nice from a distance but feels oppressive when you're stuck in the thick of it.

Tom loves it, of course. Her husband chooses design over comfort every damn time. Not her. That's one of the many reasons she was happy to leave modeling behind.

Now she's here, aimlessly flipping through a magazine that once upon a time had put her on the cover and trying not to think about drowning. Even hours later, she's still rattled.

The first thing Katherine did when she got home that day was rush upstairs to the bedroom and put on her wedding band and engagement ring. Tom gets annoyed when she doesn't wear them, which is sometimes the reason she chooses not to put them on. But back on they went, scraping over the knuckles of her ring finger as she stared at the lake from the big bedroom window.

Casey Fletcher was still out there in her boat, motoring to her house on the opposite shore. Katherine wasn't surprised to learn she was also at Lake Greene. The big surprise was that she actually liked Casey. All the tabloids had made her seem like a rampaging drunk. Someone to avoid at all costs. The person Katherine met was the complete opposite. Capable. Quietly sardonic. Not to mention misunderstood.

And sad.

And lonely.

That's what really drew Katherine to her.

She saw the loneliness in Casey's eyes and realized it resembled her own lost gaze.

After showering and changing into fresh clothes, Katherine stared at her reflection in the bathroom mirror, in the unlikely hope she was wrong about the similarity. Instead, she didn't recognize herself.

Literally.

She truly had no idea whose face she was looking at. It was the same thing she experienced when coming to in the water. Disorienting blankness, followed by a sudden recognition, as if a flashlight had been flicked on inside her skull.

"You are Katherine Royce," she said, even though she didn't quite feel like herself.

She still doesn't. Something seems . . . off. A persistent ache has infiltrated her body, leaving her joints stiff, her muscles tired. Her heart flutters at irregular moments, thrumming to its own strange beat. That's been happening a lot lately, but never like this.

Plus, there's a new worry to contend with. Everything from her waist to her neck feels unsettled. Like something is moving inside her. Something that shouldn't be there.

I'm pregnant, she thinks. An alarming prospect. Also unlikely. She's on birth control, and she honestly can't remember the last time she and Tom had sex. It's more likely she's coming down with a stomach bug or, frankly, simply unnerved by the day's events.

Katherine rises from the couch and goes to the living room window. And wall, she guesses, seeing how they are one and the same. An expanse of glass rising from floor to ceiling, separating the pristine inside from the wild outside. Staring through the glass, Katherine sighs. She might be ambivalent about the house, but there's no question about how much she adores the lake. She loves its silence, its beauty, the way the water changes colors throughout the day. Right now, it's dusted by the light of sunset, rippling in shades of pink and orange.

She loves it enough that it was easy for Tom to suggest they come here for a week or two and make it sound like it was her idea.

"I think you'd love to go back to Lake Greene for a little bit, wouldn't you?"

"I guess so," Katherine had replied. "I bet the foliage is gorgeous right now."

Tom kissed her forehead. "You always know the best time for us to take a break."

Casey Fletcher's cottage sits right against the water's edge, quiet and cozy. That's the kind of lake house Katherine wants. A place where appearances aren't important. A place where she can simply be herself.

Katherine drifts to the living room bar and pours herself a whiskey. She takes a sip, returns to the wall of glass, looks back across the lake. This time, her gaze skips to the other house on the opposite shore. The one where Boone Conrad is staying.

Similar to Casey's place, his cottage is rustic and cozy. She liked it immediately. She liked Boone, too. He was easygoing and even easier to talk to. She never felt like she had to impress him. Just being herself was enough. That's why she continued to go over there, even when it became clear Boone thought something more was happening between them. Definitely *not* her intention. Sure, he's hot, but she's a) married; b) not a cheater; and c) pretty sure they wouldn't be a good fit even if A and B weren't factors.

Still, she feels bad about the way she handled things. So bad that she pulls out her phone and, after listening to confirm that Tom isn't lurking nearby, dials his number. It rings five times before going to voice mail.

"Hey, Boone. It's Katherine." She cringes. Of course he knows it's her, which is likely why he isn't answering. "I'm sorry about earlier today. I shouldn't have come over there. It was wrong of me to just show up like that. Especially just to tell you to leave me alone. You do, but I definitely could have phrased it better. You're a great guy, but nothing is going to happen, for many reasons, so it's just best—"

A noise rises from the next room. A creak so faint she's not sure it's even real. On the edge of her vision, she sees something reflected in the great wall of window.

Tom.

In the dining room.

Just standing there.

Katherine ends the call, puts the phone behind her back, turns to face him.

"Who were you just talking to?" Tom strolls toward her, not a hint of jealousy in his voice. That would be easier to deal with—and far too simple for Tom, who enjoys being inscrutable. Most times, Katherine's never quite sure what he's thinking. When she told him she'd almost drowned, for example, she couldn't tell if he was shaken or unsurprised.

"I was asked to consider a photo shoot," she says as she slides the phone into her back pocket and raises her hands in innocence. "I told them I was flattered but that my modeling days are over."

"I was hoping you were talking to Casey Fletcher," Tom says. "I think we should go over there tonight and thank her."

"I did thank her."

"I didn't. Don't you think I deserve the opportunity to thank the person who saved your life?"

"It's just that I'm not feeling too great," Katherine says. "Maybe another time?"

"It won't be long." Tom gives her a look, his mood still unreadable. "Why don't you want us to go over there?"

Because she's ashamed of him, that's why. A realization that brings only more shame. Tom is never *not* hustling. Always too eager to impress, to strive, to get more, more, more. She had admired those qualities once. When they got married, she was perfectly fine with letting him be the ambitious one. Years later, she finds it more exhausting than endearing, and she's not eager to subject Casey to Tom's particular brand of intensity.

Then there's the fact that she truly doesn't feel great. All her symptoms—if that's what they can be called—have grown worse in the past five minutes.

Her head pounds.

Her heart gallops.

Something seems to twist around her organs.

"Something's wrong with me," she wants to tell Tom. She doesn't because she's not quite sure it's true. This could all be in her head. Her imagination running wild after a brush with death.

"I do," she says instead, forcing a smile. "We'll go after dinner. It's a great idea."

III.

It was a terrible idea.

She realized it the moment they arrived. Tom did exactly what she feared and came on too strong. Instead of impressing Casey, it made her shrink in his presence. Katherine didn't help matters by adding her own weirdness to the mix. When she spotted a pair of binoculars on Casey's porch, she was hit with a sense of déjà vu. She remembered buying a pair, clutching them in her hands, holding them to her eyes. The feeling was so strong that she said, "Oh, wow. I used to have a pair just like those."

She had no idea where it came from. She has never owned a pair of binoculars in her life. Yet the words popped out of her mouth, unplanned, unstoppable, and unnerving. Katherine felt like a ventriloquist's dummy. A horrifying sensation that blessedly went away as quickly as it came.

The downside was she had to keep up the ruse, asking Casey about birding and pretending to be annoyed at Tom. By the time his ridiculously expensive wine was finally poured, she needed a drink so badly she downed a whole glass in a single gulp. Another terrible idea.

Now Katherine is slumped in an Adirondack chair by the fire pit, regretting both the visit and the wine. Still, she tries to pretend she's enjoying herself, which isn't easy. Not with Eli asking her about how she almost drowned earlier and her unwisely bringing up that girl who vanished last summer.

"Sue Ellen," Eli says solemnly. "Sue Ellen Stryker."

Hearing the name summons an image in Katherine's mind. A sweet girl with a shy smile. Katherine instantly knows it's Sue Ellen, even though she's equally sure she's never seen a picture of her. But she had to at some point, right? How else would she know what she looked like?

"Tom and I were renting a place there that summer," she says, hoping it masks how unsettled she feels. "It was all so awful. Did they ever find her?"

"No," Eli says.

Katherine gets another mental picture of Sue Ellen, this time submerged in water. Her eyes are wide-open and her body is completely still as she sinks, drifting down until she disappears. Accompanying the image is another slithery feeling in her gut, rising upward, circling her heart and snaking between her lungs.

"So awful," she says, describing both the feeling inside her and the vision of Sue Ellen vanishing into the depths.

"Only swim at night," Eli says. "That's what my mother told me. She heard it from her own mother. My grandmother was a very superstitious woman. She grew up in Eastern Europe. Believed in ghosts and curses. The dead terrified her."

Casey sits down next to him. "Eli, please. After what happened to Katherine today, I'm not sure anyone wants to hear about that right now."

She's wrong about that. Katherine enjoys the prospect of a campfire tale. She hopes it will take her mind off this strange feeling inside her. She reminds herself—somewhat hopefully—that it could all be a combination of shock, stress, and too much wine.

"I don't mind," she says. "I actually like telling ghost stories around the fire. It reminds me of summer camp. I was a Camp Nightingale girl."

She shivers, thinking about that camp and the three girls who vanished there a few years after she stopped going. So many missing girls. A sobering thought. At least, it should be. Yet Katherine feels anything but sober. Her head, already spinning after downing that glass of wine, now whirls even faster.

"And I'm curious why swimming at night is better than daytime," Tom says.

Eli jerks his head toward the lake. "At night, you can't see your reflection on the water. Centuries ago, before people knew any better, it was a common belief that reflective surfaces could trap the souls of the dead."

"I read about that. In the Victorian era, people used to cover all the mirrors after someone died," Tom says.

"They did," Eli says. "But it wasn't just mirrors they were worried about. Any reflective surface was capable of capturing a soul."

Katherine's entire body clenches.

"Like a lake?" she says, trying to hide the urgency of her question with a smile.

Eli touches the tip of his nose. "Exactly."

The thing inside Katherine twitches. There *is* something there. She's certain of it now. That slippery slick movement is definitely *not* her imagination.

"And it wasn't just the Victorians and their superstitious relatives in Eastern Europe who thought this way," Eli says. "The tribes that lived in this area long before any European settlers arrived believed that those trapped souls could overtake the souls of the living, and that if you saw your own reflection in this very lake after someone had recently died in it, it meant you were allowing yourself to be possessed."

Possessed.

The word looms large in Katherine's thoughts. That's what this feels like. Something foreign. Inside her. Taking over.

But that's ridiculous. What Eli is saying is nothing more than a ghost story, frightening only to little kids with big imaginations.

Yet that doesn't mean there wasn't something in the lake.

Katherine's seen the clickbait horror stories about tapeworms and flesh-eating diseases and fungi that consume people's brains. Something equally as stealthy and vicious could have slipped into her when—well, she doesn't quite know what happened in that water. She was unconscious for some of it. Blind to the knowledge that her body was being invaded. And whatever it is remains there, curling around her internal organs, growing.

Her head spins even faster, fueled by wine and nerves and worried thoughts that make her only vaguely aware of what's happening around her.

Casey slamming a wine bottle against the porch steps and shouting.

Eli's soft reply.

Casey, now sounding guilty, saying something in return.

"I don't feel too good," Katherine says, her thoughts unintentionally reaching her voice. "Not good at all."

"What's wrong?" Tom says.

"I'm dizzy." Such a weak description of what she's feeling. But it's all she can muster. Suddenly too anxious to remain seated, she stands. Or tries to. Katherine feels so tired she can barely remain upright. "So dizzy."

She stumbles away from the firepit, heading toward the lake, suddenly consumed with the desire to throw herself into the water and force whatever the fuck is inside her to go back to where it came from. She makes it only a few steps before dizziness or panic or the thing squirming inside her takes over. The wineglass slips from her hands, hits the ground, shatters.

"Oh," Katherine says.

Then everything goes black.

IV.

She wakes in the dead of night, feeling like a stranger in her own bed.

She looks around the foreign room and thinks, *Where am I?*

Then she notices the man asleep beside her and thinks, *Who is he?*

Panicked, she bolts from the bed, only to be hobbled by drunkenness. She stumbles out of the unfamiliar room, down an unfamiliar hallway, to a staircase that—surprise!—she vaguely recognizes.

I've been here before, she thinks.

She lurches into the kitchen, suddenly parched, as if she hasn't had a drop to drink in years. Not true, obviously. The state she's in suggests she's had plenty to drink recently. She struggles mightily to make her way around the kitchen, searching for a glass. When she finally finds one, she drifts to the sink, fills it, and takes half a sip before being stopped by her reflection in the window.

That's not her face staring back at her.

It belongs to someone else.

Rather than fearful, she's fascinated. Whoever it is, she's lovely. A little ragged from drink, perhaps, but still gorgeous. She runs a hand down this beautiful stranger's face and thinks, *Who am I?*

She still doesn't know.

But she suspects she'll learn soon enough.

V.

Morning sun spears Katherine's eyes as she wakes from another dream. They came at her all night. The first was of her stumbling into the kitchen, not knowing where she was or even *who* she was. It was followed by snippets of time. Pleasant ones. Her and Casey, of all people, in a variety of places. At the airport, the movies, climbing to the high bluff at the southern end of Lake Greene.

But then the nightmares took over—a long parade of images as frightening as they were mystifying. She had another vision of Sue Ellen Stryker, scrambling away from her in fear. There were two other girls in two other nightmares, doing the same thing. Recoiling. Trembling. Pleading. All three ended the same way—their lifeless bodies sinking beneath the water of Lake Greene.

The final nightmare was of her also sinking into the water, staring up at the shimmering surface of the moonlit lake before being engulfed by the darkness approaching from below. Even though she's now awake, she feels drenched, as if she'd just left the water.

Katherine sits up, startled to realize she's not in bed, but on the white sofa in the living room. She springs off it, worried that it's all wet and that she's ruined one of Tom's many prized possessions. A quick check of the fabric shows that it's dry. She then touches her skin. Also dry.

Yet dread clings to her as she heads upstairs to the master bathroom. The something inside her has grown during the night. She can feel it expanding in her stomach, her chest, her limbs. While taking a shower, she feels heavy and ungainly. Afterward, when putting on something pretty in the hope it'll make her feel better, she's surprised everything still fits. Her body is the same.

Once dressed, she looks in the mirror and is disturbed by what she sees.

God, she looks as rotten as she feels. No wonder she dreamed she was someone else, confounded by the sight of herself.

"My name is Katherine Royce," she says to the mirror, as solemnly as a schoolgirl summoning Bloody Mary. "Katherine. Victoria. Royce."

Staring at her reflection, she gets flashes to the night before. Sitting by the fire, listening to Eli, feeling panicked and dizzy and sick on the boat ride back home. While all a little hazy, it's enough for her to know she embarrassed herself. Yet another thing to worry about.

She grabs her phone and texts Casey to apologize.

> Sorry about last night.—K.

It isn't until after the text is sent that she realizes she has no idea how she got Casey's number. She simply keyed in the digits automatically, as if she had them memorized. She suspects—and hopes—that Casey told her the number last night and that, for some strange reason, it had lodged itself in her brain.

> No worries, Casey eventually texts back. Who among us hasn't passed out in a stranger's yard?

Katherine's body buzzes with mortification. She has no memory of *that*.

> *It was my first time.*

> *Welcome to the club.*

Katherine struggles with her reply. At first, she types a simple *Thank you*, but deletes the text before sending it. Next, she writes, *I think I'm going crazy*. Also deleted, out of fear it will scare Casey off. She finally settles on the best summation of her feelings she can think of.

> I feel like shit, punctuated with a poop emoji.

> Need some coffee?

YES!!!!!, Katherine writes back, overjoyed at the prospect of having caffeine. Tom insists that she drink healthy things in the morning. Green tea and kombucha and kale smoothies that taste like liquefied salad.

Come on over, Casey replies.

VI.

It's getting worse.

There's no denying it now.

And Katherine *was* in denial for a little bit, after her coffee with Casey. She felt good then. Sitting on the porch. Watching the lake. Chatting like they were old friends. She felt *normal*. By the time she left, she'd started to think nothing was wrong.

But then another vision struck when she was halfway across the lake. Her and Casey in a boat, almost like the first day they'd met. But this time it was dark, and Casey looked both angry and terrified. As for Katherine, well, she wasn't herself at all. She was someone else.

A man.

Being shoved into the lake.

Splashing and sputtering and begging for help as Casey watched and the dark water took over.

Katherine was zapped back to the present, stunned and confused and scared. So unbearably scared.

Because what she just saw couldn't have been another nightmare. It was a memory. So were the others. She was certain of it.

She had experienced those things.

They had truly *happened*.

Now, after a whole day of trying to understand what it all means, Katherine sits in Tom's office, frantically using his laptop. She knows she should be sleeping. She's also afraid of going to sleep, certain there'll be more nightmares.

No, not nightmares.

Memories.

Moments she never experienced yet holds in her aching head as if she had.

Because Casey was in some of them, Katherine googles her first, finding articles about her movies, being fired from that play she and Tom saw, Casey's very public drunkenness, and, finally, the death of her husband.

She clicks on the obituary of Leonard Bradley, screenwriter, who drowned in Lake Greene. A picture accompanies the obituary, showing a good-looking man of about forty, dressed like the stereotype of a writer. Rolling Stones tee. Plain black blazer. Hair tousled just so.

That's me! Katherine thinks, and for a second, she's shocked to learn that she's dead. Her mouth drops open, a hand flies to her bottom lip, and her eyes grow wide. Surprise makes her blink incessantly.

No.

That's not possible.

She's alive.

She's Katherine Royce, not Len Bradley. And what's happening to her is all in her head. It has to be. Insanity is the only logical explanation.

Yet the thing inside her stirs and her vision blurs and a tsunami of information about Len floods her brain. His mother's favorite perfume. The feel of his father's knuckles smashing into his face. The first girl he kissed. A mouse he caught when he was eleven and beat to death with a stick just because he wanted to watch it die.

Katherine turns to the office door, checking to make sure Tom hasn't stirred. Assured the coast is clear, she starts googling things she never, ever thought she'd search for.

Missing women in Vermont.

That brings up three names and three frighteningly familiar faces she's seen only in her dreams.

Megan Keene. Toni Burnett. Sue Ellen Stryker.

Katherine keeps searching. *Haunted lakes. Ghosts in reflections.*

Swimming at night. She scans the results, finding stories similar to the one Eli told, rumors of cursed bodies of water containing the souls of the dead, accounts of people who almost drowned suddenly acting out of character.

Her stomach grows more unsettled and her head starts to spin.

It's true.

All that stuff Eli said is real and true and happening to *her*.

One of the links is to a YouTube video. When Katherine clicks it, she's confronted by unsteady cell phone footage of a teary-eyed woman speaking directly to the camera.

"Someone's inside of me," she says. "Someone I've never met. I know their thoughts. I know their memories. It won't stop. They just keep coming."

Katherine leans forward, more frightened than she's ever been in her life.

This isn't happening.

There's no way this can be happening.

Not to her.

Yet it is.

If it wasn't real, she wouldn't be experiencing the memories of a dead man. Or feeling the thing inside her expanding like a balloon. Or be so dizzy with terror that everything grows blurry. Like thick, black water is lapping at the edge of her vision.

"What's going on?"

Katherine jolts at the sound of her husband in the doorway. She slams the laptop shut, spins to face him, tries to think of something to say. She should tell him what's happening. He's her husband. He's bound to notice something is wrong, if he hasn't already.

Yet she can't bring herself to do it.

Because to say it out loud would mean it's real, and she's not ready for that just yet.

"I couldn't sleep," she says. "Thought I'd do some online shopping until I got tired. Retail therapy cures all."

"Always." Tom chuckles and scratches the back of his neck. "But it's late. Come back to bed."

Katherine stands and kisses him, pretending that nothing is wrong, even though *everything* is wrong.

And she fears it's only going to get worse.

VII.

Rather than going back to bed like Tom suggested, Katherine locks herself in the master bathroom. She doesn't want to go to sleep. She fears that if she does, she'll never wake up. Even now, the dark water keeps clouding her vision.

I'm drowning, she thinks, because that's what it feels like. Sinking into the depths even though she's on dry land.

She stumbles to the sink and the wide mirror above it. Her reflection is pale and thin and foreign to her. A mere ghost of the person she used to be.

"My name is Katherine," she chants. "My name is Katherine. My name is—"

The black water takes over now, clouding her vision, blocking out her reflection. Katherine grips the edge of the sink and closes her eyes, waiting for it to pass. When she opens them again, she finds herself facing the same reflection she saw in the kitchen window the previous night.

The stranger.

Only the person in the mirror isn't a stranger. Not anymore. It's her, only different. New and improved. Yet inside this sparkling new package is the same person she had always been.

"Len," she says as she stares at her reflection. "My name is Len."

Then she smiles.

ABOUT THE AUTHOR

Riley Sager is the *New York Times* bestselling author of six novels, most recently *Home Before Dark* and *Survive the Night*. A native of Pennsylvania, he now lives in Princeton, New Jersey.